BACK UP

BACK UP

Paul Colize

Translated by Louise Rogers Lalaurie

POINT BLANK

A Point Blank Book

First published in North America, Great Britain & Australia by Point Blank,
an imprint of Oneworld Publications, 2018

ISBN 978-1-78607-110-1
ISBN 978-1-78607-111-8 (eBook)

Typeset by Fakenham Prepress Solutions, Fakenham, Norfolk, NR21 8NN
Printed and bound in Great Britain by Clays Ltd, St Ives plc

With the support of the Wallonia-Brussels Federation

FÉDÉRATION
WALLONIE-BRUXELLES

Oneworld Publications
10 Bloomsbury Street
London WC1B 3SR
England

Stay up to date with the latest books,
special offers, and exclusive content from
Oneworld with our monthly newsletter

Sign up on our website
oneworld-publications.com

MIX
Paper from
responsible sources
FSC® C018072

For my mother, who could really jive.

We must always remember to thank the CIA and the Army for LSD. That's what people forget. [...] They invented LSD to control people and what they did was give us freedom. Sometimes it works in mysterious ways its wonders to perform. If you look in the Government reports on acid, the ones who jumped out the window or killed themselves because of it [did so] years later. So, let's face it, [they] weren't really on acid when [they] jumped out the window.

John Lennon, 1980

But I'm not here just to make records and money. I'm here to say something and to touch other people, sometimes in a cry of desperation: 'Do you know this feeling?'

Keith Richards, *Life*

1: DON'T SAY A WORD

Larry Speed stepped off the plane at Palma airport, mid-afternoon on Saturday, March the eighteenth, 1967.

Emerging from the aircraft, he squinted, donned a pair of sunglasses and removed his leather jacket. When he'd left Tempelhof a few hours before, Berlin had been shrouded in fog, and the temperature barely 5°C.

The day after the recording, he'd told the other three members of Pearl Harbor about his plan to take a few days' holiday. With three grand in Deutschmarks and fifteen months' work weighing heavy on his system, he reckoned it was more than well deserved. Besides, living at such close quarters had brought the inevitable tensions and shoot-outs. Some distance would be good for them all.

The others agreed.

That same afternoon, he called into a travel agency on the *Kurfürstendamm*. The manageress suggested Majorca, Greece or Istanbul. Speed rasped his reply, with a knowing wink.

'Whichever has the, uh, *friendliest* natives, if you take my meaning…'

The Balearic Islands, the lady informed him, smoothly. There were some seats left on the Saturday flight.

When Saturday came, Speed piled a few things into a bag, placed his Fender in its case and called a taxi for the airport. He had made sure to take his portable Teppaz record-player and a few LPs, including *Fresh Cream*. The super-trio's album had been the soundtrack to his room for the past three months.

Larry Speed, real name Larry Finch, was the leader of Pearl Harbor, the rock group he had formed three years earlier in London, while living south of the river in Battersea. He was an only son, born out of wedlock, and never knew his father – an incorrigible womaniser who disappeared overnight shortly after Larry was born. Larry had spent his childhood and most of his teenage years in a second-floor flat in a modest house on the Queenstown Road, worshipped and protected by his omnipresent mother. For almost twenty years, the four huge chimneys of Battersea Power Station, on the banks of the Thames, had marked the horizon of his world.

In rock'n'roll lore, bass players were pugnacious types, quick to lash out when crossed. But Larry was slight and delicate, with gaunt features, a pill-pale complexion and little taste for a fight. Encouraged by his mother, he had taken music lessons, learning piano from the age of eight. Four years later, he progressed to jazz guitar, and the bass soon after, like his hero and role model Charlie Mingus.

Larry retained the discipline and precision of his classical music training, earnestly maintaining that the finest bass lines were composed two hundred years ago by Johann Sebastian Bach and never bettered, except by Jack Bruce. Quiet and introvert, Larry disliked company – and people in general – but hid his awkwardness behind a false smile and a killing line in sarcasm. Things were different on stage: there, he transformed into a flamboyant, frenzied bundle of energy.

Shortly after four o'clock, Speed reached the Punta Negra, a brand-new hotel atop a small headland on the Costa d'en Blanes, about twelve miles from Palma de Mallorca. He checked into his room, opened his bag and spread its contents over the floor. Half an hour later, he appeared at the hotel pool, where his tired complexion, long, black hair and fringed shirt, open to his bony chest, contrasted starkly with the tanned, well-fed bodies of the holiday-makers relaxing on their sun loungers. The eye-opening motifs on his heavily tattooed arms completed the effect.

The hotel residents exchanged quiet words, casting suspicious, sidelong glances. Unfazed, Larry leaned an elbow on the bar and ordered a beer, drinking it down in one. Astonished by the cheap price, he decided to rev things up with a gin and Coke. By 6:00p.m., with the sun low on the horizon, he had swallowed enough drink and plied the barman with enough tips to enquire about the possibility of spicier entertainment. The bartender told him that in the fifteenth century, the ladies of Mallorca attracted mariners from twenty thousand leagues around. The tradition of hospitality was undimmed today, he added. Two establishments, the Mustang and the Bora-Bora, were singled out for particular praise.

Back in his room, Larry ordered half a roast chicken with chips and peas, and an ice-cold bottle of rosé. Residents to either side later attested that he had eaten his meal with the television on, imitating the Spanish commentator at the top of his voice. After that, he had listened to a few LPs, apparently leaping around to the music. At 11:00p.m. a taxi took him from the hotel to the Mustang Ranch in Bajos, in central Palma.

At the night club, Speed flirted with a number of girls before settling on a woman with jet-black hair, older and more curvaceous than the others. He bought her a glass of champagne, and the two danced a little. Discussions ensued, and at around 2:30a.m. Speed ordered a taxi, dived into the back seat and set off in the direction of Punta Negra. The night porter saw the pair enter the hotel at around 3:00a.m. He reported later that both appeared to be in a state of advanced inebriation.

Around 5:00a.m., the woman appeared at reception and asked the porter to call her a taxi. She was swaying slightly, but did not seem distressed or anxious. Questioned later, she confirmed that Larry had been fast asleep when she left.

The hotel groundsman began work at 6:30a.m. as he did every Sunday morning. At around 7:45a.m. he was about to clean the pool when he saw the body of a man on the bottom. He called for help immediately. Two kitchen staff and a waiter came to the rescue. The men heaved Larry Finch from the water, but saw straightaway that he was dead.

The medical examiner diagnosed traumatic asphyxial death with pulmonary edema. The time of drowning was estimated at around 6:00a.m. Marta Rego, the woman from the night club, noted in her statement that Larry had drunk a great deal, and had shut himself in the bathroom for a few minutes. Despite some torrid language during their love-making, she had found him quite *amable*. To her surprise, he had demonstrated normal, even disquieting sexual prowess. In addition to over three grams of alcohol per 100 millilitres of blood, the test reports noted the presence of codeine, Diazepam, morphine and lysergic acid, a synthetic hallucinogen better known by the acronym LSD.

The police concluded that Larry Finch had come down from his room to swim, and drowned from the shock of the cold water.

When Larry's mother was informed of his death by telephone a few hours later, she ran a warm bath, got into it with a photograph of her son, and cut her wrists. As her life ebbed away, she murmured the words of the lullaby she had sung when he was a little boy.

'Hush little baby, don't say a word...'

2: IN THE MIST

Will God forgive me for what I have done?

He knows the truth. He knows I never wanted it that way. What happened was just fate. An unfortunate series of events.

God will believe my story, the story no one would, the story whose pages have disappeared, the story I turn over and over in my head, so the details won't vanish in the mist.

3: X MIDI

The call came through to the emergency room at 6.12p.m. A woman reported that a pedestrian had been hit by a car on Avenue Fonsny, near the entrance to Brussels Midi station.

The call handler asked the usual questions, assessing the urgency of the situation.

'Are there any others wounded?'

'No.'

'Is he conscious?'

'I don't think so.'

'Is he moving? Any movement in the legs or arms?'

'Not that I can see.'

A call went out straightaway. An ambulance was despatched to the scene. Saint-Pierre Hospital was contacted to send an Emergency Medical Team.

Information about the incident was relayed to police head-quarters. A patrol set off for Midi station, siren wailing. The car weaved through the traffic, drove up onto the concourse and came to a halt close to the station entrance.

The officers cut the siren but left the roof light spinning. They emerged from the car, adjusted their uniforms and walked unhurriedly towards a cluster of people. About twenty onlookers stood in a semi-circle around a taxi. The vehicle was blocking the access route to the station, provoking a chorus of horns. A man broke away from the group and hurried towards the two policemen, visibly shocked.

'I don't know what came over him, he crossed all of a sudden, just threw himself under the cab. I braked the second I saw him, but it was too late.'

One officer moved everyone back, while his colleague ventured into the traffic, trying get the jam moving.

Crowds of passengers poured out of the station at regular intervals, dispersing along the street. Some joined the onlookers, others hurried past, indifferent to the drama unfolding before their eyes, eager for home, or a chance to unwind in one of the nearby cafés. A handful of students observed the scene with a detached air, plugged into their smartphones, each in a private musical bubble.

The ambulance arrived seconds later, followed by the emergency team's fluorescent yellow 4x4.

A doctor hurried to kneel beside the man lying half under the taxi. He bent over, gauged the victim's breathing, checked his eyes, spoke a few words in his ear, waited for a reaction. He examined the arms and legs, lifted a wrist. His assistant joined him.

'So?'

'Pulse is weak, but his GCS is a 4.'

'What do we do?'

'Work on him in the van. Too many people here and it's almost dark. About to pour with rain, too.'

The nurse looked up at the sky. Fat drops of rain splattered his face.

'Okay, I'll get the scoop.'

Carefully, the doctor raised the man's head and positioned a neck brace. He discovered a gash along the top of the scalp.

His colleague returned, armed with a metal stretcher.

The doctor took the man's arms and crossed them over his stomach. Next, he slid one hand under his shoulders and the other under his buttocks, lifted slightly and pulled the man towards him. The nurse slipped the stretcher under the body. He puffed his cheeks and breathed out heavily.

'Jeez! He hasn't seen a shower in a while! Second street sleeper I've dealt with this week.'

The victim wore an overgrown beard and long, filthy hair matted with water and blood. He was dressed in a thick, shapeless coat pocked with holes.

The crowd of onlookers had swelled. Witnesses to the accident were giving their versions of events to the newcomers. Rain was falling steadily now. A few umbrellas had popped open. A gang of skinheads in jeans and leather jackets elbowed their way to the front. One overstepped the police cordon, inspected the scene and eyed the police officer.

'Fucking hobos. Stupid bastard deserves to snuff it.'

The officer eyed him back, but gave no reaction. The standoff lasted a moment or two. The ringleader rolled a mouthful of spit, expelled it and headed back the way he had come, shadowed by his clique.

The emergency team carried the victim to the ambulance. With the stretcher safely inside, the police officer approached the doctor.

'Life in danger?'

The doctor nodded. 'I'll give you his papers in a minute.'

He climbed into the ambulance, took a pair of scissors, cut away the man's clothes and searched his pockets. Two cigarette butts, a throwaway lighter, a couple of bank notes and some coins. He called to the police officer.

'That's it. No ID.'

The doctor examined the man's chest and lungs, reporting his findings to the nurse.

'Abdomen soft, pelvis stable...'

'Legs?'

'No immediate sign of fracture, but his head hit the ground, or another vehicle. He's bleeding slightly. I'll check the neuro status.' He pinched the man's shoulder muscles.

'No reaction. He hasn't opened his eyes.'

'No reaction in the arms or legs, either.'

'Hook him up to the drip, we'll put him out.'

The nurse prepared the anaesthetic while the doctor applied electrodes to the shoulders and stomach. He adjusted the saturometer on one finger, and fastened the blood-pressure monitor around the top of the man's arm. With careful confidence, the doctor opened the patient's mouth and inserted the endotracheal tube, glancing at the instruments.

'You're right, he smells pretty high. And the fumes, like a barrel of brandy. He must have been blind drunk.'

The doctor called the hospital resuscitation unit.

'Jacques? It's Guy – on my way with a cranial trauma. Patient intubated and ventilated.'

'Okay, standing by.'

The vehicles shuddered to life and made their way in a tight convoy down Avenue Fonsny, threading through the early evening traffic towards Rue Haute and Saint-Pierre Hospital, less than two kilometres away. They passed through the hospital gates and beneath the portico leading to the emergency department. Two junior doctors lent a hand, placing the victim on a trolley and wheeling him to a cubicle. One of the nurses removed his remaining clothes. He pulled a face.

'Where'd you find this one, in landfill?' He hooked up the monitor, replaced the saturometer, checked the man's blood pressure one more time.

The doctor frowned.

'Couldn't find any papers. Have you got anything?'

'Nothing.'

The team injected a contrast agent and set about examining

the stomach and chest. They made a scan of the spinal column and brain.

The doctor gave his diagnosis.

'Cerebral contusions, two broken ribs, a head wound. There's a bit of blood in the tube. He's stable. See if there's any space in intensive care.'

At 6:57p.m., the man was transferred to intensive care. The duty team made another complete examination. Two auxiliaries washed him from head to foot, but the sickening smell persisted.

The neurosurgeon visited the patient mid-evening, noted his observations and went to the duty doctor's office.

'Withdraw medication, let's see if he wakes up.'

Around midnight, a police officer called by for an update. No papers had been found, but one of the auxiliaries had discovered a clue: letters and numbers scrawled in marker pen on the man's left hand: A20P7.

The officer shrugged.

'Won't get far with that. We'll wait a few more days. See if anyone files a Missing Person report fitting his description. Apart from that, there's not much we can do.'

The following morning, the admissions clerk completed the man's paperwork. He had been admitted to hospital on Thursday, February the eleventh, 2010 at 6:45p.m.

Under 'Family Name' she wrote *X Midi*.

4: PICK UP THE THREAD

Grand Funk. *It seems they were part of it, too. The chaos, the sirens. 'Paranoid'. A monolithic intro, fuzz pedal max'd out on the bass guitar, growling over the drums.*

Grand Funk. They make a great noise.

Now, I must be ready. Retrace the course of events. I'll account for the deaths to God. He'll understand it was fate that took me to that Berlin basement, on that apocalyptic night.

Hiroshima.

That's where it all began. That's where I must pick up the thread.

5: A STREET SLEEPER

One week after his admission to intensive care, the man still hadn't regained consciousness.

The medical team had stopped administering anaesthetic and begun close monitoring. No response was observed, and electrophysiological exploration revealed little hope of any change for the better in the short term.

The CT brain-scan report mentioned subarachnoid bleeding confined to the right sylvian fissure, with no cerebral contusion and no deviation of the ventricular system.

The MRI detected diffuse axonal injury in the midbrain, and a strategic lesion affecting both cerebral peduncles.

Lastly, blood tests indicated the man had been in a satisfactory state of health. Indicators of diabetes, but that was all. He had a tendency to high blood pressure, and scarring from an old wound to the left shoulder.

Curiously, he showed no signs of vitamin deficiency, as street sleepers often did.

Before the night team handed over their shift, the chief physician fetched X Midi's notes, called the nurses and stood with them at the man's bedside.

He consulted the file and spoke to the night nurse.

'Have you noticed any response over the last few hours?'

She confirmed not.

'No reaction at all. No sweating, no signs of agitation.'

The doctor leaned over and examined the man's pupils.

'He's stable. I'm going to take out his tube.'

It took less than a minute. Once the tube was out and the oxygen mask in place, he spoke to the second nurse.

'Contact the neuro team and ask them to prepare a room. We'll keep him here for now and if there are no complications, we'll send him up at the end of the morning.'

'Okay, Sir.'

'Keep a close eye on him for the next hour. Check his GCS again before he's transferred. And keep on with the intravenous nadroparin and paracetamol meanwhile.'

She nodded.

The second nurse glanced at the patient, then lowered her voice.

'There's something I should tell you, sir.'

The doctor followed her gaze. He looked surprised.

'Friend of yours?'

The night before, two police officers had fingerprinted the unknown man, and taken photographs, in hopes of identifying him. So far, no family members had come forward to report the disappearance of a man answering his description.

The nurse gave a thin smile.

'No, it's not that.'

He took her to one side.

'Go on.'

'Before coming here, I worked at César de Paepe for three years. They held a drop-in clinic for the homeless each winter. Street sleepers could get free treatment in the evenings. I did shifts there a few times.'

'Yes, I've heard of it.'

'The men I treated all showed similar characteristics. Whatever their age and general state of health, they had bad teeth, and their toenails would be in a very bad state. They developed a kind of second skin, all over their body. We would wash them four or five times before they started to look okay. And they all showed signs of vitamin deficiency. There was one other indicator that identified the ones who had been sleeping on the streets for a long time.'

She paused, searching for the right words.

The doctor supplied the phrase.

'Their personal hygiene?'

She nodded.

'Yes. People sleeping rough long-term lose the most basic habits of personal hygiene.'

'And what's your conclusion?'

'Despite appearances, I'm certain this man is not a street sleeper.'

6: MY MOTHER'S SMILE

Hiroshima.

My mother said my birth put an end to the war. She said it with a smile. I was sitting in the kitchen, gazing at her. I didn't know what she meant. I must have been happy.

She was preparing a meal. She dried her hands on her apron and her smile broadened.

I was born on August the sixth, 1945.

Later, I learned that Little Boy killed almost a hundred thousand people that day. A hundred thousand innocent people murdered, massacred, burned alive in the space of a few minutes while I was emerging from my mother's belly. I never understood how anyone could rejoice at such horror. I never glimpsed the bright future people associated with that event, only the heavy price to be paid.

I retain only vague impressions of my childhood, a handful of memories, blurred at the edges. From time to time, images, smells or sensations emerge from the black hole that has filled my life.

They surface for a moment, signalling to me. I see them with astonishing clarity. I could describe every tiny detail.

Then they sink out of sight. Some come back to taunt me, enchant me, touch me. Others come in a dazzling flash, then disappear forever. Whole segments of my life obliterated in the mists of time.

It was hot. Perhaps my mother's radiant warmth made it seem that way? The radio was playing classical music. Life felt easy, I was in touch with reality.

We lived in a small apartment over a garage, on Avenue de la Couronne, not far from the police barracks.

I was sitting in the kitchen, drawing new worlds with my coloured crayons. The crayons, my Dinky trucks, my Meccano and a pack of cards I won in a raffle: these were all my toys, my whole world.

The highlight of the day was the ride-past of the mounted police. At the sound of horses' hooves on the cobbles, I would rush to the window. Everyone did the same. The neighbours would appear on balconies, or at their windows.

We watched the horses walk sedately, in rows of two, three or five. The cars would pull over to let them pass.

People had time to spare.

On rainy days, the riders wore long cloaks that fanned out over the horses' hindquarters. Sometimes they paraded in dress uniforms. They looked very fine with their battle-standard and their black fur hats.

No one seemed to bother about the piles of dung the horses left behind.

When they rode out to patrol a march in the city centre, the police wore helmets and carried long truncheons.

Later each morning, I would look out for the green cart from the Union Économique. My mother and I would go down to buy our daily loaf of bread. I would walk up to the horse, but never dared stroke him. He wore blinkers. I would lean forward, trying hard to catch his eye. He made me feel afraid.

Around noon, we heard the soup-seller's bell. I would run to the window and watch people busying themselves at the back of the van, saucepans in hand. When they had gone, I went back to the kitchen.

I sat and watched my mother to-ing and fro-ing. It seems I spent my entire childhood in the kitchen, watching my mother.

In the afternoons, I took a nap. I stretched out on my bed and my mother would pull the curtains. I fell asleep straightaway.

I woke to the grinding of the mill, and the aroma of coffee. I would *get out of bed and go to my mother. A slice of buttered bread would be waiting, coated in black fruit syrup. I devoured it greedily.*

Once a week, on a Friday, my mother waxed the parquet floor. She would spread the wax, leave it a while, then polish the wood with a hand-operated polisher that weighed a ton. The smell of beeswax always takes me back to those happy Fridays. I was content. Time took its time.

My mother loved me. I think she was the only woman who ever did, besides Mary, I suppose. My brother loved to terrorise me. He told me wild beasts and creatures from outer space were hiding under my bed, waiting until night-time, when they would come out and attack me.

When my father came, he smelled of beer and tobacco. I had to keep out of sight, in my room. He was bad-tempered, and he had bad days at work. He would go down to the cellar to fetch a sack of coal, and stoke the boiler. Then he would tell my mother he wanted a beer, and the brats could leave him in peace.

My mother would do as he said.

My father was hardly ever in a good mood. When he was, he would pinch my mother's bottom, or pass behind her, pressing against her and grasping her breasts. My mother would laugh and pretend to look shocked. But I could see she didn't like it really.

I was disturbed by it, though I couldn't say why. I would disappear into my room, fuming. I wanted to stand up to him, but I said nothing.

One day, the earth shook beneath my feet.

It was late summer. My mother told me I would be going to school next day. This was good news. I would learn all sorts of things.

I didn't want to go. I cried, I yelled. My brother swaggered like he'd seen it all before, and poked fun at me. I kicked the furniture. My father slapped me and I calmed down.

Next day, I put up a heroic fight. I cried again at the school gate. I didn't want my mother to leave. I shook with rage. I wanted to go home with her, and sit in the kitchen with my coloured crayons and see her smile.

I tried to make a deal. I would stay if my mother could stay too, and sit beside me, on the next bench. They said no.

My schoolmaster was Father Martin, but I was to call him Father. If I wanted to speak, I had to raise a finger. I refused to cooperate, and never said anything.

When we took dictation, he would loom up behind me and lean over me. I felt his breath on the back of my neck. The muscles in my hand would melt. I was incapable of writing, unable to grip my pen or dip the nib in my inkwell.

I wanted to go home, and see my mother's smile.

That's about it.

All that remains of my childhood. My mother's smile.

7: AND THAT'S ALL

I was about ten years old when I first heard the words 'rock and roll'.

The lady with the French pleat, at the record shop, where we went from time to time, spoke them disdainfully as she handed me a record by Chuck Berry. She said it was new, it was called 'rock and roll'. And she pursed her lips.

Who was the first official rock'n'roller? Or the first rock'n'roll song? I never knew. I never got into arguments about that.

For me, it was Chuck Berry and 'Maybellene'.

And that's all.

8: 105 KILOS

Ten days after the accident, the police were forced to admit they were getting nowhere.

The district officers had uncovered nothing in the neighbourhood. None of the locals had seen X Midi before. The street sleepers around the station were questioned, to no avail.

On the off-chance, an ID request had been issued to the national offices of Interpol in Brussels. X Midi's fingerprints were sent for analysis by the Judicial Identification Service, but there was no match on their database.

A police cryptanalyst had studied the letters and numbers found on the unknown man's hand. Several leads had been followed up, but all were discounted.

A police team visited the hospital and asked for the man to be shaved. More photographs were taken, with unsatisfactory results. The man's unnatural expression – his slack features and closed eyes – made him hard to recognise.

They took his measurements. X Midi was a force of nature. He was 1.92 metres tall, and weighed one hundred and five kilos.

9: LAUGHING OUT LOUD

I was one of the smallest and skinniest in my class. Father Martin retired and was replaced by Mr Christian, an irascible lay teacher with an excitable, nervous disposition.

Teachers smoked in class back then, breathing smoke into their pupils' nostrils and slapping anyone who fell out of line.

Such practices were tried and tested. We knew nothing else. No one dreamed of getting angry or challenging them. The more so because the exact same discipline was meted out to us all at home.

Short trousers were compulsory. Even in the worst of the winter, the teachers seemed quite unmoved by the sight of their pupils' thighs trembling blue in the cold.

One of my classmates stood a full head taller than the rest of us. We called him Taurus, the bull. Winter or summer, his great, meaty thighs were ruddy and robust, over catch-wrestler's calves and cart-horse ankles that disappeared into his military boots. He was the uncontested king of the schoolyard. He commanded our profound respect.

Taurus claimed to know how babies were made, but would only tell the secret to members of his gang. He alluded to his theory with an air of great mystery, suggesting blasphemous revelations wreathed in hell-fire.

I was still on the birds and the bees, and that suited me fine.

The pupils' latrines were tucked away at the back of the school-yard: a row of boxed-in stalls built against the perimeter wall. They were fitted with doors that left the user's feet and head in full view when standing. The metal hooks that served as locks had for the most part been ripped off by bad boys in acts of retaliation.

Privacy of a kind was secured by holding the door in place with one foot while using the toilet. This required intense concentration and excellent coordination.

On the morning in question, Taurus had a brush with one of the teacher's pets. An acid exchange ensued, and the pet had the last word.

A harmless incident – but not when Taurus was involved.

During break, Taurus spied the swaggering pet and waited for him to shut himself into one of the stalls. For reasons unknown, he came over to me, gripped me by my jacket collar and ordered me to tear open the door so that everyone could see the little pisser's arse.

He rallied his little gang. They reported for duty and stationed themselves in front of the toilet door. I was trapped between fear of being caught by one of the supervisors, and visceral terror of Taurus's reprisals if I disobeyed.

I was rooted to the spot, stammering, unable to think. Taurus came back at me. He stood with his feet planted firmly apart, face close to mine, fists on hips. What was I waiting for?

I couldn't do it, I stammered. We'd get into trouble.

He felled me with a sharp kick in the shin, and did the job himself.

Cowering on the toilet, exposed for all to see, the poor kid began squealing like a stuck pig. Taurus and his gang doubled up laughing.

A supervisor came running over. He saw what was happening and rounded on the assembled company. Before he could ask who was responsible, Taurus singled me out with an accusing finger. The attendant clipped me hard around the ears and sent me to the headmaster, who asked why I had done such a thing. I replied that it wasn't me, and refused to reveal the true culprit, earning myself another couple of sharp slaps.

I was sent back to class and told to stay behind after school the following Saturday. I was told to write a thousand times that I mustn't open the latrine doors when they were being used.

When my mother came to collect me, the headmaster called her into his office. He told her what had happened and lamented the change in a pupil whose behaviour had been exemplary until now.

My mother listened wordlessly, thanked the headmaster and told him that she knew what she must do. She told my brother to go home by himself, took me by the hand and led me off in a different direction.

As soon as we turned the corner, she took me in her arms. She knew I was incapable of bullying.

I was furious. I shook with rage. I wanted to burst out crying, to kill Taurus, the yard attendant and the headmaster. I wanted to explain what had happened, lose myself in her arms, forget everything. But not a word nor a teardrop came.

She suggested we go to the record shop, promised me I could choose a record just for me and no one else, told me it was just a bad experience that would soon pass. I should forget all about it.

The lady in the record shop said it was called 'rock and roll'.

We took Chuck Berry's record home. My mother said she wouldn't tell our father. She would tell him I'd been invited to a friend's house on Saturday afternoon, and we would listen to the record the Thursday after that.

I had no idea of the risk she took, by choosing not to tell my father what had happened.

My father talked of nothing but war. Not the war I had put an end to by being born, but the conflict that loomed between Russia and America, the one that would destroy the planet with atomic bombs.

My brother was uninterested in either the impending war, or music. Pop-eyed, his cheeks aflame, he spent his time poring over a magazine that he stuffed under his pillow whenever I entered our room.

A few days later, I went to confession, as we were all required to do *every week. We went in groups of five, during school time. The church was next to the school.*

Having delivered myself of my venal sins, I spoke to the curate in the semi-darkness. I told him what had happened at school. I wanted to know why God had not come to my aid, because God is all-seeing, and God is just, and God punishes wicked people.

He took my question as an affront to the name of the Lord, and expressed grave reservations as to the salvation of my soul if I persisted in such blasphemy. He sent me away, adding a few Our Fathers to my penance.

That evening, I took my Bible and hurled it under my bed, throwing my Catholic upbringing, and the remnants of my faith, to the wild beasts and the creatures from outer space. That week, I turned the page on a chapter in my life. My blind confidence in humanity and the Church disappeared into thin air.

The following Thursday was a half-day at school. We took the record out from its hiding place, and went into the living room together, my mother and I. We opened the lid on the record-player.

It was a monumental item of furniture: a radio and turntable combined. It smelled of new wood and beeswax. The turntable was equipped with a system allowing you to drop several 45 rpm discs one after the other, so that you didn't have to keep going back to change the record. The lid had a brass inlay, showing a dog sitting next to an old-fashioned phonograph.

We positioned the disc and set the turntable in motion.

My whole body tingled at the sound of the opening chords. I felt an irresistible urge to get up and move, to throw my arms around, and shake my backside and every bit of me that could be twisted and shaken about. I had no idea why just these few notes had such an effect.

That was it. Rock and roll.

I turned up the volume. Chuck's guitar blew me away.

My mother was shaking her bottom, too. My brother came to see what on Earth was going on. He joined in as well.

There we were, dancing like savages, all three of us together, in the middle of the living room. We turned the volume up as far as it would go. We laughed and shouted until our stomachs hurt.

Rock came into my life that day and it never left.

That afternoon is one of the happiest memories of my life, Ma in her pretty yellow dress, dancing to rock'n'roll and laughing out loud.

10: CRASH INTO THE CROWD

No one imagined Steve Parker would ever do the deed, though his suicidal threats were well known to his entourage, and to the members of Pearl Harbor, who spent every day in his company. They reflected the darker side of his nature, the side that had earned him a reputation as a troubled, nervy character.

The slightest disagreement – a difference of opinion on a choice of chord was all it took – and he would fly into a rage, cursing the whole world and threatening to bust his amp if his demands weren't met.

Excessive behaviour like this was just the way Steve functioned. People around him were used to his eccentricities and treated his threats like the tantrums of a spoiled child. With time, no one paid them much attention or took him even half-seriously.

More shocking even than his death was the fact that nothing suggested he knew about the death of his friend Larry, just the day before.

Larry Finch was the founder and uncontested leader of Pearl Harbor, but Steve Parker was its *éminence grise*. It was he who took the decisions affecting the future of the group. After mulling them over, he would inform Larry, taking him to one side, after which Larry would relay them to all concerned, with strict orders to comply with the directives, the first of which was the band's insidious choice of name, imposed by Steve on the other members.

Steve was viscerally anti-American, blaming the Marshall Plan for making Germany the economic winner of the war. He also blamed eight long years of post-war rationing in Britain for creating a generation of small, thin, spotty, violent teenagers, fodder for the gangs of Teddy Boys that wreaked havoc in the Fifties. Throughout the same period, the German people had prospered thanks to an economic shot in the arm, from America.

Steve maintained that the wave of British rock'n'roll groups crashing onto the US market and filling the top spots in the Billboard chart constituted a second assault on Uncle Sam after that fatal Sunday in December 1941.

Oblivious to the irony at their expense, the American G.I.s who formed the backbone of Pearl Harbor's devoted Berlin following saw the name as a tribute to their strength in adversity.

Steve Parker had played guitar since he was eight years old. He had inherited a Fender Telecaster and a Stimer amp from a jazz-loving uncle.

He showed an aptitude for the instrument early on, and progressed quickly, though he took no lessons and couldn't read a note of music.

At age thirteen he began writing lyrics, which he set to music and sang, accompanying himself on his guitar. Acerbic, angry stuff, lashing out at the British Crown, the school system, Harold Macmillan's Conservative government and what he called the British people's 'blind submissiveness'.

His response to criticism generally included foul language and declarations to the effect that he refused to communicate with 'ordinary people'.

At fifteen, he was prone to a variety of tics – nervous spasms that tightened his features. He would scratch himself, pull at his hair and wring his hands convulsively. Pupils at the school he attended began to avoid him. They said he was a nervous wreck, and called him a poof.

His parents worried about his aggressive, anti-social nature and mood swings. They took him to see the family doctor.

The GP referred him to a psychiatrist who diagnosed manic depression and prescribed antidepressants. In addition to his manic-depressive symptoms, Steve suffered acute pain from a curvature of the spine.

At seventeen, he was addicted to a cocktail of antipsychotic drugs and painkillers, and regularly took more than his prescribed dose.

Steve Parker and Larry Finch got together in the spring of 1963.

Steve lived about five miles from Battersea at the time, near the Hammersmith Odeon, the famous concert hall that had hosted Ella Fitzgerald and Louis Armstrong. He had quit studying and was working nights in a bakery.

One morning, he spotted a small ad placed by Larry in *Jazz News*, calling for anyone interested in forming a rock group. Steve had sent off a few demos, without much hope.

To his surprise, Larry asked him to come over the following week. They hit it off, and recruited a third guitarist to form The Weapons, their first band. The trio had no drummer because, as Larry had predicted, none replied to the ad. Kits were expensive, and there was a shortage of amateur players.

After a few weeks, the third member was fired due to temperamental differences, and The Weapons disbanded.

Rather than hunt for a new rhythm guitar, Steve decided on a different line-up: drums, bass and two lead guitars instead of the usual back-up rhythm and solo lead combo. The two leads would answer each other's solos in a kind of dialogue. Two years later, listening to Keith Richards' and Brian Jones' intertwining guitar work on 'The Last Time', he reckoned the Rolling Stones had stolen his idea. He even considered suing them, briefly.

It took three months to find a guitarist up to the task, and four more to find a drummer. Pearl Harbor's definitive line-up was finalised in May 1964: Larry on bass, Steve as lead singer and guitar, Jim on second guitar and Paul on drums.

Steve was eighteen now, and smoking his first joints.

His back was giving him more and more pain. An X-ray revealed a slipped disc. The doctor said his long periods standing, and the weight of the guitar, were aggravating the condition. He was told to stop playing, or to play sitting down.

At twenty, just before Pearl Harbor secured their Berlin contract, he swallowed twenty Benzedrine tablets in a failed suicide attempt.

It took the police several days to establish Steve Parker's movements between leaving Berlin on Friday the seventeenth of March, and his death in Hamburg on the night of the nineteenth to the twentieth of March,1967.

Steve had left Berlin late in the morning after securing a couple of bootleg tickets for Jimi Hendrix's show at the Star Club on Sunday the nineteenth of March.

He had taken the train, reached Hamburg by early evening, and checked into the Kastanien Hotel in the heart of Sankt Pauli, on a street parallel to the Reeperbahn, the notorious artery that was home to the city's frenetic round-the-clock club and music scene.

On the night of Friday to Saturday, numerous bar owners reported seeing him enter their establishments and leave after a glass or two. One said Steve seemed to be looking for something. Another assumed he was out to visit as many places as possible.

He had concluded his tour with a visit to the Hotel Luxor, well known for the services of its exotic hostesses. Parker had a particular fondness for Thai girls, and his companion remembered him thanks to the generous tip he had left her.

He had spent Saturday in his room, and left the hotel around 3:00p.m.

Towards the end of the afternoon, he had a brief altercation with a drunk who jostled him in a bar. Words were exchanged, and then insults, and following the insults, blows. The fist-fight was settled after a few punches, leaving Steve with a black eye.

He had sought treatment in a pharmacy, then went to an Italian restaurant. After that, he had drunk several beers at the Top Ten Club and ended the evening in a strip joint.

The hotel porter saw him return at around 5:00a.m.

On Sunday, he left his room only to go to the Hendrix concert. After the show, he had visited another well-known Sankt Pauli establishment, where his companion confirmed that he seemed drugged, and had been unable to see their evening through to its natural conclusion.

He had returned to his hotel at 6:30a.m.

One of the hotel residents had come down to reception at around 10:00a.m., claiming to have heard a shot fired at about seven, but with no clear idea as to where the sound had come from.

The maids had knocked at Steve's door around midday, despite being told to clear off on the other mornings of his stay. They had expected the usual volley of insults, and were surprised by his silence.

Faced with a locked door and no response to their calls, they had contacted the hotel manager, who used his pass key.

Steve Parker was sitting on the floor, leaning against his bed with his head thrown back. The bedroom ceiling was splattered with blood.

The police investigation concluded a verdict of suicide.

Steve Parker had shot himself in the mouth using a large-calibre hunting rifle. The police suggested that the gun had been bought on the black market, and that it was easy enough to find a weapon like that in a city like Hamburg.

Toxicology tests established 1.52 milligrams of heroin per litre of blood.

Two months later, overcome with grief at his death, Steve Parker's parents hired a private detective. They told him of the events surrounding their son's death, and their doubts about the conclusions of the German police enquiry.

The detective travelled to Hamburg and conducted his own investigation, which unearthed a handful of elements to discredit the suicide theory.

The first was the quantity of heroin found in Parker's blood. According to the detective, the dose would have rendered him incapable of firing the gun.

Second, the shotgun's barrel was so long that Steve would have had to pull the trigger with his toe. Even then, he was found wearing shoes. The source of the weapon was another mystery. It was claimed that Steve had not brought it with him from Berlin. The detective could see buying a gun in Hamburg was easy, but a person still had to know where to look. And this was Steve's first time in the city.

Third, the detective felt that the relative lack of fingerprints found in the room, and especially on the gun, compounded the suspicious circumstances surrounding Steve's death.

Last of all, the few words the singer had scrawled on a scrap of paper on the bedside table were ambiguous and seemed to have been dictated.

Steve's parents referred the detective's observations to the police. Despite this, the report and its conclusions were unchanged. The police closed the case, recording a verdict of death from a self-administered shot to the head.

Steve Parker's mysterious farewell message stated that it was better to explode in mid-flight than to crash into the crowd.

11: THIS UNKNOWN MAN

On the twenty-fifth of March 2010, six weeks after the accident at Brussels Midi station, the directorate of operations for the judicial police asked the Crown Prosecutor to issue a search notice across all media.

Two photographs of the man, one bearded and one clean-shaven, were broadcast a few minutes before the evening news bulletin on both national TV networks.

The photographs drew few responses.

Besides the usual fantasists, three leads were followed up. After checking, one was found to concern a resident of Furnes who had died in 1999, and whose death could in no way be called into question. The other two led to men who were still alive, and quickly identified.

Photographs of X Midi and a description of the accident were also posted on the judicial police website, under 'Unidentified Persons'.

Despite this, the chances of securing an identification dwindled daily.

At the debrief, the inspector in charge of the enquiry delivered his conclusions with a shrug of the shoulders.

'If you want my opinion, no one but him, if he ever wakes up, can tell us the identity of this unknown man.'

12: THE BEST IN THE WORLD

The records came thick and fast after 'Maybellene'.

'Sweet Little Sixteen', 'Roll Over Beethoven', 'Johnny B. Goode', and more. They took all my pocket money.

The lady in the record shop where I spent more and more of my time showed me the new titles and urged me to buy them. They were flying off the shelves, she said. She predicted the craze for rock'n'roll would never last, and that something else would soon take its place.

But while we waited for whatever might dethrone him, Chuck Berry was my god. His records were played over and over again in the apartment on Thursday and Sunday afternoons, when my father joined his friends at the café.

Not content with shaking my backside and tapping out his relentless beat, I would mime his guitar playing, armed with a stick of wood. I shadowed his spasmodic solos, legs stuck out and feet turned in, my hair falling into my eyes.

One day, while I was in the kitchen and Chuck was presiding in the living room, I had the idea of tapping along with a crayon against a glass. The results were convincing. I took a second crayon and drummed along in time.

I noticed that the emptier the glass, the deeper the pitch. Seized with sudden inspiration, I fetched several glasses and filled them to differing levels, to produce a variety of notes.

After that, I perfected my technique with a range of kitchen utensils. I placed a salad bowl, a saucepan and a frying pan in a half-circle around the glasses, balancing the saucepan precariously on top of a candlestick.

It was a fine old racket to begin with, but my dexterity improved as the weeks went by, with the encouragement of my mother and (rather more hypocritically) my brother, who seized the opportunity to take refuge in our room with his new girlfriend.

At Christmastime, heart thumping, I discovered a drum kit under the tree. My mother's eyes shone. My father's too, but for different reasons. He took me to one side and ordered me never to play it, at least not when he was around.

It was an Italian kit, especially for children. It included a stool, a bass drum, a snare drum and a ride cymbal of sorts.

I had no idea what their proper names were. I called them 'boom', 'chak' and 'tsing'. The sound was appalling, but it was better than the substitutes I had played on up to then.

I quickly familiarised myself with the characteristics of each. With practice, I managed a few rolls. I tried hard. I didn't want to play any old how – unlike one of my classmates, who had an identical kit.

It must have been that year's bestselling toy. He invited me over to compare our skills. We took it in turns to play along with Elvis Presley (my friend's personal god) on 'Tutti Frutti', the song he stole from Little Richard.

When it was my turn to play, I did my best to distance myself from my friend's banging and crashing. I tried hard to recreate the right effects at the right moments.

All around me, people were talking more and more about Elvis Presley. To me he was just a truck driver with greasy hair who writhed obscenely while pretending to play guitar. Not for one minute could I picture him as the successor to Chuck Berry, Eddie Cochran or Buddy Holly.

I practised whenever the occasion presented itself, chiefly on Thursdays and Sundays, but also whenever my invented headaches kept me home from school.

I made good progress. My speed and precision impressed more than a few, but I still needed to master my strokes if I was to drum with a more even beat, and greater intensity. Day after day, I worked at the fundamentals: control, coordination and the independent movement of all four limbs.

Apart from my mother, my fan base included my cousin – and one of my aunts, who would laugh as I played, clapping her hands and declaring that I had quite a talent. My harshest critics were the tenants in the apartment above. More than once, my mother went upstairs to parlay.

The garage on the ground floor, below, meant we were mostly left in peace, a privilege countered by the blasts of exhaust fumes that filled the apartment from time to time. I can smell the grease and motor oil even now.

Sometimes, the screech of tyres and the shouts of the mechanics rise from the depths of my subconscious, and ring in my ears.

My record collection grew little by little. I owned a few hits by Fats Domino, Jerry Lee Lewis and Little Richard. I was fascinated by an older song, too, from Bill Haley and the Comets, entitled 'Rock Around the Clock', a forgotten B side that came to light when it was chosen as part of the soundtrack to a film that was showing in all the cinemas.

I was disappointed by the way Bill Haley looked on television. He was pudgy, with a mechanical smile that never reached his eyes, and he wore a strand of hair curled and stuck to his forehead in a half-moon shape. Nothing like the menacing, pugnacious rocker of my imagination.

To keep up with the influx of 45 rpms, and to help memorise my home-grown arrangements, I began to write my own scores.

The first attempts were rudimentary notes of the elements I needed to play, in order, on a single line. Boom chak chak, boom chak chak, boom chak chak, tsing. The limitations of my method soon became clear.

Little by little, I learned to listen and count, and to identify the beats and the tempos they composed. My scores became more sophisticated.

Now, they consisted of three parallel lines identified by the initials B, CH, and TS. I divided them into bars and sections. Most rock songs are in four-four time. For each beat, I marked the sounds to be combined, with a cross.

Later, poring over books of theory, and learning about the musical stave, I realised my intuition had served me well.

My drumming improved, and my school results worsened. I spent more time thinking up new variations than learning my lessons. My all-consuming passion, and with it my growing scorn for human nature, began to worry my teachers.

I set myself apart in my own private world, avoiding contact with my schoolmates and replying evasively to any questions that came my way. During break, the attendants watched me keep my distance in the farthest corner of the yard, or walk jerkily up and down the central line of trees, nodding my head.

My mother was called in. Supportive of my tendencies, and preoccupied by the frequent escapades of my brother – who was experiencing a difficult adolescence – she answered that she knew what she must do.

When I wasn't playing the drums, I shut myself away in a book.

My brother was reading The Diary of Anne Frank at school. I read it in a few hours, incredulous, but comforted in my distrust of human nature.

The books I read for my own enjoyment were a far cry from the inane nonsense devoured by my classmates – Enid Blyton's Famous Five or the unlikely adventures of Henri Vernes' hero Bob Morane. I immersed myself in classics borrowed from the municipal library, claiming they were for my mother. Salinger, Dostoyevsky, Victor Hugo, and the rest.

I didn't understand everything, far from it. Certain turns of *phrase, words or situations escaped me, but deep down I felt enriched by my contact with such fine writing.*

I bought myself a drumming method, eager to progress further. Rock-music classes were non-existent, but a rigorous jazz method did the trick.

I slowed up on my record buying, too, in order to complete my drum kit with a sorely needed tom-tom.

With the method open in front of me, I began practising a few fills, simple enough to start with. Then I learned my first flams.

I bought a metronome to perfect my beat. I was ashamed at having to use a 'cheat' device to keep time. Later, I learned that plenty of drum heroes played with a metronome plugged in their ear.

My classmates wanted to be firemen, fighter pilots, doctors, hairdressers, or whatever their fathers were.

I dreamed of being a drummer. But not just any rock drummer. I dreamed of being the most gifted, the most ingenious drummer ever, the best in the world.

13: LOCKED-IN SYNDROME

X Midi was transferred to the sixth floor of Saint-Pierre Hospital, to a four-bed room on the neurology ward.

His immediate neighbour was a man in his seventies, hospitalised following a stroke that had lost him the use of one side of his body. The man was experiencing trouble with language, and had great difficulty expressing himself. He spent his days staring at the sky, or the comings and goings in the room. He had few visits and called the nurses frequently, on the slightest pretext.

Late one afternoon, when the last visitors were leaving, he activated the call button. He pressed it again a few seconds later.

When the nurse arrived, she found the man in a highly agitated state.

'What is it, Sir?'

The man pointed to his neighbour, but was unable to form the words.

The nurse bent over him.

'Yes... Is something the matter?'

The man opened his mouth, held it gaping for a moment, then managed to get a couple of words out.

'He moved.'

The nurse shot a glance at X Midi, but could see no significant change.

The neurologist in charge of X Midi's case was informed of the incident when he came on duty next day. He went to his patient's bedside, examined him carefully but could see no sign of a change in his condition.

He questioned the man in his seventies. It took him more than half an hour to piece together the scraps of an answer.

The man was no longer quite convinced about signs of movement as such, but assured the doctor he had seen his neighbour open his eyes.

The neurologist opted for a fresh battery of tests.

The patient had risen from 4 to 5 on the GCS. X Midi still showed no verbal responses or movement, but the opening of his eyes – or rather, the flickering of his eyelids, previously noted only in response to pain – now occurred as a reaction to certain noises.

The doctor decided to carry out further assessment of the man's brain stem reflexes, for a more accurate prognosis.

He noted a decrease in heart rate when he pressed on the man's eyes, and contraction of the pupils in response to light.

The electroencephalogram – which had previously recorded slow electrical brain activity – now showed a response to aural stimuli. The neurologist also recorded posterior basic rhythm in the alpha frequency band. Lastly, a functional MRI scan was carried out. The examination aimed at identifying the presence of deafferentation syndrome, as distinct from deep coma or persistent vegetative state.

Several doctors and nurses came to X Midi's bedside and spoke to him, hoping to see his eyelids flicker in response to words or phrases he might understand.

The patient responded when addressed, but failed to engage when invited to close his eyes firmly once for 'yes', and twice for 'no'.

He was addressed in other languages, but each time, his response was a single blink of the eyes.

By the end of the day, the medical team was certain that X Midi was conscious. He could hear what was said, he understood French, English and even German, but was refusing to cooperate.

The tests concluded that X Midi was awake and fully conscious. His intellectual faculties and memory were intact. He could see and hear but was unable to communicate due to a state of total paralysis. All he could do was blink. His particular set of neurological symptoms was better known as Locked-In syndrome.

14: BACK THERE

A shaft of light bored a hole in the dark, burning my retina.

I heard a low hubbub of noise. I could distinguish sounds, and murmurings. Unfamiliar words. Tetraplegic. Dysarthria. Sensory loss. I don't want that all over again. The questions. The treatments. The drugs. The isolation. The fear.

Hands examine my body. An object moves across the soles of my feet. Instinctively, my big toe stretches out straight. More voices. More words. Bilateral Babinski sign. Soft abdomen. Pupillary reflexes. Faces enter my field of vision, looming larger, wavering. Mouths open and twist in grotesque, slow motion. Blink!

I am poised between the comfort of death and a life that's no longer my own.

I know their traps by now, and how to avoid them. I know their questions, their manipulations, their drugs.

One blink! Two! I try to turn my head. I follow the movement of their white coats with my eyes. I've told you everything already. You didn't believe me.

You'll have nothing from me but silence, and tears that flow of their own accord. You won't send me back there.

15: FOUR DAYS AND FOUR NIGHTS

At night, shouts and groans of pain reach my ears, through the walls. From time to time, the sharp shriek of an alarm rings out. Shouted orders. The corridor echoes with the beat of hooves.

Each night, death stalks. She slips into my room. Brushes me with her shadow, her silhouette swirls in the semi-dark. She reminds me I'm on borrowed time, that she will come for me soon enough.

I was thirteen years old when she gave me her first sign.

The Cold War was being waged in space. Europe trembled. Sputnik, Explorer. The Russians and the Americans vied for technological supremacy.

In Brussels, after two years of titanic construction work that had disfigured the city, Expo 58 opened its doors to the public. Brussels was the centre of the world. The newspapers and radio talked of nothing else. Jubilation masked the onset of war.

The Golden Sixties were on their way. We had more money now. My father took on new responsibilities, and was often away from home. He would travel all week, come home on Friday evening, and leave again first thing on Monday morning.

We had left our modest apartment on Avenue de la Couronne for a ground-floor apartment with a garden, on a smart avenue in Uccle, a stone's throw from the Bois de la Cambre.

I was in high school, having managed to escape the Catholic education system. I convinced my mother to enrol me at the Athénée, a less strict, more open-minded institution. My natural zest for learning was yet to manifest itself at school, however.

Drumming was still my main interest. Little by little, as the months went by and my pocket money mounted up, I had assembled a complete drum kit, and installed it in the cellar. I had compiled it in stages, from second-hand pieces in an assortment of different colours. The bass drum was an Olympic, the snare drum, the high and low-mid tom-tom were Ludwigs and the low floor tom-tom was a Premier. The cymbals and the hi-hat were similarly mismatched.

If you wanted to pass for a drummer in the know, you had to take sides. Like the guitars (Gibson or Fender) it was Ludwig, Gretsch or Premier. And once your choice was made, you would defend it to your dying breath. Not me. Musically, my mix-and-match drum kit didn't bother me. But I couldn't see myself joining a group with a set-up like that.

The record-shop lady's predictions proved wrong. Rock lived on, delivering a fresh load of hits, month after month. I remained loyal to Chuck Berry, but I had other favourites, too: musicians like Jerry Lee Lewis, or the Everly Brothers.

I still couldn't get along with Elvis Presley, though his song 'Hard Headed Woman' was a huge hit. He had a powerful, tuneful voice, but I didn't like his stage act, nor his clothes.

Our neighbours on the first floor, a party-loving couple with no children, ordered vats of Burgundy wine, which they bottled in the next cellar to ours. Some Saturdays, they would invite friends round to help with the bottling, to the sound of my drumming.

Late in the afternoon, tipsy on wine fumes and repeated tastings, everyone would clap and laugh out loud. For years, my rim-shots conjured the aroma of Puligny-Montrachet.

Whenever I had enough money, I would visit the music store on Place Saint-Jean to add to my kit – mostly small percussion pieces, bells or chimes.

To replenish my funds, I had taken a job delivering papers for a bookshop and newsagent on Rue Vanderkindere.

I made two rounds a day, early in the morning, around 6:30a.m., and again in the evening at about 6:00p.m. On Thursday and Saturday afternoons, I made an extra round to deliver the weeklies, and children's magazines.

The bookshop provided me with a big, black bicycle fitted with a metal basket and a large bag at the front. It was heavy and difficult to manoeuvre, especially at the beginning of each round, when the bag was full of newspapers.

The accident happened on a sunny Saturday afternoon in May.

On Saturday mornings, the Athénée gave pupils a choice between two hours of study or a trip to the swimming pool. With the exception of kids who were 'chicken', or being punished, almost everyone chose the pool.

We had to be at school half an hour earlier than usual, meaning I had to hurry to finish my morning round.

Two buses were waiting for us, double-parked on Avenue Houzeau, their engines ticking over. We went to Saint-Gilles and the Bains de la Perche, an old-fashioned open-air pool with three storeys of individual changing cubicles all around. The damp air and the smell of chorine assailed us as we stepped through the door.

In the pool, the novice swimmers were harnessed like fairground ponies and kept afloat by means of a rod and line. We mocked them and joked at their expense as we walked by.

The lifeguards went about their work, oblivious to our sarcasm. I can still hear their instructions ringing out around the poolside area: 'one, bend your knees, two, three.'

The place was thronged with kids. Different schools would arrive, in quick succession. We shared changing cubicles between two, even three. As soon as we were changed, we lined up in single file to go through the showers. It was a tense, frightening moment. The great challenge was to catch the boy in front of you unawares and pull down his swimming trunks, to general hilarity.

On the Saturday in question, I shared my cubicle with a tall, well-built boy from one of the classes above. He must have been two or three *years older than me. He undressed in silence, and I saw his erection, good and hard. He waited until I had undressed, and whistled in admiration. Then he reached out, stroked me and dropped to his knees. Impossible to sweep ten years of indoctrination under the bed with my Bible. I saw fire, and flames, demons bearing tridents, the faces of sinners twisted in agony; terrifying pictures from my catechism. I felt guilty, and thrilled to the core. Very quickly, it was over. A repugnant jolt of pleasure shook my body, and I supposed it was my turn, in the inalterable rules of the game. He groaned, and shook. I gagged on the bitter taste and the bleach. I wanted to be sick. He called me a 'pussy' and cracked the top of my skull with his fist before leaving the cubicle.*

I was in a trance, lightning danced before my eyes. I had committed a sin of the flesh. I tried to shut out the images and words instilled in me all through my childhood.

God was all-seeing, all-knowing, he knew our innermost secrets. The Evil One had triumphed; I was bound for the fires of Hell.

I said nothing to anyone. I said I felt unwell. I didn't swim.

I went home.

My mother said I looked pale, and odd.

I went to the bookshop.

I took the bike.

I rode full tilt down Rue Ernest Gossart. My legs were spinning, my heart was thumping and my brain boiled.

In the street, people stared at me as if they knew. I couldn't get the taste out of my mouth. I felt humiliated, filthy, destroyed. I wanted to turn back time, start from scratch and carry on living a normal life. I wanted to die. I didn't see the car door open into my path.

Eyewitnesses said I didn't brake. I woke up on the emergency ward at the Sainte-Elizabeth Clinic. The doctor said I had concussion, and that I was very lucky.

God's retribution was swift. The dread Angels of Justice took me to a dark room with no chink of light.

I stayed there for four days and four nights.

16: IN THE EARLY AFTERNOON

At the beginning of April, the neurology team met with their chief consultant to discuss X Midi's condition.

Recent studies of Locked-In syndrome had identified three categories: total LIS, partial LIS and fake LIS.

In the case of total LIS, the patient is the victim of a primary, massive, brain stem lesion. In the first months, he can do nothing except open and close one eyelid, sometimes two.

In partial LIS, the lesion allows for partial recuperation of one brain segment, and part of one limb.

Fake LIS is declared when the damage is to the cerebral lobes or cerebellum, and lesions to the brain stem are secondary.

The doctors had observed X Midi stretching his mouth and making slight rotations of the head, suggesting he was coming out of total Locked-In syndrome.

He was no longer dependent on a ventilator, but was breathing thanks to the tracheotomy performed when he arrived in hospital. A cannula had been implanted at the base of his neck, between the second and third tracheal ring.

From these few, admittedly slender clues, the team diagnosed partial LIS in X Midi's case. With intensive, multi-disciplinary re-education, he could hope to regain motor control. In the best-case scenario, a long period of re-adaptation would lead to partial tetraplegia with some speech and swallowing difficulties.

But in most cases, the prognosis remained bleak. Massive

neurological deficits of this kind prevented patients from eating or moving, and exposed them to multiple complications, often resulting in death.

X Midi required treatment in a neuromuscular re-education unit. Finding one was difficult at the best of times, but securing somewhere prepared to take on such a difficult case would be little short of miraculous given the patient's poor clinical prognosis, and the likelihood of his hefty medical bill remaining unpaid.

His doctors outlined the key points of the case, detailed the treatments administered, noted their recent observations and assigned a social worker to contact the relevant specialist institutions.

In addition to his neurological condition, the report noted that X Midi was being fed intravenously and had been fitted with a urinary catheter, that he was suffering with tetraparesis and paralysis of the face and throat, anal incontinence and congestion of the tracheal cannula, requiring frequent aspiration.

The social worker began making enquiries for a bed. She was prepared for a hard fight in the face of the usual objections and administrative inertia.

She was unprepared for the discovery that LIS was something of a curiosity. The condition both perplexed and intrigued medical teams worldwide.

Three days after sending out her request to centres across the country, two institutions replied that they were ready to take on X Midi: Brugmann Hospital in the Brussels district of Laeken, and the Derscheid Clinic in Hulpe, south of the city in the Greater Brussels region.

The latter seemed the more motivated to tackle the case, and was informed that X Midi would be transferred early on the afternoon of Thursday, April the eighth, 2010.

17: A MAN

The doctors said my concussion had left no serious after-effects. But at times, I still felt a kind of disconnection between reality and the way I saw things. Sometimes, it seemed I was watching a badly-dubbed film: the actors' words failed to match the movements of their lips.

I liked solitude. I had few friends. A few classmates, some neighbours and acquaintances. Drumming and books filled my time. Little by little, I fell out of synch with the outside world.

I was approaching my seventeenth year. My school results were disastrous. My teachers complained about my introversion and distant manner, which they took as a sign of arrogance and an anti-social nature.

I was biding my time: only recently, the school-leaving age had been raised from fourteen to sixteen. As soon as I turned sixteen, I announced to my parents that I was giving up on education, as permitted by law. I expected tears from my mother, and a thorough beating from my father.

All I got were my mother's tears. My father raised his hand to me and I stared him in the eye, ready to take the beating I deserved, without flinching. He thought better of it. My stature and silence had already impressed more than a few. For the first time, I was saved from my father's violent temper by my own physical authority.

My mother scurried into the kitchen. My father gave me three months to find a job, or he would throw me out on the street without a second thought. Once I had found a job, he would take a portion of my earnings for food and board. He had already decided on the amount: half of my future salary.

Later, I understood that this was a desperate attempt to get me to change my mind. I accepted his conditions and set about finding a job.

With no qualifications and no skills, I had no hope of any decent work. What would I do if I found nothing? How would I survive if my father threw me out? I worried that I would be unable to keep my drum kit. More than anything, I hoped he wouldn't stop me from seeing my mother.

I read hundreds of advertisements in Le Soir and La Libre Belgique. I wrote a host of letters and went for interviews in every corner of the capital. I faced insults and suspicion.

Two weeks before the appointed deadline, when I had given up hope, I secured a contract as a warehouse assistant with a Peugeot car dealer, not far from our old apartment.

The central parts shop covered almost a thousand square metres, in a basement beneath the garage and showroom, where the 403 and the more recent 404 paraded for the public.

To get to work, I drew on my savings and bought myself a second-hand, 2-stroke Puch scooter. It was a sluggish machine, but it gave me a feeling of freedom nonetheless.

I joined a team of twenty stock-boys, all older than me. Some were in charge of customer sales over the counter. These were the plum jobs. They left their chairs only when a mechanic or coachbuilder showed up, to search the catalogue for the reference numbers of the parts required, and fetch them from the shelves.

Two employees manned the workshop counter. The mechanics would come down at regular intervals and line up the parts on the counter-top, their hands filthy with oil. They would take advantage of the break to smoke a cigarette and exchange a few pleasantries.

I liked one of the mechanics a lot. He had a brilliant smile and a body like a catch-wrestler. He laughed all day long, at anything and everything. He was black, and so of course everyone called him Snow

White. No one took themselves seriously back then, you could crack a joke without fear of being called a racist or a fascist. He never took offence.

From time to time, the workshop foreman would come down and call everyone to order, with much hurling of insults and threats.

I was responsible for preparing the mail orders received each morning from the other Peugeot concessions. Some ran to several pages. I moved up and down the aisles pushing a trolley and loading up the parts ready for mailing.

No waiting about, no cigarettes, no joking for me. If I managed to complete my orders, I was told to sweep the aisles or put the newly delivered parts in their proper place.

When my hour of deliverance came, I resurfaced, hungry for light and air. The sun hurt my eyes and the fresh air made my head spin. I would climb aboard my Puch and head for home, exhausted.

The hierarchy was clearly defined. Stock-boys like me wore grey overalls, the more experienced staff wore blue, and the bosses wore white. The head warehouse-man was a former soldier, a stocky Frenchman with a brusque manner and a southern accent, eager to tell anyone who'd listen that his sons were both brilliant students at university somewhere in France.

With my tousled hair and unbuttoned overalls, my untucked shirt and meagre work experience, I was the very prototype of everything he detested: a lazy, uneducated, flippant, undisciplined kid, one of the new generation who would take the world to rack and ruin. He had no idea I spent my spare time reading Balzac, Hugo and Zola, or that I could recite entire passages of Racine's Andromaque by heart.

He took every opportunity to humiliate me. If one of the other dealers called on the telephone to report a mistake in his order – an incorrect reference number or quantity – he would call me in to the manager's office, staffed by four women in charge of stock control and accounts. They never greeted me. We belonged to different worlds.

The military man would give me a harsh dressing-down in front of

the ladies, airing his grievances and threatening to end my contract if
it ever happened again. Then he would send me back to work.

I weathered his attacks stoically, inspecting the tips of my shoes
while I waited for the diatribe to end. When I shut the door behind
me, he would crack a joke to his audience, and everyone would burst
out laughing.

As the weeks went by, I realised my job was not at risk. I was his
whipping boy, and essential to his survival.

I gave half my salary to my father, so I took a second job to ease things
along. From half-past seven until eleven at night. I worked in a bras-
serie on the Chaussée de Waterloo. I was a barman, paid under the
counter. I mixed aperitifs, opened bottles, rinsed glasses.

I kept a list to hand, detailing the contents of the cocktails. I
pictured myself in Boris Vian's novel L'Écume des Jours, in which
each note of the piano is assigned a drink, and the resulting mixtures
depend on the piece being played. I began tasting each concoction, out
of curiosity. Soon, I was sampling the unfinished glasses when they
were brought back. I liked the alcohol-induced euphoria. I started
drinking.

The couple who owned the restaurant had two sons and a daughter. The sons were younger. The daughter was my age. She was
flirtatious, and liked to hang around me, taking innocent-seeming
opportunities to reveal her legs or brush her breasts against my body.

One evening, after my shift, she asked me to see her home. She
claimed a man had been lurking around the house for a few days. Her
brothers were already in bed and her parents wouldn't be back until
1:00a.m.

Outside her house, she asked if I'd like to come in. I hesitated, so
she took me by the hand and led me upstairs to her room. Instinctively,
I knelt between her thighs. I didn't want to make a fool of myself, but
she guided me with her voice, her groans, her fingers, then took me
inside her.

She held me against her. She had enjoyed it, but I should shave and buy some condoms. She had taken a risk. The rhythm method wasn't reliable. I rode home stunned, happy, at peace with humankind.

At the garage next day, I was called to the manager's office.

A dealer was complaining that he hadn't received a series of parts. The little Frenchman gave me a thorough ticking off. It was my second mistake of the week.

This time, I held his gaze. When he had finished, I reminded him that to err was human.

Hardly a thunderbolt of a reply, with hindsight, but as I left the office, I felt the breath of Victory blowing over me.

When I closed the door behind me, the women did not burst out laughing.

I had become a man.

18: FORTY-FIVE MINUTES

Few people could claim to have seen Jim Ruskin in a bad mood, miserable or annoyed.

With his long, mousy hair and multi-coloured leather outfits, his collection of medieval rings and a wry grin forever pasted across his cherubic face, Jim Ruskin was Pearl Harbor's official joker.

Lively, talkative, with a taste for the good things in life, he delighted in countering the outrageous displays of Steve Parker and Larry Finch. When the situation demanded, he would defuse simmering tensions with a piece of nonsense from his personal repertoire. He would stand on tiptoe, adopt a series of pained expressions, then let out a loud fart, or rattle off jokes in an endless string of foreign accents.

Once the storm had passed, he would thump his chest with his fists and declare himself Pearl Harbor's little ray of sunshine. He reckoned that without his enthusing presence and well-placed words, the visceral in-fighting and tension would threaten the group's existence.

Mostly, his antics amused the other members, though they weren't always to Steve's taste, especially when Jim hung on his neck or jumped into his arms.

During their first show in London, Jim had dropped his trousers onstage, turned around and treated the audience to a flash of his backside, painted with a Union Jack. On another occasion, in a Soho club, he had shaken the audience out of what he saw as their unwarranted apathy by unhooking a fire extinguisher and spraying it all around the room.

Jim Ruskin was the youngest musician in Pearl Harbor, and the most gifted. He was a left-hander with perfect pitch, and the guitar was second nature to him. He practised little, and rehearsed only when forced, but was always note-perfect.

He was born in Epsom in 1947. His father was an accountant and his mother a secretary. He spent a happy childhood, in comfortable circumstances.

When he was ten years old, he heard Elvis Presley's hit 'Baby, Let's Play House'. The track's raw energy left its mark. He went home straightaway and fetched down an old Spanish guitar that was mouldering in the attic. By evening, he was playing a few chords he had picked out by ear.

After that, he took private lessons from a teacher in the neighbourhood. Jim claimed that within four weeks, he was playing better than his instructor.

He was so remarkably at ease that a few months later, his parents bought him his first electric guitar, a second-hand Grazzioso, quickly replaced by a new Fender Stratocaster.

Jim's melodic guitar countered Steve's aggressive, raging solos with soaring cadenzas and dynamic riffs inspired by Jimmy Page, a kid from his neighbourhood with whom he had spent hours dissecting solos by masters like Scotty Moor, James Morton or Cliff Gallup.

On the day after the recording, unlike the others, Jim Ruskin had decided to stay in Berlin.

He loved the city, its cosmopolitan atmosphere, broad avenues and vivid night life. He loved walking under the trees or sitting on a bench in the Tiergarten, getting into conversation with the first person who came along, or watching the rabbits frolic on the grass.

Jeans and long hair were frowned upon, but Jim was well-liked by the Berliners he spent time with. He had learned the language, spoke like them, ate and drank like them, boycotted the S-Bahn – the regional rail network operated by the East Germans – and rejoiced from the bottom of his heart whenever a resident of East Berlin confounded the Volkspolizei and made it over the Wall.

In the small hours, when Pearl Harbor had finished playing, he would disappear into the night, going from bar to bar before heading for home at first light, to a deep, dreamless sleep.

Jim was a lover of women. He had met a Berliner, Birgit, and fallen for her easy physicality and unbridled sexual appetite in the space of an evening. Birgit worked at KaDeWe, the huge department store on the Wittenberg Platz that prided itself on selling hundreds of items unobtainable anywhere else.

Jim would join Birgit late in the afternoon, when she finished work. They would eat at a neighbourhood restaurant, then go back to her apartment. There, they would smoke joints and make love until it was time for the evening set with Pearl Harbor.

Late in the morning on Monday, March the twentieth, 1967, Jim was woken by someone hammering on the door of the apartment he shared with the other members of Pearl Harbor, a minuscule three-roomed affair on the seventh floor of a dilapidated building in Zehlendorf, in the American sector.

Through the door, the shop-keeper from the ground floor told him someone was waiting to talk to him urgently, on the telephone.

Jim was half awake, with a burning pain in his skull. Bleary-eyed and befuddled, he didn't realise his three friends had left. He was alone in his bedroom.

He shouted that someone would come down, and went back to sleep. When he emerged later that afternoon, the exasperated shop-keeper told Jim that eight urgent calls had come through, and that he was not the group's messaging service.

Jim took the list of numbers, dialled the first and got through to Larry's aunt. She told him about Larry's death, in Majorca.

Shocked at the news, he called none of the other numbers, convinced they were all close relatives of Larry, anxious to tell him what had happened.

Stunned, unsure what to do, he wandered down the avenue, entered a bar, drank two coffees, then continued along the boulevard and plunged into the U-Bahn.

As his thoughts cleared, he grasped the full ramifications of the news. Larry's death meant the end of Pearl Harbor, the end of their Berlin contract and the end of his relationship with Birgit.

For a moment, he thought of contacting the others to get their reaction to the news and with it, perhaps, a shred of hope, but he had no idea how or where to contact them. Steve was on the loose somewhere in Hamburg, and Paul had left for Ireland.

His mind a blank, he wandered the passageways of the U-Bahn and headed for a platform, though he had no idea which destination it served.

When the German police questioned the train driver early that same evening, the man said the accident had occurred at peak rush-hour.

Like every evening, hundreds of people were standing on the platform when the train came in to the station. The driver had spotted a movement in the crowd, and a man had flung himself under the train. He had slammed on the brakes straightaway. But despite the relatively slow speed, he had been unable to stop in time. The man's body had tumbled under the engine and been dragged along for a few metres. His shrieks had sparked a wave of panic on the platform, and many people had run out of the station.

One passenger had tried to help him, but the man's lower half had been caught in the wheels and his legs were partly crushed by the metal cogs. The man was conscious but in acute pain and unable to speak.

The emergency services had arrived just a few minutes later. Faced with the gravity of the situation, they had called a specialist team to get the man off the track.

At the scene, the team were pessimistic as to the length of time required. The man was losing blood fast: the doctors tried to operate in situ, but were forced to abandon the attempt.

Despite all their efforts, the emergency team were unable to extricate the man from his metal cage.

Jim Ruskin lay dying for forty-five minutes.

19: LIKE A CHILD

In October, the Cuban missile crisis broke. The Russians had installed missile silos on the island of Cuba, within easy striking distance of the US mainland.

Hour by hour, the TV and radio commentators reported the escalating tension in increasingly hysterical tones.

Day-to-day activity was on hold. Shops were emptied of their goods. People were preparing for war and stocking up on provisions. There was no sugar, rice, flour or tinned food. The crisis overshadowed everything. Everyone gave vent to their uncertainties and predictions, which were mostly catastrophic. One thing seemed certain: we were all going to die.

My father cancelled his business trips so he could wait for the apocalypse in the bosom of his family. His old fears had proved right: we were on the brink of war. He spent his evenings sunk in an armchair, moaning in front of the television. No one could speak to him, talk or make the slightest noise in the room.

When the television channels went off for the night, he would turn on the radio, and sit with his ear to it, tuning in to one station after another until late into the night.

The crisis lasted for two weeks. Two weeks during which the world stood poised for nuclear war.

When Krushchev relented, my father seemed more forlorn than reassured. He quickly predicted that this was only a temporary reprieve: the Russians would never lose face as easily as all that, and they were certainly planning more of their twisted tricks.

Things had reached crisis point in the world of rock, too. The record shop lady's words were proving true.

My idols had botched their entry into the 1960s. Buddy Holly and Eddie Cochran had gone to heaven, taking Ritchie Valens with them (which was reason to be cheerful, at least; 'La Bamba' was one of the worst things I had ever heard).

Little Richard had found mysticism, Chuck Berry was in prison for taking a fourteen-year-old girl across a state line in the US, and Jerry Lee Lewis was in disgrace after marrying a girl of thirteen. Even if I had wanted to, there was no way I would transfer my loyalties to Elvis, who was cosying up to a very young girlfriend himself and had gone to Hollywood to concentrate on his film career.

A few months earlier, an ex-chicken plucker called Chubby Checker had started a new craze, the Twist. It was short lived, but for a while the whole world shook its ass to 'Let's Twist Again'.

In this downbeat climate, my brother came home with a new 45 rpm single: an unexpected shaft of sunlight breaking through the clouds after a storm. It was early November. He winked at me, showed me the record and said it was going to 'do some damage'.

I had my doubts. At first, I thought he was teasing. Our musical tastes diverged. He had a liking for chanson and inane French variety artists like Marcel 'the Mexican' Amont or Richard Anthony, a lugu-brious balladeer.

I glanced at the sleeve. The A side was a song called 'Love Me Do'. The group were four complete unknowns calling themselves the Beatles. The photograph showed four pensive types posing like a set of quadruplets, two sitting on chairs and two standing. They all wore the same mouse-grey suits and identical haircuts, long and brushed forward into their eyes. The style reminded me of the circular mop my mother used for the kitchen floor.

I put the disc on the turntable, positioned the needle and the angels came down from heaven.

It was rock, for sure, but rock like nothing any of the others played.

It was melodic, energetic, and its simplicity bordered on genius. With its haunting harmonica and close vocal harmonies, the song's amazing, fresh quality left me speechless with admiration. The guys were plainly enjoying themselves tremendously, and their sense of fun was infectious indeed.

The B side was every bit as convincing. I listened to the whole record several times over, eager for the key to its magic.

Another time, I listened closely to the drumming. The drummer was called Ringo Starr. His playing was understated, lacking any great originality, but effective. No flourishes, but an implacable, catchy beat. Later, someone told me that it wasn't Ringo, but Pete Best, on drums when the single was recorded.

Later, in London, I met a drummer called Andy White, who confided that he was the one playing on 'Love Me Do'. Ringo Starr had just replaced Pete Best, but the Beatles' producer didn't like his drumming. Andy was a session drummer. To defuse the row, he took over the drums for the final session. He never got a penny from sales of the record, and had to buy his own copy when it was released.

I knew nothing of all this that day, and wouldn't have cared. The rock'n'roll of my childhood had aged beyond recognition and the Beatles were there to dust things down. Pop was born, and I celebrated with one of the greatest hangovers of my life.

In mid-December, shortly before the Christmas holidays, the girls' school near our home organised its annual fête, to be followed by an evening dance – an unmissable opportunity for the young males of the neighbourhood. A band had been hired. They were called The Drivers, and devoted themselves to playing cover versions of hits by The Shadows.

Like everyone else, I had bought a copy of 'Apache', when it came out. I could see The Shadows had talent, especially the guitarists, but I couldn't agree with their label as 'Europe's foremost rock band'. Their compositions were mostly instrumental, mechanically executed, cold and unemotional. I found their playing pedantic and academic. I hated their ridiculous stage act, the way they all turned to one side and lifted a foot with military precision. When they weren't performing on their own account, they backed a singer called Cliff Richard, a smart, polite young man, but too limp for my taste.

The Drivers were amateur musicians of my age, who didn't take themselves too seriously. One of the guitarists, the lead, was a talented musician, but poorly supported by the rest of the group. The bass player was a spotty beanpole, plainly out of his depth, and the second guitarist, who sported a huge pair of black-framed glasses with no lenses, the better to resemble his idol, mostly stood with his back to the audience, to hide his hesitant playing.

The drummer was a rich kid with a brand-new Ludwig kit and no idea how to play it. His breaks were basic, his rolls repetitive and he made far too much use of the cymbal, the last resort of a dismal drummer. After playing for an hour, he was clearly in difficulty. He couldn't keep time, and was holding up the show.

He asked the others for a break so he could rest and massage his wrists. Fifteen minutes later, he tried to get started again, but quickly dropped out.

After anxious discussions at the side of the rostrum, one of the organisers came to the mic and asked, to my great amusement, if there was a drummer in the room. Fingers were raised. I stared into the crowd, but couldn't see who was being singled out. At last, I understood the fingers were pointing at me.

I turned scarlet. I shook my head, but the kids wanted a party and would hear none of it. They propelled me up onto the stage.

The solo guitarist's name was Jean-Claude. He leaned over and whispered in my ear, thanking me and asking me to take things easy.

We began with 'Blue Star', a fairly slow piece. My hands were shaking, and I could barely hold my sticks. I did any old thing, easy stuff, like the rich kid. I was pouring sweat. Little by little, I found my bearings and a semblance of authority. I made it to the end of the

piece, and was greeted with a ripple of applause. Jean-Claude told me
I had done OK. He suggested we play a second, faster piece.

We did 'Shadoogie', and 'Nivram', and a couple more.

The more I played, the better I felt. I tried a few things, and pulled
them off. I varied my playing, and at the end of each piece, it seemed
the hall was warming up, and the applause was stronger.

After ten or so songs, I noticed that the bass player, Marc, had
begun to wake up and Michel, the second guitar, wore a broad grin.
Jean-Claude was having the time of his life. He clapped me on the
back and said we would treat ourselves to 'Little B'.

I shuddered. 'Little B' was a trick piece. It started sweetly enough,
with some drum rolls and a nicely rounded guitar riff, but these were
just the build-up to an extended drum solo.

On the Shadows' album version of the song, the solo lasted five
whole minutes. I never knew whether it was Tony Meehan or Brian
Bennet on the recording. Unlike many, I wasn't convinced by the solo.
It was overly cyclical. But I never thought I would roll it out myself,
and certainly not in front of my first live audience.

In the general euphoria, egged on by the beers I had drunk between
pieces, I nodded. I added that I would do it my way, and it was sure
to be a complete flop.

Jean-Claude and Michel played their hearts out. Marc was wide
awake now. When the guitars fell silent I attacked the solo simply
enough, cross-sticking on the snare drum and the Charleston.

Gradually, I let rip. Double stroke roll. I was somewhere else, lost in
time and space. Buzz roll. I hit harder and harder, faster and faster.
Flam rolls. My body vibrated to the beats. The beer had gone to my head,
I was transported, out-of-body, communing directly with the gods of
rock. I was enjoying myself like never before. I had twelve arms. Cross-
stick, paradiddle and five stroke roll, single stroke, rim-shots, sticks on
sticks, I threw in every technique I had ever taught myself in my cellar.

I played for almost half an hour. When I stopped, the applause
thundered.

I looked up. I was soaked with sweat. The hall was packed, the audience had tripled. People were whistling, shouting, waving. The Drivers were applauding too. Even the rich kid spoke a few encouraging words.

I was on another planet.

I have no idea what came over me. I got to my feet, walked through the crowd and out of the school. I ran all the way home without stopping, shut myself in my room and threw myself onto the bed.

I buried my head in the pillow, and sobbed like a child.

20: DELIVERING VEGETABLES

The ambulance charged with X Midi's transfer had exited Brussels' peripheral expressway, the Ring, and was driving now along a narrow, winding, forest road, the only access route to the Derscheid Clinic.

Few people came to the institute, besides the clinical staff and visitors. Most of the sixty thousand motorists passing close by every day didn't know it was there. The occasional hiker would stumble on it in surprise, hidden amongst the trees.

The hospital porter, a scruffy, recently qualified youth, looked doubtful and turned to the driver.

'Sure it's here?'

The driver rolled his eyes.

'Yes, quite sure. Been here several times before.'

He was about fifty, and had driven for the ambulance company for twenty years. On this, their first outing together, the porter had made a disastrous impression with his piercings and snide tone of voice. But the sector was in crisis, and it was harder and harder to find qualified staff prepared to do the job.

They drove on for a few hundred metres, past an elegant Anglo-Norman villa, and reached the entrance to the clinic's grounds.

An imposing four-storey building rose before them.

'Grim old place! Doesn't look like there's anyone about, either.'

With its eerie silhouette, long conservatory and a bell tower topping the roof, the *Pavillon Laennec* looked like an abandoned hotel.

The driver sighed.

'That's not it. There's nothing in there any more, they're talking about demolishing it.'

The porter grinned.

'What a waste! The perfect setting for a Belgian remake of *The Shining*.'

The driver gave a thin smile.

'The buildings are all early twentieth century. It was a sanatorium to start with – the first in Belgium. Then a convalescent home, and a psychiatric hospital. The Pavillon Laennec was still in use a few months ago, but they transferred some of the patients to another centre just opened in Wavre.'

'I get it. Keep all the crips and nutters dumped out here in the woods.'

They drove past what may have been a chapel, and reached their destination, at the far end of the grounds: a three-storey, ochre-coloured building in the same style as the lodge near the entrance.

The place looked deserted apart from a few cars, and a nurse smoking a cigarette in front of the main door.

The driver pulled up outside the ambulance entrance.

'Here we are, the *Pavillon Vésale*. When the place was a sanatorium, this was the women's wing. It was opened about ten years after the first section.'

'Ha! Treat 'em mean, keep 'em keen...'

The driver stared at him.

'Watch your language and attitude, kid. I'm going to the office for the paperwork. Get the trolley ready.'

'OK, chief!'

The driver climbed down from the vehicle and slammed the door.

As soon as he had gone, the porter climbed down, walked around to the back of the ambulance and let down the tailgate.

'Here we are, mate. Journey's end. Welcome to your new home.'

He considered the man's face for a moment, then bent over him.

'Don't have much to say, do you? What happened, then? You a crip, or a nutter? Or a bit of both?'

The driver returned with two porters pushing a hospital bed. They slid the trolley out of the ambulance and transferred the patient to the bed. The driver signalled to the young man.

'That's it. We can go.'

They climbed into the front of the ambulance.

The porter sank into his seat and put his feet on the dashboard.

'Think I'll catch a nap. Wake me up when we're there.'

The driver twisted around sharply, shoved the kid's feet to the floor and held up a threatening finger.

'You're beginning to annoy me, you know that? What the hell do you think you're doing here? Sure this is the right job for you?'

The porter winked.

'I'm beginning to wonder. Thought I'd be saving lives. My girlfriend thinks I'm George Clooney, but I spend all fucking day delivering vegetables.'

21: FORTY YEARS OF MY LIFE

The colours were brighter, the sky was a deeper blue, the air was clearer. The world has aged, but I recognise this place. I didn't know it was populated with crips and nutters, I thought it was a retirement home, or some kind of hospice.

Her name was Sylvie, or Sylviane. Maybe Sylvia. We weren't together long. A few weeks, a month or two at the most. It was just before I left.

I would pick her up on my Puch. She would wait outside the door, with a teasing smile on her lips. Then she'd climb aboard and wrap her arms around my waist.

In fine weather, we would come here, my scooter coughing and spluttering with the effort. We would come across old people walking along the tree-lined paths in the park, in their dressing gowns.

There were benches behind the building, on the edge of the forest. We would sit on the last one, Sylvia and I. It was peaceful. No one bothered us. She'd get out the tube of glue and the plastic bag.

Sylvia looked like a boy. She had blonde hair cut short, big blue eyes and tiny breasts. We would get fantastically drunk together, but she wanted more. She introduced me to powerful cough mixture and pills. We swallowed prodigious quantities of both, but they offered no particularly strong sensations. We would feel blurry-headed for a day or two. Nothing more. We could hardly even say we were high.

It was Humbrol 77. I remember. Model-making glue. I can still see the yellow and silver tube. She would squeeze out a small quantity, *spread it on the inside of a matchbox, then drop it into the bottom of the plastic bag.*

We would take it in turns to sink our faces into the bag and breathe the fumes.

She said the flash was as intense as LSD, even if the effects were short-lived.

But what did she know?

LSD was something else. LSD was the gates of heaven and a day trip to hell.

The colours were brighter, the sky was a deeper blue, the air was clearer, life was simpler. I came here from time to time.

When Sylvia came back to Earth, she would look deep into my eyes and ask me to caress her. She was kind of crazy, but I liked her a lot. That was before the men stole forty years of my life.

22: NO QUESTIONS

The Derscheid Clinic had become the *Clinique de la Forêt des Soignes* in 2009, but most people still called it by its old name. The new team had abandoned the outdated facilities in the *Pavillon Laennec* and modernised the *Pavillon Vésale* as the focus of all the centre's activities.

The clinic was organised into four units. The main unit – the general psychiatry service – treated patients suffering from anxiety, depression or bipolar disorder. Older people with behavioural problems were grouped together in the geriatric psychiatry unit. The third unit cared for people suffering from alcohol- or substance-induced psychosis.

The fourth unit, known as the rehabilitation service for patients with cognitive disorders, was the smallest, with twelve beds. X Midi was admitted here on Thursday, April the eighth, 2010.

The next day, the chief consultant called a meeting of all staff to determine the treatment plan for the new admission. First, the team resolved to carry out a meticulous case review and a check-up to identify any psychopathological issues.

Next, they would see if any changes were needed to the current treatment. While waiting for the conclusions, they would continue to administer an anti-spasmodic, to prevent the muscles from stiffening, together with low doses of an antithrombotic, for improved circulation. Subcutaneous injections of an anticoagulant would also be continued.

The rest of the meeting was spent defining individual tasks and responsibilities. In total six individuals or groups were assigned to X Midi's case.

They began by confirming the medical team's mission. One psychiatrist, a general practitioner and an intern were put in charge of overseeing X Midi's rehabilitation programme.

The care team, consisting of the nurses, care assistants and physios, were in charge of administering basic care twenty-four hours a day, and for liaison between the various agents involved in the treatment. The ergo-therapist would follow X Midi's progress and offer specific activities depending on the evolution of his condition. The psychologist would maintain regular contact with the teams involved, across all disciplines. Given X Midi's pathology, she faced a difficult and delicate task. The social worker would see to the paperwork required to regularise the patient's administrative situation, and continue efforts to discover his identity.

Lastly, the physios would work with the patient on a daily basis, and up to three times a day as required.

X Midi would be placed in an individual room, to minimise the risk of hospital-acquired infection.

The meeting concluded with a read-through of the various decisions. There were no questions.

23: IN HER ARMS

They've brought me here because they don't know who I am, or where I'm from. Their only clue is the address I wrote on the palm of my hand. Apart from that, I have ceased to exist.

Even if I'm released from this prison, I won't remember a thing. Time has already erased the data. Perhaps it will reappear, like these images I thought were forgotten, but which resurface now.

I was about to turn eighteen. I had given up school and couldn't post-pone my military service any longer. I knew the papers would come that summer, sometime around my birthday.

I dreaded the impending date. I didn't want to learn to kill, or to obey orders. I didn't want to stop reading and playing the drums for fifteen months.

I comforted myself by deciding I would think about all that when the time came, that I would find a way out. There were rumours of ways to get yourself declared unfit.

A few weeks after the school dance, Jean-Claude came looking for me. Snow was falling. I was reading at the window, watch-ing the neighbourhood children throw themselves into a snow fight.

I didn't recognise him. Snowflakes had settled on his frizzy hair. In the school hall, I hadn't noticed he was half-caste.

He wanted me to join The Drivers. He assured me he would come to an arrangement with the current drummer, who wasn't good enough and was making no progress. He was particularly concerned that the band's rehearsals were held in the rich kid's cellar and they would need to find somewhere else.

Meantime Marc the bassist had started taking lessons, and Michel had left the group. Jean-Claude had found a guitarist and singer to replace him – Alex, an older guy who had already played in a few bands.

I accepted the offer. Jean-Claude had ousted the drummer, so we gathered in Marc's cellar for our first rehearsal. He lived a few hundred metres down the road from me. The night before, I had moved my drum kit over piece by piece.

The cellar smelled of damp and the only light was a feeble bulb hanging from the ceiling. There were no electric sockets. We caught our feet in the assortment of cables snaking across the floor.

That was the day I met Alex. He showed up an hour late. He gave no explanation, and began tuning his guitar without once glancing around him.

He took his time. The wait was interminable. I watched him out of the corner of my eye. He had swept-back blonde hair and black glasses with thick lenses. He seemed distant, like someone who has known tragedy or had an extraordinary experience of some kind.

When he was ready, at last, he asked what we wanted to play. Jean-Claude wanted to stick with The Shadows, Marc wanted to play rock. As for me, I wanted very badly to cover the Beatles. Their second single, 'Please Please Me', had just been released, and was even better than the first.

Alex waited a moment, smiling. In a few seconds, he had the measure of the group.

He nodded and said he was going to teach us the blues. The Shadows were dead, the Beatles not quite born yet, and he couldn't bear what he called 'slicked quiff rock'. He preferred Memphis Slim or the pacy, electric blues of Jimmy Reed. Similarly, he thought 'The Drivers' was outdated and renamed us The Four Fours.

He picked up his guitar, cleared his throat and intoned Reed's song 'You've Got me Dizzy'.

It turned out he could play, and sing in tune. Childishly, we all clapped when he'd finished. Next, he gave us precise instructions and left us to practise. That evening, we mastered a few numbers including

'Down in Virginia', and 'Every Day I Have the Blues'.

From one Saturday to the next, we made steady progress. Our repertoire grew and I began to like the blues.

Despite our regular meetings, Alex remained a mystery to me. He seemed even-tempered, ready to listen, sure of himself and the things he said.

When we couldn't follow or do what he wanted of us, he would stay calm, stop and smile. He would explain over again what he wanted, and we would take up where we had left off, encouraged to see him clicking his fingers and nodding in time.

No one knew what he did for a living. Jean-Claude said he didn't work. He had travelled around and done various jobs. He knew a lot of people and was part of some sort of fraternity.

During one of our conversations, he discovered I liked to read.

There was a book that had made a big impression on him. He wanted to lend it to me. He suggested I come over to his place on Sunday afternoon.

He lived on the top floor of an old building with no lift, on a street parallel to Avenue Churchill. He shared an apartment with friends, splitting the cost.

I arrived mid-afternoon. He greeted me with his usual smile. The apartment was in semi-darkness. Long red net curtains filtered the daylight. Music was playing quietly in the background. A sweet smell floated on the air.

Two guys were talking in low voices in the living room, sitting cross-legged on the floor. There was almost no furniture. Mattresses had been thrown down. A girl lay stretched out on one of them, apparently asleep.

Alex saw me looking at her. Her name was Marianne. She was on a beautiful journey and would join us later.

We went into the kitchen. Alex offered me a beer and gave me the book, The Naked Lunch, by William Burroughs.

Then he launched into a long speech touching on politics,

nonconformism and revolution. He maintained that we didn't have to let ourselves be downtrodden by the greats of this world, we should refuse to accept our lot. War was not inevitable.

He said that young people had something to say and would seize power one day to create a new order under which the world would live in peace. It was just a matter of time.

I didn't understand all the terms he used, and some of his concepts seemed confused or idealistic. As far as I was concerned, you had to be an adult to exist properly in this world. But I was fascinated by his self-assurance, and the conviction behind his words.

He spoke with poise, choosing his words carefully. His assertions were backed up with examples from current affairs. I watched him, and listened. He had an aura. I was hypnotised.

The other two guys joined us. We drank more beers. Alex kept talking and we listened without interrupting him.

Later, Marianne came over. She was tall, slim and very beautiful. She moved with supple grace. Her feet hardly seemed to touch the ground. Silently, she moved between us, placing her hands on our shoulders and kissing each of us on the mouth. Her kiss was more than a friendly greeting.

She made a thick, aromatic soup. At the end of the evening, Alex rolled a kind of cigarette and held it out for me to take.

He smiled. It was red Lebanese. The joint was passed from hand to hand, in a kind of ritual. I should have been surprised, or suspicious, but I saw it as a form of sacrament, a fraternal act that reminded me of Holy Communion.

The others inhaled, drew the smoke down into their lungs several times and held it there. Second time around, I did the same.

Little by little, I was overcome by a feeling of total happiness. I felt great. My thoughts were clear. My brain, heart and body were in perfect harmony. We talked, smoked and drank until late in the night.

Late in the night, Marianne took me by the hand. We lay down and I fell asleep in her arms.

24: AS A SMALL BOY

Paul McDonald didn't believe that bad things happen in series, nor in extraordinary coincidences.

On the morning of Tuesday, March the twenty-first, 1967, while trying to contact Jim Ruskin by telephone, he learned from the shop-keeper on the ground floor of their building that his three flatmates had all lost their lives in the preceding forty-eight hours, in different places and from different causes.

The shop-keeper added that several people had been trying to get hold of him since the deaths, and that he should contact the Berlin police immediately, or the local authorities.

Paul McDonald had no doubt the deaths were connected, and that natural causes had played no part whatsoever. He concluded, naturally enough, that he was next on the list.

After fighting down his rising sense of panic, he tried to identify a motive for the three murders, and to assess the potential threat to his own life.

Several leads presented themselves for his consideration. Larry and Steve were sarcastic and provocative, and had made plenty of enemies in Berlin. Night club owners, dealers, pimps, not forgetting the endless ranks of G.I.s they had insulted whenever they were on stage. All would have liked to see them come to a sticky end, and Paul himself was no exception.

Nicknamed the Mammoth by his close friends – and proud of it – Paul was well over six feet tall and weighed about twenty stone. Unlike Larry and Steve, he never settled scores with insults or murderous sarcasm. When he decided the limits of his patience had been reached, he would twist his goatee beard, slope over to whoever was contradicting him and smash his nose with a headbutt or his notorious right hook.

Born in Dublin in April 1940, Paul McDonald was the oldest member of Pearl Harbor.

At six years of age, he had organised a collection in his neighbourhood, to get hold of as many Mackintosh's sweet tins as possible. Next, he arranged them on his attic floor in order of size and began hammering at them with rudimentary sticks, in an effort to recreate the style of his heroes, Gene Krupa and Buddy Rich.

His mother bought him a drum for his tenth birthday. He carried it with him everywhere for two whole weeks, only putting it down when he went to bed. He got his first drum kit at fifteen, for his birthday – a second-hand Premier that his father had bought from an unscrupulous dealer, and which quickly succumbed to rust.

After leaving school, Paul worked with his father in the building trade. He learned bricklaying, but also the shot-put, and boxing. He joined a few local bands, as drummer.

In 1958 he married Margreth, a childhood sweetheart who delivered a baby boy one year later, baptised Jason. Their marriage quickly floundered, and they were divorced two years later.

Towards the end of 1963, as the tide of Beatlemania swept across Europe, and British groups were increasingly talked about, Paul left Ireland and headed for London, to try his hand as a professional.

He experienced a few setbacks before finding a job as a bouncer at Ronnie Scott's Soho jazz club, and a position as a part-time drummer with a group known as Black Spirit.

One thing led to another. He heard that Pearl Harbor were looking for a drummer, and joined the group in May 1964.

Paul McDonald stayed up late and rose early. On average, he never slept more than four hours a night. Despite this, and the phenomenal qualities of alcohol he consumed, he always seemed in Olympic form. Asked what his secret was, he would say 'sobriety – avoid it like the plague.'

One evening, before beginning their set, Larry Finch had showed up with a tube of horse sedatives and bet him twenty quid he wouldn't make it to the end of the show if he took half a tablet. Paul doubled the stakes by swallowing an entire pill, with a glass of cognac. Half an hour later, he collapsed over his drum kit. An ambulance was called. He spent the next three days in a wheelchair, brushing off the jibes of the other three.

His drumming was powerful and impressive. He used the longest, heaviest sticks ('my trees' as he called them). He drummed so hard he sometimes broke the skins on his kit. He was possessed of Herculean strength, and used two twenty-six-inch bass drums to further enhance the effect. Not content with that, he had taken out the batter skin on his bass drums, so that he could hit them harder, and produce a drier sound.

Once he had recovered some semblance of calm, Paul tried to reason things out.

No one knew he had been in London. He had told the others he was going to see his son and visit his family in Dublin. In fact, he had been for an audition. Stuart, one of his closest friends, had told him that a promising new group called Fairport Convention were looking for a drummer.

He had arrived in London on the Saturday, settled into a hotel and headed out into town. The audition was arranged for the following Wednesday and he had planned to make the most of his return by treating himself to a good time.

He decided it was unwise to contact the German police. Two weeks earlier, he had smashed up a bar in Berlin. The owner reckoned he had had too much to drink and was bothering the other customers. Wrecking the bar had gone hand-in-hand with a thorough beating, and the bar owner had ended up in hospital.

Furthermore, it seemed to Paul that carrying out three murders in a such short space of time, in three different places, took qualified personnel and skilled organisation. He couldn't exclude the possibility that the police or some other German organisation was behind it all.

He could have dialled 999 and confided his fears to the London police, but during his stay in London he had got into a row with a young motorist who had almost run him over on a pedestrian crossing. He had pulled the kid out of his car and taught him a lesson he wouldn't forget, in front of a number of eyewitnesses, all of whom were reluctant to intervene. He had left the reckless driver half-conscious on the pavement and attacked his car, with his fists, elbows and feet. Then he had disappeared into the crowd, just as a police car arrived on the scene, its siren wailing.

Best to disappear without trace, lie low for a few days, and see how things turned out. The British press were sure to seize on the affair and set their hounds on the trail.

He called Stuart and told him he was leaving London. That same evening, he took the night train to Glasgow. Next day, as soon as the banks were open, he entered a branch of Barclays on Buchanan Street and emptied his account. Then he took the train back to London.

Covering his tracks still further, he booked into a different hotel, the Samarkand in Notting Hill, where he registered under his mother's maiden name.

He spent the next five days holed up in his fifth-floor room, only going out to buy newspapers, eat in a local restaurant, or for more booze.

On Tuesday, March the twenty-eighth, at around 6:00a.m., the driver of a butcher's delivery van making his way up Lansdowne Crescent saw a man fall from the fifth floor of the Samarkand and crash to the ground.

The emergency services arrived quickly and pronounced the man dead at the scene.

The police soon identified the victim, and parallels were established between the latest accident and the deaths of the other three members of Pearl Harbor.

The investigation revealed that Paul McDonald had bolted his door, thereby excluding the possibility that anyone else could have entered the room.

Blood tests revealed that in addition to 2.5 grams of alcohol per litre of blood, the victim had swallowed ten Vesparax, a powerful barbiturate. The police also found numerous pools of vomit on the carpet.

They concluded that Paul McDonald had lapsed into an alcoholic coma. He had vomited in his sleep, which had woken him up. He had gone to the window to get some fresh air, and had lost his balance.

Despite protests from McDonald's family, they recorded a verdict of accidental death by defenestration.

Paul McDonald's funeral took place one week later, at the church of St Lawrence O'Toole in Dublin, on what would have been his twenty-seventh birthday.

At the funeral, Paul's son Jason, aged eight, beat time to the funeral march on the drum his father had been given as a small boy.

25: DOWN THE DRAIN

I found my military service papers on the table in the dining room. I had been waiting so long, I'd forgotten all about them. But there they were, mocking me, folded in four in a brown envelope with no stamp.

I had just finished a day of stocktaking, a particularly exhausting ordeal. Once a year, we checked the difference between the book inventory balance and the counted stock. The operation took place over two weeks after the store had closed for the summer, and before reopening again in September.

The stock-boys were each given a series of cards. They would make their way down each aisle, checking that the quantity of items recorded corresponded to the actual number in stock. They would check for discrepancies due to coding errors, loss or theft. For this reason, the operation was carried out in twos, one partner checking the other's work.

The head warehouse-man had teamed me up with Jacques, a hard-boiled man of thirty with a thick moustache and brilliantined black hair. He was sour-tempered and always ready to pick a fight. One evening, I saw him settle a personal score with his fists, at the back of the store.

One thing was clear: we were not the head warehouse-man's personal favourites. He disliked Jacques's aggressive nature and my apathy in equal measure, and exacted his revenge by assigning us to Small Nuts and Bolts, the most thankless task of all.

It was our job to count the nuts, bolts and myriad minuscule washers kept loose in big, metal drawers. In most cases, the card indicated several hundred items, and it fell to us to confirm the accuracy of the information.

We worked in complete silence at first, our exchanges limited to the comparison of the two figures. Jacques would call out the number of items recorded on the card and I would count the contents of the drawer by hand. In some cases, it took me fifteen or twenty minutes. Once I had finished, I gave him the result.

While I tackled the washers, Jacques would smoke a cigarette or fire cutting remarks at the other stock-boys passing within earshot. We had several hundred reference numbers to check. The way things were going, we stood no chance of meeting the deadline.

From time to time, something would happen to break the monotony. One day, a group of mechanics took Snow White by surprise and shut him in a huge cardboard box, which they sealed with duck-tape.

From inside, Snow White roared with laughter. Rather than try to escape, he puffed cigarette smoke through a series of small holes he had drilled with a screwdriver. The show attracted all the stock-boys, and some of the mechanics. We all laughed out loud, until the workshop foreman arrived on the scene.

Loudspeakers played music at low volume over our heads. One morning, they played 'Lucille', by Little Richard. Jacques shook his hips, muttering that the idiot ought never to have given up singing. I told him the story about how Little Richard had seen a fireball in the sky and taken it as a command from God to quit devil-music and devote himself to gospel instead.

Jacques stared at me, transfixed. He asked me how I knew about that, too. We discovered our shared passion for rock music.

In the space of a few hours, Jacques was transformed and stocktaking became fun. We talked, and argued, and hummed the occasional number while we got on with the job. Time flew by.

Like me, Jacques loved Chuck Berry's guitar playing, and Jerry Lee

Lewis's wild beat. I knew Lewis had married a thirteen-year-old girl, but Jacques told me more: this was Lewis's second marriage, the first having been contracted when he was just fourteen. Jerry Lee Lewis said you had to be either hot or cold because if you were lukewarm, 'the Lord would spew you forth from His mouth'. Jacques told me, too, that Chuck Berry was the meanest man who ever lived. When he gave a concert abroad, he would keep an eye on the dollar rate, adjust his fee if it went up and only play if the money had cleared in advance. He told me that Chuck had overdubbed on one of his tracks, to avoid having to pay a second guitarist.

More than anyone, Jacques adored Eddie Cochran, who he reckoned embodied the essence of pure rock. In just a few songs, he had captured the atmosphere of an era, and the attitudes of a generation. What was more, like James Dean, he had passed into legend by dying at the right time. Jacques reckoned that in the year 2000, our children's children would still be listening to 'Summertime Blues'.

He was blown away by what the Beatles were doing. Their first album had been released that spring. Ten tracks recorded in half a day for the pathetic sum of four hundred pounds. Ten small masterpieces packed with chiming guitar work and catchy tunes. 'Twist and Shout' was my favourite. The track was a cover of a song by Medley and Russell, recorded at the end of the session when an exhausted John Lennon had barely any voice left.

By the end of the week, we had made good progress, but we still had half the cards to check and the boss was getting impatient. Jacques suggested we switch roles.

We changed our working method. I called out the reference number and he would march over to the drawer in question. I would read out the quantities given on the card: 613, 223 or 458. He would pull out the drawer, weigh it in one hand with an expression of intense concentration, and declare that the amount tallied, or we were three washers short. I would note the result. The whole operation took about fifteen seconds at most. We doubled over laughing. Having *ignored me for almost a year, he had adopted me in the space of three days.*

At the end of September, I reported to the Petit-Chateau barracks for my statutory three-day induction.

The site was near Avenue de la Couronne, where I had spent my childhood years. Everyone talked about the 'three days at Petit-Chateau', but in fact there were only two.

I had decided to try a plea of 'insanity'. My expert sources told me I should play my 'concussion' card, and convince them that the accident had done irreversible damage. I was further advised to talk gibberish and grind my teeth during the electro-encephalogram. Best of all, I should try to pick a fight or refuse to cooperate with the guys in charge.

That morning, I stood in the middle of the parade-ground, surrounded by a hundred other guys. Most were older than me and had finished their studies. Like me, they were clutching suitcases and looking lost.

Like me, they were deeply unenthusiastic at the prospect of spending fifteen months enlisted under the flag. Many had taken part in the unrest that accompanied the general strike of 1960. Listening to them talk amongst themselves, I knew the era of nicely brought-up, meek young people, conforming to strict parental and school rules, was coming to an end. Their talk made me think of Alex.

I began by answering a lengthy questionnaire. The soldiers asked me if I had a preferred weapon? Did I want be a non-commissioned officer? I refused any suggestion of officer status and opted for the air force, which was reputedly more open-minded than the land army.

At the end of the morning, I was given a metal identification tag on a chain. I was to wear it around my neck at all times, under my clothes. It bore my matriculation number, my name, my initials, my date of birth and the words Armée Belge. An officer came to explain that if we were found dead, the badge would be broken in half along the marked line, and sent to the ad hoc unit.

Next, we went for our medical check-up. We all stood naked in a row. We had to urinate into a flask and bend forward for the doctor to examine our arse-holes.

My file noted that I had suffered concussion, and I was sent for an electro-encephalogram. I looked dazed and rolled my eyes back as if I were half-mad. As soon as the examination was underway, I ground my teeth as instructed. The doctor called me to order and told me to stop taking him for a fool.

In the afternoon, we watched a film about war, the uses of morphine and the dangers of syphilis, backed up by a truly terrifying collection of photographs. We ended the day with a series of psycho-technical tests full of squares and circles and cogs. In the evening, I watched François Truffaut's The 400 Blows, *one more time. It was the only film they possessed.*

After dark, a few guys took out their hipflasks of liquor. We poured the filthy stuff down our throats and engaged in a gigantic pillow fight that ended in the small hours of the morning. Next day, they took a group photograph and informed us that the cost would be deducted from the money we would receive for our two days. At the end of the day, I stood in line and walked into an office where a military doctor announced I was fit to serve. I received the verdict with a mixture of incredulity and resignation. For better or worse, I knew those few words would change the course of my life.

I collected my things and left.

At the corner of the street, I tossed my ID badge down the drain.

26: GUILTY OF SOME OFFENCE

The Derscheid Clinic's chief consultant was an energetic woman in her forties, with a powerful voice and striking good looks.

On Wednesday, April the fifteenth, she attended X Midi's bedside with the entire multidisciplinary team. The latest reports she had seen suggested the man was ready for their visit.

She positioned her face in the man's line of vision and tried to hold his gaze.

'Hello, my name's Marie-Anne Perard. I'm the clinic's chief consultant.'

She paused, watching the man's eyes.

'I know you can understand me. I'm going to tell you what's happened to you, and explain what we are going to do.'

She stopped, turned to her assistants and indicated with a nod of the head that the man was clearly conscious. She turned to him once more and moved her head slightly to the left.

The man's eyes followed her.

'You have had an accident, Sir. We call it a cerebrovascular accident or CVA. It has affected your brain stem.'

She let the information sink in.

'Briefly, the brain stem is part of the central nervous system. It's located between the brain and the spinal cord, and it channels the nerves leading to and from your brain.'

A thin trickle of saliva escaped from the man's mouth.

'I'll be frank with you. For the moment, you're totally paralysed, but there is hope. You're responding well to the initial
treatment. You've begun to move the fingers of one hand,
which is a sign that you are entering the recovery phase – your
body is gradually reawakening. Your condition can improve. If
this continues, we can…'

She paused, seeking the right words.

'We can prolong your life. We may be able to help you
recover some of your faculties. But you have to help us.'

She passed a hand in front of X Midi's face.

The man's eyes widened.

'Can you sense my hand over your face? If you can feel my
hand, blink once.'

The man showed no reaction.

'I know you can understand me. We can communicate with
you, and you can communicate with us. We will ask questions
that require only a "yes" or "no" answer. To say yes, blink once.
To say no, blink twice.'

The man continued staring at her. She thought she could see
fear in his eyes.

'You need to trust us, there is hope, but you have to help us.
Are you ready to help us?'

She moved closer.

'I don't know what happened to you before the accident, but
you're safe here. Nothing bad can happen to you. I will come
and see you regularly. I can't force you to communicate with us,
but it will help us if you agree to cooperate.'

The man tried to avoid her gaze.

She stepped back and signalled to her team. They fell into
single file and left the room as quietly as possible, as if guilty of
some sort of offence.

27: AGAINST MY HEART

Scraps of the world before come to me. Sounds, colours, a few indistinct images. During the day, they inflict the television on me: cartoons, idiotic game shows or repeats of old football matches. The sound is turned down so low I can't grasp what's going on.

Yesterday, a rock group burst onto the screen. Four crazed guys. No idea which century they were from. I opened my eyes wide. I concentrated hard to try to hear them. The guitarists pulled faces and writhed like demons, the drummer was fired up, shaking his head all around, the singer twirled and waved in a flood of light.

A few notes and a thin, reedy voice were all I could hear, but for a moment, I felt alive.

Someone entered the room and switched off the TV. Overstimulation is to be avoided.

Sometimes they stroke my skin lightly, bend over me, feel my muscles. One of them works hard, pummelling and kneading my carcass. But his hands do some good. He massages my legs, feet and back, and the nape of my neck.

A woman asked me to pucker my lips, as if I was going to give her a kiss. She opened my mouth with her fingers. I had to slide my tongue along my palate. She said it was good, I was making progress.

Another woman came to talk to me about hope.

What hope? The hope of escaping one prison for another? Imagination and memories are my only escape. Nothing else.

If they only knew how much I value freedom. For freedom, I gave up everything I cherished most in the world.

My call-up papers arrived in late autumn. Two gendarmes called first thing in the morning, to deliver them in person. It was raining. There was a strong wind. The trees were skeletal, their leaves swirled along the street.

I was to report to the Dossin barracks in Malines on the second of January 1964, before 10:00a.m. The papers said I would spend three months there before joining a unit as a typist, at the operational head-quarters of a mobile evacuation hospital near Cologne, in Germany. A train ticket was included with the forms.

Next day, I told my boss I would be leaving work to complete my military service. He stared me up and down and declared it would knock some sense into me.

At lunch break, Jacques took me to one side. He could see I was anxious, and miserable. To cheer me up, he told me about his own adventures in military service, with the Paracommandos. He had intervened in the riots in Leopoldville, shortly before the Congo secured independence, and witnessed the events that followed.

He promised my own service would be much less challenging. I'd spend a couple of days in the cells, be knocked out once or twice and experience some memorable hangovers, and an agonising dose of the clap.

In December, I spent most evenings over at Alex's. I brought supplies of food and beer. In exchange, Alex supplied me with hash and marijuana.

We ate listening to Bo Diddley, B.B. King or the Beatles, whose second album had been released a few weeks earlier, on the day that Kennedy's assassination in Dallas shocked the world.

Alex was unconvinced by the Beatles, despite the definitive tracks on their second album, like 'I Want to Hold Your Hand' and 'She Loves You', with its stream of 'yeahs'.

After eating, we would light a joint under the earnest gaze of Che Guevara, and Alex would start talking. He knew my mind was made up, but he compounded my firm belief that I was doing the right thing.

He told me the story of a decent kid of seventeen, a Midwest farmer's boy, well-liked by all, who found himself embroiled in the Hell of Vietnam, against his will.

One of his comrades was killed in an ambush by the Viet Cong. A few days later, they found the body. His balls had been cut off and stuffed into his mouth. Then his head had been cut off and stuck on a bamboo spike.

Next day, the decent kid from the Midwest walked into a peaceful village and massacred an entire family by smashing their heads with his rifle butt. The women and children weren't spared. When his officer came to put an end to the carnage, he blew his brains out.

According to Alex, it was possible I could react like that kid, in a comparable situation. War turned men into animals and monsters. The CIA was training secret death squads whose job was to terrorise South Vietnam by killing civilians.

We couldn't stand by while crimes like these were perpetrated, he said. We shared in the guilt if we let such atrocities go unprotested. It was our duty to revolt. Young people had to seize power, stop the slaughter and encourage men to act like human beings again.

He explained all this calmly, with a strange light in his eyes, as if he had witnessed the events he was describing.

On New Year's Eve, I played with Alex and The Four Fours for a private function near Ohain, in a hall hired for the occasion by a well-heeled crowd. The party had aspirations to 'decadence', with an Ancient Roman theme.

Everyone was in fancy dress, us included. The men posed and camped it up in their immaculate togas. Women plastered in outrageous make-up laughed uproariously, their breasts all but bared.

To me, the atmosphere of wild excess felt indecent, and out of place. On the other side of the world, children were being scorched by napalm bombs, Buddhist monks were pouring petrol over themselves and burning to death in the hope of raising humanity's awareness of their plight. Innocent people were dying every minute, on both sides.

We finished playing at around five thirty in the morning. The last guests had gone, and the van collecting our stuff wasn't coming until the next day.

I needed some time alone.

Alex and the others had left.

I carried on playing. I thrashed my drums to the point of exhaustion. Around noon, I went home. But I couldn't sleep. Late that night, I packed my case. I took a few clothes, my wash kit and the dozen books that mattered to me the most.

When everything was ready, I sat in the kitchen and waited for the night to be over.

We had kept the old furniture from our apartment on Avenue de la Couronne. On the table, I could see the scratches and spots of colour from my childhood.

My mother found me half asleep at around 6:00a.m. I told her it was time, that I had to go. I stood up and held her in my arms. I can still feel the press of her body against mine. I feel her warmth, the smell of her hair.

She knew I was in a bad way. But she couldn't know what what really tormented me. She told me not to worry, that it would be all right, everything would always be all right.

I hugged her tight, unable to let go. There were tears in my eyes. She stroked my face.

My father didn't join us. I could see him watching from the shadows of the living room. My mother told me he wished me good luck, and that he looked forward to seeing me again in my smart uniform, when I came home on leave, standing tall and proud with my hair cut short.

I picked up my case and left the apartment. I found the strength not to look back. My mother's face at the window would have broken my resolve. I never imagined that was the last time I would hold her tight against my heart.

28: DESTINATION BERLIN

A few days after reading the detective's report into the death of their son, contesting the verdict of suicide, Steve Parker's parents contacted the families of the other members of Pearl Harbor to propose a meeting.

Larry Finch's aunt declined the invitation. Her sister, Larry's mother, had killed herself shortly after receiving the news of her son's death, and Larry's aunt was unable to overcome the pain of the loss of her two closest relatives. She didn't want to think about it ever again, and was trying to forget the circumstances surrounding the tragedy. She gave strict instructions to be left in peace and cut the call without further ado.

Jim Ruskin's parents agreed to the request, with a mixture of bitterness and relief. The police investigation's conclusion, that the deaths of the four musicians were an extraordinary coincidence, was unacceptable. Jim's father was unconvinced by the explanations he had received from the chief of police when he travelled to West Berlin to collect his son's remains.

Since the events of March, he had studied a number of books on the law of series, probability, significant coincidences and synchronicity.

He was certain the deaths were connected, and suspicious. He had put forward a number of theories, but was unable to identify a single coherent motive. The call from Steve's parents confirmed his view: other people were questioning the police's conclusions. He would not stand alone in the face of suspicion and the impenetrable wall of officialdom any longer.

Dirk and Caroline McDonald, parents of Paul the drummer, also agreed to meet, and invited their son's ex-wife to join them. Jason, their grandson, refused to accept the theory of accidental death, and was convinced his father had been murdered.

The McDonalds were alarmed by the account of their son's movements in the days prior to his death. He had behaved like a man on the run. Paul was afraid of nothing, his father said. He wouldn't hesitate to face up to adversity and take a stand if necessary. He was not one to shut himself away in a hotel room for no good reason.

The meeting took place in London, at the Parkers' home, on Saturday, July the fifteenth, 1967.

None of the guests knew one another, they had never had occasion to meet and no one had attended the funeral of another member of Pearl Harbor.

They felt an immediate closeness, united by the pain of losing a child.

When everyone had arrived, Steve's father, Gary Parker, made a short, emotional speech evoking the agony of a father who outlives his son. When he had finished, his wife served refreshments. The first hour was spent sharing memories of the dead. Some had brought photographs, which were passed around.

Next, the Parkers introduced the assembled company to George West, the detective hired to investigate Steve's death.

West set out his reasons for questioning the outcome of the police investigation. He shared his findings, and the conclusions drawn. Amongst other things, he cited the tiny probability that four men sharing the same apartment and doing the same job could die within such a short space of time without some cloud of suspicion surrounding their deaths.

Next, he invited everyone around the table to say a few words. The families shared the facts at their disposal.

West listened attentively, took notes, asked questions. When he had collected all the available information, he made a few remarks.

There had been inadequate coordination between the German, Spanish and British police. No organisation had taken the possibility of a connection seriously, each death had been treated in isolation. If the four deaths had been handled by a single police force, he had no doubt a more thorough-going investigation would have been launched.

He collected his notes and highlighted a few points he had picked up during the round-table discussion. He noted that the hotel porter in Majorca had observed all Larry's comings and goings, but had not seen him come down to the swimming pool between five and six in the morning, despite being still on duty at that time.

Why hadn't he seen him? How had Larry reached the pool? Why hadn't he taken the shortest route, via the hotel lobby?

As for Jim Ruskin's supposed depression, cited by the Berlin police, this seemed surprising in a man whose even temper, optimism and enjoyment of life were well known. He was unlikely to have killed himself on a whim. Ruskin had just heard about the death of the group's leader, Larry Finch, and the news would doubtless have affected him, but not to the point of suicide, particularly given his lack of awareness of the death of Steve Parker.

Jim had talent, and his Berlin contacts would certainly have enabled him to pursue his musical career. His volatile friendship with Larry was an insufficient motive for suicide.

Finally, the train driver's testimony gave no explicit reason to suspect Jim had thrown himself voluntarily onto the tracks.

As for Paul McDonald, the fact that he had bolted his door from the inside had led the police to the hasty conclusion that no one else could have got into the room. But how could they be certain Paul hadn't let someone in, of his own accord?

West knew the Samarkand Hotel. Paul's room was on the fifth or sixth floor. An escape across the rooftops would have been child's play.

He concluded with a question. Where had the money come from?

The musicians had all complained about their meagre salaries, and the difficulty they experienced making ends meet. Yet at the time of their deaths, Larry Finch was staying in a four-star hotel in Majorca, Steve Parker had treated himself to the charms of several hostesses around Sankt Pauli and a very expensive, bootleg Hendrix ticket and Paul McDonald had purchased a plane ticket to London and installed himself in a luxury hotel.

When West had finished, Steve Parker's parents outlined their proposition. They suggested to all present that they extend the detective's contract and pay for his continued enquiries, sharing the costs amongst themselves.

Contrary to their expectations, everyone refused.

Jim Ruskin's mother was aware of her husband's doubts on the matter. But she would rather accept the verdict of suicide than discover her son had committed some other, unspeakable act. She was still grieving and couldn't face any further torment. She knew Jim drank and took drugs, and she thought that may have something to do with his death. She wanted to remember him as a gentle, playful, lively lad.

Paul McDonald's parents said they were facing financial diffi-culties and were in no position to fund an investigation, the outcome of which remained uncertain, despite the evidence. Paul's ex-wife Margreth bitterly regretted the situation, but she was on the dole and couldn't contemplate any extra expense.

The Parkers weren't in a position to pay the detective on their own. West had no intention of negotiating his fee; he was in high demand and his many clients were more than happy to pay what he asked.

As he was leaving, Jim Ruskin's father suggested taking their story to the papers. Until now, not a single journalist had shown an interest in the serial deaths.

The proposal was adopted.

They drafted a letter detailing the facts, and signed it jointly.

The letter was dispatched to the main London daily papers, but attracted no favourable replies. The families shifted their focus to smaller papers and the regional press, still to no avail.

Just as they were about to give up, a journalist from the *Belfast Telegraph*, to whom Dirk McDonald had sent the letter in a last-ditch effort to attract some interest, got in touch with the group and suggested a meeting.

The Ruskins and the Parkers gathered at the McDonalds' home in Dublin on September the eighth, 1967, for a late afternoon meeting with Michael Stern, the journalist in question.

At first, all were somewhat disconcerted. On a first impression, Stern had none of the calm assurance of George West. He was short, bald and shifty-looking. He squinted as if in bright sunlight, and pushed constantly at a large pair of glasses that slipped down his nose.

They were encouraged by his apparent empathy, however, and his willingness to listen.

After their interview, the journalist confirmed his interest in the affair and promised to get the green light from his editor-in-chief, to begin investigating the suspicious deaths.

A few days later, Stern announced that he had secured the go-ahead, and asked the families to give him everything they had in relation to the case. He hoped to try to reconstruct each band member's movements from the moment Pearl Harbor was formed, until March 1967. He was optimistic, he said, and ready to pull out all the stops to shed light on this murky business.

On Monday, September the eighteenth, 1967, Michael Stern boarded a plane, destination Berlin.

29: THE WAY I LOOKED

I took the tram to Brussels Midi. The station was on a more human scale back then. None of the gaudy shops and gangs of threatening youths I saw on my return.

In the main hall, I felt as if everyone was watching me, as if the word 'deserter' was written all over my face.

I walked to the platform, head down, clutching the ticket I had bought. I climbed aboard the train and moved along the corridors, searching for a seat with no one opposite.

I checked my watch constantly. My feelings of guilt increased with each passing minute. I imagined the consternation of the military authorities, the call to my parents, the missing person notices. I felt worse still when the ticket controller and customs officers entered my compartment. They studied my face and papers, then left.

The time of innocence was past. I had broken the law, and needed to be constantly on my guard.

I reached my destination around noon. Alex had told me that Paris was livelier than Brussels, but the difference between the two capitals, less than three hundred kilometres apart, was beyond my imagination.

The streets were thronged with people. The boulevards were choked with slow-moving traffic that roared and belched thick smoke. People walked and ran in all directions, gesticulating and talking loudly. My head spun. I entered a maelstrom of unfamiliar noise, colour and smells.

Around me, Paris bubbled with life, and I was alone in all the world.

I went down into the metro. I was disorientated. I boarded a train going in the wrong direction and became lost in the labyrinth before finding my bearings and alighting at Saint-Michel in mid-afternoon. I headed for Chez Popov, a bar on Rue de la Huchette. My stomach was empty. I was ready to go back on my decision.

By chance, the elderly Russian couple Alex had told me about were there. When I told them he'd sent me, they welcomed me with open arms.

They showed me the back room. Sleeping bags littered the floor. A lanky young American lay stretched out on one. He was reading Jack Kerouac's On the Road *and smoking a cigarette. The book was in tatters. He greeted me as if my arrival was the most natural thing in the world. In strongly accented French, he asked me where I had come from and if I liked Bob Dylan. I had no idea who he was talking about, and replied that I hadn't read anything of his yet. He told me I had a sense of humour and that we were sure to get along.*

He had a round, pink face like a soft sweet, and smiled all the time. Everyone called him Candy. We ate, and hit it off there and then. After the meal, he leapt to his feet and announced we would go find the others.

We walked to the Square du Vert Galant, at the tip of Ile de la Cité. The others were a bunch of guys like him, young men who had decided to break with convention and hit the road. They had come from all over. As well as French, there were English and Americans, and a few Dutch. They massaged one another on the public benches. They seemed to have occupied the space and chased out the passers-by. Some were lying under the weeping willow, wrapped in large blankets. Others were sitting on the stone quayside, backs to the wall. Joints were passed from hand to hand. Most people had nicknames. Finger, an American, had had the last phalange of his index finger ampu-tated, to avoid being called to serve in Vietnam.

A fair number of them reminded me of Alex. They spoke and looked like him: indolent, and scruffy, with long hair. One or two were almost thirty. An old guy from Nantes, known as Cheyenne, was over sixty. He had a deeply lined face and faded blue eyes. He wore a beard, and long white hair parted down the middle. His nickname came from a coloured bandanna he wore tied around his forehead.

He wasn't the group leader, but a kind of sage, respected by all. Whenever the occasion presented, he would take a book by Rimbaud from out of his pocket and lose himself in its pages, looking up only to call for silence and read us a passage out loud.

I spent my first weeks with them. I followed them from morning to evening and late into the night. In addition to the Square du Vert Galant, their favourite spots were Saint-Germain-des-Prés and the quaysides along the Seine.

In the evening, everyone would meet at Place de la Contrescarpe. They would sit along the fountain rim or directly on the cobblestones. If it was too cold, they would crowd around a table in one of the bistros. They talked politics, literature, music. They discussed human nature and God. The spectre of war was everywhere. The Americans talked about Vietnam, the war their country's young people were confronting head on. The French talked about the last wars, and Indochina, and Algeria: open wounds that seemed to have scarred their memory. Everyone talked about the coming war, the one that would destroy planet Earth.

They talked all day long, in sombre, grandiose terms. They would get carried away, raise their voices, disagree furiously, slam their hands on the table and issue dark threats, even when no one contradicted them.

From time to time, they would get into a discussion with someone from the other camp, the ones they called the 'bourgeois reactionaries'. Things would quickly turn sour. More than once, they almost came to blows.

I never got caught up in the conversation. I listened. I wanted to form my own opinion before defending theirs. Often, they would seek my approval of the theories they put forward. But even if I had an opinion, I wasn't able to put it into words. Eventually, they accepted my status as a taciturn observer.

Their arguments were often confused, or contradictory. They said they were anti-war, and their badges preached disarmament or anti-militarism. But many wore items of American army uniform: khaki shirts, parkas, military caps and boots.

They tried to explain the symbolism behind their choice. But I never understood their logic. They said they were pacifists but they walked around dressed like soldiers.

In the same way, I felt respect for the late John Fitzgerald Kennedy, and couldn't picture him as a bloodthirsty warmonger, manipulated by the demonic McNamara – as they maintained he was.

I didn't want to spark a fight and find myself rejected by the group. I said nothing.

Money-wise, I was getting by. I had brought all my savings with me. I had taken Alex's advice and converted my Belgian francs to dollars. A thick wad of green slumbered at the bottom of my case. I changed a note from time to time, to cover my needs. I thought my funds would see me through until I found a stable job.

Events decided otherwise, and the money quickly vanished. The group said that money drove the economy, and the economy drove the war. They were proud not to have any, and were all the better for it.

Encouraged by the group, I squandered what I had, to match their free-wheeling status. I financed the group's lifestyle. I paid for meals, drinks and grass. When there was nothing left, I did as they did, and asked for money on the streets. Begging was frowned upon, and I had to watch out for the police.

Candy played guitar – mornings down in the metro, afternoons on café terraces. One day, I offered to join him. He hesitated, then agreed.

I had brought my sticks. At first, I watched him for a day or two. I kept an eye on the coins people tossed into his guitar case.

One morning, I felt confident enough to try. I waited until he launched into a blues, and drummed along, beating on the ground. He loved it. He didn't know I was a drummer. He liked what I was doing, and so did the public.

I let rip after that. On bistro terraces, I would bang on the ground, the walls, the pipework, bottles, table-tops, the waiters' trays, whatever was to hand. I whirled around Candy like a satellite in orbit.

On the pavement, people would stop, tap their feet, clap their hands, sing along with us. Some afternoons, we would gather an audience of about fifty. We made money, but the crowd attracted the police and more than once we had to make a run for it.

Candy knew my situation, and covered me when I ran off. He would slow down and let himself be taken in my stead. His American passport was a magic ticket. He never spent more than an hour in custody.

On one of our escapades, we met a diaphanous youth who played like us, on the steps of the Sacré-Coeur. He was a singer and guitarist, pleasant, open and hugely talented. I saw him again years later, on TV. He had cut and dyed his hair, and become the French pop star, Michel Polnareff.

From then on, Candy and I played together every day. At the end of the evening, we would count out the money and share it. Then we would eat, get drunk and smoke joints. We would go back to Chez Popov just before dawn, and set out again a few hours later. I was free, I felt great, though I was hungry and getting thinner by the day.

I liked our autonomous lifestyle, but the ersatz drumming was losing its appeal. I missed playing for real. I had itchy hands and feet.

The Paris rock scene was unlikely to fulfil my aspirations. The Beatles were a massive hit in France, especially after playing the Olympia earlier that year. Other British bands like the Rolling Stones and the Spencer Davis Group were being talked about, too, but the French remained focused on their beloved héxagone. They were determined to protect their home-grown stars, rather than embrace real rock.

France had its yéyés – named for the Beatles' 'yeah, yeah, yeah' – an insipid bunch singing insipid songs. Some of them fancied themselves as real, hard rocker: dilettantes like Johnny Hallyday, Eddy Mitchell, or Dick Rivers. I gave them two years at most, before they sank into oblivion. They thought that by anglicising their names, covering English and American rock standards and half-heartedly wiggling their hips, they could be real rockers. Eddy Mitchell's insipid cover of 'Maybellene' brought tears to the eyes.

Even Sylvie Vartan, a dumb blonde of about my age, who had shared the spotlight with the Beatles at the Olympia, assured everyone quite seriously, on the radio, that she was singing rock and roll.

A few years earlier, in the Fifties, Henry Cording had been France's first self-proclaimed rock singer. His music was beneath notice, but his lyricist was the poet and novelist Boris Vian. Now, under the name Henri Salvador, the same singer was squeaking and gibbering his way through an appalling series of novelty hits, not least an abysmally mawkish song about a little mouse called Minnie.

One thing led to another. Cheyenne discovered I could play drums and was looking for a job with a band. He was a musician himself, and had played trumpet in a jazz group after the war. He told me there was a musicians' labour exchange of sorts, on Friday evenings at Porte Saint-Martin, near the Théâtre de la Renaissance. Instrumentalists looking for work would swap tips and openings, and people in work could find replacements as required.

I found the place, but it was deserted. A bistro owner told me the exchange had moved to Pigalle. I stopped by several times but came away with nothing. I had almost given up on the idea of drumming for a living when, by pure chance, Candy took me along one evening to the Cigale jazz club.

The place was full of music lovers, and jazz fans in particular.
Candy introduced me to Maurice, a musician he knew from the
Antilles. He played trombone with a small line-up, and invited me to
jam the following evening, in a cellar on Rue de Clichy.

I went along. I played all night, alternating with another drummer,
a somewhat aloof Frenchman who called himself Mike. By the small
hours, I was exhausted and happy. I had reconnected with my old
sensations. My technique was intact, as if my hands had a memory
all their own. One of the guitarists came over to ask if I would play
with him. He was called André and wanted to form a rock group. He
knew a good bass player, and had his eye on a singer. What was more,
he had a new drum kit I could play.

Two weeks later, we began rehearsing. André lived on Rue de
Provence. We called ourselves Les Tourbillons – the Whirlwinds. We
weren't bad. The singer knew a few people, and got us some gigs.

We played several times at the Golf-Drouot, on a Friday night. Five
or six groups took turns over the course of the evening. We had forty-
five minutes to convince the public and earn the chance to come back
the following week. I had some great times there. It was the high
temple of Paris rock, with an audience of true music fans. They were
great teachers, and we made great progress.

A few weeks later, we played a rock festival at the Tabarin, a caba-
ret at the foot of Montmartre. The bill included big names like Vince
Taylor and the Chats Sauvages.

After our set, a man in his forties, dressed in a suit and tie, came
over and asked if we would like to record some studio demos. We
showed up a few days later, in Seine-Saint-Denis, on Paris's north
rim. Not really a studio, just a bare room with a tape recorder and a
Neuman mic standing in the middle.

The man was waiting for us, with a technician and a sour-looking
woman who stared me up and down. He gave us a few sheets of
music, recent English and American hits for the most part.

We positioned ourselves around the mic, and the technician did a quick sound check. We played about ten numbers from the repertoire, and a couple of André's compositions. The two men and the woman listened, stroking their chins. They sat on rickety chairs off to one side, all in a row. From time to time, they would whisper in one another's ears.

The man got to his feet in the middle of a number and signalled for us to stop. He called André over. They left the room and came back fifteen minutes later. The band was hired to record a single, but the man didn't want me.

My playing wasn't the problem, but my personal style was. He didn't want a beatnik on his books. He would find another drummer to play with Les Tourbillons. André was sorry, but he couldn't pass up an opportunity like that. He fired me on the spot.

I went back to Candy and the others, and my recitals on the grands boulevards.

Autumn was drawing to a close, and my second Parisian winter loomed. The English guys headed back to London one by one. There was a lot going on. Young people were making themselves heard. London was The Place to Be. A new craze was sweeping the music scene – rhythm'n'blues. New groups were emerging every day. People talked about The Animals, The Kinks and The Who.

The Who positioned themselves as dangerous competition for the Beatles. They had a drummer who played like no one ever before.

What was more, a pirate radio station called Radio Caroline was spearheading a revolution. Broadcast from a boat anchored outside territorial waters, Caroline played great music all day long, a thousand miles from the never-ending diet of Tom Jones and Engelbert Humperdinck, as authorised by the stiff-shirted big-wigs at the BBC.

For the first time, you didn't need a well-known name, a contract with a big-time label or a government-approved sound to get airplay.

I liked Paris, but I knew I would have to cross the Channel if I was to keep playing drums and not get fired for the way I looked.

30: ON THE SCREEN

The month of June was marked by an unusual heatwave. Despite air-conditioning, many patients suffered from the high temperatures, and the clinic regretfully recorded a number of deaths.

X Midi seemed unaffected, however, and was making good progress.

Each afternoon, the porters would install him in a wheelchair, and one of the care staff would walk him along the corridors in the clinic. Weather permitting, they would walk outside, along the avenues in the park.

Every two days, he was taken to the physiotherapy unit to be verticalised. The therapy consisted of strapping the patient to a tilt table and gradually moving him into an upright position. The treatment promoted respiratory mobility and helped decrease spasticity. It was also thought to have psychological benefits.

Thanks to the verticalisation sessions, and daily bronchial draining with the physio, X Midi was now able to breathe unaided.

The occupational therapist had noted more ample rotations of the head, and firmer movement in the fingers of the left hand. The man was now able to stretch the corners of his mouth. A speech therapist set to work, and detected the emission of a few sounds.

Marie-Anne Perard made one of her regular visits, on Tuesday, June the twenty-eight, towards the end of the morning. She was accompanied by a tall, well-built therapist, wearing a broad smile.

The chief consultant stood beside X Midi.

'Hello. My colleagues tell me you're making encouraging progress. Congratulations.'

The man stared straight into her eyes.

'Are you hot?'

No reaction.

'Are you in pain anywhere?'

The man continued staring at her, without blinking.

'You still don't want to communicate with us?'

She turned to her giant of a colleague and beckoned him to come forward. She stepped aside so that he could enter X Midi's field of vision.

'This is Dominique. He's just joined the team and will be your physio from tomorrow. Dominique is French, he's worked at the clinic in Garches and has experience of cases similar to yours. I'm sure you'll get along.'

The man's eyes moved, and rested on the physio.

Dominique's smile broadened. He winked at X Midi.

'She's right. I'm sure we'll get along fine.'

The chief consultant stepped back into view.

'Thanks to Dominique, you'll be able to visit our pool. We've allowed for two or three sessions a week. It will do you a great deal of good.'

Dominique winked again.

'You'll see. Pool sessions with Dominique – the best thing!'

Now it was Marie-Anne Perard's turn to smile.

'I hope Dominique's enthusiasm proves infectious. I hear you can move your fingers – is that right?'

No reaction.

'Are you hot? Would you like us to take off your gown for a few minutes?'

The man shifted his eyes to the television screen. An American soap was playing with the sound turned down.

'Well, I'll leave you in peace. Keep up the good progress.'

She left the room. Dominique stayed behind, alone with X Midi.

He moved close to the bed, smiling broadly.

'So, it's just the two of us now. I suggest we both get along on first-name terms – what do you say?'

X Midi continued staring at the television.

'If you're in agreement, blink once.'

No reaction.

The physio laughed heartily.

'You are some joker! You understand what I'm saying, but you don't want to answer, is that it?'

X Midi ignored the question.

'OK, you don't want to talk. You'd rather watch rubbish on TV?'

He had an idea.

'Know what, if we do some good work together, you and me, I can help you get some more movement in your fingers. Once they're agile, we'll teach you to use the remote. You can choose what you want to watch. What do you think?'

The man detached his gaze from the TV and stared into the physio's eyes.

Dominique wagged his head, his eyes open wide in triumph.

'Aha! That's got you interested!'

The man stared at him intently.

'You'd like me to work with you so you can stop watching this crap and choose whichever programme you want?'

The man shifted his gaze back to the images on the screen.

31: FIRST TRAIN TO CALAIS

They lay me out on a plastic mat. On top, they lay a square of blue, synthetic material. The heat prickles my backside. They wrap me in a gown that makes me sweat.

They know what they are doing. It's a stratagem to get me to talk.

They've sent me Snow White, but I'm not fooled. Snow White was younger, though they are alike in other ways – the same enthusiasm, the same laugh. He's been trying to blackmail me, almost from the first moment I saw him.

He has them take me to the pool. It's an ordeal, I hate it. The men in white burst into my room unannounced and take me to a white-tiled room. A sort of spider's web is lowered from the ceiling. They truss me up in the net and dip me into a pool filled with warm water. For a moment, I feel like one of the kids learning to swim at La Perche.

When the night is over, they take my temperature and blood pressure. They administer their drugs through the gastric tube. They hook up a plastic bag filled with brownish liquid. When the bag's empty, they take me out of the room, down a labyrinth of corridors. One day, a few notes of music floated from one of the rooms. 'A Day in the Life'. The nightmare came back to haunt me.

In the corridors, I cross paths with the others. Crips. Nutters. Death-cheaters. Poor sods with no legs, no arms, twisted faces, mouths stuck in a hideous leer.

When they see me, they stare. I can read their eyes.

A kid so thin it's frightening stations himself near the entrance, huddled in his chair. He reads comic books out loud. In the lift, I met a young woman in a wheelchair. She was beautiful. She smiled at me. Her chest was strapped into a corset. She had only one leg.

After the TV weather report, they take me to a big room. They hoist me up in the middle like Christ on the summit of Golgotha. They exhibit me for all to see. At my feet, the crips gesticulate, and pedal, and sigh, and groan, and lift their eyes to me.

And then – sacrificed, powerless, entirely at their mercy – I think of Floriane. I see her smile, her misty gaze, the open gift of her body. I hear her voice breathing my name in the half-light.

I never understood it was a call for help.

Winter came, and 1965 was almost upon us.

I was drinking more and more. My daily intake of hash or grass had become a vital need, and money was short.

Jimbo, the dealer who supplied my dope, suggested I work for him. He hung around Rue de la Huchette, plying his trade from group to group.

He boasted of living in the same building as Chester Himes, on Rue Bourbon-le-Chateau. He must have been five or six years older than me. A port-wine stain slashed his forehead. He was incapable of standing still, always fidgeting and glancing around, as if afraid someone might appear out of nowhere.

It was my job to hang around the bistros near private schools attended by the offspring of the wealthy bourgeoisie, and pass on his merchandise.

In France, back then, plenty of stuff was produced and trafficked, but it wasn't widely used. In Paris, there were still a few opium dens, and a handful of night clubs in Montparnasse where you could sniff or inject heroin. In Pigalle, the blacks smoked 'Marie-Jeanne' in the basements of certain bars, but this was nothing to what I found later, in London.

I hesitated, but Jimbo set me straight. I would be doing the kids a service, expanding their consciousness, opening the doors of perception to another place, far from the materialist consumer society that rotted their souls in the here and now.

For the others, grass was just another component of their philosophy of anti-institutionalism, freedom from constraint and intellectual enquiry far off the beaten track. Jimbo's words reflected their thinking. They made sense. I agreed to work for him.

Next day, I began prospecting. After a few fruitless attempts, I found a good spot, a bistro on Rue de Londres, not far from a well-known private school. At lunch break, and after class, the bistro filled with hordes of pretentious, reckless kids.

For the first few days, I made a show of ignoring them, absorbed in a book I took along for the purpose. I chose titles likely to attract their attention – On the Road, The Catcher in the Rye, *or* The Naked Lunch, *but also texts by Sartre, or Cocteau. I bought a book by Françoise Sagan, too. I heard she had been a student at their school for a time.*

With my nose in my book, I listened to their talk. Mostly platitudes and chit-chat, but they would discuss current affairs, too, or philosophy, or politics. They took themselves tremendously seriously, and seemed convinced they were part of some sort of élite.

One day, I insinuated my way into the conversation. They were surprised at first. My appearance and way of talking were disconcerting, but they had got used to seeing me around, and let me have my say.

I did the same over the days that followed. They found my ideas attractive, even seductive, and finally, fascinating.

All I did was rehearse the broad lines of the arguments put forward by other members of our group. I repeated what I heard every day, with conviction. I talked about the counter-culture, about ignoring tomorrow, about freedom, peace and love. I told them about writers I had met. I told them about myself. I invented a past life with my philosopher parents, in some mysterious country on the other side of the world.

Day by day, my aura blossomed. I grew in their estimation, from marginal, to original, until finally I acquired the status of guru. When I walked into the bistro, a group would form around me. They would wait for me to arrive, and press me with questions.

I would look inspired, talking quietly, with great serenity, just as I had seen Alex do. They seemed unbothered by my persistent stumbling, over certain words. Sometimes I would answer with a stream of nonsense. They drank it in. I was astonished by the influence I exerted over them.

Meanwhile, Jimbo was becoming impatient.

I told him I was making progress, but that it was important to take things step by step.

One thing led to another, and the question was broached: what could help them attain the level of consciousness and lucidity they so envied in me?

I told them to meet me one Thursday afternoon in the Saint-Lazare train station, nearby. We found a quiet corner. I rolled a joint in front of them and told them to pass it around, explaining how to inhale the smoke.

The effects were soon felt. One by one, they got high as kites.

Next day, they placed their first order.

Floriane was one of them. She was my age. She was beautiful, with long blonde hair, freckles that devoured her face and big, blue eyes that called out in distress. She was an only child. Her father was a high-powered businessman, and her mother had taken a lover.

She became one of my best clients. Her personal consumption increased steadily, and she brought new recruits, demanding greater and greater quantities.

After a few weeks, she wanted to take things to the next level. I was reluctant, but she insisted, so I spoke to Jimbo.

He told me she was quite right. Puffing a joint was a joke, compared to shooting up. Intravenous was best, he said. He talked about 'the flash'. He could get what she wanted.

I had no idea what he was talking about. He said he would admin-
ister her first shoot, and show her how to do it herself.

I spoke to Floriane.

A few days later, she told me to come to her place that night. The
timing was right; her father was away on business, and her mother
was sleeping elsewhere.

That evening, I went to her place with Jimbo. He brought two
friends along, Fuzzi, a guitarist I saw from time to time at Chez
Popov, and Roman, an angular type with a beaked nose, who I had
never seen before, and who was introduced as a childhood friend.

Floriane was waiting with a friend, Pascale, a brown-haired girl
with generous breasts and a wild look. Floriane lived next to the Parc
Monceau, in a big apartment painted entirely in white. The carpet
was white, too. Colourful pictures hung on the walls. A huge, gleam-
ing, black grand piano took pride of place in the sitting room.

She put on some music. We sank into deep, raw leather sofas. We
got to know one another, smoked and drank. Jimbo prepared a pipe
crammed with a dark, thick, viscous substance. He called it dross and
said we could tell him what we thought of it, later.

Things soon hotted up. I was very drunk, and half stoned. Floriane
took me by the hand and led me to her parents' bedroom. As soon as
she had closed the door, she pressed herself against me and kissed me
on the mouth.

I had no idea what Jimbo had put in the pipe, but we were both
very turned on. I hadn't slept with anyone since leaving Brussels. She
knelt. I climaxed almost immediately, and again when we made love,
responding to Floriane's small cries of pleasure.

Then she got up, opened the door and called to Jimbo. He entered
the room, looked at me and smiled.

He held a bath towel, which he spread over the bed. He assembled
the syringe and filled it. Floriane looked anxious. He told her he was
used to this, everything would be all right.

He strapped her biceps, tapped on her forearm, found a vein, inserted the needle and pressed down on the syringe. Floraine shuddered, her eyes rolled back and her whole body jerked.

Jimbo told me to leave the room and fetch Roman.

In the sitting room, Fuzzi was flirting with Pascale. They were half-lying on the divan, licking one another's lips. He had one hand under her sweater, caressing her breasts. Their cheeks were on fire.

I poured myself a whisky. I wandered into the library. I staggered along the corridor. My perspective was distorted. I lost all notion of time and distance.

When I came back to the sitting room, Pascale was kneeling at the foot of the sofa, one hand moving under her skirt, while Fuzzi hunched over her mouth.

I heard sounds from the bedroom. I hesitated at first, but thought I heard a cry. I pushed the door. Floraine lay sandwiched between Jimbo and Roman. She looked absent, inert, her body jerking with the movements of the other two. She turned to look at me and stretched out a hand. The scene was blurred, unreal, distant.

I didn't understand that it was a call for help.

I left and closed the door. I was close to passing out. I had a vague sense that what was happening in the bedroom was not right, that rules had been broken. I was aware of it, but unable to summon the energy to feel outraged or do anything about it. I stood for a long time in front of the closed door.

A long cry rang out. Jimbo and Roman emerged from the bedroom. They were shouting at one another. In the sitting room, they came to blows. Fuzzi and Pascale had disappeared into one of the bedrooms. Jimbo and Roman were trading blows, making no effort to shield themselves from each other's swipes. The punches made a dull, thudding noise. Jimbo was bleeding from the nose. Blood spurted, staining the white walls and carpet. Roman carried on hitting him. Jimbo swayed. His face was covered with blood.

I took fright and left. I ran. People stared at me in the street. I must

have looked like a madman. I managed to get home. Candy and I were
sharing a fourth-floor room in a building on Rue de la Harpe. I hid
under the covers and sank into unconsciousness.

Candy shook me awake at dawn.

Jimbo was outside on the street.

I had a headache. Images from the night before came to me in
waves. I felt as if I had woken from a nightmare. I put my head out of
the window. Jimbo looked half-crazed. I went downstairs. He was
covered in bruises. Something had gone badly wrong. My girlfriend
had thrown herself out of a window. The police were looking for
witnesses. He was leaving for Marseille.

I packed and locked my case in two minutes flat. I took the metro
to the Gare du Nord and boarded the first train to Calais.

32: SOMETHING QUITE EXTRAORDINARY

Dominique quickly became a valued member of the clinical team.

In a short space of time, he established himself as something of an attraction with the nurses. His unshakeable good humour, infectious enthusiasm and jokes delighted the carers and patients alike.

Shortly after arriving early each morning, his catchphrase would ring out along the corridors.

'...the best thing!'

Some of the patients liked to take up the refrain, imitating his sing-song tones.

A few of the doctors thought his bonhomie went a little too far: he would do better to adopt a more discreet approach, especially in an establishment like the Derscheid Clinic.

Dominique was unbothered. Out of earshot, he mimicked their stuffy attitude and referred to them as the Grouches.

His professional skill was universally praised, on the other hand. He never had to look for the sites of pain in a patient's body: he said he could *sense* them. They presented themselves to him, he could feel them in his fingers, as if the pain was his own. He did more than ease the muscular aches and contractions, he drew them out, made them his own and relieved the sufferer of them completely.

Several patients had adopted him as a valued confidant, in

recognition of his expert treatment, and his ability to boost their morale.

He never questioned the concerns people confided to him, any more than he would belittle the suffering his patients told him they endured. He never patronised, never claimed to 'know what they were feeling', but would listen, eyes wide, a smile on his lips. For some, the mere sight of his face was therapeutic. He convinced his patients they were strong and tenacious, with the energy they needed to battle on and overcome their pain.

In many cases, his methods proved beneficial.

Since joining the clinic on the thirtieth of June, Dominique had spent at least two hours a day with X Midi.

He tracked the latter's progress, and administered the sequence of treatments prescribed by the doctors. The initial efforts to get X Midi out of bed and into a wheelchair had been a success. Now he had to work on the patient's balance and autonomy when seated.

After that, they would tackle the wheelchair controls, if the man chose to cooperate. Dominique worked on X Midi's breathing, too, helping to him to recover maximal movement in his thoracic cage.

Their close contact, day by day, led to the development of an unusual strategy.

Before entering X Midi's room, Dominique would announce his arrival with a simulated quick-fire dialogue, out in the corridor. His voice carried all around, and the tragi-comic exchanges delighted the occupants of the neighbouring rooms.

'Good morning, my friend! Good to see you, did you sleep well? Sweet dreams?'

'Morning Dominique! Well, I dreamed I was swimming with you!'

'Aha! In the pool?'

'No, the Caribbean.'

'In the Caribbean, with me? My-oh-my! No sharks, I hope?'

'Plenty! Great White Sharks.'

'Uh-oh! The ones with stethoscopes around their necks? The worst thing!'

He would burst out laughing, then poke his head through the door, often catching X Midi by surprise. Alerted by the sound of Dominique's voice, his patient would be looking out for him, from the corner of his eye. Entering the room, he would glance at the TV and pass comment.

'Seen this episode, the gardener did it.'

Standing at X Midi's bedside, he would slip the remote control into the patient's hand.

'Let's try another channel, just press one of the buttons.'

The occupational therapist reckoned X Midi was capable of using the remote now, and the controls on the electric wheelchair. But still he refused to make the effort, and seemed uninterested in the possibility of greater autonomy.

Dominique would wait a few moments, then take back the remote.

'Fine, well in that case I'm putting on MTV. Music while we work!'

Next up was the name game.

'So, we're still on the letter A, is that it? André? Your name's André?'

He waited for a reaction.

'Not André? Albin, like in *La Cage aux Folles*? Antoine, like the singer?'

The treatment began with a gentle massage of the ankles, toes and knees, combined with passive mobilisation. Little by little, the massage became firmer and more insistent. Dominique knew from experience that LIS patients often felt 'chopped up' into parts. Vigorous massage could help them feel whole again.

Throughout the treatment, he kept up a stream of talk, hoping to incite a reaction.

'Albert, like our beloved monarch? Don't say you're called Albert? Really? That's so funny!'

Next came work on X Midi's joint mobility, as a preventive treatment for spasticity.

'Tomorrow, we're off to the pool, Albert. Swimming with Dominique: the best thing!'

Sometimes, he would lower his voice and speak into X Midi's ear.

'I really would like to know your name, my friend. If it begins with an A, blink once, OK?'

On Monday, the second of August, during the weekly team meeting, Marie-Anne Perard asked everyone present to summarise X Midi's case from their particular perspective.

The accountant spoke first, delivering a statement of X Midi's care costs. The man's identity remained unknown, hence there was no supplementary healthcare plan. His treatment was wholly at the expense of Belgium's Public Centre for Social Welfare, who were slow to reimburse the outlays and were issuing more and more requests for justification. She supposed that a portion of the costs would be charged to the clinic's own profit-and-loss account, squeezing an already tight budget.

The roundtable was almost complete, and Dominique took his turn to speak. Unlike his colleagues, he did not go into detail regarding X Midi's medication and treatments, or their likely outcome. But his words struck home.

'This man has lived through something quite extraordinary.'

33: THE CENTRE OF THE WORLD

My only memory of the Channel crossing is the ceramic toilet bowl, pressing against my heart like a life belt. Kneeling on the floor, I heaved and heaved again, hoping to rid myself of the sick feeling that left me gasping for breath.

I had sobered up, but my temples were caught in a vice, from the after-effects of the dross. I could no longer feel the ground beneath my feet. Each step was a dive into a bottomless pit. Jimbo's words circled round and around. Something had gone badly wrong. My girlfriend had thrown herself out of the window. The words hammered against my eardrums, and each time they resounded, the rush of adrenaline flooded my chest and limbs, even to the tips of my fingers.

What had gone wrong?

Why had Floriane jumped?

Elaborate, improbable scenarios presented themselves. At best, I was an indirect witness, at worst, an accessory to murder.

I thought constantly of my mother. I thought of the pain she would feel if she knew what I had become. I wanted to hold her in my arms and confess everything, to tell her what had happened, tell her I hadn't understood it was a plea for help.

Arriving in Dover, I was so dazed that I failed to realise the police were asking for my papers. Fortunately, they thought I'd been suffering from seasickness. They glanced briefly at my passport, shared a joke and let me through.

I had to get new papers. I knew they could be bought in London.

Stepping down from the train, at Victoria Station, the effects of the drug began to wear off. In better spirits, I set off to discover the most amazing city on the planet.

Clapton is God. My first memory of London. The words were written on the wall of an Underground station. I had no idea who Clapton was. Nor that I would soon be meeting the greatest guitarist of all time.

In less than an hour, I could see why the English guys had been eager to get home.

In the summer of '65, London was an unprecedented cocktail of revolutionary stirrings and extreme, entrenched conformism. The traffic was denser even than Paris, but no one sounded their horn. There was no attempt to squeeze past the other vehicles; everyone drove in a disciplined manner, determined to keep things flowing by a kind of mutual consent. On the Underground escalators, people stood to one side so that passengers in a hurry could walk up next to them.

No one seemed shocked by my appearance, as they had up to now. I hadn't cut my hair since leaving Belgium, and wore a ponytail, with the beginnings of a beard. My clothes were crumpled, and pocked with holes. But still I passed unnoticed. There were none of the disapproving looks and mockery that had been a fact of everyday life in Paris.

On the pavements, gentlemen in black suits and bowler hats rubbed shoulders with Buddhist monks in orange robes, turbaned Sikhs, Kenyans in brightly patterned kaftans, Chinese in strange, skimpy suits and ladies seemingly from a different century. As if all the nations of the world had decided to live together in harmony.

But the streets were thronged with young people, too. Their wild looks exuded freedom. I was in London. I was alive.

I felt that young people would seize the reins of power, and that I had found the centre of the world.

34: THE SURFACE OF HIS MIND

Michael Stern, the journalist from the *Belfast Telegraph*, stayed in Berlin from the eighteenth to the twenty-third of September.

He had assumed everyone in West Berlin spoke English, but was forced to find an interpreter at the last minute, which lost him an entire day.

The statements he eventually collected confirmed his belief that the deaths of the four musicians were no coincidence.

First, he spoke to the Turkish shop-keeper on the ground floor of the building where the group had shared their three-roomed, furnished flat. He was disappointed not to see the flat itself – it had been emptied and let to new tenants.

According to the shop-keeper, the flat had contained few personal belongings. After the events, the owner had deposited what was left out on the pavement, and it had all been taken away with the refuse.

The shop-keeper said that if the flat had been his, he'd have done the same. He would probably have thrown the hotheads out long ago, anyway. They were noisy, foul-mouthed and totally lacking in respect. They would come back in the middle of the night, blind drunk or drugged and hollering in the stairwell. Each band member would come home at a different time, waking everyone in the building several times a night.

Once, one of the other tenants had come out of his

apartment in a rage to call them to order. He was lucky to have escaped being lynched.

They bought nothing in the shop, but treated it like a public call-box, having given the telephone number to all their contacts.

When the man had vented his outrage, Stern asked about the musicians' comings and goings during their last days in Berlin.

The shop-keeper remembered that in the space of twenty-four hours, three of them had left the city for unknown destinations, and that only the one he called Ringman, the politest of the four, had stayed behind. He remembered Larry Finch coming into his grocery shop on the Saturday morning, wearing a leather jacket and dark glasses. He wanted to use the phone to call a taxi.

After cutting the call, he had shocked the other customers by declaring in bad German, with gestures to match, that he was off to dance flamenco and have a good time with the ladies of Majorca.

Unusually for him, he had left a five-mark note on the counter.

The shop-keeper didn't think there had been more calls than usual for the group, in the days before they left. No one had visited the band members, he said. As a rule, he never saw anyone else – male or female – going up to the flat. Apart from the telephone calls, and the postman, no one had ever asked for them.

He hadn't noticed anything strange in their behaviour, though they may have seemed a little more excitable than usual. Ringman hadn't seemed anxious or disturbed after his friends left, at last not until he learned of the death of one of them, and threw himself under the U-Bahn.

Stern questioned one or two of the building's other

residents, who corroborated the shop-keeper's story, but added nothing new.

An elderly woman on the sixth floor, directly underneath Pearl Harbor's apartment, said that she knew their days were numbered, well before the series of accidents. They all smoked, took drugs and drank like hobos. She had heard one of them vomiting for a whole evening.

Stern managed to contact the apartment's owner by telephone. He complained that the four hellraisers had paid no rent since the beginning of the year. He had nothing further to add, except that he wanted to hear nothing more about them, ever again.

Next, Stern visited the bistro where the group had played, in the English sector, on a street adjacent to the *Kurfürstendamm*, West Berlin's liveliest thoroughfare.

Known as the Yoyo bar, the place was a curious mix of pizzeria, concert hall and night club.

The club's owner was surprised to see a journalist devoting time to a series of unremarkable accidents. Though he admitted, with a knowing wink, that the conspiracy theory was likely to shift copies. He agreed to answer some questions.

The musicians would arrive around 7:00p.m. They would eat, do a few try-outs and begin their set around 8:00p.m. They were scheduled to finish at midnight, but would play on until two or three depending on the crowd, and the mood, making a total of seven hours on stage, with a ten-minute break every two hours. They were paid by the hour, so there were no complaints.

The place was frequented by a handful of students and hordes of servicemen, mostly American G.I.s, who came to listen to good old rock standards from back home. Pearl Harbor had carved a niche, covering standards from the American songbook, with a twist all their own.

The bar owner told Stern the musicians were an unmanageable crew who had caused their share of mayhem. But he had kept them on because they could warm up a room and fuel an atmosphere like no other group.

More than once, he had had to intervene to calm things down. They would holler at one another, hurl bottles into the audience, insult them or provoke fights.

They played seven days a week, but had asked for an exceptional day off on March the fourteenth, giving no precise reason. They had given just two days' notice, which left him in a spot.

He had granted their day's leave with bad grace, sensing that to refuse would only spark another fight. He had found a replacement band at the last minute, and the evening had been a fiasco. The audience had booed the stand-ins and demanded Pearl Harbor's return.

Next day, Larry Speed, the bass player and leader of Pearl Harbor, had called to say that all four were taking two weeks' holiday. The furious bar owner had threatened them all with dismissal if they didn't show up for work that evening. Larry had replied that that was how things stood, and if he didn't like it, he could 'go fuck himself'. Finch's response had troubled him, not for the language, he was used to that from them, but because the band had always been desperate for cash and clung to their residency, until now. The bar owner confided to Stern that most of their earnings went on illicit substances.

On the morning of his last day in Berlin, Michael Stern met Birgit, the woman Jim Ruskin had fallen in love with shortly before his death.

She gave him some information that whetted his appetite.

On Monday, March the thirteenth, Jim Ruskin had announced he wouldn't be playing at the Yoyo bar next day. The group had accepted another engagement, adding enigmatically that they were going to get their big break.

Birgit had wanted to know more, but Jim wasn't telling. He was determined the gig would take place and didn't want to jinx it by saying anything about it beforehand.

On Wednesday, March the fifteenth, Jim told her the group had taken part in a recording session the day before, and that a record by Pearl Harbor would soon be in the shops.

Larry Finch, Steve Parker and Paul McDonald had used the resulting cash to take a few days' holiday. Jim Ruskin, on the other hand, had chosen to stay in Berlin to spend more time with Birgit. He always looked on the bright side, she said. He was full of enthusiasm and knew his own mind. She couldn't believe he had chosen to end his life in what she could only assume had been a fleeting moment of depression.

Stern tried to find out more about the recording session Birgit had mentioned, but drew a blank. That afternoon, he toured a few record shops, but none had ever heard of a disc by a group called Pearl Harbor.

Before catching his flight back to Belfast, he learned that Berlin had no less than thirty-one commercial recording studios, from the top-flight Hansa Tonstudio to poorly-equipped amateur operations that could be hired by the day, the hour, even the minute.

Back in Belfast, he called each one, but none had organised a recording session on March the fourteenth with a group by the name of Pearl Harbor. Only two recording sessions had taken place in the city that day, one by a gospel choir, the other a duo of flautists.

He offered his editor-in-chief an initial article about the disturbing series of deaths, but was turned down. At this stage in the investigation, there was nothing to suggest any kind of plot. The editor advised him to keep digging, but not to waste too much time on the story.

He would review his position if anything new came to light.

Three days later, Birgit called to say she had remembered a detail, though it was perhaps of no importance. Jim had telephoned someone from her flat on the day before the supposed recording session, which was unusual.

The two had exchanged a few words in German, and Jim had mentioned the titles of a few rock songs. The man down the line was called Karl, she remembered. Jim had spoken his name several times, and addressed him respectfully.

At the end of the week, Stern reviewed progress. Several questions still needed answers.

What had happened on the evening of March the fourteenth?

What had they recorded at the session, and where had it taken place?

If a record was made, why was it never released?

And who was Karl?

Stern ran through his notes, with a vague sense that he held vital information right there, under his nose. He read everything through several times, but could find no clue.

It was a phenomenon he had encountered before. He knew that in time, the information would float to the surface of his mind.

35: A GREAT ROCK CONCERT

A succession of black guys parade across the screen, all wearing dark glasses and piles of jewellery. They move back and forth in front of the camera, gesticulating with their hands. In the background, half-naked women writhe about on the hoods of huge, gleaming American cars.

The beat is mind-numbing, the melody non-existent, the words meaningless.

Whatever happened to music?

Chess, an English guy I knew from Chez Popov, had left me an address before heading back to London. We hadn't talked much in Paris. His French was poor and I knew only a few words of English.

Whenever the occasion presented itself, he would dig in his satchel for a portable chess set and try to find an adversary. If he failed, which was often, he would play alone. It didn't seem to bother him, quite the opposite, in fact – he said he was sure to win that way. From time to time, I would answer the call of duty and sit down opposite him. He liked playing against me. Victory was even easier.

The address was a Soho pub, the Bricklayers Arms, on the street people called Strip Alley. Chess spent his afternoons there, playing his eponymous game.

I set out to find the bar, though I was painfully aware of the difficulties that lay ahead. I was a deserter, and a fugitive wanted by the police. I was alone in an overcrowded city and spoke only a few words of English, mostly what I had learned from listening to rock music.

By chance, Chess was there. He seemed pleased to see me again. I told him I had left for London sooner than expected due to unforeseen circumstances. He asked no questions. For a good while, we struggled to find words. Eventually, he confided he was 'onto a good thing' and that he would try to include me, too.

The good thing was Brian, a rich kid whose father had died of cancer a year earlier. Brian had inherited the family home in Hampstead, a collection of artworks and a hefty sum of money. He shunned his bourgeois origins and dreamed of living like us. Being a man of few scruples, he had dispatched his mother to a home and taken possession of the house.

Now, he lodged about fifteen people like us, two or three to a room. He figured this act of generosity gave sufficient credit to his claim to be one of our kind.

Chess and I went to Brian's place. The house was magnificent. Like the set of Mary Poppins. Chess went in and talked to Brian. He came out again, wearing a broad grin. Brian had accepted me, I could move in, there was a place in a room on the third floor.

Inside, the house was less smart. The air smelled of tobacco and beer. The walls were covered with writing and obscene drawings. A low cacophony of music merged from different corners of the building. Brian shook my hand and showed me to my room.

We had few words in common, but I quickly got the measure of him.

Brian was tall and thin, spotty and awkward, on a permanent quest for acceptance and approval. His hands were slender and mani- cured. He wore his hair long, like us, but in an obviously expensive cut. He had made holes in his jeans and traded his Shetland wool sweaters for khaki jackets from an American army surplus store. He had daubed the letters N and D on the back – Nuclear Disarmament – and added a phrase along the lines of 'Beatniks against the Bomb'.

None of us thought of ourselves as beatniks. The term had been coined by our detractors – a combination of Kerouac and Ginsberg's

'Beat' and the Russian 'nik', as in Sputnik. We denounced American imperialism, but that didn't make us fervent admirers of Brezhnev. It was a shorthand term that marginalised us by labelling us as left-wing extremists. We were accused of propagating subversive ideas.

But the label suited us, too. We were happy to be shunned by a society we rejected.

Brian's hospitality extended beyond a place to sleep. The kitchen was full of food, the fridge was full of beer and bottles of alcohol lined the shelves. A desk drawer in the study was stocked with grass, hash and pills. Everyone could help themselves.

Brian was proud to have the same name as the founder of the Rolling Stones. He read Faulkner, claimed to know everything about English rock groups and gulped amphetamines. When he ran out of money, he would take more out of the bank. He was alarmingly stupid, but we played along.

We knew we were trampling all over one of the fundamental principles of our philosophy, based on the renunciation of material goods, but we worked a compromise with our conscience: ours was a temporary situation, a short interval between acts. For me, the intermission lasted over a year.

At first, my feeble English meant I was able to take Brian's regular authoritarian outbursts without retaliating. Completely un-announced, he would start shouting and insist we tidy the place up, or order us to clean our rooms. More than once, his fits of temper led to the hurried departure of a housemate.

In the basement, he had installed a sort of private club, with a well-stocked bar and soft lighting. In addition to state-of-the-art sound equipment and a two-track Grundig tape recorder, the room was scattered with musical instruments: a piano, six guitars and two saxes. At the back, a virtually unused Premier drum kit stood gathering dust.

Brian couldn't play a note on anything: he hoped to lure qualified musicians and hold improvised concerts.

But beyond the recipients of his largesse, no one made a show of taking him seriously. His invitations were never accepted and the room was kept locked. No one was allowed inside.

Lucy was the house's only female. She lived on the second floor, in a room to herself, at the back, overlooking the garden. Handel's Water Music floated out from under the door.

Lucy was one of us. Before meeting her, I had never imagined a girl could be attracted to our way of life. She came from a small town in the north of England. After drifting across Europe for a couple of years, she had come back to Britain, and settled in at Brian's.

She was beautiful, but cared little for her looks. She had black hair, brown, almond-shaped eyes and dazzling white teeth. She found fun in everything, joked all day long and laughed out loud, like Dominique. Like him, she was a skilled manipulator. She kept Brian twisted around her little finger; he would do whatever she wanted.

Lucy was no whore, but in exchange for a few pounds she would deliver a blow job, nothing more. The first time I went to see her, she whistled in admiration and said she'd have to charge double. Any man could seduce any woman he wanted, she said, provided he was hung like me and had a sense of humour.

She would joke and act the fool to start with. Once, she squashed her face between her hands in an ugly grimace and asked 'Do you fancy me now?' She didn't want us to think she was 'on the game'. It was her way of letting herself off the hook and distancing herself from what she did. After these preliminaries, she would drink a mouthful of hot tea, to prodigious effect.

On my twentieth birthday, she refused to take my money and asked me to stay with her afterwards. For the first time, I realised our dealings had taken a different turn.

It took me three months to master the rudiments of English and begin to make myself understood. Little by little, I took part in the house conversations.

Each day, the papers reported that Johnson had ordered fresh bombardments in Vietnam. The Vietnamese people were dying in a hail of napalm bombs.

In the house, no one spoke much about the war. For them, the world revolved around music. The Swinging Sixties were at their height, and the wave of new British groups were the main topic of conversation. Not a day went by without some new group coming to the fore. They were all talented and creative, with bright futures guaranteed. The Beatles were the unchallenged leaders, now on their fourth album, while dozens of others lined up to take their crown.

Everyone talked music all day long, with a passion bordering on hysteria. Some swore by none but The Rolling Stones, who had positioned themselves as the bad boys of rock, and the challengers to the nice, clean-cut Beatles. Others worshipped the Pretty Things, each member as ugly as the next, who tried to mark themselves out from the Rolling Stones by making more noise and behaving still more badly.

For Chess, The Animals were the epitome of British rock, thanks to Alan Price's high-voltage keyboards, and Eric Burden's vocals, off-key but loud, passionate and wild. Manfred Mann was a favourite with quite a few. They were a professional outfit with a proper singer and a pretend drummer who held his sticks like he was beating eggs.

Brian, true to his roots, thought The Kinks had true class because they wore red hunting jackets on stage. But he disapproved of The Who for smashing everything up during their concerts, and leaving the stage like a battlefield strewn with the shattered remains of drums, guitars and amps.

It was during one of these discussions that I finally discovered the identity of Eric Clapton. After triumphing with the Yardbirds on 'For Your Love', he had gone back to the blues, with John Mayall's Bluesbreakers.

One thing was clear, whether we talked politics, sex or drugs, everything came back to rock'n'roll.

That autumn, I heard news from Paris. There was a dark side to Floriane's death, and I was wanted as a witness. One of my nicknames was known to the police, but they hadn't managed to identify me. Roman and Jimbo were wanted, too. Last heard, they had set sail for South America.

To cover my tracks, and at Lucy's request, I shaved my beard. She said a beard was very uncool, no rock star wore one apart from the pseudo-intellectual Manfred Mann. Our relationship continued. I loved to fall asleep with her after making love. She was gentle and funny. She wrote me sweet notes, or things to make me laugh, and left them in my pockets for me to find throughout the day.

Brian had no idea we were together. He would never have tolerated it, and would probably have thrown us out on the street.

The news from Paris pushed me to get fresh identity papers. I had been given the address of a restaurant on the Clerkenwell Road. Clients would order the dish of the day and slip the waiter a password.

I went there the next day. They could do me a better-than-real Canadian passport, but I'd have to wait several weeks and pay more money than I possessed.

I was forced to look for work, and began cleaning windows. I bought the equipment I needed in a hardware store and went door-to-door in the neighbourhood.

Hampstead was a prosperous area. I did my best to look willing and helpful. I explained that I was French, travelling around the world, and that I spoke only a few words of English. I soon established my clientele.

The job suited me. No one wanted to talk, beyond a quick greeting or a few pleasantries about the weather. I was in no hurry, and applied myself to the task, never trying to up the pace, as my competitors did. I never fixed a price; people were free to pay what they liked. Some took advantage, and handed over a few coins, others were surprisingly generous.

In September, one of my clients asked if I had heard of a group called the Rolling Stones. His son had a ticket for a show that night, but he was in bed with a high fever. I couldn't believe my ears. I told him I was crazy about rock music. He clapped me on the back and gave me the ticket for free.

I went back to Brian's clutching the ticket to my heart and keeping a wary eye on the passers-by. I would have placed it in a bank vault if I could. After the concert, I kept the ticket stub until it crumbled to dust. I can still see it now – a small square of blue paper. 'Friday September 24th Stalls J18. Eight shillings and sixpence'.

I had never been to a concert. All I knew of rock music was what I heard on records or watched on television.

The Stones had released their third British album, Out of Our Heads, that very day, and their red-hot single 'Satisfaction', which had been a hit in the US over the summer, had been released in Britain just a month before.

The show was at the Finsbury Park Astoria. The Stones played twice, first at about 6:00p.m. and again at nine. My ticket was for the second session. I got there an hour early. I had drunk and smoked in preparation for the event.

The hall was packed with people. Hundreds of girls screamed without a break. I supposed they would stop when The Stones came out on stage.

When the curtain rose, the screams were twice as loud. I could hardly hear Keith Richards' opening riff. My neighbour hollered the title in my ear: 'She Said Yeah'. Girls began to cry and shake their heads. Some fainted, and were carried out on stretchers. People hammered the floor, waved their arms, clapped their hands.

On stage, I couldn't take my eyes off Mick Jagger. He was wild, obscene. His thick, blood-red lips shone fit to light up the room. He snaked his hips, tossed his hair into his eyes, turned his back on the audience, bent double, shook his backside, slid the mic between his legs.

They played about ten songs, and finished with' Satisfaction', the summit, the apotheosis. The fans raced to the stage door, hoping to catch them before they left the building.

I stayed in my seat, knocked out, exhausted, amazed, terrorised.

I waited until the last people had left the hall. I wanted to drink it all in, down to the last fraction of a second. I knew nothing would ever be the same again.

When the cleaners appeared, I was still prostrate, and rapt. They asked me what I was doing.

The fog cleared.

A strong reek of urine hit my nostrils. Some of the girls had screamed so hard they peed in their pants. The floor was wet. The smell made me retch.

Later, I became accustomed to the stench. Finally, I took it as a sign of a great rock concert.

36: I LIKE YOU

On Tuesday, September the twenty-first, Dominique made his way along the corridor and began his usual routine. After the made-up Vaudeville-esque exchange outside the door, he entered the room.

He greeted X Midi, placed the remote in his hand, chose his name for the day and received no response.

He began the massage, and sensed a slight tremor in the man's arms and legs.

He watched his face.

A few drops of sweat beaded X Midi's forehead, and his lips trembled slightly. His eyes seemed unusually bright. He was focusing all his attention on the television screen, and seemed to be experiencing some degree of inner excitement.

The TV was showing a report about U2. The Irish group were playing next day at the Stade Roi Baudouin, in Brussels. The show had sold out over a year before and the concert would be played to a packed house. The group's fans were burning with excitement, and the musicians' imminent arrival had set the Belgian capital alight.

The report retraced preparations for the group's '360° Tour'. There were clips of U2 on stage, performing 'Get On Your Boots', a track from their latest album.

Dominique continued the massage as if he noticed nothing. After a few minutes he straightened up, casually.

'I've drunk too much coffee, Barnaby. Just popping to the

little boys' room. Now you stay right there, I'll be back in a second.'

He made sure the remote was firmly wedged in X Midi's hand. Before leaving the room, he switched to a telesales channel, then closed the door behind him, went a short distance down the corridor and stood waiting.

He stopped a nurse who was heading for the room.

'Would you mind coming back later? I'm conducting a small experiment!'

He waited a few minutes more, then returned.

The TV was back on the report about the rock group, and the volume had increased.

He walked to the centre of the room and froze in mock astonishment, hands on hips.

After a few minutes, the man shifted his gaze from the screen and stared straight into Dominique's eyes.

He blinked, and tears trickled down his cheeks.

Dominique knew what he was seeing. These were not tears of sorrow. X Midi was laughing fit to bust.

He bent over the man and dabbed his eyes with a tissue.

'You know what, Barnaby? I like you.'

37: HOPE I DIE BEFORE I GET OLD

His face was a picture, with his huge round eyes and fake surprise. I like him a lot, too. He eases my discomfort and makes me laugh. He talks to me like a normal person. People coming into the room often think I can't hear, because I don't speak. They address me like a child, using simple words.

More than half a century since the lady in the record shop made her dark prediction, and rock is still alive. In better shape than ever, in fact. Those Irish guys made a powerful noise.

Rubber Soul *was released at Christmastime. The press hailed it as the Beatles' most complex and accomplished album to date. But I was disappointed. The beat was softer and some of the lyrics were a drag. It heralded a profound change: a portion of the rock world was softening and starting to take itself seriously.*

Sonny arrived in the first days of 1966, on a freezing winter morning, as I was leaving for work. I opened the door. He emerged from out of the fog enveloping the street, like a vision.

I never knew if it was his nickname, or whether he really was called Sonny, but it was the name everyone used.

Sonny came from nowhere. He told me he'd come straight from Buenos Aires, where he had spent the last two years. Subsequently, I noticed his story changed depending on who he was talking to, and the circumstances.

He was small, thin and wore his hair short, with a neat parting down one side. He was bursting with energy, and always primed with some truly astonishing piece of news. He was Brian's childhood friend. He knew everyone in London, and played harmonica like a god.

He moved into my room, closely followed by fifteen suitcases.

We were polar opposites in appearance and temperament. He was always nervy and alert; I was completely laid-back. He never stopped talking; I was taciturn. He got up every morning in the best of spirits and took a wholly positive approach to life, while I treated everything with scorn and suspicion. Yet we became the best friends in the world.

At any hour of the day or night, he would take his harmonica from his pocket, encase it in his cupped hands and make it laugh or cry. I couldn't believe my ears. As if his own emotions were breathing life into the simple block of wood. I was astounded at his talent. I would stop what I was doing and listen, dumbfounded.

Sonny was a mod. London's youthful 'in crowd' was divided into two distinct, rival clans, the mods and rockers. People said you were a mod, or a rocker, or you were nothing. I failed to understand the difference in their thinking and music. Their antagonism left me baffled.

According to Sonny, mods were citizens of the world who looked to the future. They were optimistic and cool. A mod never smiled in public. Shepherd's Bush, in West London, was their rallying point.

The rockers were just an unhealthy throwback to the Teds of the Fifties, he said. Before they cleaned up their image, the Beatles had been proper Teds, picking fights and throwing punches on the slightest provocation. They had been banned from pubs across Liverpool. Lennon, the supposed poet of the proletariat, had been the most quarrelsome of the four.

The uninitiated, like me, distinguished mods from rockers by their appearance. The mods wore tailored, Italian suits. They would change outfits several times a day and rode around town on customised Vespa scooters. Their movement was the springboard for the Carnaby Street phenomenon, named for the street that became the epicentre of London's fashion scene and counter-culture in the early Sixties.

Rockers styled their hair in huge quiffs slicked with Gomina grease. They wore jeans and black leather jackets decorated with studs or chains. They rode big, British motorcycles – Triumphs, Nortons or BSAs – and gathered on the margins of the larger cities.

Mods and rockers formed two fanatical groups. The mods thought the rockers were thugs, the rockers said the mods were effeminate poofters.

Their dreaded fights had become a holy war. When they weren't working, they gathered at seaside resorts and engaged in veritable pitched battles.

Sonny never went out without his fishhook, cosh and flick knife. He concealed them in the lining of his military parka, which he wore to protect his smart suits.

When I showed him my record collection, he refused even to look at it. I had no albums by The Who, I didn't know the Small Faces or Georgie Fame. I should stop listening to studio recordings and discover real, authentic rock.

I told him about the powerful impression The Stones concert had made on me. He seemed more surprised. He was determined to perfect my musical education. He had contacts in town. He would make me see music from a different point of view.

London swarmed with clubs. The most popular for rock fans were the Marquee and the Crawdaddy. Rhythm'n'blues fans gathered at the Ealing Club, in a basement under the station. The stage was under the street, which was set with glass paving stones to let in the light. Musicians played with their feet in puddles of water, and pedestrians walking overhead. Dozens of other places brightened the London night: the Adlib Club, the Scotch, Sybilla's, the Flamingo, the Red Lion, the Bag O'Nails, the Speakeasy, the Revolution, and more still. I've forgotten their names. Each started out different, but they were all the same in the end.

The first place Sonny took me to was the Marquee on Wardour Street, in the heart of Soho. The Stones had played their first shows there, before taking up a residency at the Crawdaddy. The Marquee was run in fine style by a guy named Harold, a jazz and blues freak who had ridden the first wave of new British rock bands.

Sonny knew him well: several times, he had stood in for a well-known harmonica player by the name of Cyril Davies, who had died of leukaemia the previous year. I didn't ask how he had managed this feat, having just come back from two years in Argentina.

Sonny had boundless admiration for The Who. The group played at the Marquee every Tuesday night. The gigs were always sold out, but Harold owed Sonny a favour or two.

We went along in late January. That evening, I watched the most extreme group on the planet. I had heard what they got up to on stage, but what I saw was beyond my wildest imaginings.

Their tetchy violence was felt the minute they walked on stage. They were bad-tempered, scowling furiously at the audience and scrapping amongst themselves while they set up. Rather than keep their biggest hit till last, like the Stones, they began with the shattering 'My Generation', currently at the top of the hit parade.

The singer, Roger Daltrey, gesticulated and spun and hollered, and stammered and swung his mic round faster and faster like a lasso. Pete Townshend wheeled his outstretched arm and hammered his guitar strings with incredible force.

Their rock was noisy, instinctive and destructive. The mood in the crowd was at fever pitch. Girls were in the minority, but they shrieked even louder than for The Stones.

There was hysteria in their screams, but terror, too, as if they had been lured into a trap. I was amazed, and more than a little alarmed: at a Stones concert, one girl had thrown herself from the top gallery and died, grievously wounding another fan.

The guys, for their part, were furious at the sight of their

*girlfriends in such a state, and were eager to fight it out. Fists flew at
the back of the room.*

*On stage, I was mesmerised by The Who's drummer, Keith Moon,
the eye in that storm of decibels. I was fascinated by his charisma.
Mouth hanging open, eyes rolled back, he thrashed and thrashed, and
thrashed again. As if his life depended on it. Thrashing and thrashing
without pause, without stopping for air. His playing looked chaotic,
but it was underpinned by a prodigious technique. 'The Ox', a track
that lasted a few minutes on their album, stretched to over half an
hour and showed the extent of his genius. His tom-tom rolls made the
stage and floor shake. The two big bass drums, hammered in frenzied
rhythm, produced a rumble of thunder that echoed to the back of the
room.*

*My ears buzzed, my hands trembled. The sound he generated was
so violent, it blurred my vision.*

*For their last number, Pete Townshend pushed the volume up to the
max, grabbed his guitar and made as if to break it in two across his
thigh. Feedback spattered and whined from the saturated amps. One
of them poured smoke from behind. Daltrey slammed his mic against
the bass drum, the ceiling, the amps. Keith Moon was on his feet now,
kicking his cymbals, toms and bass.*

*For the finale, Townshend grabbed his guitar by the neck and began
striking the floor, as if he was wielding an axe. Then he attacked the
two amps. The brutal epilogue sent a wave of panic through a portion
of the crowd. Some of the audience tried to make their way to the
exits.*

*I left the club anaesthetised, deaf and groggy. Sonny looked dazed,
and tripped out. One hypnotic, inhuman phrase swam round and
round in my head.*

*After that, I would hum it under my breath. I made it my personal
creed.*

Hope I die before I get old.

38: SUDDENLY CAUGHT HIS EYE

Michael Stern was undeterred by the lack of enthusiasm from the editor-in-chief of the *Belfast Telegraph*. Obstinately he pursued his enquiries from Belfast.

He got back in touch with the family members, hoping to gather information on the recording session mentioned by Jim Ruskin's girlfriend, Birgit.

Larry Finch's aunt gave the same answer as the Parkers, when questioned: she knew nothing, and wanted to hear nothing more about it.

As for the Parkers, neither Steve's parents, nor any of his friends had heard from him in the days leading up to his death.

Jim Ruskin's father John said the same.

Stern returned empty-handed, too, from an interview with Paul McDonald's family. Paul's last telephone call dated from early March, to his son Jason.

No one had heard anything about a recording session.

In early October, Stern contacted George West, the London detective hired by Steve Parker's parents. He doubted West would cooperate, but prepared his questions nonetheless.

He wanted to know if the hostesses West had interviewed in Hamburg remembered hearing Steve Parker mention a recording session. As expected, George West said they did not.

But Stern's conversation with the detective suggested another lead worth exploring.

He returned to the question West had raised during the

London meeting: what was the source of the money the four men had suddenly acquired, the money that Jim Ruskin mentioned to Birgit on the morning after the recording?

Steve Parker had spent time with several hostesses, and had paid them in Deutschmarks. One of the women remembered receiving a handsome tip. If he had been able to buy a gun in Hamburg, as the police implied, the nature of such transactions suggested he must have received a considerable sum in cash.

Stern called the Kastanien Hotel, where Parker had stayed in Hamburg, and was told he had paid cash, in German money.

It was impossible to trace the bootleg ticket Parker had bought for the Jimi Hendrix concert, but he had doubtless paid cash for that, too.

Yet if the members of Pearl Harbor had indeed taken part in a conventional recording session, they were unlikely to have been paid on the same evening. Demo sessions were seldom paid. As a rule, and with the exception of professional session musicians, the artists would be paid later, with a percentage of the record sales.

Stern decided to pursue this line further, and embarked on a fresh series of telephone calls, which produced some interesting information.

Larry Finch had paid for his trip to Majorca in cash, at the Berlin travel agency. But there had been no movement on his bank account, which was in the red and temporarily blocked. The woman he had spent the night with in Majorca said he had a large quantity of pesetas in cash.

Paul McDonald's movements proved still more intriguing.

He had paid for his plane ticket to London, and the bill at his first hotel, in cash. On March the twenty-second, he had entered a branch of Barclays Bank in Glasgow and emptied his bank account. He had travelled back to London that same night and checked in to the Samarkand. Shortly after arriving, he had changed his Deutschmarks at reception, using the money to pay for six days up front.

The information led West to a second set of questions.

Where had the money come from, that enabled Larry to buy a plane ticket and hotel room for several hundred marks, and to pay for it in cash? The same Deutschmarks that had enabled Steve Parker to visit several prostitutes and procure a ticket to see Jimi Hendrix? The same money that Paul McDonald had spent at the British Airways desk in Berlin? And why had McDonald paid his advance bill in German currency, when he had just taken sterling out of his account in Glasgow? Why had he checked in at the Samarkand under his mother's name? Where had the money come from?

Stern also made efforts to identify Jim Ruskin's contact, the man known as Karl, who he had called from Birgit's flat.

Karl was a very common name in Germany, and he quickly abandoned the search in favour of the recording studio.

The studio where the recording was made was not one of the thirty-one listed in Berlin. Two possibilities presented themselves: if the studio was outside West Berlin, which would involve crossing the Wall – unlikely, given the current tensions, and the fact that the session seemed to have been arranged at the very last minute – then it must have been in a private house, or installed especially for the recording, which also seemed unlikely.

On Thursday, October the twenty-sixth, 1967, Stern took a call from a man by the name of Stuart Bloomfield, a resident of north London who introduced himself as a friend of Paul McDonald.

Bloomfield hadn't been able to make the journey to Dublin for his friend's funeral, but he would be visiting the city shortly.

He had called Paul's father to find out the location of his son's grave, so that he could lay a wreath.

This was how he had heard about Michael Stern's investigation. He said he had seen Paul in London before his death and wanted to help the journalist as far as he was able. Stern took a flight to London the following Saturday.

Stuart Bloomfield confirmed that he had seen Paul on his return from Berlin. He was in great shape and had just secured an audition that he was keeping secret from the other band members. The two had gone out to celebrate.

Paul was spending money like his number had come up on the Premium Bonds. Bloomfield had asked him where it came from, and Paul told him Pearl Harbor had recorded a single in Berlin.

Bloomfield had pressed him with questions, but Paul gave no details. He seemed uncomfortable, and answered evasively, or not at all.

On the eve of the audition, Paul had called him. His good mood had evaporated and he seemed anxious, nervy, on the defensive. He said he had changed his mind and was leaving London. He didn't say where he was going.

Back in Belfast, Michael Stern filed his notes and read through everything he had collected so far. It was then that a detail that had escaped his notice until now suddenly caught his eye.

39: MY HEART RACES

Sonny's arrival turned life at the house upside down.

Under his influence, Brian had switched sides, trading his beatnik disguise and tuning in as a mod. But despite what Sonny said, the movement was showing signs of fatigue.

Once Brian became a mod, he expected the rest of the house to do the same. He limited himself to the occasional word of disinterested advice at first, but quickly became more forceful.

He would stop us in passing, list our style failings and issue directives on how to adapt our behaviour and appearance to the new norms. In short, we were ordered to become mods too.

He had the house repainted and hired a cleaning lady. Bedrooms were to be kept tidy, and beds made before going out.

Several housemates fell foul of this abrupt change, not least Chess. He bowed out, and left London for New York. Chess said London was becoming a drag, and the best artists would soon be leaving England. The future lay across the Pond.

Little by little, my dealings with Brian cooled, the more so because Sonny invariably intervened in my favour when his old friend was on the attack.

Nonetheless, I made a few changes to my appearance, the better to blend in when I was out and about with Sonny. I cut my hair and bought a few smart suits. Sonny came to the boutiques with me, to offer advice. It was an exhausting business, given my height and build.

Paradoxically, the musicians playing the clubs we visited all wore tousled hair and scruffy clothes.

Sonny changed his outfit two or three times a day. In the evening, before leaving the house, he would spread out his collection of suits, try on various shirts and sweaters, change trousers, undress and dress until he found the best combination for his purposes. He would parade in front of the mirror in the hallway, check himself front and back, twist and preen and ask me what I thought. It was never-ending.

If he wasn't completely satisfied with his outfit, he would put his suits away, hang up the shirts, fold the sweaters in a neat square in the cupboard, sit down on the bed and declare there was no way he was going out. After a few minutes, he would get to his feet and start the whole ritual over again, from scratch.

When he had found the right look, he would choose what I was going to wear, to harmonise – nothing too contrasting, but different enough for us not to look like twins.

The whole business took over an hour. It was too much, and it wore me out, but it was fun all the same. Sonny took it all terribly seriously. He was a dead man, he said, if he was seen out in the same outfit twice.

One day, Sonny ordered me to stop cleaning windows. The mods spat on plebs. I should burn my overalls and come and work with him. He had got himself a job in a record shop on the King's Road. He was in the owner's good books, and managed to get me hired. The business was booming, and qualified staff were in short supply.

At first, I tidied stock in the back room. After a few days, the boss decided my odd accent had a certain charm and shifted me to the front desk, with Sonny.

My poor knowledge of the market was no obstacle: the toughest questions we fielded were confined to the release date of the Beatles' next single or The Stones' next album. When the long-awaited date arrived, the queue would stretch out onto the pavement, and our day felt like it would never end. The release of The Who's second album, A Quick One, *with its provocative title and colourful, Pop Art cover, made for some unforgettable moments.*

Sonny and I were inseparable. We were opposites in every way. I couldn't have cared less about clothes, he wasn't interested in literature. The only thing we had in common was our worship of rock music.

Under his influence, my style changed. Spending time with me, he saw the benefits of reading. I had started reading in English and realised the scale of the task ahead of me. The vocabulary was more extensive than French. I checked constantly in the dictionary for the meaning of a word or phrase. Sonny stared at me dumbfounded when I told him that Mick Jagger had slipped a phrase from James Joyce's Ulysses *into the lyrics of 'Paint it Black'.*

Lucy left one morning. Brian had pushed things too far. She left with no explanation, not even one of her notes slipped into my trouser pocket. We had been seeing less of one another, but her unannounced departure left a bitter taste. I felt frustrated, betrayed, abandoned.

That evening, I sank into a depression and told Sonny everything that had happened since leaving Belgium. We were supposed to go and see John Mayall, but he sat with me, never once getting up from his chair, never interrupting, never once glancing at his watch. He listened, wide-eyed, frowning, stunned into silence.

Then he opened up, in turn. His father was well-known in political circles. He hated them all. Utter hypocrites. He said nothing more.

We went out every night, skimming from club to club. Rock filled my nights – pure, living rock that had nothing to do with the polished product on the records we sold. In a smoky room filled with screams and the stench of beer, tobacco, sweat and piss, even the space between two rock numbers was pure rock. The wrong notes, the feedback, the swearing and the flights of inspiration were the fabric of our world.

I met plenty of groups – well-known outfits like Manfred Mann, the Spencer Davis Group or the Yardbirds, but also promising musicians making their debuts at the Marquee: people like Pink Floyd, The Action, David Bowie and Al Stewart.

We were at the Scotch of St James for a show by Jimi Hendrix. The memory of that moment is imprinted on my mind.

At first, Jimi bent over his guitar with an inspired look, eyes closed. Suddenly, he would start whirling around, writhing and playing with his teeth, his elbow, scraping the strings of his Fender against the stage. Bombs exploded, sirens wailed, Stukas strafed over London, like the Blitz at its height.

Hendrix could conjure a three-dimensional setting in sound and vision with his Stratocaster and fuzz pedal.

Blown away by his talent, we saw him again at the Bag O'Nails. Every one of his concerts was unique.

The Crawdaddy was one of our favourite venues. The Stones had been the resident group in their early days, but they had flown the nest now. Unfortunately for the band, Mick Jagger had become the most sought-after invitee on the planet. He took his role very seriously, and moved in lofty circles.

The Yardbirds had taken over from The Stones. Jeff Beck had stepped into Clapton's shoes. The bass player was a guy by the name of Jimmy Page, about my age, a phenomenal, virtuoso studio musician. From time to time, he would swap his bass for a double-neck Gibson, which he played with a bow.

We would finish up at the Adlib Club or the Speakeasy. Contrary to what was reported in the music press, the rock groups camped at the top of the hit parade knew each other well and were in no way rivals. The Beatles and The Stones were habitués at the Adlib. Hordes of rich kids hung out at the club, hoping the bands would show up. They would shoot cocaine and swallow vats of whisky, until they sank into a coma.

Plenty of musicians went along to the Speakeasy after their shows. The ones who came along didn't take themselves seriously, and were easy enough to talk to. If you proved your credentials, you could approach them and get into conversation.

The Speakeasy was where I met and befriended a few names –

Andy White, Ritchie Blackmore, Jon Lord, Jeff Beck, Bobbie Clark.

Jimi Hendrix came once or twice. He was explosive on stage, but otherwise quiet and discreet. He would sit at the back of the room and doodle on the beermats.

I drank a lot and smoked huge quantities of grass. We never went home before dawn, and the record shop opened at nine. We slept just a few hours. To keep going, we boosted the effects of the grass with Methedrine and Benzedrine pills. A simple enough recipe: a joint, a pill, a joint, a pill. Sonny showed me the way. During the war, English soldiers had been given amphetamines to stay awake for days at a time.

We often heard people talk about acid, but there was none to be had in England. It was a prestige product, available only to an elite few. Rumour had it that every artist in America was hooked on LSD.

One night at the Speakeasy, a few musicians got up on stage to jam. After a few numbers, they asked if there was a harmonica in the room. Sonny pulled a face, got to his feet and went to join them.

Two hours later, twenty of us showed up at Brian's.

Blind drunk and galvanised by his triumphant set at the Speakeasy, Sonny dragged Brian out of bed and ordered him to hand over the keys to the cellar.

We hurried downstairs, and switched on the amps. Denny Laine and another guy threw themselves on the instruments. Denny had played guitar with the Moody Blues, but he had left the group and wandered like a lost soul ever since. The other guy was a bass player. I got behind the drums, Sonny sang and played harmonica.

I hadn't played in a while. I had tried hanging around Archer Street on a Monday, with the other musicians looking for work, but never managed to sell myself. My shyness and bad English were against me, and the British players always got the gigs.

Happily, the dozens of pills I had swallowed shattered my natural reserve and defused my stage fright. I soon rediscovered the old sensations. I told myself I was Keith Moon and got to work.

We played until 8:00a.m. By the time we finished, a crowd of a hundred or so had crammed into the cellar, from God knows where. Brian had thrown on some clothes, brushed back his hair and taken control of the bar. He emptied the fridges and took a decent pile of cash.

The most frenetic time of my life began that night, and ended a few weeks later, when I met Mary.

They were wild weeks. We rushed like crazy, all day long, spending in an hour what we had earned in a week, going to gigs and hurrying down to the cellar to play what we had heard.

We spent our days playing rock, talking rock, drinking, smoking and swallowing quantities of pills.

It was pointless and destructive. But looking back, I think of that time as the moment I became my true self.

Sonny and I were a mad, mismatched, unassailable pair. He was one of my rare gifts from heaven. He taught me the beauty and richness of friendship.

When the time came, he sacrificed himself to rescue me from hell. When I think of him, my vision blurs and my heart races.

40: MY WHOLE LIFE

She walked in.

The walls swayed and the room closed in around her.

My muscles froze. I skipped my beat.

Plato says that in the beginning were androgynous creatures with four arms, four legs, one head and two faces. Zeus, fearing their power, decided to cut them in two, condemning them to a lifetime in search of their other half.

She was called Mary. She was my whole life.

41: LIKE AN OYSTER

Dominique arrived early at the clinic. He parked his car, opened the boot and took out a portable CD player. He carried it into the clinic on his shoulder, greeted the team and headed for X Midi's room.

Just outside the door, he launched into his habitual imaginary dialogue.

'Ah, Dominique! Good morning! But tell me, who are all these people you've brought with you today?'

'Don't tell me you don't recognise them!'

'They look kind of familiar.'

'You bet they do – you saw them yesterday on TV. That's Bono, there, and this is The Edge.'

'Really? U2?'

'Yes, they're in Brussels for tonight's concert. And since they were passing, I asked them to come and play for you.'

He dived into the room, glancing towards the bed with an ironic grin. X Midi was watching for him out of the corner of his eye.

Dominique switched off the television.

'So, Baudouin! You're a rock fan?'

He stood beside the bed.

'The name's Baudouin, isn't it? Blink once for Baudouin, twice if I'm wrong.'

No reaction.

'Do you like swing? We're going to work to music. Feel the beat. I've brought a few decent rock tracks with me.'

He pulled the tray table over to the bed and set up the CD player. Then he chose a CD and inserted it into the deck.

The opening chords of 'One' echoed in the room.

Dominique caught hold of the edges of his white coat, opened his arms wide and spun around.

'Do you know this song? It's U2. Voted their all-time favourite by listeners to Belgium's premier rock radio Classic 21! That your favourite, too, Baudouin?'

He bent over X Midi, eyebrows raised in enquiry.

'So, do you like that one?'

He laughed.

'Would you rather I put the TV back on?'

The man stared at him, unblinking.

'I can put another one on if you want, try and find out what you like.'

He inserted another disc and left it for a few moments.

'"With or Without You". Bet you like that one, don't you?'

He repeated the process with other discs, to no avail.

Then changed tactics.

'Of course, I'm so stupid. You prefer the older groups, am I right?'

He took ten CDs and passed their covers in front of X Midi's eyes.

'If you see anything you'd like to hear, blink once, OK?'

He held up the CDs one by one, reciting the names of the artists.

'The Cure? The Clash? Like punk, do you, Baudouin? Bon Jovi? Phil Collins? I love Phil Collins! The Eagles? Santana? Supertramp? Queen? Freddie Mercury, what a voice! Simple Minds? No, not Simple Minds, you're quite right.'

He raised his arms and dropped them again to his sides.

'That's all I've got, Baudouin. Want me to bring some other stuff tomorrow?'

The man looked away.

Dominique admitted defeat: yesterday's nascent hopes had been short-lived. X Midi had shut tight, like an oyster.

42: I DID ALL RIGHT

We played every night, and every night, more and more people joined us. Brian's cellar was the hip place to be, the private, post-concert party to which everyone who was anyone was invited.

Sonny and I had established a fine reputation as the nightbirds of the moment. The creatures of London clubland looked out for us, greeted us, offered us drinks, sought our opinion, in hopes of being invited back to Brian's.

Some nights, there were dozens waiting for us outside on the pavement.

The noisy gatherings angered the neighbours. More than once, the police were called but found nothing untoward. There was no law against invited guests, even if they showed up every night of the week. Typically, the cops would leave with a general warning to keep the peace and respect the neighbours' sleep.

When we arrived with our guests, we would go downstairs and take possession of the place. Brian would hand-pick the hopefuls waiting outside, the chief criterion being the size of the bank note proffered by the would-be revellers. Then he would come down to the cellar and instal himself behind the bar until dawn.

That autumn, Sonny and I went to Klooks Kleek, a small club located upstairs at the Railway Hotel in West Hampstead, not far from Brian's place. Eric Clapton's new group Cream were playing a show.

I had heard talk about the drummer, Ginger Baker, but had never seen him at work. When we arrived, his silver Ludwig kit was waiting on stage. The word 'Ginger' was inscribed in huge letters on one of the bass drums; the word 'Baker' was written just as large on the other.

I was intrigued by the number of accessories and percussion pieces he had added: congas, chimes, bells, but also things I had never seen on a drum kit before – like an empty whisky bottle.

The trio arrived an hour late. They walked slowly through the crowd and got up on stage.

Excitement in the room was at fever pitch. Jack Bruce and Eric Clapton wore moustaches from a past century. Ginger Baker was red-headed with long hair and a beard, and looked as if he was in the final stages of a long illness. All three wore loose-fitting, brightly coloured shirts – a new look just in from California that was sweeping everything in its path. America was taking its revenge: soon, the happening place would be San Francisco.

We expected them to play blues, and they played blues. But theirs was a brilliant combination of blues, rock, country and jazz. Their virtuoso playing did the rest.

Clapton deserved his nickname; he played like a god. Hunched over his guitar, he seemed absent, absorbed in his complex constructions. The room hung on his every note. His speed of execution was phenomenal, his solos dizzying. From time to time, his guitar would soar in lyrical flight, ending on a sustained note that sent shivers down the spine.

Ginger Baker's playing was breathtaking. With his gaunt features, chalk-white complexion and shocking teeth, he was the archetypal drummer of genius. He played as if he had only hours to live, as if he could still save his own skin if he thrashed hard enough to see off the evil eye. Open-mouthed, eyes popping, he immersed himself in endless rolls that swept the whole world along with them.

By the end of the concert, my arms and legs were shaking. I wanted to be Cream. I would grow my hair and beard. Later, I even bleached them to look more like Ginger.

We went to the Speakeasy. We knew Clapton was likely to stop by. He showed up an hour later, accompanied by his clique of hangers-on. No sign of Bruce or Baker. They installed themselves at the back of the club, indifferent to what was happening onstage or in the rest of the room.

When we left the club, fifteen or so guys followed us, habitués of Brian's for the most part. To our astonishment, Clapton came too, with a portion of his clique at his heels.

The whole illustrious crowd packed in to the cellar, and Brian almost passed out when he recognised Clapton. I froze in his presence, too. A few guys picked up guitars, I got behind the drums and we began to play.

Watching other drummers had enhanced my own playing. Most rock drummers played in four-four time on the hi-hat. But I kept the cymbals open on the second and fourth beats, the ones forming the backbeat, and let the snare drum take the lead. I was a little slow on the snare, but spot-on with the hi-hat. Each drummer's style is defined by the infinitesimal lapse between the two. That way of drawing out the bar a little longer was characteristic of my playing, and the musicians I played with liked it.

Clapton smoked and chatted, girls hanging on his every word. From time to time, he cast an eye in our direction, mechanically, like glancing at a TV tuned to a football match, with the sound turned off.

Between numbers, I swallowed pills by the handful. A few glasses later, the talk was livelier and Clapton came over to where we were playing. He picked up a guitar, tuned it, adjusted the sound and issued some instructions to the bass player. The guy winked at me, leaned in to the mic and counted four.

We played for an hour and a half. Rock and blues standards. I don't remember any of the titles, or how I interpreted them. I lost all notion of time and space.

At the end of the last number, the room went wild. Clapton turned to me, gave a thumbs-up and said I did all right.

Nothing else. But for me, there could be no higher praise.

I did all right.

Later, Sonny said I had played like a king.

I still wasn't the best drummer in the world, but I had played with Clapton and I did all right.

43: YOUR BETRAYAL

Mary appeared the day after that legendary night. If I hadn't felt encouraged by Clapton's words, I would probably have stayed tongue-tied, as usual.

Mary was born on New Year's Eve, in the last hour of the last day of 1946.

Her parents were high-minded, principled petits bourgeois, and fervent Anglicans. Despite this, they had divorced when she was ten years old. Mary had left London to live with her mother, and settled on the outskirts of a small Berkshire town. Her mother had found work in a bookshop on the high street.

Mary had signed up for drama lessons at school, where she discovered her talent for music and singing. At fourteen, she was singing on Saturday evenings in the town's cafés. Her repertoire consisted of popular folk songs. Her mother chaperoned her, and collected the tips.

Her performances were appreciated, and she began to sing on Fridays and Sundays, and then on weekdays, too. Her mother encouraged her to take singing lessons and develop her technique. Her range extended over three octaves.

She walked into the cellar with a crowd I had never seen before. I was busy playing with a few regulars. Our eyes met and I lost the beat. The guitarist shot me a questioning glance. We played on, but I wasn't with them.

Mary said her chin stuck out and her eyes were too far apart. She said so every time she looked in the mirror.

I replied that Jackie Kennedy thought the same thing about herself. She would look at me and shrug her right shoulder, always just the one, always the same way. I would add that Jackie Kennedy was one of the most beautiful women in the world. She'd laugh and tell me I was a terrible liar, but she would pretend to believe me.

They gathered at one end of the bar and ordered beers. Mary took hers and drank it straight from the bottle.

From time to time, she shot me a glance out of the corner of her eye. She could see I was floundering, and knew she was the cause.

At eighteen, she had married the son of the owner of the bookshop where her mother worked. A wild, thoughtless impulse, almost a selfish whim. She wanted to get out from under her mother's yoke. The marriage lasted less than a year. She left him and headed for London.

She began hanging out in the capital's clubs, looking for a guitarist to accompany her.

And that was how she had come across a group of rock musicians, the Frames, talented amateurs who played when they felt like it. Fascinated by her voice, and her musical skill, they had written a few songs that exploited her vocal range, and convinced her to join them. Encouraged by the success of their gigs, she had begun to write her own lyrics to rock, blues and jazz settings.

The guys she was with treated her as an equal, like one of the boys. None seemed to be paying her more attention than the others.

I watched her as I played. She talked, gesticulated and drank beer after beer. I was racked with jealousy whenever one of them spoke to her. She had been there less than an hour, but already she was mine.

She started to watch me too, with a mixture of annoyance and curiosity.

I remembered Clapton's words. I held her gaze. I did all right.

After an hour of cat-and-mouse, she spoke to one of her crowd, a skinny, bearded guy who scratched the top of his head constantly.

They came over. The bearded guy asked the guitarist if he could borrow his instrument, then went over to the bassist, to give him the chords. Mary would sing a song she had written herself, a slow four-four, kind of a Latin jazz, like a rumba. That was all I had to go on.

Mary took the mic, closed her eyes and began to sing. It was a jazzy ballad, with a catchy rhythm. Her voice was grainy, melodious, powerful.

When she sang the refrain, the back of my neck tingled. In just a few seconds, I was covered in goosebumps. Around the room, conversations paused and everyone held their breath.

She stood with her back to me, dancing lazily on the spot. From time to time, she would freeze in an alluring pose.

At the end of the song, she turned her back on the audience, looked into my eyes and dedicated the last lines to me.

I did what the words of the song asked me to do, and more. I gave her all the love I had in my heart, I emptied it down to the very last drop, like a philanthropist pouring his fortune into a lost cause.

Besides my mother, I think she was the only woman who ever loved me.

In the small hours of the morning, the cellar gradually emptied.

Mary's friends said goodbye and left. Apart from Brian, we were the only two left. Brian emptied the cash box and put the money in a small safe concealed behind the bar. He asked me to switch everything off before coming up.

We had hardly spoken.

She stroked my face with her hand. She told me she wanted me, and asked if I wanted her, too.

We went up to my room. She undressed, and undressed me in

silence. I got into bed and she lay on top of me. She placed her hands on my chest, closed her eyes and threw her head back, gently moving her hips.

She waited.

I asked her permission to let myself go.

It was an idiotic question, but she appreciated it. I was the first man who had ever asked her. She took it as a mark of respect.

I wish you were beside me now. I want you to know I forgive your betrayal.

44: HIS FIELD OF VISION

On one of his daily visits, the occupational therapist noticed a slight trembling in the fingers of X Midi's right hand, and more extensive facial movements.

She noted the observations in her report and added that these promising signs confirmed X Midi was making progress. Slowly and gradually, he was coming out of LIS and entering the recovery phase.

The notes concluded that a partial reversal of X Midi's condition was possible.

Dominique was one of the first to be informed, by virtue of his rapport with the patient.

He hurried to X Midi's bedside to give him the good news.

'Hey, Casper – I spoke to your occupational therapist this morning. She's noted some encouraging signs. We're going to get you out of there.'

His smile broadened as he showed X Midi a small pot of jellied liquid and a plastic spoon.

'Allow me to serve you your first meal.'

He stood motionless for a moment, holding the bowl level with the man's eyes, watching for a reaction.

'Surely you're not going to let yourself be fed like a baby? Haven't you had enough of that catheter? You'll have to learn to eat again sometime, sooner or later, so you might as well start with me.'

X Midi's eyes filled with tears.

Dominique bent forward and examined the man's face.

'What's up Casper? Are you crying? Are you sad or crying for joy?'

He sat on the bed, took X Midi's hand and examined it.

X Midi was in acute distress.

'I'm your friend. I'd like to help you.'

He wiped the man's eyes and ran his hand through his hair.

'I'm your friend. Me too, I'm sad. You don't seem to want to be friends. I think you've been through something terrible. I understand that you don't want to confide. People have hurt you badly, I can feel it. But I'm your friend. You can talk to me. You can trust me.'

The man stared at him without blinking.

Dominique bent closer and adopted a confidential tone.

'I'll cut you a deal. I can see you don't want to talk and I won't try and make you any more. I'll carry on talking to you, but I won't ask questions.'

He paused for a moment.

'If ever you do want to talk to me one day, you should know that I'm your friend. I'll listen, I'll answer your questions, and whatever you say will be between you and me.'

The man stared at him with sustained concentration.

'Okay? If you want to talk to me one day, if you have something to say or something you want to ask, you can count on me. I give you my word. Deal, my friend?'

X Midi closed his eyes, kept them shut for a moment, then opened them again.

Dominique stood up and left his field of vision.

45: TO THE END OF THE NIGHT

We were together from that moment on. Mary rented a small attic room in a smart townhouse in Kensington, on Argyll Road, not far from Holland Park. The owner was an old acquaintance of her mother, a long-time widow, and half deaf. She tolerated Mary's vocal exercises, her nocturnal comings and goings, feeling her way along the hall in the small hours. But she couldn't allow Mary to bring a man into her home. Mary went to fetch a few things, and stored them in my room: sheet music, a wash bag, clothes.

Brian didn't like her. The day after we met, he came to find me and said he knew her reputation, she was a whore, she'd sleep with anyone, and I should watch out. I thanked him for the warning. I would watch out. I was on my guard.

A fortnight later, Brian erupted again. It was a Sunday morning. Sonny and I were eating breakfast in the bay window. Mary had just gone out.

It was a beautiful winter morning. The sunshine was dazzling. Sonny and I squinted in the bright light. He sat opposite me, smiling. The coffee burned my palate. I was happy. Mary and I were in love.

Brian came downstairs and began to holler.

His house wasn't a hotel, let alone a brothel, he'd had enough of hearing my whore squealing like a sow all night, and he didn't want me to spend another day under his roof. If I wanted to waste my time with that silly bitch I would have to go fuck her somewhere else.

I was dumbstruck, impotent, incapable of responding to his violent outburst.

I wanted to find the right words, to defend Mary's reputation, tell Brian he had gone too far, but I was speechless.

Sonny could tell I was reeling from the blow. He got to his feet and came to my defence. Brian was exaggerating, he was rude and ungrateful. He was cashing in on the people we brought back every night, we'd made his cellar one of the hippest places in London, I'd played with Clapton, the least he could do was to leave me in peace and let me fuck whoever I wanted.

Brian refused to calm down. Quite the opposite, in fact. He reeled off a paean of praise to his own altruism and generosity. He was housing ten people at his own expense and no one had offered to contribute a penny, not even the ones with paid jobs, like the two parasites we were.

Voices were raised.

I sat and listened, unsure what to do.

Sonny wasn't stopping there. They were screaming at one another now. They spoke fast, and shouted. I didn't understand it all.

Brian was furious. Just because Sonny's father was screwing half the Cabinet didn't mean he could do what the hell he liked.

Sonny broke off in mid-sentence.

I watched as his face turned white.

His lips trembled.

I stood up and walked straight over to Brian. His eyes widened.

I threw a punch that sent him reeling to the other end of the room. He staggered backwards, clutching his nose, and crashed into the bookcase, sending books clattering down around him.

Sonny stood frozen in the middle of the room, tears in his eyes.

I took him by the shoulder. He was deeply hurt. I hugged him tight, cradling him like an unhappy child. I tried to comfort him as best I could. We'd go see the Easy Beats at the Upper Cut that evening. Brian was just a poor rich kid who didn't feel comfortable in his own skin, he was talking rubbish, I hadn't understood a word. We'd have fun, we'd get pissed and swallow tons of pills. Your harmonica will sing and we'll play till the end of the night.

46: AN UNLIKELY SCENARIO

No sooner had the previously unseen connection jumped out at him than Michael Stern grabbed the telephone and dialled the number for the Yoyo bar, the club where Pearl Harbor had played from Sunday, January the second, 1966 (the start of their contract) to Monday, March the thirteenth, 1967 (the date of their final show).

An employee answered that the boss had gone to Frankfurt for the weekend and wouldn't be back in Berlin until the following Monday, late afternoon.

Stern promised to call back, and continued his enquiries by contacting the shop-keeper on the ground floor of the four men's apartment building. There was no answer; the store was clearly shut at this late hour.

Nothing for it but to bide his time and call back on Monday afternoon.

The boss of the Yoyo bar confirmed that the musicians had kept all their dates, every night. No one had failed to show in the final weeks, right up to the day they asked for last-minute leave and never came back.

The grocer was more irascible. He couldn't talk, there were people in the shop and he had no recollection of the musicians' comings and goings in the days prior to their deaths. He repeated what he had told Stern in person, during his visit to Berlin.

When Stern said he wanted to talk to the tenant on the sixth floor, he was told she had no telephone and rarely went out. She suffered with rheumatism and was unable to make her way down six floors without a great deal of pain.

Stern suggested they arrange a time to call, and asked the grocer to help the woman down to the telephone on the ground floor. Sensing the other's reluctance, he explained that he was making progress with his investigation, that this was clearly a case of multiple murder and that her testimony could be decisive.

Later that afternoon, he telephoned at the appointed time and managed to question the lady. He muttered a few words in German and succeeded in making himself understood. She reiterated what she had told to him to his face. Shortly before the four men's deaths, one of them had stayed in the apartment for an entire evening. She had heard him walking about. She heard his coughing fits, and the sound of him retching and throwing up.

But she was unable to give a precise date.

Stern tried to refresh her memory by asking questions about her own activities that day. He suggested clues. What had she eaten? Had anyone come to visit? How had she spent the evening?

Tentatively, she remembered comparing the vomiting she could hear upstairs to a medical column she had been reading in *Der Spiegel*. The article reported that Germans ate too much fat at breakfast.

The magazine was delivered on Tuesdays, she said, and she always spent the evening reading it.

A quick call to the magazine established that the article in question appeared under the headline '*Reiner Tisch*', that it had been written by a staff writer covering health issues and that it had appeared in the twelfth edition of that year. The news weekly had gone on sale on Monday, March the thirteenth.

Subscribers would receive it the following day.

This meant the woman had heard the noises overhead on the evening of Tuesday, March the fourteenth, 1967.

Stern concluded that one of the four hadn't taken part in the recording, but had stayed at home feeling ill, perhaps with a stomach complaint.

The detail was of secondary importance, but it indicated that if the group had indeed been witness to some dark goings-on, only three of them should have been killed.

Stern read his notes one more time and tried to identify who had been absent from the recording. He called Birgit, Jim Ruskin's girlfriend, and asked her to help him make sense of the puzzle by reconstructing the group's movements.

Ruskin had spent the evening of Wednesday, the fifteenth of March at Birgit's apartment, as he had done on Thursday the sixteenth, Friday the seventeenth, and Saturday the eighteenth, when the group had stopped working and taken their leave. Jim had stayed with her on all four nights, but she had asked him to go home on Sunday evening, saying she was tired and would be going back to work the next morning.

Michael Stern noted the information and made his deductions.

The recording had taken place on Tuesday, the fourteenth of March, 1967. Only three of the four musicians had taken part. The fourth had stayed at their apartment, feeling ill. On Wednesday, the fifteenth of March, Jim had slept at Birgit's, but the other three had slept in their own beds. The same was true of Thursday, the sixteenth.

On Friday, the seventeenth of March, Steve Parker had taken the late morning train to Hamburg. Larry Finch and Paul McDonald had stayed in the apartment. On Saturday, the eighteenth, Larry Finch and Paul McDonald had left for Majorca and London respectively.

That night, Saturday, the eighteenth of March, the apartment was empty. Jim Ruskin came back alone on Sunday evening. His presence was confirmed by the grocer, who had woken him up towards the end of Monday morning.

Stern examined his notes.

They looked like a logic problem from his early years as a student.

He sketched a table, inserted the names of the four men across the top of the columns and assigned a date to each line, then filled in the information he had gathered, noting where each person was reported to have been.

The document was peppered with question marks.

Who had stayed at the apartment on the night of the recording? And why was that person dead? If he hadn't taken part in the recording, why was he, too, in possession of a large sum of money?

He couldn't exclude the possibility that someone from outside the group had been in the apartment that evening. But that seemed an unlikely scenario.

47: FIND A JOB

Brian had suffered a broken nose. He left to get treatment. When he came back, nothing more was said. That night, Mary slept with me, we made love and she cried out even louder than usual.

Apart from that, we spoke little. We were both naturally reserved.

She sang to exorcise the things she didn't say. The words of her songs expressed her distress, her anger, her dashed hopes. Her couplets railed against abandonment, violence, servility and the childhood she never had.

I did the same on the drums, my own form of words. I thrashed with my sticks to forget the fear I felt at the madness I was being drawn into.

We drank until we were sick. We started again next morning with a few harmless beers, and wine. Late in the evening, we drank spirits. We smoked grass and used amphetamines to keep going.

On her return to London, Mary had taken heroin and sang its praises to me. She dreamed of taking it again, of initiating me, but we didn't have enough money.

I didn't tell her that I had been putting money aside. I didn't want anything to do with the stuff. Since Paris, I associated it with rape, misery and death.

The image of Floriane, trapped between the two men, her arm outstretched, continued to haunt me.

We would spend long hours stretched out beside one another on the bed, churning our thoughts without exchanging a word. We listened to one another's breathing, or to The Stones, or the noises circulating in the house. When the silence became too heavy, we made love.

We spent New Year's Eve in my room. Our haven. Mary was celebrating her twentieth birthday. The house was quiet.

In the street, people laughed and shouted and whistled. Cars drove by faster than usual. We heard the cacophony of horns, and the crackle of fireworks in the distance.

We made love until we gasped for breath.

In the small hours, I told her I loved her. The words sounded strange in my mouth. I heard them over and over again in songs, but I was speaking them for the first time.

She said nothing. She took me in her arms and held me there for a long time. She seemed thoughtful.

After a while, she drew a deep breath and told me she had been pregnant.

A few weeks after their wedding, she and her husband had invited one of his friends over for dinner. They had eaten, laughed and drunk themselves crazy. At the end of the evening, they had all screwed. It wasn't unpleasurable, but she thought it was a one-off, a chance occurrence. It happened again the following week, and again after that. He was insatiable. He brought other men back, people she didn't know. Sometimes three in one evening.

One day, she was late. Her period didn't come. She went to see her doctor and he told her she was pregnant. She left her husband and got an abortion in London.

No one knew about this. I was the only person she had ever dared tell.

Her confession didn't change my feelings, but something had broken inside her.

A few days later she told me she was leaving for Berlin. A German night club agent had been sent to London to look for new artists.

He had seen her singing with the Frames. The same evening, he had offered them a three-month contract with a fashionable club. The deal included food, bed and board and a salary to boot.

They had all accepted, apart from the bass player. The German said he would find a replacement in Berlin. He took Mary to one side. So long as the singer came, everything was fine.

I told Mary I didn't want to be without her, and would come too.

She flew off the handle. Three months was nothing, I wasn't being reasonable, I had a job, I had friends, my passion, there was nothing for me in Berlin, the three months would soon go by.

I insisted. I would find a job, even if I had to serve in a bar, clean windows, deliver newspapers or sweep the pavement. Perhaps I would find work as a drummer. So many groups played in the big cities in Germany.

She stared at me, shrugged her right shoulder, just the one, and nodded.

I was stubborn. I could do whatever I liked.

I needed new papers to leave England and travel to a city like Berlin. I had enough money to buy them. I went back to the restaurant on the Clerkenwell Road, ordered the dish of the day and gave the waiter the password.

In the back room, I put my money on the table and said I needed the papers that week.

Three days later, they were ready. I was Jacques Berger, a Canadian citizen, single, born in Quebec on March the sixth, 1946.

The remaining members of the Frames were not happy to have me along. I had played with them in the cellar from time to time, but they seemed unhappy to have me with them in Berlin. They also knew full well their contract depended on Mary and that without her, they would have nothing.

We left London on January the fifteenth, 1967, destination Berlin. The other members of the band ignored me, except to say they hoped I would find a job.

48: HE'LL ONLY TALK TO YOU

On Monday, November the fifteenth, Dominique arrived at the clinic at around 7:00a.m.

As usual, he walked through the lobby, called out a greeting to all present and headed for the cloakrooms, skipping a dance step or two along the way.

One of the night nurses was sitting in the rest area, her head in her hands. She looked deeply concerned.

'Michèle? How come you're still here?'

The nurse looked exhausted.

'I've been waiting for you.'

Dominique laughed out loud.

'Waiting for me? Must be my lucky day! Watch out, Michèle, you're a happily married lady with two children!'

'I'm not joking, Dominique. X Midi had a bad turn last night.'

Dominique's smile disappeared.

'How bad? He's not—'

'No, his condition's stable now.'

'What happened?'

The nurse glanced out of the window.

There had been torrential rain all weekend. Several rivers had burst their banks. The rising water had brought serious flooding. A number of towns and villages were badly affected. Hundreds of homes had been evacuated. Fallen trees and mudslides had blocked roads and caused severe disruption to rail traffic.

On Saturday afternoon, the country's emergency response plan had been activated. Fire and rescue crews had worked day and night. On Sunday morning, the army and Red Cross had been called out to provide support.

She sighed.

'It's been one hell of a weekend. Apocalyptic! The Tubize Clinic was hit by lightning – the basement was flooded and their electricity cut out. The residents had to be transferred elsewhere. The patients here saw it all on TV, you can imagine the panic. They were traumatised. We were dealing with anxiety attacks one after the other. Things have calmed down now, thank goodness.'

'You should have called me; I'd have come in.'

She dismissed the suggestion with a wave of her hand.

'We've seen worse. Let's go out for a minute, I need a smoke. We can talk outside.'

She pulled on her coat. Dominique put his jacket back on and followed her out into the car park.

'You should stop smoking.'

'So you've told me a thousand times.'

'What happened with X Midi?'

She dragged on her cigarette, inhaled the smoke, held it for a moment in her lungs, then breathed it out.

'Last night, about 9:00p.m. The TV volume shot up in his room. I went to look. There was no one else there, but he had the remote control in his hand.'

Dominique frowned.

'He knows how to use it, but he's only done it once.'

'So I thought. He turned the sound up as far as it would go.'

'Did he do it on purpose?'

'I'm sure he did. He was motionless, but his hands were shaking, he was drooling, he was making rattling, groaning noises, and he stared at me very hard.'

She lit a second cigarette from the stub of the first.

'I checked his blood pressure and pulse. His heart was racing. He was sweating. I called the duty doctor. He said he was having an anxiety attack and gave him Valium.'

'Did he calm down?'

'No. That's what was surprising. It didn't seem to have any effect on him. Either he's a force of nature, or he's been dependent on Valium in the past. The doc waited for half an hour, but he was still agitated. He injected another dose after forty-five minutes.'

'And?'

'He began to drift off to sleep.'

'He must have seen the TV news and panicked.'

'I don't think it was that, Dominique. Something happened. I've watched the poor guy for almost a year, trapped in that vegetative state, but suddenly it was as if he'd woken up. His eyes were full of expression. Fear, impatience, astonishment, I don't know. He stared me in the eyes. It went on for ages. You'll think what I'm about to say is stupid, but it upset me. It really upset me. He seemed to want to tell me something. I've been doing this job for seven years. I see tragedy, and pain, and death every day. I thought I was immune to it, but suffering in silence like that, it really hit me. As if he had a gnawing secret that he wanted to get out.'

Dominique stood in silence.

'I think that man has suffered a great tragedy in his life. I've tried to communicate with him but he seems frightened half to death. What do you think I can do?'

'I know you like him, at least you seem to.'

He shrugged.

'Dominique likes everyone! It's in my nature. But yes, I have become attached to him. I'd like to help him. There's something he wants to confess, to free his conscience. Maybe a secret to confide.'

'That's why I waited for you.'

'You think he's ready?'

'That's what I felt last night. I don't how he'll react today but I think he's had enough of the silence. He wants to talk, and he'll only talk to you.'

49: IT WAS RAINING

Mary sang on stage the very night we arrived in Berlin. The replacement bass player showed up, as promised by the German agent. An English guy aged about thirty, from Leeds. He had settled in Berlin in the late Fifties after meeting a German girl during his military service. His name was Freddie. He hit it off with the Frames straightaway.

The club they were hired to play was the Graffiti, in Charlottenburg, near Richard-Wagner-Platz in the English sector.

It was a flashily decorated place on two levels, with a restaurant on the ground floor, serving simple food at affordable prices – pizza, hamburgers and the traditional bratwurst mit ziebeln. Big, kitsch chandeliers hung from the ceiling and the walls were covered with film posters from the Thirties.

At the back of the restaurant, a padded double door opened onto a staircase leading to the discotheque, on the floor above. The club was bigger than the restaurant. A fifteen-metre bar filled one wall.

I spent most evenings there, propped against the counter or perched on a high stool chatting to Gunther, one of the barmen. I could describe the place down to the last detail. The stage faced the bar, a metre above floor level.

The first customers would arrive late afternoon, but the majority appeared at around 8:00p.m. They were mostly military: English, Americans and French, generally in uniform. Crowds of German girls stood waiting, immaculately turned out, made up and wafting perfume. They chattered, laughed loudly and stared at me in disdain.

It was a place for fun and good times, like a lot of clubs in Soho, but unlike London, the bright veneer masked the underlying distress. West Berlin was a megalopolis of multiple, contradictory facets. By day, it seemed quiet, at peace with itself, despite the omnipresent Wall that haunted Berliners and travellers alike. The traffic flowed freely. The city was spacious and airy, traversed by broad avenues and scattered with parks including the enormous Tiergarten, in the heart of it all.

West Berlin was capitalist enclave in a Communist zone. The West made sure it was a showcase for democracy, freedom of thought and its own brand of pseudo-humanism.

The older Berliners were sullen and melancholy, caught between shame at their Nazi past, the humiliation of occupation by foreign forces and the pain of separation from their loved ones. At the sight of me, with my unkempt appearance and bleached hair, they would simply look away — a reaction unlike either the indifference of Londoners, or the Parisians' scornful stares.

The city's youth had become accustomed to the situation. They dressed and behaved like their counterparts everywhere else, but eschewed the eccentricity I had seen in London.

After dark, things would hot up in certain districts. The liveliest of all were the streets off the smart, stuffy Kurfürstendamm, packed with bars, clubs and strip shows. Numerous English groups played there. They had fled London's cultural boom and the new wave of psychedelia, in hopes of earning a decent living somewhere, having missed out on fame and glory back home.

Mary's room was on the top floor of an ochre-coloured building on Liesenstrasse, in Wedding, in the French sector, ten kilometres from the Graffiti. The other members of the group were housed in a small furnished apartment on a parallel street.

Mary would spend part of each afternoon rehearsing and writing songs. She would leave at around 2:00p.m. and I would join her early in the evening. I took the bus or the U-Bahn to Charlottenburg. Sometimes I walked, but the distance was exhausting.

We would get home at around one o'clock in the morning. Often, we took a taxi and shared the fare.

From our window, we could see the Wall where it cut through St Hedwig's Cemetery, on the other side of the street. During its construction, the East German authorities had moved the graves that became stranded in no-man's land.

At night, the strip of ground was brilliantly lit. When I was unable to sleep, I would watch the frontier guards moving back and forth like menacing ghosts.

At regular intervals, we heard the clatter of the S-Bahn running along the back of the cemetery. Apart from that, the street was quiet, with few cars.

I wasted my afternoons, moving from bistro to bistro. I would sit at the bar and try to make the manager's acquaintance. Most could manage a few words of English or French. I would order a beer and invite them to join me. They usually accepted.

I would open the conversation on safe ground – the weather, or the concert schedules. I had an encyclopaedic knowledge of both. Once contact was established, I would explain what I was doing in Berlin. I had some cards printed at the automat in the KaDeWe, the big city-centre department store. I had typed my name, Jacques Berger, and my trade – drummer. By way of an address, I had included the telephone number at the Graffiti.

Man weisst ja nie! You never know. Gunther taught me the phrase. I would drop it in at the end, casually placing my card on the bar, with a few notes to cover the drinks and a tip.

I was becoming more dishevelled by the day. My soul mirrored my decaying body, and my body mirrored the ruin of my soul. Pessimism darkened my days, hope had given way to disillusion. Mary was worried. Our love-making became laborious and infrequent, subject to the effects of dozens of pills. I was hooked on Tuinal, a red and blue capsule that helped conquer my inadequacy.

By day, I took a mixture of Dexedrine and Preludin. The latter had been classed as a drug and taken off the market, but it could be bought illegally in Germany, and I managed to find it at a good price.

I swallowed the pills down with beer. In the evenings, I smoked grass and chewed peyote buttons. The cocktail restored my prowess for a brief moment, and destroyed it the rest of the time

I had stopped reading. Not that I lacked for time, or that Berlin was short on books, but I was incapable of concentrating on a text. I would stare at the lines, unable to fathom their meaning.

I became firm friends with Gunther, one of the barmen at the Graffiti. He carried a vast beer gut and never smiled. He spoke fluent English and adored rock music. We would discourse at length on past successes and emerging trends.

My position was unchanged. Rock should be pure and hard, or it wasn't worthy of the name. I was loyal to the Rolling Stones, but the Beatles had betrayed the cause. Their latest single, 'Strawberry Fields', was a spineless morass.

Gunther maintained it was a magical progression, basic three-chord rock couldn't carry on the same way until the end of time. He liked the new, exotic sounds, and appreciated American groups like the Byrds.

One evening, just as Gunther was telling me what he thought of Pink Floyd's latest single, 'Arnold Layne', the telephone rang. He exchanged a few words with the caller, then looked hard in my direction.

I will remember that day to my dying breath. Mary's contract was coming to an end. It was March the fourteenth, 1967.

It was raining.

50: BACK-UP

Stern worked on the assumption that the recording session had taken place, and that it held the key to the whole affair.

What had happened that evening?

What had the recording unleashed?

For a moment, he wondered whether the results of the session had proved unsatisfactory, which went some way to explaining why the organisers had never released the record.

But on second thoughts, he discounted the theory. The money excluded that possibility. If their performance had been mediocre, the musicians wouldn't have been paid, yet they received the money straightaway, at the end of the session, which was unusual in the music industry. In the United Kingdom, artists were paid a percentage of sales, or a fixed fee, and the money was disbursed one year after the record had been released, or a year and a half for sales overseas.

Stern concluded that an unexpected turn of events had prevented the record's release, or that it had been intended for a different market, or a different purpose altogether.

He focused on the presumed absence of one of the musicians, the one who had been unable to attend, and had stayed behind at the apartment. He checked the table he had drawn up and proceeded by elimination.

Jim Ruskin could be discounted quite reasonably, straightaway. He had clearly been the group's point of contact with the organisers: he had a good command of German. His telephone calls from Birgit's apartment, with the man named Karl, and the things he told her the day before and the day after March the fourteenth, confirmed his likely presence at the recording.

Stern examined the profiles of the other three and concluded that Larry Finch's absence from such a major event was inconceivable. He was the founder and leader of Pearl Harbor. No group could function without a head man, especially not when it came to laying down tracks in a studio.

Steve Parker was Larry's right-hand man from the start. He played lead guitar and sang. Together, they were the heart and soul of Pearl Harbor. It was highly unlikely the recording could have taken place without one or other of the two.

That left the fourth member, Paul McDonald, the drummer.

McDonald had talked about the recording to his friend Stuart when the two met in London, but had dodged his friends' questions and given no details about what had taken place.

McDonald was a powerfully built man. He drank heavily, but he had a reputation for rude health, and an ability to hold his drink.

Michael Stern got in touch with Nick Kohn, a London music journalist he had met at a conference. He explained his approach, the context and the facts.

Kohn replied that no musician was ever completely irreplaceable for a recording session.

Many session musicians were happy to stand in, either to take the place of an absent player, or because the musical arrangement required it, or for a spot of added value on certain tracks.

In many cases, if a musician was absent, an alternative technique would be used, namely re-recording. The process involved recording the missing parts after the event, on a supplementary track.

He took the example of a recent track by Cream entitled 'Sunshine of Your Love'. Clapton had played both solo and rhythm guitar, using this method. According to him, Paul McCartney had recorded an entire song on his own, playing each instrument, and recording successive overdubs.

Kohn also told Stern that in the small world of rock, when it came to the classic line-up of three musicians and a drummer, the drummer was often considered a necessary evil. Drummers were doomed to extinction, to be replaced by the rhythm machine, a revolutionary new electronic device. And while rhythm machines still weren't perfect, he predicted they would soon prove more accurate and above all, much cheaper than their human counterparts. The first models had been developed in Japan, and many studios had begun using them.

In conclusion, and in answer to Stern's question, he figured that the player most easily replaced in any rock band was the drummer.

Before ending the call, he added that in a city like Berlin, where so many decent groups were performing, it wouldn't be difficult to find a capable drummer as back-up.

51: GET TO A PHONE

With the handset wedged against one ear, and his hand clapped over the other, Gunther listened, staring at me all the while.

I could tell from his look that the message had something to do with me. At one point, he nodded and spoke a few words, raising his voice above the din of the music. He put his hand on the mouthpiece and called me over.

The boss of the Viktoria was on the line. The Viktoria was a bar near the Europa Center, where I went from time to time to drink and listen to the resident rock group. The guy had just received a call from someone looking urgently for a back-up drummer. I had left him my card; it was worth a shot.

Gunther asked me what he should say.

I agreed, in principle.

Gunther uncovered the mouthpiece and translated my reply. The boss at the Viktoria gave him a telephone number. I should call immediately, or the job would go to someone else.

Gunther dialled the number straightaway. An overexcited voice at the other end gave the name Karl. I could hear him hollering down the line, despite the racket in the Graffiti.

I was to find a taxi straightaway and get over there. No need to worry about equipment; there was a kit ready and waiting, and three guitarists. I would get six hundred marks for the evening, and my taxi fares.

I agreed on the spot. Gunther sealed the deal and Karl gave him the address.

Six hundred marks. Good money for a few hours' back-up. But a paltry sum for the wreck of a life.

I emerged from the Graffiti. Icy rain lashed the pavement. I ran to Richard-Wagner-Platz and dived into a taxi.

The place was on Wegelystrasse, at the far end of Strasse des 17 Juni, on the west side of the Tiergarten. The taxi stopped in front of a soulless apartment block, like hundreds of others in Berlin.

A man paced distractedly outside the entrance. He was bent forward with his coat pulled up over his head, against the rain. He hurried over as soon as he saw me emerge from the taxi. His name was Karl. He seized my arm and led me towards the building.

The main doorway opened onto a spacious inner courtyard. He tried a few words in German as we ran across. I answered in English, telling him I didn't understand. He switched straightaway, spouting the words in a disorderly jumble. I got the gist.

I would be taking part in a recording session. Normally there were four members to the group, all English, but the drummer had fallen ill at the last minute. Apart from the three other musicians and Karl himself, no one knew, nor should they be told, that I wasn't the regular drummer. The less said the better. The bass player would brief me when we arrived. If I wanted my money, I should play the game, pretend to know them and apologise for showing up late. Family problems, something like that.

For 600 marks I was ready to swear my grandmother had died of an overdose.

We went down to a basement, reached through a door at the back of the courtyard. A maze of narrow corridors led to a small, low-ceilinged room.

The atmosphere was choking. The heating was on full blast and the room smelled of mould. A faint aroma of hashish floated on the air.

The guitarists were tuning their instruments and testing the equipment. Two technicians were busying themselves, one in the studio, adjusting the mics, the other in the recording booth. The latter was fitted with a mixing deck and two big tape recorders. They were Studers, the top of the range. I knew the brand, but had never seen these models before.

Besides the musicians and technicians, there were three other men in the room. They stood motionless at the back of the booth, watching the preparations. Their plain suits and conformist haircuts contrasted with the rest of the scene. Karl went to join them, and delivered a seemingly endless monologue.

The bass player came over and harangued me for showing up late. He had hollow features and a skin-and-bone figure. I mumbled a few words of apology. He pointed to the drum kit with an authoritative air and ordered me to get into position.

I did as he said, with no fuss. This was all part of the scenario. I settled down, looking suitably contrite. The kit was a Ludwig, in good condition.

While I was getting my bearings, the bassist turned his back on the booth and asked if I could count to eight. He seemed nervous, and tetchy. Without waiting for an answer, he said the session would revolve around one of their own compositions. The song was called 'Girls Just Want it all Night Long', and it opened with a guitar riff in four-four. The bass would come in after that. The second guitar and the drummer would come in after four more bars. He would tolerate one bad take, no more, I'd just have to fit in. He advised me to keep plenty in reserve for the bridge.

Finally, he said he was expecting something more than what he called 'rock for pussies.'

He wandered off and one of the other guitarists came over. Unlike the bass player, he seemed relaxed and in good shape. He smiled, as if he had just played a great joke behind someone's back. He had long, bleached hair and a ring on every finger.

While pretending to tune his instrument, he proffered some information under his breath. The gig had come out of nowhere, two days ago. Karl had come to the club where they played, and suggested they make a recording. The guitarist's name was Jim Ruskin, the bass player was Larry Finch and the second guitar was Steve Parker. I was Paul McDonald. The group was called Pearl Harbor. The real Paul McDonald had snorted poppers before coming out, to boost his performance, but had been taken ill.

Jim's guitar had just five strings. He followed my gaze. This was one of his strokes of genius, he had taken away the low E string and tuned his guitar to open G. He'd show me how to blast the guts out of a Gibson.

Discreetly, he reached out a hand and winked. He held a small, blackish pellet in his palm, and a few pieces of paper the size of a postage stamp. He asked if I'd prefer some Afghan primo or a tab of lysergesäurediathylamid. He pronounced the German compound name with evident relish.

He was carrying some good stuff. Afghan primo was the best hash on the market, but it was hard to come by. I had tried some once or twice in London. The resin was shot through with delicate, white veins. Sonny assured me it was goat shit, used as a binding agent. As for the acid, this was a chance to try my first trip. I took the pieces of paper and stuffed them into my mouth.

When everyone was in position, Larry signalled to the technicians, then turned to Steve, who was sitting on a chair, frowning, with his head in his hands. Sullenly, he got to his feet.

Larry pointed his index finger to the ceiling and waited for silence. He clicked his fingers four times, and a growl of thunder rang out.

Steve's riff was wild, fierce and jubilant. He generated feedback and saturated noise like nothing I'd ever heard. After the fourth bar, Larry's bass joined the dance, a huge, formless rumble. I put together an intro fill and came in with Jim.

All hell broke loose. Pearl Harbor had invented something completely new.

The ground shook. The whole building shook.

Berlin shook.

Their music had phenomenal power. Sustained by the demonic bass-line, their riffs came together, swirling and soaring like furious gales coupling to form a hurricane. Larry hollered until his voice cracked, telling all the world that girls just wanted it all night long. Between couplets, he went into further detail, accompanied by long, raucous howls.

It was bestial, terrifying, inhuman.

Drowning in the vortex, I thrashed and hammered like a madman.

And the more I thrashed, the more I felt overwhelmed by a mixture of spite and despair.

The acid was doing its work. I was soaringly, dizzyingly high. I began to pour sweat. I prickled with goosebumps all over. My hands left trails of light as they moved. The studio's light bulbs exploded with blinding flashes.

The atmosphere was surreal. The guitarists twisted and writhed. Karl was shaking his head from side to side. The technicians were having a fine time behind the controls.

Motionless at the back of the booth, the three stooges stood stock still, like British Bobbies policing a march.

We did four numbers straight off without stopping, barely even pausing for breath. Finally, the technicians signalled that they had what they wanted.

The world stopped.

I was lost in flight, gorged on decibels and LSD.

I came to on the pavement outside. The members of Pearl Harbor were clapping me hard on the back. Karl paid me my dues and every-one disappeared.

The rain was still falling.

I found myself laughing helplessly. I stood for some time, laughing all alone on the pavement, my nose pointed skywards, with rods of icy rain pouring over my face and trickling down my neck.

Then I began to come down.

The descent was dizzying, too.

I wanted to die. I could see the Mercedes star on the roof of the Europa Center at the far end of the Tiergarten, two or three kilometres away. It wasn't revolving slowly as usual; it changed colour, and size, and rose into the night taking the sky-scraper with it.

There were no taxis passing. I felt bad. I had no idea what to do.

The S-Bahn was close by. I could have taken refuge there, like the drunks and druggies. The West Berlin police weren't allowed there; the S-Bahn was run by the GDR, and their cops left the Western junkies alone.

I could have taken refuge in the S-Bahn and things would have gone no further. But I went back to the studio, hoping to get to a phone.

52: FIFTEEN MISERABLE SECONDS

I crossed the courtyard. The rain was beating down harder than ever, my face was soaked and my vision blurred. I walked to where I thought the studio was. I was a tiny nutshell blown about by the storm.

I found the door to the basement. I went in. I was soaked from head to foot. I fumbled in the darkness, but couldn't find a switch. Arms outstretched, eyes staring, I felt my way along the labyrinth of passages, crashing into the walls.

I found myself standing outside the studio door. It was closed. I was about to pass out, my head was spinning, my legs were wobbly. I had to get out of this trap. I shouldered the door hard, and it fell open.

I saw straightaway that I had made a terrible mistake.

A dozen people were busying themselves in the room, but silence reigned.

Everyone stopped and turned to look in my direction. The technicians I had seen during the recording had gone; others had taken their place. Some of the men were wearing baggy white overalls, skullcaps, gloves and masks over their mouths. They looked like lab workers experimenting on mice in a TV documentary.

It was colder in the room. The aroma of hash had disappeared, chased out by the smell of disinfectant. For an instant, the smell took me back to my concussion, and my stay in the clinic, back in Brussels.

The room was lit bright as day by powerful standing lamps. The drum kit had been dismantled and sophisticated-looking equipment *had taken its place, together with big metal containers topped with dials, their needles dancing. In the booth, four technicians were bent over the mixing deck with an expression of intense concentration, headphones over their ears.*

The three men in suits were still there. As throughout the recording, they were watching proceedings in the studio. They looked alarmed and furious at my intrusion.

A fourth man was standing beside them. He was older than the others. His attitude suggested he was their superior. He was almost two metres tall, with a pale complexion and eyebrows low over his deep-set eyes. His hair was as white as his shirt. The four men were wearing headsets like those used by the runway staff at airports.

I wasn't sure what I was seeing. The place and time seemed uncertain. I felt I was moving through some parallel world, or playing a role in a science fiction movie. Were it not for the four men, who clearly recognised me, I would have thought I was dreaming, or had found the wrong door. I knew LSD could produce hallucinations, but I wasn't tripping now, and these guys were real.

The tall man stared in my direction. He shot the others a questioning glance, signalling my presence with a jerk of the chin.

One moved across to where he stood and told him in a low voice that I was the drummer. He spoke English with an American accent. He looked uneasy. Once the information was delivered, he took a few steps back.

The tall man came forward and stood in front of me. He was broad enough to block my field of view. He asked me what I wanted.

I stammered a few words about the rain, the taxi, the distance, the Mercedes star soaring into the sky, whatever came into my head. Before he had time to react, I had turned on my heels and fled into the dark passage.

I've spent enough time with musicians to know that most recordings are reworked after the take. There are myriad ways to dress things up and improve the results. I knew that mixing had become part of the creative process in its own right. I knew that some musicians liked to try special effects, too.

I also knew that the process was usually carried out in collaboration with the artists.

Less than fifteen seconds had elapsed from my return to the studio to my hurried exit. Fifteen miserable seconds.

53: SANKT BONIFAZ

When I opened my eyes, it was light and Mary had left.

A delicate haze floated in the room. Confused images jostled in my head. My heart was beating hard and fast, I could hear it pounding in my ears.

Mary had left me a note on the table.

She had tried to bring me round, without success. I had come home later than her, and she had been worried. She asked me to call the Graffiti as soon as I was up and on my way.

I stared around me. For a moment, I felt I had dreamed the entire thing: the recording session had never taken place. I had taken too much dope and had a bad trip. I had smoked too much, drunk too much and swallowed too many pills. My brain was playing tricks, I had suffered hallucinations.

I splashed cold water on my face. The mirror showed my reflection: haggard and gaunt with dark, sunken eyes.

I made coffee and swallowed a couple of Tuinals. I pierced the gel capsule with a needle, to accelerate the impact. I had to distance myself from the nightmare. Its persistent aftertaste stalked me.

I found the money in my pocket as I was dressing. The notes were brand new. I counted them out. Six hundred and twenty marks.

The evidence was plain. The recording session really had taken place. Still, I needed to know whether what I had seen afterwards was real, or a figment of my imagination.

Points of light danced before my eyes. Little by little, the images became clearer. I remembered the guitarists, and the pieces of paper. Jim had assumed I was hooked on LSD, and given me enough to trip out a horse.

I went out. The staircase swayed. The fresh air did me some good. The trees were showing their first signs of colour. The rain had ceased. Cold sunlight bleached the street.

I headed for the first telephone kiosk and called Mary. She was relieved to hear my voice. I had been agitated in my sleep. Several times, I had sat up in bed, choking. I had sweated, and seemed feverish. I had spoken gibberish, in a mixture of French and English. She thought I was delirious.

For my own peace of mind, I called in at the Viktoria. The barman recognised me and asked how the evening had gone. I muttered a vague answer and placed a fifty-mark note on the counter, by way of thanks. I wanted to know how the back-up request had come through to him.

He slipped the note into his pocket and offered me a beer. He'd received a telephone call at about 11:00p.m. He didn't know the caller, but the guy knew there was a resident rock band at the Viktoria, and wanted to hire their drummer for the evening. He said he would pay the musician 500 marks and give the barman a further 250 marks for his trouble.

The caller said he was having trouble finding a player. But the Viktoria was packed, and the group were in full swing. The barman had turned down the offer, but said he would talk to the group at the end of their set, around 2:00 or 3:00a.m. The man sounded agitated. He insisted. The barman couldn't get him off the line. That was when he thought of me. There was nothing else to tell.

I set out to find Pearl Harbor straightaway. In less than half an hour, I discovered they played at the Yoyo bar, on the Ku'damm.

The place wasn't far away. I called in.

The bar had just opened and the boss was in a foul mood. I asked what time the band began playing. He replied that Pearl Harbor wouldn't be playing there any more; he had fired them that very morning. I tried to find out why, but he told me to clear off.

In despair, I headed for the Graffiti. While Mary finished rehearsing, I told Gunther all about the night before. I told him how I had gone back to the studio after the recording; that I had seen strange things. But I gave no details. I didn't want to pass for a lunatic.

When we got home, I told Mary about the previous night. She stroked my face while I delivered my story, gazing at me with the gentle benevolence of a parent listening to a child's made-up adventures. I didn't insist.

Days went by and I came round to the idea that I had hallucinated everything – the second part of the evening, at least.

Mary's contract was coming to an end and we were preparing to return to London. The boss at the Graffiti was pleased with their residency and had offered them an extension, but they refused.

I spent my last days in Berlin watching out for Pearl Harbor's single. But there was nothing. I asked at all the city's main record stores, but the disc wasn't registered, nor was it listed as a forthcoming release.

In early April, we returned to London. In just three months, everything had changed. Hippies were the latest thing. Everyone wore brightly coloured, fringed clothes. Hair was very long, and beards and bead necklaces were de rigueur. The music had changed too. Acid had made its appearance, and everything was soft and sluggish, from the beat to the way guys of my generation walked. They dragged their feet, looked stoned and spent their days sitting in front of the United States Embassy calling for peace in Vietnam.

My room at Brian's was taken, and the few things I had left behind were waiting for me in a corner of the living room. Sonny had been thrown out as well. He was living with a few friends in Chelsea, in a flat belonging to a guitarist who was on tour in Australia.

Mary returned to her lodgings in Kensington and introduced me to the landlady. She took her to one side and told her we were going to get married.

The woman was clearly a decent soul, with gentle eyes. She frowned and asked Mary to repeat what she had said. Mary said she knew it was against the rules for a couple to live together in the house. She would be looking for somewhere else right away, but begged the owner to let me stay temporarily. She begged for me to be allowed two weeks under the woman's roof, while she sorted herself out.

The landlady looked me up and down.

I felt awkward and uncomfortable with my tattered kit and unkempt mop of hair. She smiled, and her smile reminded me of my mother. She turned to Mary, jerked a thumb in my direction and asked if she really intended to marry a character like me.

Mary took me by the hand and nodded.

The woman sighed. We were to make ourselves at home, and she would give us a more spacious room that had just become vacant.

Her name was Virginia Fowler. Her husband had died in the Blitz. I remember her with a special fondness.

I asked Mary what Mrs Fowler would say when she found out she was lying. She gazed at me, shrugged one shoulder and said she was telling the truth. The full significance of her words was lost on me, at first.

That night, Mary bit me so hard she drew blood. Next morning, the dried blood had stuck my earlobe to the pillow. My ear was misshapen for life. I woke Mary, took her in my arms and told her I wanted her to be my wife.

My life bounced back. I was going to marry the woman I loved. I wanted my mother to know. For the first time, I considered a trip *home, but there were so many obstacles in my way. I was wanted as a deserter in Belgium, and as a witness to a suspicious death in France.*

Mary was enjoying more and more success. There were quarrels from the moment we returned. The bassist and drummer left the Frames, while the guitarists followed Mary. One was called Bob, an emaciated, bearded guy who scratched his head constantly. The other was a quiet, effective musician by the name of Tom.

I applied for the post of drummer. They accepted me. We began the hunt for a bassist. London was crawling with talented musicians and we soon found one who suited us. In late April, we formed a group. Four musicians and a girl singer. Mary and The Governors.

I kept in touch with Sonny. We saw less of one another now. From time to time, he would accompany us on the harmonica.

Those few weeks were the happiest and most serene of my life. I went back to work at the record shop. I had enough money coming in. I worked all day, and we played at night.

Mary had kept her existing contracts, and signed new ones all the time. She was dazzling, and her confidence grew. I played almost every day, getting better all the time.

Life seemed simple. We were in love. We talked about our future marriage and imagined a thousand different places for our honeymoon. We took our time. We made love. We drank. We laughed.

It was during this time that Mary and I discovered the many and wonderful virtues of cocaine.

From time to time, I kept a half-hearted look out for Pearl Harbor's record in the racks. Nothing appeared and gradually, I began to forget the whole business.

By early June, I was scarcely giving it another thought. Until the Massacre of Sankt Bonifaz.

54: HAND

Snow fell thickly on the night of the twenty-third to the twenty-fourth of December.

Traffic was disrupted and it was 11:00a.m. before Dominique reached the clinic, after a three-hour journey to cover the few kilometres separating his work and home.

After the stormy mid-November weekend, he had redoubled his efforts with X Midi, as the nurse had advised. Encouraged by her firm assurance, he had taken a more direct approach. He had reminded the man of the procedure: one blink for 'yes', two for 'no', and had asked him straight out if there was anything he wanted to confide.

The man had averted his gaze.

Dominique had beaten a retreat. The next day, he asked the man if their pact still held. He wanted to be certain he had his trust. The man had stared at him for a long while, then blinked his eyes once. But had taken no further initiative.

The patient had made further progress over the intervening weeks. The movement in his fingers was more supple, and he could turn his head further – ten degrees to the left, and to the right.

Dominique called out his usual greetings and headed for X Midi's room.

He was in the habit of informing his patient of his absences, ahead of each weekend, or when he took a day's leave in the week. That morning, at around 9:00a.m. one of the night nurses had called Dominique's mobile to tell him that X Midi was showing signs of distress. The man knew the hours kept by his care team, and seemed distraught when Dominique failed to show. She had tried her best to reassure him, but to no avail.

Outside the room, Dominique launched into one of his imaginary dialogues.

'Dominique! You're late!'

'I know. It's been snowing.'

'It's been snowing?'

'It certainly has been snowing! The biggest snowfall across the country for seventy years!'

He walked into the room.

X Midi was looking out for him. A mixture of fear and relief showed in his eyes.

Dominique crossed the room and took X Midi's hand in his.

'Forgive me, Eddy, I'm late. It's been snowing all night. Thirty centimetres of snow in the streets! Tonight is Christmas Eve. I was planning a trip to Paris to spend it with my family, but the roads aren't clear and the Thalys isn't running.'

The man held his gaze. He seemed to be calming down.

Dominique softened his voice.

'Where you were last Christmas? With your family, I suppose? Everyone has some family somewhere. Would you like to see yours again?'

X Midi stifled a moan and flexed his fingers.

Dominique watched him for a few moments. The man rolled his head from side to side, moving his lips.

Dominique bent over him.

'Do you want to tell me something, Eddy?'

The man stared into the physio's eyes and blinked rapidly, once.

Dominique felt his heart leap.

He moved his face closer.

'A few words from you would be the best Christmas present ever.'

The man moaned once more.

Dominique ran a hand through X Midi's hair.

'Stay calm, my friend, I'm here to listen. I made a promise, and I'll keep it. Whatever you say is between the two of us. Understood?'

The man blinked once.

Dominique felt a rush of excitement.

'You know I've been waiting for this for a long time. I've got something for you.'

He went over to the wardrobe and took out a cardboard tube. He pulled out the poster inside and showed it to X Midi.

'Look, this is an alphabet chart. Vowels on the top line and consonants underneath. They're arranged according to the frequency of their use. You know 'e' is the most used letter in French? And for consonants, 's'.'

The man stared at the poster with interest.

'See where we're going, here?'

The man gave no reaction.

'I'll explain. You're going to make words. First I'll say "vowel" and if the first letter of your word is a vowel, you'll blink once. If not, you do nothing. See, I'm making life easy for you. Then, I'll pronounce each letter, one after the other, very slowly, you'll have plenty of time. I'll wait. When I get to the letter you need, you blink once. Okay?'

No reaction.

'Okay, Eddy? Shall we give it a go?'

The man continued to examine the alphabet chart.

Dominique didn't want to pressure him. He rolled the poster back up and pushed it into the cardboard tube.

'There it is, my friend. The day you want to tell me something, I'll get the tube out. You can turn off the TV, to let me know. Now I need to go. I have other friends waiting for their treatments. I'll be back in a while.'

He turned on his heels and headed for the door. He was stepping out into the corridor when the TV went black.

Dominique walked back into the room.

'Did you turn it off? You want to tell me something?'

The man closed his eyes.

'Fine, so I'll get the chart?'

The man stared at him.

Dominique took out the alphabet, moving slowly and deliberately. He didn't want to risk making the man change his mind.

He let X Midi examine the chart for a few minutes before asking his first question.

'Vowel?'

The man showed no response.

'So it's a consonant?'

He began reciting the series of consonants.

'S? T? N? R? L? D? C? P? M?'

The man closed his eyes.

Dominique felt the adrenaline rush flooding his arms and legs.

'M? That's the first letter of your word?'

The man blinked.

Dominique was jubilant.

'Fantastic! Amazing! Edouard, you're a genius! M? M! *Mmwah!*'

He blew X Midi an extravagant kiss.

The man carried on staring at the poster, as if the exercise demanded his total concentration.

'Okay, let's carry on. If I think I've found the word, I'll make suggestions, that way you won't have to keep on to the last letter.'

He pointed a finger at the top line.

'Vowel?'

Yes.

'E? A?'

The man blinked.

'A? That's the second letter? A like *amour*? MA? That's the beginning of your word?'

The man signalled that it was. His eyes filled with tears.

'We carry on with the same word?'

Yes.

'Vowel?'

Yes.

'E? A? I?'

Yes.

'I? MAI?'

MAI was correct.

'Vowel?'

No reaction.

'S? T? N?'

Yes.

'MAIN?'

Yes.

'*Maintenant*?'

No reaction.

'*Main*? Hand? That's your first word?'

Yes.

'Shall we continue?'

No reaction.

'That's what you want to tell me? Hand?'

The man blinked once and looked away, leaving Dominique perplexed.

Hand.

55: FAR BACK

Perhaps I'll get out of this prison. I need time. I can think clearly. I know what's going on around me. I know what a hand is. I can picture a hand. I know mine are there, I can feel them again.

If I could speak, I could pronounce the word, but spelling it out is a problem. It's been so long since I read or wrote anything.

All this takes me so far back.

56: LAST ON THE LIST

Stern was convinced Paul McDonald's replacement had been a last-minute thing. The drummer was an energetic man, in robust health. Given what was at stake, he must have dropped out at the very last minute. It must have come as a surprise.

The session's organisers would have been forced to look for a replacement drummer. The London columnist Nick Kohn had confirmed that many groups played 'residencies' in Berlin. The challenge would be to find one that had recently quit, or a drummer available to step into McDonald's shoes.

For Stern, it meant listing every drummer who had played in West Berlin during the month of March: no small challenge. He gave up on the idea and asked himself what he would have done, in the organisers' place.

Logically, he would have called round the night clubs where the groups played.

A feasible enough lead.

He drew up a list of clubs, bars, night clubs and other Berlin haunts likely to have hired musicians to provide evening entertainment.

But the task proved unexpectedly tough. West Berlin numbered one hundred and thirty-nine places hiring musicians on a regular or permanent basis. Limiting the search to rock groups wouldn't help – any jazz or variety drummer would have been up to the job, too.

Stern gave his editor-in-chief a detailed progress report on the investigation, and suggested hiring a German-speaking temp reporter to carry out the search.

His request was refused. The editor-in-chief ordered him to drop the story: no one was interested.

Stern acted on his chief's instructions. He did not put up a fight.

That evening he contacted his friend George Marshall, the vice-chancellor of Queen's University Belfast, and asked him to find a German-speaking student prepared to earn a bit of pocket money by making a few telephone calls between classes.

A few days later, he was contacted by Manfred Hammer, a student from Karlsruhe, willing and able to help. Stern had prepared the work, drawing up an alphabetical list of bars and night clubs. He installed the student in his own flat, and said he would pay him out of his own pocket.

Hammer's mission was to contact the manager of each venue and ask if he had received a request for a back-up drummer on the evening of March the fourteenth.

Stern was all too aware that seven months had elapsed, and there was a slim chance of success.

Hammer set to work on Thursday, November the sixteenth, around 11:00a.m.

By the end of the day, he had made over fifty calls. Most went unanswered. Some had hung up before he had time to formulate his request. The few who heard him out answered 'no'.

Late in the afternoon the following day, just as Hammer was beginning to give up hope, he spoke to a waiter at Danny's Club. The man remembered taking just such a call. The club's resident group at the time were a rock outfit called The Sharks. The caller had been looking for a drummer for the evening, and offered three hundred marks.

The call had sparked controversy at the club. Given the large sum involved, the waiter had spoken to the drummer, who said he would take the gig. The other group members were willing to let him go provided he shared the money. The singer declared they would play an 'intimate' set that evening – no drummer: he would provide the percussion himself, on maracas and tambourine. But the club's boss had intervened and refused point blank. The discussion turned sour, and there were heated exchanges for several minutes.

The man on the line had been furious at being made to wait so long for a refusal.

Hammer thanked the waiter and called Stern immediately to announce the good news.

Stern was delighted. He was on the right track. They would continue with the calls. He asked Hammer if he could find a friend to help out. Next day, Hammer found another student, Hilde Bachmann, a Bavarian girl from Munich.

Between November the eighteenth and the twenty-fourth, they took it in turns to make the calls. They called without a break from ten in the morning to midnight, encouraging one another and stopping only for a drink and a sandwich.

Sometimes it took more than ten calls to reach the right person. Finally, they reached seven people who remembered receiving the back-up calls, but with no further leads.

On November the twenty-fourth, around 3:00p.m., Hilde Bachmann was on the line to a man by the name of Fred Weiss, the boss of the Viktoria Bar.

One of the last on the list.

57: AN UNWITTING ROLE

The events occurred on the night of the fourth to the fifth of June, 1967, in Ramstein, near Kaiserlautern, some seven hundred kilometres south-west of Berlin.

On a normal day, it would have made the headlines of every newspaper, but at dawn on the fifth of June, Israeli Mirages attacked Egypt and destroyed the country's air force while it was still on the ground. Half an hour later, tanks entered Sinaï. The Six-Day War had begun.

For the man in the street, this marked the beginning of World War Three. The morning papers all changed their headlines at the last minute, and the Sankt Bonifaz Massacre became a secondary news item, relegated to the inside pages.

The town of Ramstein was known as the home of the biggest American air base in Europe. As on every Sunday night, its military personnel were enjoying their last night of freedom after weekend leave. One of the most popular bars in the town centre was the Hula-Hoop, a huge dance hall with several different bars and restaurants.

Large numbers of American soldiers had gathered there that evening, together with French, British and Belgians garrisoned close by. A fair few Germans were also out, mostly locals.

At around 1:00a.m. a fight broke out.

Eyewitnesses said several assaults had been launched around the hall, at the same moment, mostly targeting the Germans. The military personnel threw themselves at the Germans all at once, as if an order had been given.

The victims were massacred with punches, kicks and broken-off bottles. *The soldiers seemed to have been overcome with a kind of murderous bloodlust. Seven German civilians were killed in the space of a few minutes. After lynching these poor innocents, the American and British soldiers turned against the French and the Belgians. They began fighting amongst themselves. Blood flowed. It seemed nothing could stop the wave of violence. With no one left to attack, some of the American personnel turned on their own garrison comrades.*

The military police hurried to the scene, and were attacked in their turn. Faced with a huge number of assailants, they were forced to retreat. Their aggressors pursued them through the streets. The police opened fire and killed three of the ring leaders.

Calm was restored as suddenly as the flash of violence had erupted.

Ambulances arrived. The events had taken a heavy toll. Fifteen dead and thirty wounded, some in a critical condition.

The West German authorities talked of mass hysteria.

That Sunday night, like every Sunday, was my night off. The War and the massacre were fermenting while Mary and I watched Jimi Hendrix's set at the Saville theatre. Paul McCartney was there too. Jimi opened the show with 'Sgt Pepper's Lonely Hearts Club Band', a fine tribute to the Fab Four, whose album had been released just a few days earlier.

Next day, everyone was talking about the war in Egypt. I bought a newspaper – something I never normally did. I glanced through the report of the outbreak of Arab–Israeli hostilities while drinking my coffee. I spoke good enough English, but reading still gave me a few problems. Mary translated the words I didn't understand.

After reading the article, I turned the pages of the paper mechanically, and found the section recounting the events in Ramstein.

My heart leaped.

He was there. On one of the photographs taken immediately after the tragedy. He was there, amongst the bystanders in front of the Hula-Hoop. He seemed to be watching the ambulances driving back

*and forth. He was a good head taller than the rest of the crowd. I
recognised his white hair, his martial appearance, his closed expression and deep-set eyes.*

*I should have stopped there, finished my coffee and got on with my
semblance of a life but it seemed to me that behind this slaughter lay
an appalling truth, in which I had played an unwitting role.*

58: THE CALL OF DUTY

The discovery troubled me deeply: it boded ill. I showed the article and the picture to Mary. She shrugged her shoulder and countered that it was just a coincidence, the photograph was blurry, and my imagination was playing tricks.

Mary didn't believe me, and I didn't insist. I waited until she went out.

As soon as the door closed behind her, I threw some things into a bag and pocketed the money we had stashed. I had to get to Ramstein, and nothing would stop me.

I left Mary a note. I was not mistaken. It was no coincidence.

I took the bus to Heathrow. At the Lufthansa counter, I bought a ticket to Frankfurt.

I was distracted, dazed. Had I made the right decision? I felt guilty about Mary. Lost in thought, I moved through passport control and customs without a hitch.

I arrived in Frankfurt mid-afternoon. From there, I caught a train to Ramstein, and arrived at nightfall.

The sense of tragedy was palpable. The station was packed with people, but silence reigned. I saw faces stricken with grief, terrified stares; slumped, defeated figures. The events had occurred less than twenty-four hours before, and many relatives were only just arriving.

The hotels were filled with families and journalists. Dozens of people were sitting on the station hall floor, half awake, staring into the void. The families of victims sat alongside the families of the *attackers. Some appeared uncomprehending, or in denial. Others showed deep sorrow.*

I mixed with the crowd. I passed myself off as the brother of a wounded Belgian soldier. It suited my purpose. I felt a hypocrite, taking cover in such circumstances, but the alibi was useful to try and understand what had happened. Using my French and English, and the few words of German I had picked up, it enabled me to approach witnesses.

Each time, I repeated the same questions.

Eventually, one survivor, traumatised by the images seared on his memory, produced the fragment I dreaded but had been expecting.

Shortly before the outbreak of violence, he had seen the disc-jockey talking to a young man in civilian clothes, in the doorway of his booth. The man had handed him a round metal box, like a film reel canister. My witness couldn't tell me anything more – he had left a few seconds later, just as the trouble broke out.

My blood froze. Propelled by some unseen force, I left the station and set out on the road to hell. I found myself outside the Hula-Hoop. I have no idea how.

Men and women stood silently collecting their thoughts outside the entrance to the club. Notes scribbled hurriedly on scraps of paper had been pinned to the door. A carpet of flowers was spreading in front of the building. A tape recorder crackled classical music. Hundreds of candles had been placed on the pavement, their flames wavering in the icy wind.

Drowning in the midst of such distress, I trembled with rage and cold. I was like a survivor after an atomic bomb-blast, wandering amongst the ruins of a city whose every corner was redolent of death.

I headed back to the station. Everywhere I went, people were talking unreservedly, trying to find the words that would help them understand and release their sorrow.

By dint of asking, I found the disc-jockey. He was the same age as me. He was sitting at a table in a bar in town, haggard and staring into space. This was the beginning of his second sleepless night. Alcohol was helping to erase the nightmare. He was surrounded by friends, each trying to help him draw breath and return to the world of the living.

I sat at his table. I told him the story about my wounded brother. He spoke a little English. He listened without listening, haunted by the scenes of the night before. He would never sleep again.

I asked no questions. We drank and talked like people united in grief.

Deep in the night, he gave me his version of events. When the fighting broke out, he had been targeted by a group of American soldiers. They were hurling things at the glass screens around his booth – bottles, glasses, chairs. He locked himself in and took refuge under the mixing desk, to escape being killed.

He remembered people screaming. He remembered the murderers exhorting their comrades to fight. He heard the agonised groans of the victims as they lay dying.

His story was long and painful.

I asked him if he had any idea what might have sparked the violence. He did not. One question led to another, and I steered him to the clue I had picked up. I asked if he remembered what record he was playing when the attacks began. He couldn't remember. After a moment, he looked up, stared defiantly at me and asked why I wanted to know. I replied that it was something that had just occurred to me, nothing more.

Prompted by the question, he recalled a simple, harmless incident. A punter had sought him out during the evening, handed him a record in a metal case and asked him to play it. The sort of thing that happened all the time. As a rule, it was the regulars who put in requests, but he had never seen this man before.

As always, he listened to a few bars on his headphones, to make sure the request wasn't a joke. The brief snatch he heard was fine; it was a decent rock track. He thought the fighting had probably broken out while that record was playing.

We sat in silence, pondering the implications of what he had told me.

Without knowing it, I had begun the long, grim hike into the darkness that engulfs me still, today.

I had witnessed the aftermath of a dress rehearsal. The worst was yet to come. But nothing could have been further from my mind.

Just as I was leaving the bistro, a man walked in. He wore the gaunt expression of a person who has reached the end of the line. People knew him: he was a local police officer. All day long, as a representative of the German authorities, he had witnessed the assailants – mostly American soldiers – being questioned by the military police.

Their reactions left him baffled. Most seemed completely unaware of the gravity of their actions.

Asked what motive had driven them to murder, most had given the same, enigmatic answer: the call of duty.

59: THAT ENDLESS FINAL CHORD

I was awake all night. I wandered the streets of Ramstein like a stray dog. I went from one bar to the next, drinking glass after glass and trying to listen in on the conversations around me. When each bar closed, I left and followed the silhouettes wandering in the semi-darkness, in search of the last bistro to close, or the first to re-open.

Early next morning, I returned to the station and bought a ticket for Berlin. I wanted to find out what the members of Pearl Harbor had set in motion, with their recording.

The journey took a full day. I changed trains in Mannheim, and again in Hanover. My appearance intrigued the authorities. Time and again, I was asked to present my papers and answer a string of questions.

I showed my ID so frequently, I became convinced of its authenticity. Even the most diligent police officers seemed reassured.

I reached Berlin early that evening. I was hungry. I was suffering the effects of my sleepless night. I had spent half my money and made do with a hunk of bread and a sausage from a street stall.

I went to the Yoyo bar. This time, the boss seemed in a good mood. He had a full house, the room was packed and punters were elbowing one another to the bar.

On stage, the resident group were on fire, thrashing and writhing and making some great noise.

I fought my way to the bar, ordered a beer and signalled to the boss. He nodded and carried on dashing from one end of the bar to the other. I waited a good while before he granted me his full attention.

He asked what I wanted. I hollered over the din: I wanted to contact the guys from Pearl Harbor.

A few days after being fired, Larry Finch, the bassist, had been found dead at the bottom of the pool in a luxury hotel near Palma de Mallorca. He had died of excess alcohol and dope.

The next day, Steve Parker, one of the guitarists, had put a bullet through his own head in a hotel room in Hamburg.

A few hours after that, Jim Ruskin, the other guitarist – the one who had given me the LSD – had been crushed under a train in the U-Bahn at Thielplatz station.

Lastly, the drummer Paul McDonald had thrown himself from the fifth floor of a hotel in London, one week later.

The police had come asking questions at the Yoyo bar, but there was nothing he could tell them. The deaths had occurred quickly, one after the other, but the police had been unable to establish any connection between them. They had completed their routine enquiry by closing the case on Jim Ruskin.

The Yoyo bar's boss said my visit was a coincidence. Just a few days before, he had taken a call from a man by the name of West, an English detective hired by Steve Parker's family to open an investigation into their son's suicide. The boss looked sceptical. He reckoned Steve Parker's parents were trying to clear their own consciences by advancing a classic conspiracy theory. There was nothing suspicious about the series of deaths, as far as he was concerned. The guys were crackpot alcoholic junkies, dedicated to abusing themselves and every substance known to man, right down the line.

Before returning to his clamouring clientele, he asked why I was looking for them. I told him I'd lent the group some equipment. But my story was unconvincing. I was too disturbed by what I had just heard. The boss clearly didn't believe a word I said, though this didn't seem to bother him in the least.

I got out of the Yoyo bar fast. I hardly knew where I was. My head was spinning. My stomach heaved with an inrush of fear.

I couldn't believe the deaths were a coincidence, or some appalling example of the law of series. My intuition told me there was a connection between the domino deaths and that stormy night of March the fourteenth.

The more I thought about it, the more the certainty gnawed. I should have been dead by now. My unplanned return to the studio had sparked this carnage. I was responsible for the deaths of four men.

I found Gunther at the Graffiti. He was surprised to see me. He had put on still more weight. The place was jumping, but he was as unsmiling as ever. The crowd were going wild but the group that had replaced the Frames were musical midgets by comparison.

During our many conversations, Gunther had explained that the fervour that seemed to grip West Berlin was connected to the unique situation in which the population found itself. On the other side of the Wall, Soviet tanks were preparing to invade the city, and the whole of Europe after that. It was a matter of weeks, days, hours. Everybody knew it, and wanted to make the most of their last moments of freedom.

Gunther had predicted the Soviet invasion would take place on the day of the inauguration of the Television Tower, one of the few attractions in East Berlin that could be seen from the West.

The East German authorities were building a gigantic tower, rising to a height of over 350 metres: the tallest watchtower in East Berlin. Gunther said it was planned as a symbol of Soviet supremacy that would afford the Communist authorities a panoramic view of the reunited city.

He offered me a drink and I told him about the tragic fate of the members of Pearl Harbor. I told him I was convinced that what I had witnessed after the recording was somehow the cause of it all.

He thought for a moment. There were things on certain tracks, he said. You couldn't hear them, but they were there.

I had no idea what he was talking about. He asked if I had heard the Beatles' latest album. I said I had. I wasn't really a fan, but I could see Sgt Pepper's Lonely Hearts Club Band *was a major piece of work. It had been selling like hot cakes since its recent release, and was playing continuously at the record shop.*

Gunther suggested I listen carefully to the last track on side B, the already famous song 'A Day in the Life'. The cacophonous, symphonic ending had sparked widespread comment, most of it wild approval.

I should listen through to the very end, he said, to the very last seconds, and carry on listening beyond that endless final chord.

60: IN GREAT DISTRESS

Dominique had been turning X Midi's strange message over and over in his mind for days. He tried several times to communicate with his patient, in hopes of obtaining further information, but without success.

Was he experiencing pain in one of his hands?

Did he want to make use of some object?

Perhaps feed himself?

Would he like someone to hold his hand?

Dominique scrutinised X Midi's medical notes.

No mention of a scar or injury to either hand. But he noticed that the man had reacted when he was addressed in English during the initial tests at Saint Pierre.

Could he have spelled out an English word?

'Main'? Dominique pondered the possibility for a moment, but quickly dismissed it as unhelpful. He read through the notes one last time, but could find nothing likely to shed any further light on the matter.

The medical notes weren't exhaustive, however. Dominique knew that. In the first week of January, he contacted the team at Saint-Pierre Hospital and asked to speak to whoever had taken charge of X Midi when he was admitted.

The usual administrative barriers held firm, but he pushed hard and eventually obtained a vague promise that one of the care staff on duty at the time would call him back as soon as possible.

Then silence. Dominique decided to take a trip to Brussels, on a day off.

On Thursday, January the thirteenth, he walked into the admissions service at Saint-Pierre Hospital and asked to speak to a fellow physio.

After half an hour, a young colleague appeared. She listened and agreed to help.

The physio took Dominique to the emergency service, where they found a nurse who remembered X Midi.

She described some letters and numbers on one of his hands, but had no idea what they meant. The information had been passed to the police, however, and the details had been recorded in their report.

Dominique went straight to the relevant precinct, on Rue Marché au Charbon, near the hospital.

He held out no great hope, but was surprised to be greeted warmly by the officer in charge: Gérard Jacobs, a man in his early fifties, with a fine moustache and a gravelly voice.

Dominique explained what he was after, and Jacobs gave him immediate access to the report, including a note to the effect that X Midi's left hand bore a series of letters and numbers: A20P7. The officer informed him that a group of IT specialists and a codebreaker had analysed the formula but had been unable to clarify its meaning. He passed Dominique the information held in the file, and noted that the police's various attempts to identify the man had ended in failure.

Dominique promised he would pass on anything he turned up.

Next day, Dominique hurried along the corridor and burst into X Midi's room.

His patient eyed him with curiosity.

Dominique sat himself on the bed.

'A20P7.'

The man closed his eyes. They were blurred with tears.

'That's what you wanted me to find out, wasn't it? Are you ready to tell me anything more?'

X Midi seemed to hesitate for a few moments, then blinked once.

Dominique walked over to the cupboard and brought out the alphabet board.

'Remember? You remember how this works?'

The man indicated that he did.

Dominique placed the board in full view and gave X Midi a few minutes to take it in.

'All set?'

The man continued staring at the board.

'Vowel?'

No reaction.

'So it's a consonant! S? T? N? R? L? D? C?'

The man blinked.

'C? Okay! That's your first letter. Vowel?'

The man seemed unsure.

'Vowel?'

He blinked.

'E?'

Yes.

'CE. Got it.'

The man closed his eyes and kept them shut. The exercise was exhausting. He remained motionless for some minutes, then opened his eyes once more.

Dominique started over, immediately.

'Shall we carry on? Vowel? No? Okay. S? T? N? R? L? D? C? P? M? Okay! M is your third letter. CEM?'

Again, the man closed his eyes.

Dominique sensed he was closing himself off once more. He bent down and took X Midi's hand.

'You must help me, my friend. I don't know any French words beginning with CEM. Do you want to help?'

The man seemed to have dozed off.

Dominique waited a few minutes more, motionless at the foot of the bed, holding the alphabet board.

At length, X Midi opened his eyes.

'Shall we carry on with the word?'

X Midi showed no reaction.

'Do you want to try a new word?'

Yes.

'Vowel? No? Consonant.'

They went as far as the letter X.

'You're sure? X? CEM X?'

The man blinked.

Dominique battled on.

'Vowel?'

X Midi broke into a sweat.

'Consonant?'

Dominique launched into the sequence of vowels. The man stopped him at the letter L.

'CEM XL?'

Yes. X Midi closed his eyes and kept them shut.

Dominique bathed his eyes, speaking softly.

'CEM XL. Is that all?'

Slowly, X Midi opened his eyes once more. And Dominique saw he was in great distress.

61: THE POWER TO END MY OWN LIFE

I won't communicate any further with the rest of the world. These exercises demand a superhuman effort on my part. I have read so many, many books, but now I can barely construct the simplest word. Consonants and vowels fight it out, relentlessly.

They have achieved their goal. I am reduced to silence. I am no longer a threat. My story will sink into oblivion forever.

They can find me now. It doesn't matter. I must fulfil my self-imposed duty, the reason I stayed alive through all those years on the run.

I could have departed in peace if they had not robbed me of my last freedom, the power to end my own life.

62: IN HIS NOTEBOOK

When Michael Stern learned that his student helper Hilde Bachmann had found a promising lead, he raced to the telephone and booked a flight to Berlin.

It was almost the weekend, and his trip would pass unnoticed. Stern's obstinate pursuit of his investigation had irritated his editor-in-chief. His boss had asked recently if he had indeed closed the case, and Stern had replied in the affirmative.

Since when, a portion of Stern's own money had been sunk into his ongoing enquiries, with no proof to date of a single motive connecting the band members' deaths.

His wife was becoming annoyed, too. After hiring two students to make hundreds of international calls from their home phone, her husband had left for Berlin to continue the investigation himself, paid for out of their own savings.

He seemed nervous and irascible lately. He was becoming obsessed with the whole business.

Michael Stern stepped off the plane at Tempelhof on Saturday, November the twenty-fifth, 1967, in the middle of the afternoon. He took a taxi, swung by his hotel and headed for the Viktoria Bar.

Fred Weiss remembered the telephone call that evening in March. The man who called had sounded frantic, under pressure. He had been looking for a musician as back-up for the same evening. He knew the Viktoria had a resident rock band, and wanted to hire the drummer.

The call had come through towards midnight; the place had been in full swing, with a packed house. Weiss had refused to call the session to a halt and send the drummer over. The man on the line had insisted and offered enough money to make him change his mind, but he had stood his ground.

That was when he had remembered one of his regular clients. A Canadian guy who said he was staying in Berlin while his girlfriend sang in a group. He was a drummer. He had let it be known he was available for temporary bookings, and left his card.

The man on the line was impatient, and Weiss couldn't find where he had left the card. He asked the man to leave a number, promising that he would contact the drummer, and get him to call.

Weiss confided that this was more a tactic to get the man off his back than a favour to his customer, who only called in occasionally, and who he found odd and not particularly pleasant.

The drummer had come by to thank him, next day. He said the evening had gone well. This was how Weiss knew the back-up gig had taken place.

Stern asked if Weiss had kept the drummer's calling-card. Weiss wasn't sure. There were dozens of cards pinned up over the bar. Stern insisted. Weiss studied them, frowning. Finally, he took one down and handed it to Stern. It was succinct and to the point:

Jacques Berger
Drummer – Batteur

A telephone number had been pencilled on the back.

Weiss said that was the number he had dialled. The call had gone through to a club whose name he couldn't remember. He had spoken to one of the barmen. By chance, the drummer was in that night. He had given him the caller's telephone number, thrown away the piece of paper on which it was noted and hung up.

Michael Stern placed a twenty-mark note on the bar and asked Weiss to call the club where Jacques Berger had been drinking that night.

Reluctantly, Weiss did as he was asked.

Stern hurried straight over to the Graffiti, arriving there at about 7:00p.m.

He went first to the restaurant, where he spoke to the waiters, trying to make himself understood as best he could. No one knew who or what he was talking about. One of the men directed him to the night club on the first floor.

The place was busy, already. A loud rock group were making heavy work of it onstage. The rest of the room was in semi-darkness.

Stern spoke to one of the bartenders, ordered a drink and asked if Jacques Berger was in.

The man didn't know any Jacques Berger. He spoke a little English, so Stern gave him a few more details. The bartender said Berger was most likely Mary's boyfriend. She was the lead singer with the Frames, an English group who had played there at the beginning of the year. They had left Berlin a few months ago.

Stern wanted to know more. The guy directed him to another bartender, a fat guy with a bad-tempered look. The man listened for a moment, frowning in annoyance, then cut him short and asked why he was there. Stern had to shout to make himself heard. He explained he was a journalist, and outlined the main stages of his investigation.

The man seemed uninterested. He wiped glasses while he listened to Stern, interrupting him frequently to serve other customers.

When Stern had finished, the man said he couldn't see how he or Jacques Berger could possibly be mixed up in this business. He told Stern that Berger had got himself a drumming gig with a band that had left for a tour in some far-flung place on the other side of the world. He didn't know the group's name.

Stern knew the man was covering his friend's tracks. He would get nothing further here. He left his card all the same and asked the barman to tell Berger to get in touch if ever he heard from him.

Outside the club, he quickly scribbled the words 'Mary' and 'Frames' in his notebook.

63: MY LAST IMAGE OF HER

I returned to London on Wednesday night. Mary wasn't at the flat. I hadn't slept for three nights. We were playing at Ronnie Scott's that very night and I needed to rest, if only for an hour or two. I was counting on my small stash of Pervitin pills to see me through.

I thought Mary would come home, wake me up, and that we would go to the gig together. But Mary didn't come back.

I woke up the next day, around noon. I was confused. I had slept for over twelve hours. The light hurt my eyes. I felt I was returning from a long journey to a distant land, and rediscovering the real world.

Mary was still not back, and I was overcome with anxiety. Suddenly, I realised the implications of what I had done. I had left without warning, I had taken our money and given her no choice in the matter. I had jeopardised the group. They must have scrambled to find a back-up drummer and keep our bookings.

I called Bob, one of the guitarists. He cut me off angrily and hung up before I had spoken barely a couple of words.

I should have gone to look for Mary straightaway. Things would have turned out differently. I sensed my absence had brought its share of consequences, but I refused to face reality. Naïvely, I thought things would become clear in time, that tensions would subside and the problems would be resolved in a matter of hours.

I went to the record shop, and was greeted with a furious tirade. The manager gave me a warning, and a direct threat: next time I went AWOL I'd be fired immediately. I said I was sorry, and got to work. Sonny was there. He gave me a reassuring wink.

The news from the War was discouraging, to say the least. The Egyptians had attacked an unarmed American ship and it was feared the US would join the fighting, on the Israeli side.

While World War Three brewed, an endless stream of carefree London youth filed through the shop. One after another they came in and left with a copy of the Beatles' Sgt Pepper's Lonely Hearts Club Band, or 'A Whiter Shade of Pale', a syrupy single by a band called Procul Harum.

At closing time, I put 'A Day in the Life' on one of the turntables. I listened right through to the end, as instructed by Gunther.

When the reverberations of that final chord subsided, a twenty-second silence was interrupted by a kind of squeaking noise, followed by crackling, and the chatter of sing-song voices on a loop. I couldn't make out what they were saying. It made me think of a stuck record, with the needle going round and round in the same groove. The sequence ended with something like forced laughter.

I listened to it a few times, trying to decipher what was being said.

I called Sonny and the other assistants over. One of the storeroom guys had sat in on the recording sessions and knew what it was all about. We clustered round, and for the first time, I heard about backmasking.

The process involved inserting recorded sounds or words backwards. According to our colleague, John Lennon had discovered the technique by accident when manipulating tapes while he was high on dope.

The Beatles had used it several times after that, adding phrases or noises, even running a guitar solo backwards on one song. It was just playing around, a favourite trick of their producer, George Martin.

The technique used on 'A Day in the Life' was more complicated. The symphonic part was played by forty musicians from the Royal Philharmonic and London Symphony orchestras. McCartney had asked them to play the lowest possible note on their instruments, and then to get to the highest note possible, in loosely defined stages over twenty-four bars.

He said the mysterious final groove contained a hidden message, consisting partly of a reversed tape and partly of a whistle that was inaudible to humans but which could be picked up by dogs, to make them bark.

Under normal circumstances, I would have found the conversation amusing, and intriguing. But now, the theory opened up disturbing possibilities.

Was it possible to insert messages or sounds, inaudible to the human ear, which could be decoded by the human brain? Could the messages bypass the conscious mind, to reach our subconscious, and affect our behaviour?

I returned to the apartment, my head full of puzzles and contradictory facts. A quick glance around told me that Mary had not been there all day.

I panicked. I swallowed a couple of Pervitin and hurried over to Soho, to Ronnie Scott's Club. The manager told me that last night's concert had been cancelled due to my absence. The guys hadn't found a replacement drummer, and Mary had disappeared.

I made the rounds of our usual haunts, pushed doors, spoke to people who knew us. I must have looked half-crazed – I could read the fear and discomfort in the eyes of the people I questioned.

Gradually, I learned that she had been seen with Gab, a Jamaican we hung out with from time to time. He had tried to sell us heroin on several occasions, and I had always refused.

I knew where to find him. I went to his place. He lived in Brixton. A street drunk pointed out his pad, in a small, two-storey building on Angell Road.

My nerves were raw. The door to the building yielded to a shove from my shoulder, and I raced upstairs. I knew he had a gun, like most dealers, and didn't want to give him too much warning. I hammered on his door.

He came to open it. He was bare-chested, and had hastily pulled on some jeans. His skin glistened with sweat. He had the distant gaze of a person sky-high on heroin. The gun was in his hand.

He asked me what I wanted. I wanted to know where Mary was. I read the answer in his eyes. He sensed danger and tried to close the door, but I pushed on it with my full weight. It flew open and I hurried to the bedroom with Gab at my heels. He was hollering, thumping me from behind, threatening to shoot.

Mary lay on a mattress at the back of the room. A threadbare cover did nothing to hide her nakedness. She seemed to be sleeping, but her eyes were open and she stared at me, without seeing me.

The image of Floriane, in Paris, burst into my consciousness.

I spun around to face Gab.

He was pointing the gun at me.

He fired. I felt the bullet enter my shoulder. I kept walking towards him. He had no time for a second shot. I tore the gun from his grasp, grabbed a fistful of his hair and slammed his face into the table. I saw red. I pulled him back to his feet. Still gripping him by the hair, I smashed his face against a wall, once, and then a second time. I heard his skull splinter, I saw his flesh torn open. My hands were red with his blood.

When I had finished pummelling him, he was an inert mass, limp in my hands. I couldn't tell whether he was alive or dead. My shoulder didn't hurt. It was pouring blood and my shirt was soaked.

Mary was on her feet and watching the scene.

She moved forward, naked, into the middle of the room. She walked like an automaton, her expression absent. She stared at me, then looked down at Gab, lying at my feet. She had reached the end of the road, the frontier of madness.

Suddenly, she realised what had happened. He eyes widened, she raised her hands to her mouth.

My last image of her.

64: MY DIGNITY

The gunshot had alerted the neighbours. The wail of the sirens was intensifying. Brixton was a notorious area, and the police were never far away.

I cursed Mary. I cursed her for betraying me. I cursed her for causing me to commit an irreparable act. I cursed her and I cursed me, too. It never occurred to me that the meth coursing in my veins was in large part responsible for my uncontrollable access of rage.

Despite my feelings, I should have wrapped her in a blanket and carried her off on my shoulder, far, far from there. I should have spared her the suffering and harassment, the grief.

My rage and fear got the better of me. I panicked and took to my heels.

I wandered the streets until dawn. I hugged the façades of buildings and lurked in their shadow. I was disorientated. I was crying. I was drunk with rage. The pain had awoken and I suffered agonies in my shoulder. The Pervitin was still at work. I was supercharged, brimming with hatred. I wanted to attack the drunks I came across. I had to keep control, forced myself not to grab them by the neck and pummel them senseless, as I had done with Gab.

Sunrise came early. It was almost the summer solstice. I made my way to Brian's. I knew he kept a complete first-aid kit to hand. I rang the bell. He came to the door but wouldn't let me in. I forced my way in, grabbed him by the neck of his dressing gown and forced him down to the cellar.

He was squealing like a rat, begging me for mercy. I demanded he *open the safe hidden at the back of the bar, behind the mirror. I took all the money. Brian was crying like a baby, shaking and drooling. He'd even pissed himself. I took a bottle and broke it over his head. He collapsed like a dead weight.*

I went back upstairs. I dressed my shoulder one-handed, as best I could. The entry wound was level with the top of my arm, but the bullet was lodged inside, against the bone. I emptied a box of antiseptic powder into the wound and applied a bandage. Each movement provoked a groan of pain.

Next, I began looking for clean clothes, and dope.

I swallowed dozens of pills and packed a few things I found lying in an unoccupied bedroom. Before leaving, I went down to the cellar. Brian was still lying unconscious, but his heart was beating and he was breathing. His eyes were rolled back and there was blood on his face.

I felt a fresh surge of rage. I kicked and elbowed and knee'd the guitars, the drum kit and the amps. With my good hand, I took each of the bottles lined up on the shelves and hurled them across the room, breaking everything I could.

When I climbed the stairs once more, a handful of guys were standing at the top, their faces tired and sleepy, but wide-eyed in terror. They said nothing, and made no attempt to go down to the cellar.

Mid-morning, I burst into the restaurant on the Clerkenwell Road. It had just opened. I didn't order the dish of the day. I gave the password to the server who came to greet me, and told him it was an emergency.

He took me into the back room, where three men were seated at a table, reading the newspaper. I laid my identity papers and a wad of notes on the table. I told them I would need new papers by nightfall. I laid a second wad of notes beside the first and asked them to find me a doctor to extract the bullet lodged in my shoulder.

They saw I meant business and didn't try to negotiate. One of the men got to his feet, pocketed the money and told me to come back around midnight.

I left the restaurant and visited several different pharmacies, to stock up on antiseptics, painkillers and bandages. I took refuge in the Underground for the rest of the day. I emerged from time to time, to go to a bar and change my bandages in the toilets.

Little by little, the bleeding stopped, but the pain was still keen and I was worried the wound would become infected.

In the early evening, I called Sonny. The police had come to the record shop and questioned everybody. The cops knew my identity – the one on my false ID. Sonny didn't know what had happened, and hadn't heard anything from Mary.

I thanked him and hung up.

I got my new papers that evening. From now on I was René Schnegg, a French citizen, born in the Alsatian city of Colmar, on July the thirty-first, 1945. They had found someone to treat my wound, too: a vet aged about sixty whose red-veined nose announced the extent of his alcohol dependency. He slipped on a pair of glasses, and a headlamp, administered a local anaesthetic and began digging about in my shoulder. The three Italians looked on, visibly wincing.

He extracted the bullet and stitched the wound. It had damaged my shoulder, and he was doubtful whether a full recovery could be achieved without effective physiotherapy. I was likely to find certain movements difficult, he said.

I was very far from imagining he would be proved right, and that I would never play the drums again.

The Italians must have been satisfied with the money I had handed over: they let me use a room above the restaurant.

I turned back and forth on the squeaky bed, incapable of sleep.

Next day, I took the first train to Glasgow. Heathrow airport would be under surveillance and I would be stopped the instant I set foot in the place.

I planned to fly to San Francisco, with a few stopovers to cover my tracks. My new ID reduced my risk of arrest, but for all I knew, I might be wanted for murder now, and would have to exercise the utmost caution.

In Glasgow, I took a taxi to Prestwick airport and bought a ticket for Geneva. The flight left late in the afternoon. I curled up in a corner of the terminal and tried in vain to sleep.

I was shaking with fever. An acute, throbbing pain pierced my shoulder.

On arrival in Geneva I headed for the Pan Am desk to buy a ticket to New York. A poster caught my eye. It showed a close-up image of a saxophonist. A jazz festival was opening the following week, in Montreux.

I changed my plans and took a train to Montreux. Two hours later, I reached my destination. I stepped down from the train.

I was alone on the platform.

And then the realisation struck. I had lost everything in the space of just a few hours: the woman I loved, my best friend, my identity, my dignity.

65: THE MAN CLOSED HIS EYES

It took Dominique almost a month to decipher the riddle X Midi had posed.

CEM XL

Without a singular stroke of luck, he might never have succeeded.

Initially, he had focussed on the three first letters, thinking they might be an abbreviation. He had searched dozens of directories, hoping to find something that might correspond.

CEM was listed, amongst other things (in French), as *cours élémentaire moyen* (a primary school grade), *chef d'état-major*, a business specialising in applied microwave technology, or an automatic classification algorithm.

As for XL, Dominique was convinced the letters indicated 'extra-large'.

It was during a treatment session with another patient that it occurred to him the last two letters might mean something else.

He had been asking the woman about her age, her career and where she came from. She replied that she came from Ixelles, and had spent most of her life there.

At first, Dominique paid no attention, and made no connection with the coded letters. The possibility only struck him at the end of the session; he asked the woman to repeat the name of her home town.

She did so, further noting that Ixelles is one of the nineteen municipalities of Greater Brussels and that it was often written simply as XL, even in certain official documents.

In a flash, Dominique thought he saw the solution. X Midi wanted him to consult the *carte d'état-major* or land registry for the commune of Ixelles. A20P7 – the letters and numbers inscribed on his hand – were very likely references allowing him to locate a particular square on the map.

He began hunting, but quickly gave up. Not only could he not find a *carte d'état major*, or a topographical map of Ixelles, but A20P7 corresponded to no map or GPS reference he could identify.

De Rouck, the indispensable Brussels street map carried in every Bruxellois' glove compartment before GPS came along, was of no help either.

The second flash of inspiration was equally unexpected, following a death at the clinic.

Dominique was in the clinic's main office when staff from a local funeral parlour came to collect the body. Along with the documents for the transfer of the patient's body, and the certificate from the commune where the burial would take place, was a paper indicating the grave plot:

Cimetière de Verrewinkel
125 avenue de la Chênaie, 1180 Brussels
Allée 9, Pelouse 16, Emplacement 53.

With the cipher A20P7 fixed firmly in his mind, Dominique had taken to poring over every combination of letters and numbers that came his way.

He started visibly at the sight of the paper.

X Midi had given the reference to a grave.

The A and P corresponded to the cemetery's pathways and greens. The theory fitted for CEM too. The man spoke English.

Given his confused state and his evident difficulty manipulating the alphabet, he must have confused *cimetière* in French with the English *cemetery*. Which would also explain why he hadn't attempted to complete the word.

At the end of his shift, Dominique called the cemetery in Ixelles. The clerk confirmed that there was, not an *Allée*, but an *Avenue* 20 and a *pelouse* (or 'green') No.7. It lay on the east side of the cemetery, not far from the railway line, and contained a hundred tombs.

Next day, Dominique entered X Midi's room with none of the usual preliminaries.

He sat on the bed without saying a word, and waited for the man to catch his eye.

'Good morning, my friend.'

The man stared at him in curiosity.

'Would you like me to pay a visit to your green, No.7? On Avenue 20, in Ixelles cemetery?'

The man's eyes conveyed the same distressed appeal as when he had first given Dominique the message.

'You want me to go there, is that it?'

Yes.

'I will go, my friend, but there are a hundred tombs on that green. I need the plot number.'

The man looked panic-stricken.

'I promised you this is strictly between ourselves. Do you trust me?'

The man blinked once, then looked away and lost himself in the television screen.

Dominique waited.

After a few minutes, X Midi seemed to have calmed down.

Dominique addressed him.

'Do you want to talk?'

The man blinked once. He did.

Dominique rose to his feet, opened the cupboard, took out the alphabet board and placed it on the bed, facing X Midi.

He began by counting up the sequence of numbers, but X Midi showed no reaction.

'You don't know the number, is that it?'

Yes.

'In that case, give me a name.'

The man opened his eyes wide and began to perspire.

Dominique pretended not to notice, and began the sequence of vowels. He continued with the consonants, but X Midi didn't stop him.

'Can you think? Wait a few days? You want to be sure I am your friend?'

The man seemed to hesitate.

'Do you want me to start over?'

Yes.

Dominique began the sequences again. The man seemed to be racking his brains at each letter, as if he was dreading he might make a mistake, or finding it hard to remember the name he was spelling out.

The exercise took over half an hour, and resulted in five letters:

O-D-I-L-E.

X Midi was sweating profusely. He was exhausted by the effort of concentration.

Dominique sponged his forehead.

Now he had the first name, he needed the family name. But he didn't insist. It would be bad luck indeed if several Odiles lay buried in the same plot of grass.

'I'll go tomorrow afternoon.'

The man stared hard at the alphabet board.

'Do you want to add something?'

X Midi was exhausted, but he indicated that he did.

The first letter was F.

The second, L.

Dominique interrupted the exercise.

'You want me to take her some flowers?'

The man closed his eyes.

66: A POOR, CRAZY GUY

If I'd had a friend like him, my life would have been different. I needed structure, a framework. My ideas weren't always clear and I didn't know how to express them. I needed a guide. Someone to listen, understand and advise me.

There was Sonny, of course.

He helped get me out of there.

With hindsight, I don't know whether I should thank him or blame him.

Sonny was just a poor, crazy guy.

67: THE MAN FROM THE BERLIN SESSION

Michael Stern was forced to wait until Wednesday, December the twentieth before he could get to London.

On that day, the British Foreign Secretary, the Right Honorable George Brown, returned from a meeting of the Council of Ministers of the Six to inform the House of Commons of 'the action to be taken by the Government' following the refusal (by France) of the United Kingdom's latest application to join the European Community.

Foreign affairs were not Stern's speciality, but since no other journalist on the *Belfast Telegraph* had agreed to go, he put himself forward to cover the story.

On his return from Berlin in late November, Stern had had a lively exchange with his wife, who accused him of neglecting his family life and depleting their savings to finance an enquiry that his editor-in-chief had not approved. Eager to avoid another row, he had agreed to drop the affair.

He let a few days pass, then returned to his enquiries with the utmost discretion.

In early December, he re-established contact with Nick Kohn, the London music columnist, and asked him to find out about an English group who had played in Berlin at the beginning of the year. The band were called the Frames, and their singer was called Mary. He also wanted to know if Kohn knew of a Canadian drummer called Jacques Berger.

Before cutting the call, he begged Kohn to keep his request secret. Kohn said he would.

A week later, Kohn called him back.

He had found the information with ease. The Frames were a five-piece English pop-rock group: four musicians and a girl singer. Apart from the latter, who was called Mary-Ann McGregor, the line-up had changed fairly frequently. The group had broken up after their return from Berlin, and a new combo had formed shortly after, known as Mary and The Governors. Mary, and one of the guitarists from the Frames, formed the core of the new group.

A drummer – the aforementioned Jacques Berger – a bassist and an English guitarist had been hired immediately.

The group was promising, but a personal drama had halted their ascent. In June, the drummer had left a small-time Brixton drug dealer grievously wounded in a fight. He had been on the run ever since. The singer, who had been present at the time, was traumatised. She had been treated for a form of nervous depression, but was well now, and singing again.

She was leading a quieter existence, and had changed her repertoire and stage name, calling herself Mary Hunter. She had a residency at the Dorchester, the luxury hotel on Park Lane, where she performed seven days a week during happy hour, to the delight of wealthy tourists and businessmen. Twice a week, she sang a late-night set at a Soho bar, the Village, where she was accompanied by Bob Hawkins, a former guitarist from the Frames and The Governors.

Stern thanked Kohn for the information.

The newshound in him was pleased to have picked up Berger's scent, but just as he thought he was closing in, the man had gone on the run, and no one knew where he was.

On December the twentieth, after conducting a few interviews connected with the George Brown story, Stern made his way to the Dorchester.

Mary Hunter was a frail-looking young woman with a pale complexion. She wore a long black dress that didn't look as if it belonged to her. She wore no make-up, and no jewellery.

Stern was seduced straightaway by her voice. She exerted a powerful fascination from the opening notes of each song.

He noticed that, unusually for a venue like the Dorchester, the clientele stopped drinking and talking to listen to her.

Her accompanying pianist laid it on pretty thick, frowning, gesticulating, taking the applause as if it was meant for him.

When the set was over, Stern approached Mary and asked if he could speak to her. Instinctively, she recoiled from the small, insignificant-looking man, with his forced smile. He explained that he was a journalist, investigating a story about a series of events that had taken place in Berlin while she was playing there with her former group.

Reluctantly, she agreed to talk, and suggested they go somewhere else. Stern left the bar and waited for her outside the hotel entrance. She reappeared a few minutes later, wearing jeans and a big woollen sweater. The outfit made her look frailer still. Stern noticed she had a slight turn in her eye.

They went to a pub near the hotel, where she supplied brief answers to his questions.

She had been in a relationship with Jacques Berger. They had been together less than a year. While he was in Berlin with her, he had played a back-up gig, a last-minute replacement for the drummer of a rock group who were due to make a recording. The record had never been released. They had separated in June. She'd had no news since.

This was all she had to say on the subject of Berlin and Jacques Berger.

Stern could see he would get nothing more; once again, his investigation was stalling. He told her about the four members of Pearl Harbor and their strange deaths, just days apart. He told her everything he had found out, omitting nothing. Finally, he confided that in his opinion, the recording session was directly linked to the suspicious deaths.

The young woman's attitude changed completely. She seemed genuinely frightened by what she heard.

She said she had thought Jacques Berger was imagining things, that he had hallucinated the whole incident. She saw now that he may not have been mistaken. She said she still loved him. She wanted to know what he was doing, and she was ready to help the journalist with his investigation.

Stern ordered a fresh round of drinks, and Mary Hunter began her version of the story, from the beginning.

During the recording session, one of the musicians had offered Jacques some LSD. He had never tried it before. He had taken it and had a bad trip. Next day, he was confused and told her a far-fetched story about how he had gone back to the studio and surprised a group of men tampering with the tapes. She'd thought he was still tripping, and paid no attention.

By early June, they were back in London. Berger had read a news item in one of the daily papers. The article told of a mass brawl that had broken out in a German club, leaving several people dead.

In a photograph taken at the time, Berger had thought he recognised one of the men present at the Berlin recording session. The picture had upset him. He suspected a conspiracy and was convinced the man had orchestrated the massacre. On the same day, he had quit London, leaving her a note that explained he had to find out the truth.

He had come back three days later, and found her at a friend's place. Berger had gone mad, breaking down the door.

The two men had gotten into a fight. Berger had seriously injured her friend, and made a run for it. The police enquiry concluded that Berger had acted in legitimate self-defence, but he was not around to testify.

She hadn't heard from him since that night.

Stern asked if she had any, even the vaguest, idea of where Berger might have gone.

She told him Jacques Berger was an alias, but she didn't know his true identity. He was a secretive, introverted, uncommunicative man with often muddled ideas. He had told her very little about his childhood, or his past. She knew he had grown up in Brussels, but that was about all. He had been attentive and thoughtful, and she missed him a lot.

Stern wanted to know if anyone else might be able to tell him more.

Berger had a friend called Sonny. She didn't know if it was his real name, or a nickname. She hadn't seen him since. The two had worked in a record shop. That might be one avenue worth exploring.

Thin pickings. Stern couldn't see much use for the information he had gathered. He decided to spend the night in London, and visit the record shop next day.

He would find his wife an adequate excuse for postponing his return to Belfast.

Before leaving Mary, he gave her his card and asked if she could remember the name of the newspaper in which Berger had seen the photograph of the man from the Berlin session.

68: MY OWN STORY

I had expected to find Montreux buzzing with excitement just a few days ahead of its jazz festival, but all was calm.

Night had fallen. The lake seemed to be sleeping, the shop windows were dark and the streets deserted. I wandered around town, my footsteps ringing out on the paving stones. Besides the posters, nothing suggested any degree of excitement, or the slightest preparation for the event.

I took a room in a small hotel in the centre of town, in the quarter known as Les Planches.

The receptionist was a guy named Andrew, but everyone called him Andy. He had a beanpole figure, carrot-red hair and a relaxed, easy manner. He was four or five years older than me. He came from New York, and had left his native city to travel around the world, stopping over from time to time to work for a few weeks, so that he could finance the next stage of his trip.

I asked him if there was any work to be had in Montreux. Defeated by the pain in my shoulder, I had given up on the idea of finding a back-up gig during the festival.

Andy scratched his head. The taxi firm was looking for drivers, but I didn't have a licence. The grand hotel was looking for a night concierge: theirs had left them in the lurch just days before the festival opened.

With my decent English, fluent French and smattering of German, he reckoned I stood a chance. But not looking like I did right now.

Next day, I shaved and got a haircut. I went to the bank and changed my pounds for Swiss francs. Then I made a tour of the boutiques and bought trousers and jackets, shirts and a series of ties. I tried nothing on. My wound was hurting too badly.

To finish, I swapped my boots for classic English brogues. My purchases took their toll on Brian's windfall, leaving me with just a few notes.

I passed unnoticed on the street. I barely recognised myself in the mirror.

I had been nobody. Now I was Everyman.

I took two capsules from my stock of Tuinal, from Brian's stash, and showed up at the Palace Hotel. I met the Head of Reception, and the director.

I had no references, and don't remember performing brilliantly at the interview, but I was hired on the spot. The fast-approaching festival was a factor in my favour.

The job required no particular skills beyond staying awake from 10:00p.m. to 8:00a.m., deciphering the room numbers announced in a variety of languages by the hotel guests, no matter how drunk, and presenting them with the right key.

The Swiss officials accepted my false papers without a second look. While waiting to regularise my situation, I could begin work on the eve of the festival.

All I remember of those three days of jazz is the image of a handful of artists crossing the lobby, some staggering dangerously. The stars of that first festival were Keith Jarrett, Jack DeJohnette and Cecil McBee, names that meant nothing to me.

Perhaps they came to collect their keys. Perhaps they were shocked at my indifference. Insurmountable walls separated the worlds of jazz and rock.

Throughout the festival and the days that followed, I was seconded by a member of the hotel staff, who had done my job before moving over to room service. He was a cold, distant Swiss by the name of

François. He taught me the rudiments in tones loaded with condescension and scorn.

As well as handing out keys, I made several tours of the hotel during the night, to check the fire doors were closed. I was to turn out the lights in places where they weren't strictly necessary, and switch on the night lights instead.

In addition, I had to be able to answer the telephone, and take accurate messages without asking the caller to repeat themselves. I would complete the check-in formalities if people arrived late, and take clients' bags up to their rooms.

If asked, I would book taxis, order newspapers, give directions, advise on restaurants or bars, and venues for other nocturnal entertainment. I could also arrange for such entertainment to be sampled at the hotel.

I needed to know how to do all of this, but above all, I was never to question a client's request, however extraordinary. I was to respect my superiors, show absolute discretion and find solutions to any and every problem.

My pay wasn't great, but the hotel provided me with a room in an annexe. I was allowed one meal when I arrived on duty, and a copious breakfast when I finished each morning.

Before leaving the hotel, the cook would slip me some delicacies for the rest of the day.

The job suited me fine. The last waiters left the hotel around midnight, leaving me in sole charge. Apart from the occasional client, there was no one to talk to, and that suited me fine, too.

The hotel was home to two distinguished guests. The celebrated Russian novelist Vladimir Nabokov and his wife had made the Palace their principal residence for several years already. They occupied a suite on the top floor.

Like everyone, I had read Lolita and Pale Fire. I was dazzled by Nabokov's poetic style and boundless imagination. I admired him tremendously. He devoted every morning to writing. In the afternoon, he would go walking in the hills, or play tennis.

Journalists came at regular intervals from all over the world, to interview him. He would receive them in the Green Salon. Towards the end of the afternoon, he would settle into a chaise longue beside the pool.

By the time I came on duty, Nabokov had retired for the night. I saw him only a few times, but his haunting presence in the hotel is doubtless what inspired me to write my own story.

69: A FEW DAYS AFTER THE EVENTS

Michael Stern quickly laid hands on the newspaper Mary had mentioned.

The article recounting the tragic events in Ramstein was published in the *Daily Telegraph* on Monday, June the fifth, in the international news section. Other daily papers had also run the photo, in which Jacques Berger thought he recognised one of the men from the Berlin recording session.

In the same picture, an emergency response team crowded around three stretchers covered with sheets. Ambulances were parked in the background, their rear doors gaping open. To the right, two policemen were holding back a crowd of curious onlookers. A good thirty or so people stood craning to see what was going on. The small format and poor definition made it impossible to make out their faces.

How could Berger have identified the man from such a poor reproduction of the photograph?

Stern persisted nonetheless. There was no way of proving that one face in the crowd belonged to a man who had been present at the Berlin studio on March the fourteenth, but the coincidence was certainly troubling.

Before hearing Mary Hunter's story, Stern had suspected the recording might have triggered the deaths of the members of Pearl Harbor. Now he was convinced.

Something had happened – probably Berger's reappearance

after the other band members had left – and their deaths were
the result.

Berger had talked about individuals tampering with the
tapes.

But why? What could be the connection between this and
the Ramstein massacre?

Berger's identification of the man in the photograph was
tenuous, but worth exploring.

Stern wanted to know every detail concerning the events in
Ramstein, and the conclusions of the enquiry.

He contacted Hans Bühler; the Bonn correspondent for the
Belfast Telegraph. Bühler hadn't been following the story person-
ally, but he knew the main points.

The police enquiry had concluded that the events were a
case of mass hysteria leading to uncontrolled violence.
A comparable situation at a football match in Turkey had led to
the deaths of forty spectators, twenty-seven of whom died
from knife-wounds.

But this was the first time such unrestrained violence had
been seen in a night club. The final death toll was eighteen.

Stern was struck by this final piece of information: articles
published at the time had mentioned fifteen deaths.

Hans Bühler explained that two people had died from their
wounds, and that an employee of the night club – a disc-jockey
– had subsequently committed suicide.

He had been found hanging at his home, a few days after the
events.

70: MY IDEA TOOK SHAPE

I worked six days a week. Andy and I were both free on Wednesdays, and spent the day together.

We would meet mid-afternoon in front of the church on Rue du Temple. From there, we would take the Sentier du Télégraphe, climbing on foot to Glion, a small village perched high on the road to Caux.

The village was home to a bistro run by a Belgian, where we would drink Stella and smoke joints. Andy knew where to get them: they were more expensive than in London, but the quality was worth it.

Thanks to my new lifestyle, I was smoking less and less dope. I still used speed, but more in order to stay awake all night than for the sensations it delivered.

Late in the afternoon, when the beers and dope were taking effect, I would talk to Andy about rock music. I had bought myself a portable turntable and a few albums. Hendrix, Cream, the Grateful Dead and Jefferson Airplane were top of the pile.

Andy talked to me about his twin passions, photography and painting. Between us, he did most of the talking, often with his trademark sing-song, theatrical delivery. Andy was gay, but that never blurred our friendship. One day, I told him about my experience in the swimming-pool cubicle. Nothing more was said.

Often, Andy would preface a remark with the words, 'When I'm rich and famous…'

He had studied art at university in Washington State, and later at

Yale. He had secured a grant to study in Rome before setting off on his world tour. Montreux was only his second stopover.

He said he was going to launch a new movement in painting: hyper-realism. He would be its leader; other artists would follow in his wake. He would stage vast exhibitions in the world's most prestigious galleries, and the whole planet would applaud in wonder.

When he talked about art, he used complicated expressions: affective subjectivity, illusionism, pictorial decoys.

He figured photography was the midpoint between art and reality. He wanted to break with the predominant trend for abstract art. I listened, understanding nothing.

One day, I asked if he would show me his paintings. He seemed reluctant. He tended to send them all back to the States once they were finished.

He had been working on an ambitious project for several weeks. He agreed to show me the work, but only when it was absolutely ready.

On one of our Wednesday afternoons, Andy posited a theory about our respective centres of interest. Sight and hearing were the only senses engaged by the arts. Sight allowed us to perceive reality, to see objects, describe them and be aware of their presence. It was the basis of scientific reasoning.

Our sense of hearing, on the other hand, could only transcribe the information it received in temporary form. The fleeting quality of sound was precisely the reason why certain sounds, especially music, had such an emotional impact. Andy reckoned that our sense of hearing appealed more to the emotions than to the conscious mind.

I failed to register the implications of this at first, but he had given me the elements of an explanation for what had taken place in the Berlin studio.

Next day, I registered at the library in Montreux, near the hotel.

I subscribed to various scientific magazines. I became fascinated by anything to do with sound – its physiology and psychology, acoustics, psycho-acoustics, geophysics.

What little money was left at the end of each week, I spent on books that couldn't be found at the library.

I read them at night, while on duty, and I took notes.

When I felt ready, I began to write my story, supporting my theory with examples and technical data culled from my reading.

Little by little, my idea took shape.

71: ONE YEAR TO THE DAY

As soon as he had finished his rounds, Dominique climbed into his car and drove to the cemetery in Ixelles.

He was curious and impatient to see what awaited him there. Odile was not a common name, but what would he do if several Odiles were buried in the plot?

He parked on Avenue des Saisons, went into a florist's shop and bought a magnificent bouquet.

He checked the plan at the entrance to the cemetery and headed down the broad central path. At the circular intersection, he took Avenue No. 3. At the second intersection, he turned left onto Avenue No. 20.

Plot No. 7 was at the top of the path.

Dominique paused and looked around. It was mild for early February, and he squinted in the bright sunshine.

The cemetery was in the middle of town, yet the silence was broken only by the cries of children at a school somewhere out of sight.

The ground sloped gently towards to a box hedge masking the railway line beyond. In the distance, the office towers on Boulevard du Triomphe barred the horizon.

The plot held a hundred or so tombs, arranged side-by-side in rows. Most dated from 1991.

Dominique moved carefully along, reading the first names one by one. In the middle of the third row, he crouched down to read one in particular:

ODILE CHANTRAINE
ÉPOUSE R. BERNIER
1920–1991

A shock ran through his body.

His heart beat fast. Beneath the inscription was a photograph of the deceased, in black and white. The very image of X Midi.

The grave looked neglected. The tombstone was streaked with blackish mould. There were no candles or flowers.

He laid the bouquet and took a few photographs.

A woman paying her respects at a nearby grave walked across, hobbling slightly. She was small, barely a metre fifty in height, and must have been about eighty.

Her face radiated tenderness.

'Pardon me for bothering you, sir.'

Dominique gave her a broad smile. She wore a wig, fixed on backwards.

'No bother, Madame, how can I help you?'

'It hasn't rained for days. I want to water my flowers, but the watering cans and taps are down at the end of the path, and I have trouble walking.'

'Shall I fetch you a watering can?'

'That would be most kind. It's for my husband. I've been coming to see him twice a week, for the past thirty years.'

She glanced at Odile Bernier's tomb.

'Is this someone from your family?'

Dominique realised the watering can was a pretext. The old lady was curious.

'From the family of one of my patients, at the clinic where I work.'

The woman's eyes widened. She pushed down the corners of her mouth in admiration.

'A clinic?'

'Yes.'

'You're a doctor?'

Dominique laughed.

'No, I'm not clever enough for that. A humble physiotherapist.'

Another admiring pout.

'A phy-sythrapist treated my husband when he was ill.'

'Physio-thera-pist.'

'Yes, yes, it's difficult to pronounce!'

'What happened to your husband, Madame?'

The woman pursed her lips in grim resignation.

'Cancer. He was gone in less than three months. He was barely fifty-seven. Never drank a drop of alcohol, never smoked. And he played tennis twice a week.'

'I'm very sorry, Madame.'

She swept the air with a fatalistic wave of the hand.

'Such is life. What can one do? I make the best of it. And he was a fine-looking man. I never went with another man after him. But I was still beautiful when he died, and there were a few who were after me.'

'You are a sainted woman, Madame.'

She gave Dominique a knowing wink.

'There were one or two before him, though.'

Dominique winked back.

'It'll go no further!'

She sighed.

'It's been a long while since I saw anyone attending to Madame Bernier.'

Dominique felt his heart leap.

'Did you know her?'

'No.'

'Yet you mention her by name.'

'I know the names of all one-hundred-and-eight people resting here. I've been coming twice a week, for thirty years.'

'Do you know what happened to her?'

'Well, I know that she has no immediate family, now. Her husband died a few years before her. She had a son who came from time to time, but he died too.'

'Was there only one son?'

She seemed surprised by the question.

'Yes, and no daughter. That's why no one has been for a long time.'

She assumed a detached expression.

'Except perhaps the family member being treated at your clinic.'

Dominique had no desire to play the old lady's game. He walked to the end of the path, filled a watering can and carried it back.

'A very good day to you, Madame, and thank you for the gift of your charming smile!'

'Good day to you too, Doctor.'

He thanked her and left the cemetery.

Back in his car, Dominique took out his mobile and retrieved the card that had been handed to him by Gérard Jacobs, the police officer. He punched in the number.

Jacobs recognised his voice straightaway.

'Hello! Any news?'

'Yes, I believe I've identified our man.'

The policeman paused.

'He's able to talk?'

'No, but he is managing to communicate with me.'

Dominique explained everything, and told Jacobs about his visit to the cemetery.

The policeman noted down the information.

He waited for Dominique to finish his story, then cleared his throat.

'Well played, Sir. The cryptanalysts wondered if the cipher might be the coordinates for a cemetery, but there are several hundred across Belgium. I'll see what I can find about Odile Bernier-Chantraine, and I'll call you back.'

He spoke again, before Dominique could cut the call.

'Oh, and you're aware of today's date?'

The question took Dominique by surprise.

'February the eleventh. Why?'

'Your man was knocked down outside Midi station on February the eleventh, at 6:00p.m. A year ago to the day.'

72: GHOST WORDS

Michael Stern took advantage of a few days' holiday between Christmas and New Year to turn his attention to a decisive question: exactly how had the men Berger surprised at the studio tampered with the tapes?

He fixed a meeting with Chris Reynolds, a gifted and voluble sound engineer he had got to know as a student. Reynolds was working for Radio 1 now, and supervised studio recordings for the Ulster Orchestra. He was often called in by promoters to record rock or pop concerts.

Stern visited Reynolds at home, a small bungalow with a pistachio-green façade, on Avoniel Drive. Reynolds offered tea and, not without some difficulty, cleared him a place to sit in the living room, which was crammed with books, records and magazines.

Stern saw straightaway that he would need deep reserves of patience to extract the answers to his questions.

With plentiful gesturing and sound effects, Reynolds launched into a detailed account of the Hendrix and Pink Floyd concerts he had supervised at Whitia Hall that November.

Next, came an overview of his major productions and social ascent since leaving university. After that, he expounded on his personal vision for the future of rock and pop music in the short, medium and long term. The monologue took over an hour.

Stern was a very good listener – a fine quality in a journalist. He sipped his tea, champing at the bit.

When Reynolds asked Stern the reason for his visit, he stated his question in plain terms, to avoid further procrastination.

Was it possible to tamper with a recorded tape?

And if so, could the tampering influence anyone listening to it? Reynolds stared at the ceiling for a moment, then got to his feet, left the room and returned with a piece of paper on which he drew a cross section of a human ear.

His explanation was delivered in solemn tones.

The ear enabled us to capture sounds, but the information received was only decoded in the brain.

Armed with a pencil, Reynolds continued with an explanation – based on the diagram – of how sound vibrations are channelled along a conduit leading to a fine, strong, elastic membrane less than half an inch in diameter, better known as the tympanum or eardrum. The membrane vibrated at the slightest sound.

Tapping on the paper with his finger, Reynolds noted that each sound received sent a nerve impulse to the brain, corresponding to its particular frequency. The oscillations encountered a thin partition, the basilar membrane, covered in thousands of nerve cells, which transmitted a 'sound picture' to the brain.

The science was far more complex, of course, but he would spare Stern the details.

Reynolds explained that human hearing had its limits, just like human vision. We couldn't hear all sounds, only those with a frequency of between 20 and 20,000 hertz (the lowest and highest respectively). Anything below 20 hertz was referred to as infrasound, and anything above 20 kilohertz was ultrasound.

With an air of mystery, he declared that while it was impossible for us to hear anything outside this range, it did not mean that infra- or ultrasounds had no effect on the human brain.

Take elephants, for example. They used infrasound to ward off their enemies. The giant beasts were also capable of communicating with one another in this way, across distances of between five and thirty miles.

Reynolds continued with an anecdote that sent shivers down Stern's spine: In the early 1960s, two English researchers in acoustics tested the effects of infrasound during a concert in London. They had introduced very low frequency sounds into specific pieces of music, and then asked the audience to describe their sensations. A majority of those questioned reported feeling unexpected emotions such as nostalgia, anguish or heightened aggression.

Powerful infrasound waves could be highly destructive, both mechanically and physiologically. Experiments had been carried out during the war, with the German army. Low levels of infrasound produced significant physiological symptoms, leading to nervous or psychological disorders.

Noting Stern's evident fascination, Reynolds got to his feet once again and searched through his bookshelves. He took out a scientific review and summarised one of the articles.

In the 1950s, two American doctors studying the effects produced by certain waves in the brain had been visited by agents of the CIA. The government agency had taken over their project and appropriated their technology for its own labs.

He continued with an article by one Allan Frey, published in 1962 in the *Journal of Applied Physiology*.

The article reported that the use of extreme low-density electromagnetic energy had caused both deaf and non-deaf subjects to hear sounds. The effects had been observed several miles from the antenna used to transmit the waves. With slight variations to the parameters, it was possible to recreate the sensation of a brutal blow to the head.

When he had finished reading the article, Reynolds delved into his bookshelves once more and emerged triumphant, with a patent application from an American researcher in Norcross, Georgia.

The patent described a silent communications system based on inaudible sound waves of very low or very high frequencies. The description of the process explained that the intended message would be transmitted using acoustic vibrations, and 'planted' in the brain of the recipient by the use of loudspeakers or headphones. The carrier waves could be transmitted 'live', in real time, or recorded and stored on mechanical or magnetic supports.

To complete his demonstration, Reynolds fetched a large Revox tape recorder and placed it on the table, in front of Stern. He disappeared into another room and returned a few minutes later with a spool, which he positioned on the machine. He slipped a set of headphones over Stern's ears and asked him to listen.

The tape turned for about a minute, but Stern heard nothing.

Reynolds stopped the machine, wound the tape back and played it again, but faster.

This time, Stern heard a collection of sounds that sounded for all the world like some kind of dialogue. Reynolds explained that it was a lovers' conversation, between two elephants.

His conclusion was clear; it was possible to record or insert infrasound onto magnetic tape, but powerful equipment was required for it to have any effect on the listener.

Reynolds launched into a new topic: sound illusions, beginning with the Doppler effect.

The phenomenon explained why an ambulance siren seemed to become more and more high-pitched as the vehicle approached, and more low-pitched when it was moving into the distance.

He elaborated further with a sketch explaining that the phenomenon was due to the space between each wavefront.

On now to musical illusions: the tritone paradox, the Shepard tone and the 'melody of silences'.

The tritone paradox showed that it was difficult to determine where a note was situated in the octave when it was played simultaneously across five octaves. The paradox occurs when the note is followed by a second note played in the same way but separated from the first by an interval of six semitones. Because the listener has no precise information about the note's position on the octave, some will state that the second note is lower than the first, while others believe it is higher.

The more Reynolds talked, the more excited and animated he became. He took a fresh sheet of paper, to demonstrate the Shepard tone. He drew a diagram of a piano keyboard and described Shepard's experiment, conducted in 1964, resulting in a scale that seemed to rise continually. The scale had been used on occasion to compose pieces of music.

By the time Reynolds got on to the melody of silences, Stern was half-exhausted.

Reynolds left the room and returned with another spool for the Revox.

The tape played a sort of background noise in which Stern thought he could make out a melody.

Reynolds was exultant. The melody didn't exist, but was created in the brain by the silences between the notes. He embarked on a complex explanation peppered with a host of technical terms – tonic and phasic receptors, coding of the duration of stimuli and the brain's adaptation to the latter.

Stern was dazed.

He could take no more and was about to say so when Reynolds moved on to the most impressive aural illusion of all.

He fetched a third spool of tape and slipped the headphones back over Stern's ears.

This time, Stern heard sounds coming alternately from the left and right. He heard a woman's voice pronouncing an unknown, two-syllable word, the same word on each side, but a short interval apart. Little by little, Stern began to hear other words, interspersed between the original word, and finally a complete phrase accompanied by a kind of melody.

Reynolds was enjoying himself immensely.

The words, phrases and melody that Stern heard were not on the tape. The phenomenon was due to the human brain's constant search for meaning in the things its hears.

The meaningless syllables were associated by the brain with known words, then combined to form other words, or even complete phrases.

Scientists called the phenomenon 'ghost words'.

73: THE CALL OF DUTY

Days passed. Autumn came, and winter soon after. Snow covered the mountains on the opposite shore of the lake.

Rock music was more and more strung out. Tracks were getting longer and longer, and I was beginning to tire of it all. The Doors and Pink Floyd were leading the field. The Beatles' latest album, Magical Mystery Tour, marked the beginning of their end. 'Nights in White Satin', a terrible single by the Moody Blues, oozed endlessly out of every radio.

For my part, I stuck with pure, hard, fast-paced rock, like 'Sympathy for the Devil', from The Stones.

I settled into the routine of work at the hotel. I earned my share of comments, criticism and reprimands, and I learned my trade. The hotel guests found me discreet and efficient, and the management were satisfied.

I began to talk. Mostly stock expressions of politesse or answers to standard queries. But I could address a person and look them in the eye.

The pain in my shoulder gradually eased, but a stiffness remained. Broad, sweeping gestures were impossible. I refused to contemplate the thought that I might never play the drums again. I told myself I would get physiotherapy later, when my life was properly settled.

I came off the drugs. No more dope, beyond the few joints I smoked with Andy on my Wednesdays off. Alcohol was my intimate friend, but it took a vast amount for me lose touch with reality. I took sips of drink all night long. I was sober when I came on duty, and left before the morning shift arrived. My habit went unnoticed.

Each time we met, Andy would announce his imminent departure. With that out of the way, he would talk about his painting, and I would talk to him about rock music.

On New Year's Day, he told me his latest project was ready at last. He agreed to show it to me before shipping it to New York.

I went to his room for the first time – an attic at the top of an old building on Rue d'Etraz. He begged me to ignore the bewildering mess.

A huge colour photograph, two metres by three, filled the end wall. It showed a big, blue American car parked in front of a shoe store in a big American city, evidently New York. He must have used the print as the inspiration for his work. Andy asked me to move closer to the picture. I could see now that the huge picture was composed of individual elements, each about fifty centimetres square.

I moved closer still, and stood open-mouthed. Never before in my life had I seen such a realistic painting. The car's reflection was visible on the glass of the store window, each element of the composition, every object was reproduced in a wealth of extraordinary detail. The effect was striking. I hardly dared imagine the time such minutely detailed work would take.

I stepped back and sat down. I stared in admiration at the masterpiece for over an hour, examining every part of it.

Andy was delighted. He danced around me as I looked. He asked if I understood now why he would be rich and famous one day.

By night, at work, I pursued my research. I noted my observations and linked them to the events I had witnessed. When I felt sleepy, I would turn on the TV.

The more I read, the more I learned. I became an expert on hearing, sound and acoustics.

I can scarcely recall the countless articles I read at the time, but my conclusion was clear: the guys at the studio had tampered with the tapes of 'Girls Just Want It All Night Long'.

I concluded that their work was subtler than the insertion of a few *phrases recorded backwards, though they may have used that tech-nique, too.*

I focused on 'ghost words', as the specialists called them: non-exist-ent words generated by the human brain, from sequences of phonemes. I reckoned they had been linked together at very low frequency, making them undetectable. Low frequency sounds, inaudible to the human ear, explained why animals could sense the onset of natural disasters. At the subconscious level, the frequencies could bring about profound alterations in behaviour.

The ghost words explained why only a section of the audience in the night club in Ramstein had responded to the stimulus, as not everyone would have been able to understand English.

The truth came to me one night in February 1968.

I had just finished my tour of inspection. I had fetched a glass of beer and switched on the television. It was almost midnight and the channels were shutting down for the night. I watched a report by a team of journalists working for a Swiss station.

The studiously impartial report gave a detailed picture of the daily life of G.I.s in Vietnam. The camera had followed a number of units. Mostly, the military authorities had ordered them to stop filming and sent them packing.

But they had nonetheless succeeded in infiltrating an American camp a few kilometres from Hue. The Tet offensive had just begun, and the American authorities were in over their heads.

The journalists had seized the opportunity to film the installations and preparation for a mission. Soldiers were seen running in all direc-tions, priming their weapons and equipment, paying no attention to the camera.

A few notes of music were heard.

One of the journalists questioned a G.I., a spotty young kid. Laughing, he told them the song was their anthem. It was played every time they set out on a mission. The officers had fixed loudspeak-ers to the half-tracks and the choppers.

My blood froze.

Amongst all the to-ing and fro-ing, I heard that wild, ferocious, jubilant noise. Steve's riff. Larry's bass entered the dance. I felt an icy wave run through me, to the very tips of my fingers and toes. Transfixed, I heard my own intro fill, and Jim's opening bars.

While the kid joked about the anthem, Larry Finch hollered until his voice cracked. The bass guitar, and my big bass drum, kept the beat.

On the screen, the G.I.'s face was transformed. His eyes became wide and staring, his features set hard. He added that the rock track gave them courage, and brought Charlie out in a cold sweat.

Then he turned on his heels, muttering that he had to go. The call of duty.

74: CLASP HIS HAND

Dominique stopped for groceries on his way home from the cemetery. He was emerging from the supermarket when Gérard Jacobs called back.

He couldn't resist a joke when he recognized the police officer's voice.

'You Belgians are quick off the mark. I thought the police were supposed to be slow to respond?'

'Well, we have been trying to identify this man for an entire year,' Jacob quipped. 'Without you, we'd still be at square one.'

'Anything new to report?'

'Yes. It seems to match up. Odile Chantraine was born in Brussels in 1920. In 1942, she married Roger Bernier, a Belgian citizen, born 1917, in the Namur region. They had two children, both boys. Pierre, born September 1943, and Jacques, born August 1945.'

'The woman I met at the cemetery said one of the sons was dead.'

'Absolutely. The elder boy, Pierre, died in 2006. Roger Bernier died in 1988, and his wife in 1991. Pierre Bernier was married, with one daughter. His wife died, too, but his daughter is alive. She's forty now, married and living in South Africa.'

'So Jacques is my patient?'

'Very likely.'

Dominique gave a long sigh.

'Jacques. I was almost there. We'd gotten as far as Isidore.'

'What?'

'Sorry… Nothing. So X Midi is Jacques Bernier?'

'That's not all. Jacques Bernier disappeared in 1964.'

'Disappeared?'

'On January the second, to be precise. He was supposed to report for military service in Malines. He never showed up, and there's been no trace of him since.'

Dominique did the figures quickly.

'He's been missing for forty-seven years?'

'I can understand you're surprised. But we register around a thousand missing persons every year, about three a day.'

'And they're never found?'

'Usually, they are. Most are runaway minors, which would have been Jacques Bernier's case at the time. We Belgians only decided 18-year-olds were adults in 1990! Many are confused, or have dementia, and go wandering. But there are suicides, too; accidents, and family fights. The Missing Persons Bureau has over sixteen thousand case files, and about eight hundred have never been closed.'

Dominique could hardly believe his ears. He stood beside his car, his shopping bags at his feet.

'What's he been doing for forty-seven years?'

'I couldn't tell you. But according to the file, he never got in touch with his parents, though they were a happy enough family, it seems.'

'What do you know about him, apart from his disappearance?'

'Very little in the file. A decent kid, quite quiet. He was involved in an accident when he was about fifteen, and suffered severe concussion, which may have had long-lasting effects. That's one of the theories in the case file. He was declared fit for military service, though.'

Dominique was deep in thought.

'So he came back after forty-seven years? Why? To ask his ma to forgive him, and put roses on her grave?'

'He may have thought his time was up. Criminals often react like that. A last wish to get something off their conscience.'

'No, that's not it. That doesn't feel right to me.'

'Then keep communicating with him. Try and find out more. I'll try and find out if there's any other family left. You should get in touch with his brother's daughter. I'll call you if there's anything new.'

Dominique ignored his day off and turned up at the clinic next morning.

He walked into X Midi's room unannounced, lifted him with both arms and sat him upright in bed. Next, he placed his laptop on the trolley table and wheeled it to face him. He opened the image viewer and showed X Midi the picture he had taken the day before.

Then he sat on the bed and took his hand.

The man's eyes misted over.

For the first time, Dominique felt X Midi clasp his hand.

75: THE WRONG I'VE DONE

Your smile is the smile I've always known. The years haven't taken their toll. I can go now. I hope you forgive me for the wrong I've done.

76: TO SUPPORT HIS THEORY

After visiting Reynolds, Michael Stern was certain that Pearl Harbor's deaths were connected to Jacques Berger's unexpected reappearance at the Berlin studio.

Berger hadn't been tripping. The men he described to Mary Hunter weren't imaginary. They were there in the studio, tampering with the tapes.

Stern was convinced, too, that the events in Ramstein, and the death of the night club disc-jockey, were linked to the affair.

But his own firm belief wasn't enough. No journalist worth his salt ever exposed a topic without a minimum of facts, and he had no tangible proof that would change his editor-in-chief's mind.

Jacques Berger could well have been killed himself, by now. The men in the studio had no idea he'd been standing in for the group's regular drummer, which explained why Paul McDonald had been eliminated. But they would certainly have discovered the truth later, and hunted him down. As to the motive for all this, it was plain as day. Stern was something of a history nut. He knew that the world's great powers had sought ways to galvanise their troops, or weaken their enemies' defences, since the dawn of time. The history books were full of examples.

One ancient text, *The Art of War*, and its mysterious author Sun Tzu, declared that war was based on trickery.

Sun Tzu recommended the use of propaganda and disinformation, to convince the enemy that defeat was inevitable. He suggested other tactics to undermine morale or increase stress levels.

In the eleventh century, the Ismailis practised a secret science that was thought to confer magical power: knowledge that was revealed only to the initiated, by degrees. Apprentices at the first level learned how to use hashish to develop their physical courage and achieve enlightenment.

The Mongol lord Genghis Khan was known for leading hordes of bloodthirsty riders across Russia and Europe. His reputation for total command was reinforced by the psychological conditioning to which his troops were subjected.

Hatred of the enemy was all-important, but for his men, the knowledge that they were free to pillage, kill and rape – a favourite spoil of war – was a useful boost to morale.

More recently, in the Second World War, the Nazis had injected their soldiers with testosterone to heighten their aggression. The Wehrmacht's doctors distributed tens of thousands of doses of amphetamines to keep their men awake and bolster their fighting spirit.

After the Second World War, the US army hired behavioural psychologists, following the results of a study that showed the majority of combatants were reluctant to kill, even on the field of battle.

To alleviate the soldiers' feelings of guilt and increase their aggression, they had established a battery of drills designed to condition individuals to think and act as a group, transforming them into a kind of killing machine that was better able to consider the enemy as non-human.

It was rumoured that early in the Vietnam war, the US army had experimented with LSD.

After taking the drug, troopers showed symptoms of psychotic schizophrenia, and could be pushed to commit violent acts against others.

Another rumour held that the experiment had been a disaster, and that the military authorities were now testing more sophisticated methods: psychotronic weapons, devices that used electromagnetic waves that could make people act unconsciously, and unleash their aggression.

For Stern, the tragedy that had unfolded in Ramstein was the result of an experiment with new technology, designed to programme human beings: a finely-tuned system capable of stimulating aggression in one section of a mass of people, and weakening the defences of the other.

It remained to gather the evidence he needed, to support his theory.

77: THE NUMBER I KNEW BY HEART

I would have gone home, if I hadn't been arrested. My identity crisis was coming to an end, I was no longer in revolt, I was becoming reconciled to the human race, little by little.

I thought of my mother every day, of the pain she must feel, the same gut-wrenching pain that I felt. I thought of my father and my brother, too. Distance and time had erased the grievances I held against them.

I would have gone home, I would have held my mother in my arms, I would have clasped her in my arms, without a word. She would have asked nothing of me.

I would have overcome all the obstacles. I would have justified myself. I could do that now. I would have expiated my misdeeds. I would have trusted to justice. I would have taken responsibility for my actions and accepted my punishment.

The Swiss television report had left me shaken. I knew what was afoot now, I knew what they were up to. I wanted to shout it out loud, to tell it to every single guest I encountered at the hotel, but there was no one I could talk to.

I could have confided in Andy. Our friendship was frank and sincere, but he knew nothing about my past. I had made a clean break, and invented some half-baked story that floored me whenever he asked.

Sometimes, I failed to answer when he called me by my name. He was the only person who knew me as René. Everyone at the hotel called me 'Monsieur Schnegg'. This was a new difficulty: when I ordered my first fake ID, I had deliberately chosen a name similar to my own, to avoid precisely that eventuality.

I carried on writing my story over the days that followed.

There was enough to support my theory. The further I got with my text, the more convinced I became; I was tormented by the urge to speak out.

One night, when I had drunk more than usual, I could keep the secret no longer. It must have been three or four in the morning when the inspiration came to me. I knew who I needed to speak to. I knew who would listen.

I picked up the telephone and dialled the number I knew by heart.

78: RECORDING SESSIONS

In early February, as Michael Stern struggled to corroborate the facts, he received a telephone call from Jim Ruskin's ex-girlfriend, Birgit.

She seemed well. Jim's death had affected her deeply, but almost a year had passed, and life went on. In October, she had met a man with whom she hoped to form a long-term relationship.

She asked Stern if he was still investigating the deaths of the members of Pearl Harbor. Stern told her he was.

She was calling to tell him about an incident in Berlin, with a clear link to the events of March 1967. The incident had occurred a few days ago, but had only just been reported in the papers.

She fetched a newspaper and read the gist of the article over the telephone. The Berlin river police stated that they had recovered what seemed 'in all likelihood' to be the body of a German rock agent, Karl Jürgen, from Munich, who had been reported missing on March the eighteenth, 1967. The fifty-two-year-old's body was discovered in a canal lock near the Mühlendamm bridge, in the centre of Berlin.

The police communiqué indicated that there were no suspicious circumstances – the death was probably suicide. The investigators hoped that the autopsy would shed further light on the affair. Enquiries so far suggested personal reasons. The police excluded any political motivation.

The man had left his apartment in Charlottenburg, in West Berlin, very early in the morning on March the eighteenth, 1967, and had not been seen since. His wife had reported him missing the same day, and told the investigators that her husband had been suffering from depression.

Following the death, the police had issued a call for witnesses in the neighbourhood. The couple had been living in Berlin since November 1966, and had few social contacts. Two divers had searched a lake near the couple's home, without success.

Karl Jürgen had been an agent for a number of rock groups, mostly still waiting for their big break.

He handled contract negotiations and booked recording sessions.

79: IN SCOTLAND

Sunday. As luck would have it, Gunther was still behind the bar. Berliners hated Mondays, and the Graffiti club would often stay open until the small hours on Sundays.

The music in the background was quiet enough, and Gunther seemed in relaxed mood.

He said he was surprised and delighted to get a telephone call from me, and I knew this was no standard, polite greeting – bubbly enthusiasm was not one of his most marked characteristics.

The last customers had just left, and he was making ready to close up. That weekend, West Berlin had hosted an international congress against the war in Vietnam. Fifteen thousand people had marched through the streets. Rudi Dutschke, a Marxist activist, had given a rousing speech that had sparked extraordinary, chaotic scenes.

After that, it had been a quiet evening, with only a few people in the bar.

Gunther launched into an account of the situation in Berlin. Revolution was in the air. Youth movements had been infiltrated by Communist agents and were being manipulated. Soon, the much-heralded revolution would gather speed; East German tanks would invade the city, and then the rest of Europe.

I let him finish, though I had heard it all before, word for word.

On to rock music. Gunther reckoned Pink Floyd were the flagship for the psychedelic rock movement. Their first album, The Piper at the Gates of Dawn, was a brilliant success, though he couldn't see himself playing 'Astronomy Domine' or 'Interstellar Overdrive' at the Graffiti any time soon.

Next, my own news. I told him I'd found a job in a Swiss hotel, but refrained from saying exactly where. It was in French-speaking Switzerland, I told him.

Then I got to the point. I reminded Gunther of the last time we had spoken. I told him I now knew what had really happened at the recording sessions on March the fourteenth. I had proof that the deaths of the four members of Pearl Harbor were no accident. They had been murdered. And I knew the motive.

I told him everything I knew. I had my notes to hand, and consulted them from time to time, to back up one significant detail or another.

As I had expected, Gunther seemed unfazed by my revelations. He was similarly underwhelmed by my explanation of ghost words and infrasound, and the conditioning of US troops in Vietnam.

When I had finished my concluding remarks, he said my argument was convincing, and that it supported his own belief, namely that World War Three was brewing. He returned to his own theories and expounded them for several minutes more.

I didn't mind. I had exorcised my obsession. He had listened without interrupting, and he hadn't told me I was mad.

I was ready to bring our talk to a close when Gunther interrupted me suddenly, as if he had just remembered something, albeit nothing of any great importance.

In November, he had been visited by a Scotsman who said he was a journalist. The man said he was investigating the deaths of the four members of Pearl Harbor. He had outlined his case and told Gunther he wanted to get in touch with me. Gunther had told him he could go to hell.

But the man had left his card.

Gunther asked me to wait a minute. I heard him place the receiver on the bar and rummage through the jumble stashed underneath.

He came back to the telephone, out of breath. The man's name was Michael Stern and he was a reporter for the Belfast Telegraph.

I made a note of his number. I didn't know what to think. Was this one of the men from the studio? Had they realised their mistake? Had they tracked me down? Was this a subterfuge to get in touch with me?

My head cleared instantly. I had to take the information on board and think about what to do.

I thanked Gunther. I didn't bother to tell him that Belfast wasn't in Scotland.

80: THIS LATEST MYSTERY

Gérard Jacobs contacted Dominique in the middle of the following week, to share his latest information.

He told him that his superiors weren't prioritising the investigation. But he remained committed to it. He had invested a few hours of his own time to take things forward.

On the preceding Saturday night, he had spoken on the telephone to Jacques Bernier's niece, who was living in Johannesburg, in South Africa. The woman knew very little about the uncle she had never met. After he disappeared in 1964, her grandparents had tried several times to trace him, without success.

Her grandfather and father rarely spoke about him. But throughout her childhood, when she visited her grandmother and they were alone together, the old lady would tell her stories about Jacques, how he played the drums on the tops of biscuit tins, or an afternoon when they had danced to rock'n'roll records. She refused to believe he was dead. To the end, she was convinced he would come back one day.

She had heard he was a troubled character. When her father talked about his brother, and their childhood, he had few good words for Jacques. He called him a crackpot. The mad, stammering drummer. She never knew exactly what he meant, and hadn't bothered to find out.

The police officer had also managed to contact one of Jacques Bernier's old schoolteachers.

The man was eighty years old now, and had known Jacques in 1961, but remembered him well. A shy, reserved boy who had a speech impediment and seemed to live in his own world. He read a great deal, but never talked about the books he loved.

The secretary at the cemetery in Ixelles had confirmed that a man had telephoned several times in February 2010, to ask about the location of Madame Bernier's grave. The woman remembered that the man sounded confused. He had called several times in succession, to ask the same question.

Lastly, Jacobs had obtained a copy of the medical report drawn up in September 1963 when Jacques Bernier had spent three days at Petit-Chateau, ahead of his military service.

The report noted that the psychometric tests and medical examinations showed Jacques Bernier suffered from minor behavioural problems. He had been in good physical shape, and the electroencephalogram carried out at the time had revealed nothing abnormal. The doctors suspected he had simulated the symptoms of aprosexia in order to be declared medically unfit, hence they had discounted the diagnosis. He had been declared fit for service.

In conclusion, Gérard Jacobs told Dominique that he had released the man's identity to the press and that some of the daily papers would be publishing the information.

The news presented Dominique with a dilemma. He had given Jacques Bernier his word. He had promised never to reveal the information they exchanged. But he had to act with integrity vis-à-vis the rest of the medical team.

He went to see Marie-Anne Perard, the director of the clinic. He told her about the approaches he had tried with X Midi, and the results obtained.

Marie-Anne Perard thanked him for being frank with her and made no comment on his silence thus far. She understood that he had kept his word, and assured him it would go no further. She told him, once again, that the patients praised his enthusiasm and excellent treatment very highly.

Dominique decided to talk to X Midi straightaway. His patient had made no attempt to communicate since seeing the photographs from the cemetery.

Dominique sat on his bed.

'I have something to tell you, my friend.'

The man frowned and stared the physio in the eye.

Dominique took a deep breath.

'I can't keep our secret.'

The man's eyes widened.

'I know, I promised, and I understand your disappointment, but I can't do otherwise. I know something of your story, but I don't know everything. I know your name is Jacques Bernier and that you disappeared a long time ago. There are sure to be people looking for you somewhere. People who love you. A woman, children, or friends who would love to see you. For them, and for you, I can't keep our secret.'

A look of panic came into X Midi's eyes. He shot a glance at the cupboard.

Dominique understood straightaway.

'You want to talk?'

Yes.

Dominique took the alphabet board and began listing the letters. Bernier focused his concentration, as if terrified of making a mistake.

It took over fifteen minutes to compose the first word: MICHAEL

The second word came more quickly: STERN

Bernier stared at the television. He seemed relieved to have got the words off his chest.

'Michael Stern? Do you know where I can find him?' Dominique asked.

No reaction.

'Is he a friend?'

No reaction.

'Does he live in Belgium?'

Jacques Bernier kept his eyes fixed on the screen.

Dominique tried a few more questions, without success.

Then he had an idea.

He stared at the television, too.

'He's been on TV, is that it?'

The man turned his head slightly and blinked twice.

'He hasn't been on TV, but there's a connection?'

Bernier signalled 'yes'.

'He's a film star? Or a journalist? Something like that?'

The man signalled 'yes' and closed his eyes.

Dominique understood there would be nothing more, this time. He would have to investigate this latest mystery.

81: SAY ANOTHER WORD

Three weeks had gone by since Birgit's call, and Michael Stern had made no progress with his investigation. He began to lose heart. He had no idea which lead to follow next. All led to a dead end.

The victims' families contacted him regularly for an update on his research. And each time, he told them things were moving forward little by little, but that they shouldn't hold out any great hope.

Towards the end of the month a bulletin announced that a United Arab Airlines Ilyushin aircraft had crashed in Aswan, in Egypt. Michael Stern was chosen by the *Belfast Telegraph* to cover the event.

He was making preparations to leave when the switchboard operator announced an incoming call. She added that the caller had refused to give their identity, and the reason for the call. He went back to his desk and picked up the receiver.

For a few seconds, he thought the caller had hung up. He was about to hang up himself when he thought he heard a faint creaking sound, followed by a man's voice pronouncing a few words he didn't understand.

After a few seconds, the man said his name was Jacques Berger. He had been told the journalist was trying to get hold of him, and he wanted to know why.

Michael Stern felt a sharp, adrenaline rush. The man's speech was confused. Some of his words were barely comprehensible. English wasn't his mother tongue, he spoke with an accent, but not the nasal tones of a French Canadian.

Stern could tell the man was in a state of high stress. He had just a few seconds to earn his trust. He told Berger he knew who he was, and what had happened to him, and that he wanted to help.

The man appeared to think for a few moments, then asked Stern to tell him what he knew.

Stern struggled to contain his nerves and speak calmly.

He knew that Berger had played a back-up gig in Berlin on March the fourteenth, last year. He had replaced the drummer of a group called Pearl Harbor, and had taken part in a recording session, after which he had surprised several men who were tampering with the tapes. After that, the four other band members and their agent had been killed.

The man seemed to hesitate.

He asked Stern to repeat the last phrase. As he did so, Stern realised that the agent's death was news to Berger. He explained that earlier that month Karl Jürgen's body had been found by the Berlin river police.

The man absorbed this latest shock, saying nothing for a few moments.

When he spoke again, he asked the journalist for his version of events. He wanted to know what conclusions Stern had reached.

Stern told him about the ghost words and the connection he had established to the events in Ramstein.

The man stammered at the other end of the line.

He spoke vaguely about a helicopter, soldiers, the Vietnam war, then said his life was in danger, that the men behind the plot were capable of anything, and wouldn't hesitate to end his life.

Stern seized the moment. He agreed, and repeated his offer of help.

The man raised his voice slightly. How did he think he could help?

Stern was careful to speak in calm, measured tones.

The best way to stop the men in their tracks was to reveal what they had done, expose it. It was the only reasonable course of action.

The man said he would think about it. He hung up before Stern could say another word.

82: A NORMAL LIFE

I turned the information over and over in my mind, in the days that followed.

How had the journalist followed the trail back to me? Was it a trap? Should I call him back or steer clear?

I ordered a copy of the Belfast Telegraph. Michael Stern's name was amongst the list of contributors, but that didn't mean he was definitely the man Gunther had spoken to.

One evening, I called the paper's number. It was late. The offices were empty apart from the switchboard operator. Michael Stern wasn't there. The duty reporter asked if he could take a message. I wanted to ask him if Stern had travelled to Berlin the previous November, but I couldn't find the words.

I subscribed to the newspaper. On February the twenty-sixth, Michael Stern's byline appeared on a report of a summit that had been held in Dubai.

Two days later, at our weekly get-together, Andy told me he was leaving Montreux for real. He had got a job in a hotel in Vienna and would be leaving in early March. He wanted to continue his round-the-world trip, see the work of Vienna's early-twentieth-century masters and study their technique.

I made my decision the next day. I went to a call-box and telephoned Michael Stern.

He seemed unsurprised to hear me. His calm, even tone helped me to calm down, too. I asked him a few questions, to be sure I was speaking to the right person.

He was very familiar with the case, though I was ahead of him in understanding exactly what the men in the studio had developed.

But he told me something I didn't know. Something that confirmed the theory we shared: Karl, the man who had organised the recording session, and who had greeted me at the entrance to the studio, had been found dead – drowned – in Berlin. He had died almost a year ago, at the same time as the members of Pearl Harbor.

Stern suggested reporting the affair, and promised to help me. He thought this was the best way to curtail the men from the studio and protect my life.

By the end of the conversation, I felt confused and overwhelmed. I told him I would think about it.

I hung up and called Andy to tell him I was coming with him to Vienna. I was afraid he'd say no, but he agreed.

I didn't tell the hotel manager what I was doing. I felt I was in danger. The men surely knew they had got the wrong person in Paul McDonald, and would be looking for me now. If a journalist had tracked me down, they would do the same.

I made preparations to leave, in the days that followed. Andy had a furnished apartment waiting for him in Vienna, which he had rented through an aunt. In Andy's circles, people were well accustomed to helping one another out. He was happy for me to stay until I found work, and somewhere to live.

On the morning of Monday, March the eleventh, 1968, I called Michael Stern back. I had planned what I wanted to say. This time, I did the talking.

I told him I had written an account of the facts, proving the existence of the plot. The text also shed light on the mass manipulation techniques used by the men. The whole thing ran to a hundred pages, packed with detail.

He sounded impressed. We agreed to meet in London on the following Monday, March the eighteenth.

He would meet me at the airport and ensure my safety. In the *afternoon, he would introduce me to some of his colleagues in the London press. Then, in the early evening, he would arrange an interview with a handful of influential political personalities. We would expose the scandal and stop the plot in its tracks.*

He told me to be careful, and to guard the notes with my life.

His last words.

That afternoon, Andy and I took the train. By evening, we were in Vienna, settling into a charming apartment in Prater. I could see the big wheel from the window.

Next day, he took me to visit the Vienna museums. Andy went from picture to picture, dancing with delight, kneeling before them, jumping up to peer closely at each canvas, telling me anecdotes about the artists' lives, or commenting on the techniques they had used.

At the Belvedere, his excitement reached fever pitch. The museum's centrepiece was Gustav Klimt's Kiss. *The canvas was displayed in a glass case, and lit to accentuate the vivid colours and gold leaf. Andy said that Klimt had produced a much bolder version of the picture a few years beforehand, which had mysteriously disappeared.*

I made a show of listening, but all I could think about was the meeting arranged for March the eighteenth. My mind was made up. Once I had unburdened myself of the secret, I would go home, and turn myself in.

I was convinced the outcry surrounding my revelations would act in my favour and encourage clemency.

When I had paid my debt, I could lead a normal life.

83: UNUSUAL FOR HIM

First thing on the morning of Thursday, March the fourteenth, 1968, a year to the day after the events in Berlin, Michael Stern marched into his chief's office.

He confessed straightaway to going against orders, and said he had continued with the enquiry he had begun six months earlier, into the deaths of the four members of the band known as Pearl Harbor. He outlined the different stages of the investigation, and provided conclusive proof that the deaths in March 1967 were linked to, indeed part of, a CIA plot designed to programme human beings for military purposes.

Finally, he told his chief about his recent contact with the back-up drummer who had been present at the recording. And he concluded by announcing that this key witness would be coming to London the following Monday. The man had compiled a document recounting the facts and explaining the techniques used by the US agency to manipulate behaviour *en masse*.

The editor-in-chief waited for him to finish. He got to his feet and picked up two recent copies of the *Belfast Telegraph*.

He began reading the article Stern had written about the Ilyushin air crash in Aswan. Stern had concluded his dispatch by suggesting that in light of the Cold War between the United States and Russia, the accident was very likely no accident at all.

The second article, also by Stern, had been published two days earlier. Stern had been sent to report on the disappearance of a Soviet K 129 submarine. The vessel had been carrying three nuclear ballistic missiles. It had left its base in Ribachyi on the Kamchatka peninsula towards the end of February, and had disappeared without trace on the eighth of March, off the coast of Hawaii.

Stern had propounded the theory – contested in some sections of the media, supported in others – that the sub had been torpedoed by the US navy.

When he finished reading, the editor-in-chief was loud in his exasperation.

A journalist reported facts, nothing but the facts, without exaggeration or understatement, without distortion or extrapolation in support of some lunatic conspiracy theory. He insisted that the *Belfast Telegraph* was a proud, independent paper, not an organ of the Communist party.

And hard on the heels of these two infringements of the basic laws of journalism, here was Stern again, digging up an old, highly dubious story in an effort to reveal yet another CIA plot.

Stern began to object, but his chief cut him short and warned that no way would his paper make a fool of itself by publishing a 'scoop' that was both hypothetical and obviously partisan.

He ordered Stern to take a few days off and think about his future career. Because the *Belfast Telegraph* wouldn't compromise its reputation any further by publishing his paranoid fantasies.

And with that, he called the interview to a close. Stern left the room, slamming the door behind him.

Early that evening, Stern's wife called the newspaper office.

She was worried. Stern wasn't home yet. They had guests, and he had promised he'd be home early. He hadn't called to say he'd be late, which was unusual for him.

84: I LOST CONSCIOUSNESS

The day before my departure for London was a very special day in my life. But I would only know that the day after.

Andy had started work at his hotel. I got up late and wandered aimlessly through the streets, deep in thought about what lay ahead.

It was a Sunday. In the centre of Vienna, the majestic façades were resplendent in bright sunshine that would have warmed the people out walking, were it not for an icy wind.

The city basked in its old-world glory. Trams made their way along the broad avenues, the first of the day's tourists were taking their horse-drawn carriage rides, and coachmen strutted in their top hats and riding coats.

In front of the opera house, smartly-dressed couples waited in line, carrying folding chairs, in hopes of cheap, standing-room tickets.

I walked along the Graben, allowing myself to be picked out by street conjurors and acrobats. I stopped to eat a sausage and drink a beer at one of the kiosks.

I felt free, I could breathe. Everything seemed so simple. I was very far from imagining what had occurred some nine thousand kilometres away.

With a hundred of his men, Lieutenant William Calley, commander of Charlie company, had surrounded the small village of My Lai, in Vietnam. Calley had rounded up the population, set the village alight and ordered everyone killed. Almost five hundred civilians were slaughtered in cold blood. Wounded children were murdered trying to escape. Thirty women who emerged from one shelter with their hands in the air were killed, with their babies. Even the dogs and cats were killed.

Calley's men seemed to be in a kind of trance. It was said the carnage had been carried out to the strains of hard rock music, played through loudspeakers mounted on helicopters.

I hadn't slept all night. As if the news had somehow been imprinted on my subconscious. Next day, I took a taxi to the airport. Mv plane left around noon and landed in London one and a half hours later.

Michael Stern would be there to meet me. We had arranged to meet by the Mini Cooper display in the arrivals hall. We would both carry the latest edition of the Belfast Telegraph under one arm. I would find a copy at one of the news stands.

My stomach clenched tight as I presented my passport on arrival. The officers barely glanced at my papers. I hurried to meet Stern, buying a copy of the Belfast Telegraph on my way.

I circled the Mini Cooper with the paper under my arm, but there was no sign of Stern. I felt ridiculous, walking round and round the car. I unfolded the newspaper and prepared to wait.

My heart stopped. I read the banner headline and knew instantly that Stern would not be coming. I had walked into a trap.

I hurried towards the exit.

I was a few metres from the glass doors when an electric shock left me rooted to the spot. An iron grip closed around both my arms. One of the men standing either side of me spoke into my ear, in a low voice. I was coming with them, quietly. No fuss.

We turned around and crossed the hall, back the way I had come. We disappeared down a corridor. They opened a door and pushed me into a windowless office, flooded with bright, violent light and furnished with nothing but a metal table and two chairs.

Behind one of these stood the man from the recording studio. He looked taller than I remembered. He stared at me just as when we had first met, with complete indifference. He seemed incapable of emotion.

He stepped forward, positioned himself in front of me and spoke two words. 'The Book.'

My mind raced, but I couldn't find the words, and said nothing.

The man signalled to his acolytes. One of them tore the ruck sack from my back and tipped its contents onto the floor, sifting them with his foot. The document was not there. They ordered me to undress.

I did as they asked, and stood naked in front of the three men. They made a meticulous search of my possessions, but found nothing. One by one, they took each item from out of my bag and examined it. Then they tore the lining, shredded my clothes and took everything in my toilet bag to pieces.

They were empty-handed. The giant planted himself in front of me once more and stared me in the eye. He seemed neither furious nor exasperated. He heaved a great sigh. If anything, he looked mildly irritated – as if my refusal to cooperate would make him late for his next meeting.

The man standing behind me hollered straight in my ear.

'The Book!'

I saw this was my only hope of salvation. So long as they failed to lay hands on my text, there was a chance I would live.

I said I had no idea what they were talking about.

I felt a slight movement. A shock. Something broke inside me, and I lost consciousness.

85: THE MYSTERY WAS DARKER STILL

Dominique supposed that Michael Stern – the name Jacques Bernier had spelled out – had been a close friend or associate.

Perhaps Bernier had been a journalist himself, and the man was a colleague. But he might equally be a friend, or merely an acquaintance. Unless Stern had once written an article concerning him, directly or indirectly.

Whatever the reason, Bernier had given Stern's name because this person could help him, and perhaps explain what had happened before his accident.

He began with an Internet search. If Michael Stern had ever written an article or a column of interest, there would be references to it on the Web.

He typed the journalist's name into the Google search window and pressed 'Enter'.

The results astounded him.

Michael Stern was far from unknown. If this was indeed the man Jacques Bernier was talking about, then the mystery surrounding his past life had just thickened even further.

Michael S. Stern was born to a working-class family in Derry on October the twenty-fifth, 1938. He studied journalism at Queen's University Belfast, and joined the *Belfast Telegraph* in September 1963. The *Telegraph* was Northern Ireland's biggest paper at the time, with a circulation of over one hundred thousand copies.

Early on the morning of Monday, March the eighteenth,

1968, he had walked into the office of his editor-in-chief, Roger McGuinness, and killed him with three shots to the head. Next, he had killed Greg Ryan, a colleague who tried to tackle him, and seriously wounded Stephen Jones, a radio announcer who was present at the time. Security had intervened and managed to disarm him.

A few days before, Stern had a serious row with Roger McGuinness, who had accused him of political bias in a number of articles, and delivered a strong warning. Several witnesses had seen Stern leave the premises in a very bad temper.

His wife reported that he had not come home that night, and hadn't contacted her.

Questioned a few hours after his arrest, Stern declared he had acted under duress. He said he had been abducted by a group of men, and kept in isolation for several days. He claimed to have been brainwashed and programmed to commit the murders. He cited an extensive plot, organised by a foreign governmental agency, aimed at controlling human conscious-ness and using mass manipulation to further their imperialist ends.

The experts dismissed his far-fetched claims. There was no plea of diminished responsibility.

He was tried, found guilty of murder with malice afore-thought, and sentenced to life imprisonment.

Stern was held at Belfast's Crumlin Road Gaol until 1976, when he was transferred to the so-called H-Blocks at the Maze prison. There, he took part in the hunger strikes of 1981.

He engaged in a number of other actions designed to draw public attention to the miscarriage of justice he claimed he had suffered.

Throughout his detention, he persistently claimed his inno-cence, and stuck to his version of the facts.

He was found dead in his cell on the fourth of March, 1987. The autopsy concluded he had suffered a heart attack.

Dominique consulted several sites giving details of all this. They all gave the same account of the facts. There was no mention of Jacques Bernier.

Stern had killed his editor-in-chief over forty years ago. Jacques Bernier had been twenty-three years old.

Why had he brought up this man's name? Had he known him in prison? Had they shared a cell?

Dominique thought he had found a possible meaning behind Bernier's message. But now, the mystery was darker still.

86: MY HANDS BEGAN TO SHAKE

The day before my arrest was my last day of freedom. My last hours as a human being.

The fog came down, and took possession of my soul.

My consciousness altered, slowly. My brain was blurred, I never felt fully awake. A kind of nagging, drugged sensation destroyed my faculties and neutralised my will. I was living in a parallel world. My hands were no longer my own. I would look at them, and try to recognise them. They had become strangers to me.

I felt my face for signs of the physical blows I was sure I had suffered, but could find nothing. They persecuted me, but the treatments inflicted upon me left no trace.

I saw the things around me. I recognised them, but I could no longer name them, nor recognise what they were for.

They shut me in a kind of sparsely-furnished bedroom. They would come in at regular intervals, in pairs. They were faceless. They would grab me by the arms and take me to an interview room, different each time.

They would make me sit. Men would examine me, and ask me questions.

The book.

They spoke politely, with deference, as if anxious to be seen to be sticking to the rules.

The book.

The book.

They invented scenarios. I had given it to someone on the plane. I had posted it to an address in London before leaving Vienna. I had deposited it in a bank vault. I had hidden it at the airport.

I programmed my responses. I clung to my last hope, silence. I had no idea what they were talking about. I knew nothing about the book. Gradually, I forgot what I had written.

Other questions came. Who had I spoken to? Who had I spouted my nonsense to?

I thought of Mary, and Gunther. If Stern had spoken to them, they would know. I had to protect Mary. I prayed they hadn't heard any mention of her name. As long as they remained in the dark about the whereabouts of the book, there was a chance I would live.

Silence.

Oblivion.

I thought of nothing else.

Keeping quiet and forgetting.

They would come to fetch me, and ask the same questions each time.

Where?

Who?

When they brought me back to my room, I would check my hands, feel my face.

I became impotent. I was incapable of situating myself in time. There was no clock, no mirror, no window. Men in white coats would come into my room. They forced me to swallow pills. I underwent examinations. When they left, I would sleep. Each day, the fog thickened.

I don't know how many days, or weeks, or months it lasted.

They came for me without warning. They took me to a large hall where fifteen or so people were waiting.

Everyone spoke loudly and emphatically.

They described who I was. They told me I was a deserter, a drug trafficker, that I had been involved in the death of a young girl in Paris, that I had killed a rival in London, that I had attacked and robbed a British citizen. They spoke words I didn't understand.

I hadn't known for sure if Gab was dead. I didn't want to believe it even though I knew I had gone too far. I felt bitter regret.

I wanted news of Mary, but couldn't allow myself to speak. My hands grew bony, my head spun.

They declared that I was suffering from diminished responsibility, and sent me to Dartford. The fog became impenetrable. My hands began to shake.

87: THE PERPETRATORS WERE NEVER QUESTIONED

On Sunday the seventeenth of March, 1968, shortly before speaking to students at the University of Kansas, Senator Robert Kennedy announced his candidacy for the White House.

The news was greeted with enthusiasm in Berlin, where his brother, JFK, had been welcomed in June 1963, and famously declared 'Ich bin ein Berliner'.

That evening, the Graffiti had enjoyed one of its best and most profitable nights of the year. Despite a renewed onslaught of winter weather, Berliners were out partying in force. The club's new resident rock group, a bunch of energetic English guys, had taken the atmosphere to fever pitch, and the punters had partied into the small hours.

The last diehards had left at 6:00a.m. – when the sun was already up.

As he did every Sunday, Gunther Krombach had set about closing the bar. He emptied the cash register, slipped the bank notes into a stiff cardboard envelope, poured the coins into a metal box and headed downstairs to stash everything in the restaurant safe.

There he found Pablo Fermi, the manager, closing the restaurant.

Once the money was safely stowed, the two made themselves a dish of pasta. They often spent an hour philosophising and talking politics before heading home.

Shortly before 7:00a.m., while Gunther Krombach was

fetching his jacket, three men in cagoules burst into the restaurant. They wore long, black coats and military boots, and they were armed with pump-action shotguns.

They held up Pablo Fermi and insisted he hand over the takings. While the manager carried out their orders, in fear of his life, one of the men left the group and headed upstairs.

A few moments later, Fermi heard two loud shots. The man reappeared. He nodded to his colleagues, and the three dashed outside. Paolo Fermi heard the rumble of a powerful engine and the screech of tyres.

Paralysed with fear, he waited a few seconds before racing to the stairs leading to the night club.

He found Gunther Krombach's lifeless body spread-eagled behind the bar, with two bullets to the head, shot at point blank range.

The police were quickly on the scene.

Three similar attacks had taken place in the past month, but this was the first time the gang had opened fire on a victim.

The police found a gun hidden under the bar. The manager explained that it was used to help pacify aggressive customers, and prevent fights.

Nothing in the position of Gunther Krombach's body suggested that he had tried to grab the concealed gun, or shown any resistance.

In his statement, Paolo Fermi confirmed that the man who had addressed him spoke German without a foreign accent. The other men had said nothing.

The police found no spent cartridges. The ballistics expert concluded that Gunther Krombach had not been killed by a pump-action shotgun, but by a handgun firing 9-millimetre bullets.

The attack was the last of the series to occur in Berlin.

The perpetrators were never questioned.

88: I HAD BECOME HARMLESS

My first memory of Dartford is the black-and-white tiled floors of the corridors I walked down, flanked by men in white coats. These brief, return trips were the only time I saw my fellow inmates.

With my nose to the ground, I would stare at the chequered floor. I thought of chess. I imagined the pieces moving across the board. I anticipated offensives and devised strategic defences. To no avail. The end result was always the same.

Sometimes I would look up.

I saw empty-eyed men. One glared at me with real animosity. He was pale, with twisted features. His mouth folded in upon itself. I looked away.

Others stood motionless in the corridors. They would throw their heads backward and forward or burst into crazed laughter.

I can still smell the odour that seeped from the walls and under my door. The sweetish reek of excrement mixed with the smell of urine, disinfectant and boiled vegetables. I thought I would get used to it eventually, but the opposite was true: nausea haunted me day and night, though day and night were indistinguishable to me.

They thought I was dangerous, and kept me in isolation. I was shut in a tiny cell with no furniture other than a bed fitted with straps. There were steel bars at the window.

My rare waking moments were peopled with nightmares.

From scraps overheard here and there, I discovered I was in Stone House Hospital in Dartford, in the county of Kent, about sixteen miles from London. One of the oldest and best-known psychiatric *hospitals in the United Kingdom. Jacob Levy, a butcher suspected of being Jack the Ripper, had been a resident, and died there from syphilis.*

At the end of the nineteenth century, Dartford was England's dumping ground. The town was home to leper colonies, hospitals for infectious diseases, gunpowder magazines and asylums. There were many such institutions locally. Darenth Park, a hospital for mentally handicapped children, and Stone House vied with one another for the most sinister reputation.

Dartford was also the birthplace of the Stones. Keith Richards' childhood home was just a short distance from my prison.

Noises came through the walls. Mostly groans. Occasionally, a shriek of terror would ring out. I lay stretched out in the dark. A man would come to my door and tell me to keep quiet.

They had made me believe I was mad.

From time to time, sirens would wail, usually a sign that a madman had escaped.

Panic in the corridors, people running in all directions. The inmates would begin hollering in unison. As if a cat had been let loose in a kennels. Some would destroy anything that came to hand, or hammer their heads against the walls.

The breakouts never lasted more than a couple of days. They would be found hiding in a park, dead or frozen stiff.

Each day, each week, each month, men would come to question me. They promised I would be kept in better conditions if I agreed to cooperate. I had no idea what they were talking about.

One day, the visits stopped, and they took me out of solitary confinement. I had become harmless.

89: SOME KIND OF THREAT

Dominique had continued his investigations into the events of the eighteenth of March, 1968, and the murders committed by Michael Stern. He had read through a number of websites in English, dictionary to hand, but found nothing new.

The shocking discovery had occupied his weekend, but try as he might, his obsessive ruminations threw up no obvious link between Michael Stern and Jacques Bernier. Each hypothesis seemed more improbable than the last.

On Monday morning, he printed out a sheaf of pages summarising the affair, and headed for the clinic, hoping that on sight of the information, Bernier would be encouraged to tell him more.

He entered Bernier's room, cracked a few jokes and began the usual treatments.

'Have you seen the news, Jacques? First Tunisia and Egypt, and now the threat of an uprising in Libya. But knowing Qaddafi, he won't go quietly.'

No reaction.

'And the football, Jacques? Do you like football? Standard lost against Ghent, and Westerlo beat Anderlecht, did you see that?'

Bernier was impassive.

Dominique continued his massage, detecting a fair degree of tension in the leg muscles.

His patient was distant, lost in his own inner world.

Towards the end of the session, Dominique broached the subject he really wanted to discuss.

'I took a look on the Internet, Jacques. I know who Michael Stern is. I know what happened to him. But I don't understand what that has to do with you. Did you know him, or one of his victims?'

The question drew no reaction.

Bernier seemed cut off. His eyes rolled, unfocused. He seemed to be reliving some interminable nightmare.

Dominique tried another tack, adopting a brighter tone.

'Have you seen the sun? Spring's come early this year. I'm going to get you into a chair and we'll take a little walk out in the forest, would you like that? And after that, the pool.'

He didn't wait for a reply. Away from his usual surroundings, Bernier might feel more at ease, and agree to answer his questions.

He called a nurse to help him manoeuvre X Midi into the wheelchair.

Bernier was still visiting the pool, and receiving verticalisation sessions. He had shown encouraging progress in the first months of treatment, but recently there had been little change. His treatment team described his condition as stationary, perhaps even regressing slightly.

Dominique headed down the corridors towards the main entrance to the clinic.

The sun was bright, but it was still cold. He called a nurse, asked her to watch X Midi for a moment and went to the dispensary to fetch some blankets.

On the way, he met Marie-Anne Perard.

'Morning, Dominique.'

'Good morning, Madame.'

'Where are you hurrying off to?'

'I'm taking X Midi for a walk.'

The clinic director checked her watch.

'The staff meeting begins in ten minutes. I need you there. Walks are in the afternoons, and it's too cold to go out.'

Dominique did not protest. He retraced his steps, reinstalled Bernier in his bed and headed for the conference room.

Marie-Anne Perard greeted the meeting's participants and ran through the agenda. To Dominique's surprise, X Midi's case was at the top of the list.

'To begin, I'd like to address the case of the patient known to us as X Midi.'

She paused and looked at Dominique.

'I'm delighted to inform you that Dominique has succeeded in communicating with him.'

Most present were already aware of the news, but greeted it with applause nonetheless.

Dominique was embarrassed.

'Thank you.'

'Well done, Dominique, you should be proud.'

'Thanks, everybody.'

The director continued.

'Dominique has succeeded in creating a climate of trust that encourages communication. With patience and tenacity, he has obtained information that has enabled us to identify our patient. X Midi's name is Jacques Bernier. I would ask everyone to address him as such from today, and to update all our files and documents accordingly. We still know relatively little about him. M. Bernier is Belgian, born in 1945. He was reported missing in January 1964. The police have opened an investigation, which will, I hope, enable us to find out more. A call for information appeared in several newspapers this weekend, inviting anyone who knows him to come forward.'

Dominique cursed himself for forgetting to check the announcement in the press.

Marie-Anne Perard paused again, and waited for complete silence before announcing her news.

'I'm happy to inform you that the article has already produced results, and that I received a telephone call this morning from England.'

Dominique flinched in his seat.

'I spoke to the assistant of a Dr Philip Taylor, a psychiatrist and professor in London. He treated Bernier until late summer 2009. He will visit us here tomorrow.'

Dominique couldn't be sure why, but he received the news as some kind of threat.

90: I HAD MET THIS MAN SOMEWHERE BEFORE

Each day lasted a year, each year passed in the space of a day. In the park, the trees changed colour sometimes. They were my only point of reference.

I had a bigger bedroom, and furniture was installed in addition to my bed. Three nutters were moved in with me, doubtless in hopes of forcing me to acknowledge I was now one of them.

Mostly, they kept silent. One of them lay stretched on his bed for hours at a time, staring at the ceiling, a thin line of dribble trickling from his mouth. The other two would come and go. We lived cheek by jowl, but never spoke.

I came and went, too. I wandered the corridors, staring down at the chequered tiles. I tried to get away from the smell and the shouting. To no avail.

One of the men in white would appear from time to time. They didn't question me now, but they would search me and talk amongst themselves as if I didn't exist.

There were a great many suicide attempts. Few succeeded. Mostly, people tried to hang themselves with their shoe-laces or a twisted length of sheet.

I can still see one poor sod, who set himself alight. He had managed to get hold of a big container of white spirit or disinfectant. He poured a fair quantity down his throat, then splashed his face with the rest and set it alight.

The tragedy occurred in the courtyard, in front of several witnesses, including some visitors. The guy started running around, hollering, his head and the top of his chest consumed in flames.

Several people tried to catch him, immobilise him and put out the fire.

All around me, the nutters were going wild. Two or three took advantage of the chaos to try to escape. Sirens wailed. There were scenes of panic. That evening, everyone got a double ration of pills.

I never heard if the guy had died. I never saw him again.

From time to time, I heard the slow movements of a symphony coming from some unknown source, a swelling of violins that sparked a feeling of profound anxiety. Apart from these gloomy notes, there was no rock or music of any kind, no radio and no TV at Stone House.

It was snowing the day he arrived. He was an old man, over sixty. He walked at a snail's pace, step by step, shaking all over. He made his way along the corridors, inch by inch, staring ahead of him with empty eyes. He stopped at regular intervals to catch his breath.

I observed his gentle features, the slight smile that played around his lips and the unruly mop of hair sticking up on top of his head.

Little by little, a face emerged from out of the fog. I had met this man somewhere before.

91: SEVERAL INDIVIDUALS

With the exception of *Rolling Stone* magazine and the *New Musical Express*, Mary Hunter never read the newspapers. She took no interest in politics or economics, still less in football and the antics of celebrities, splashed across the tabloid newspapers that Londoners loved to read.

When she reached the Dorchester late in the afternoon, she knew nothing about the shocking events that had occurred in Belfast a few hours before. The pianist greeted her with a copy of the *Daily Mail*, and asked if the man on the cover wasn't the journalist who had come to interview her last December?

The headline took Mary by surprise. Michael Stern's picture appeared under a headline announcing what had happened. She shuddered, with hindsight, at the thought that she had spent an hour and a half alone in conversation with this seriously unbalanced individual.

Feverishly, she pored over the article. There was no reference to the investigation for which she had been interviewed.

For a few moments, she pondered whether she should go to the police, and tell them about his visit. The pianist dissuaded her straightaway. When he asked her what she had discussed with Stern, she merely replied that it was to do with an old story that she was connected with only indirectly.

If she spoke to the police, he said, she could expect long hours of questioning and a thorough investigation of her private life.

Mary was living now with Bob Hawkins, the guitarist who had followed her from the beginning. He was consumed with unwholesome jealousy over Jacques Berger. The drummer had forced the group's split, and made Mary suffer. He had stolen her savings, got into a fight with Gab and fled London, leaving Mary alone. She had become depressed, and stayed that way for weeks. The police came regularly to ask if she had any news of Berger.

There was no point opening old wounds. She decided not to go to the police.

Deep down inside, she knew she was still in love with Berger. He was a taciturn, unstable, disturbed character, but he had been an attentive lover. He had always respected her, and treated her with consideration. He was different from the other men she had known.

She regretted what had happened. At the time, she believed he had left her for good and taken their money with him. She had been in despair, and allowed herself to get dragged along, thinking heroin would help her overcome her distress. She had felt partly responsible for the drama ever since.

Mary had spent a few weeks trying and hoping to find Jacques. She had contacted people she knew in Paris, Brussels and Berlin, but there was no trace of him.

Not a day went by when she didn't hope for some news, or a sign from him. But if he did get in touch, it would bring a whole new set of problems. Jacques Berger was still wanted in connection with his attack on Gab. The Jamaican had survived, but lost the use of one eye.

Around 10:00p.m., at the end of her set, she left the Dorchester and headed for Soho to meet Bob Hawkins and a few friends in a pub.

Around midnight, after Mary had failed to show up, Hawkins called the Dorchester. The receptionist confirmed that Mary had left the hotel two hours before. She had seemed tired, had almost lost her voice and hadn't received her usual warm ovation.

Hawkins waited until the following morning. Towards noon, he went to the police to report his girlfriend missing.

Mary Hunter's body was discovered three days later, on the afternoon of Friday, March the twenty-second, by a team of dockers working at the port of Newhaven on the south coast of England, near Brighton. Her corpse was found aboard a freight train from London.

The body showed traces of numerous blows, bruises and burns. The medical examiner dispatched to the scene estimated she had been dead about forty-eight hours.

The police concluded that Mary Hunter had been abducted and incarcerated, before being killed.

The autopsy revealed a high concentration of heroin in her blood, but few associated molecules. This, combined with the low levels of the substance in her urine, suggested that death had occurred quickly, from an overdose.

Samples also indicated that she had had sexual intercourse with several individuals.

92: WHISPERING MY NAME

I heard what sounded like a cry of pain, a long groan of despair. I listened out. A thin strain of music floated along the corridor.

I followed it.

At the far end of one dormitory, an old man was huddled on a chair near the window, his eyes turned to the sky. He held a harmonica in both hands. The notes he played were laden with sorrow.

No one but him could make a harmonica weep that way.

I moved nearer. He stared at me. He recognised my features. He stood up, still searching my face, and his memory.

As for me, I had found him.

Slowly, he opened his arms.

I knew Sonny cried easily, but I never imagined I would see him sob like a child. He held me in his arms for a long time, whispering my name.

93: WE NEED TO TALK

The day after the meeting, Dominique got to the clinic earlier than usual. He wanted to be there when Dr Taylor showed up, and was determined to announce his arrival to Jacques Bernier.

As soon as he appeared in the entrance, a night nurse hurried to greet him.

'Here already, Dominique? Thank goodness! Mme Desmet is complaining of pains in her legs. She's asking for you. And M. Bernier is very agitated; he's running a fever, and hasn't slept all night.'

Dominique flashed a smile.

'Thanks, Léna. I'll take care of it. I'll go and see Mme Desmet, it won't take long, and after that, M. Bernier.'

He took a step back, made of show of examining the nurse from top to toe and sighed.

'You look tired, Léna, you should take some time off.'

Her turn to smile.

'I'm going to the seaside this weekend. A girlfriend is lending me her apartment in Le Coq. Want to come along?'

Dominique widened his eyes and pressed a hand to his throat, pretending the offer had taken his breath away.

'Le Coq? This weekend? With you? Why not? Let's talk later!'

She came closer, placed her hands on his shoulders, stood on tiptoe and whispered a few words in his ear.

Dominique laughed out loud.

'Have no fear! I'll bring a sleeping bag and take the sofa.'

Léna had been working at the clinic for a few weeks now. She brimmed with energy and enthusiasm. Her overtures to Dominique had been the object of endless corridor gossip and comment. The more so because he was strikingly good-looking, and far from impervious to her charms.

Dominique visited his first patient and gave a series of massages, to relieve the pains in her legs. Then he headed for Bernier's room.

Unusually, Bernier wasn't looking out for his arrival. His mouth was half open and he was staring at the ceiling.

Dominique approached the bed.

The man didn't seem to notice his presence. He was sweating and his eyes darted left and right, as if watching a horror film projected above his head.

Dominique bathed his forehead.

'Jacques, my friend, we need to talk.'

94: IN THE FLAMES

We found somewhere out of sight. We didn't want them to know we knew one another – they would become suspicious, and we would be separated.

We arranged to meet near the laundry, along a path in the grounds, behind the chapel. Together, we felt stronger. We would spend long moments sitting on a bench in deafening silence, savouring our companionship, with only the water tower to watch over us.

Sometimes, Sonny spoke to me. He would lean over and speak in a low voice, articulating each syllable as if I was a complete moron.

I couldn't understand what he said. I couldn't answer. I formed the words in my head, but I was incapable of expressing myself. Thanks to them, I had unlearned the power of speech.

During one of our meetings, Sonny gave me a wink and showed me his clenched fist. Slowly, he opened his fingers. He held some pills in the palm of his hand. He took one, placed it on his tongue, shook his head and spat it out. I should stop taking them.

The men in white brought them morning and evening. They were set out, in order, in a small box. They would tip them into my hand, give me a glass of water and wait for me to swallow them. Before I was declared harmless, they would look down my throat with a small torch to make sure I had swallowed them down.

I stopped taking them from one day to the next, just as Sonny had advised. I waited until they had left the room, then made myself sick into the toilet bowl. I was careful not to be noticed. I was suspicious of the lunatics they had infiltrated into my cell, to spy on me.

Slowly, I began the journey back. I emerged from the fog. Colours and sounds returned. The men in white had faces now. I could tell them apart. Only the smell persisted.

I began to decipher Sonny's messages, but I found it hard to communicate with him. I wanted to question him, find out what had happened to him. I wanted him to confess whatever sins had brought him to Stone House. I wanted to know how he had managed to make himself look like an old man.

Little by little, I began to mutter a few words. Early one morning, when the cleaners were going about their work, Sonny waited until they were looking the other way, and led me by the hand into a store room.

A sink with a mirror over it stood against the back wall of the room. Sonny positioned me in front of it. I stared at the reflection in the glass. Sonny looked the same as usual. Next to him stood an old man I had never seen before. He was taller and broader than Sonny. The old man was staring back at me in amazement.

Bit by bit, Sonny retraced his story. After his wild years, he had met a woman. They had married and had two children: two boys, Thomas and William. He had found a job with a car-hire company. His wife worked in a boutique, selling clothes.

They were an ordinary couple, like thousands of others in England. They paid their taxes, went on summer holidays and followed the football.

One morning, Sonny had left for work. His sons were already grown up; one had left home and got married. Sonny's boss told him the firm had been sold, and there was no longer a job for him there.

The police had found him three days later. He had locked himself in a toilet in Liverpool Street station and was methodically tearing a magazine into tiny pieces. He had no recollection of what he had been doing.

That was the first time he went AWOL, the first hole in his memory. I thought the story was quite amusing, but he was not smiling.

Other walkabouts, other holes followed. He had been found huddled in a foetal position at the back of a wardrobe in a furniture store, and another time in a confessional. The police got to know him; he had quite a record.

He had spent two months in a psychiatric hospital – his first stay. A few days after returning home, he had taken some food and hidden under his own bed. For almost two days, he watched his wife come and go, heard her weeping and wailing, spied on her telephone conversations, listened to the diagnoses of the police and doctors.

He went back to the first hospital, until his family decided to have him permanently incarcerated. I was sorry.

I told him my story, in return. I told him about the deaths of the guys in Pearl Harbor, about Floriane's death, Gab's death, Stern's death, my back-up gig in Berlin, the death of the disc-jockey in Ramstein, the ghost words and the infrasound that had killed innocent civilians in Vietnam.

I got everything mixed up, for sure. Sonny didn't seem convinced.

One day, I plucked up all my courage and asked him if he had any news of Mary. His answer was evasive. He had come across her once or twice, but they hadn't spoken, and he had no idea what had become of her.

I could tell he was hiding the truth. He knew something, but he didn't want to be the one to tell me. He spoke of her the way people talk about someone who has died, lowering his eyes, in sad, resigned tones.

I didn't insist. I wanted to picture Mary alive and happy.

It was several weeks, maybe over a month before I regained something approaching clear-headedness. I liked Sonny. We were united. We supported one another through moments of great doubt, but little by little, his presence and his concern were no longer enough. I wanted my freedom. And I wanted to see my mother.

Sonny reckoned she would be about eighty-nine. If she was still alive.

One of Sonny's sons came to visit from time to time. His name was Thomas, and he was the chief accountant for a building firm. He was a well-built, confident type, the opposite of his father. Sonny said he was a very capable boy. He suggested we ask him to see what he could find out.

I wanted to know. It had taken me a while to piece together the information scattered all around my head. I had forgotten who I was, my name and where I had lived.

Thomas came, and I spoke to him. He left with the information, promising his father he would make enquiries and tell no one what he was doing.

A few weeks later, I learned that my mother had died in the early 1990s, and that she was buried in the cemetery in Ixelles. I learned that my father had died, too. I wanted to disappear into nothingness that day, to die of shame and despair.

Day after day, hour after hour, I turned the news around and around like a dagger in a gaping wound. It was obvious to me now. I couldn't stay where I was. I couldn't end my life like this. I had a duty to fulfil before I could leave this world.

Day after day my conviction grew. I had to get out of this place. I had to make my peace with my father and beg my mother's forgiveness.

I told Sonny what I had determined to do. He was quiet and thoughtful for several days.

One morning, he told me he was going to get me out of there. He had it all planned. The end of summer was approaching, it was the night before the full moon, the night when anything was possible.

I don't know if the phases of the moon really do have an effect on the behaviour of lunatics, but when the full moon approached, things would get completely out of hand at Stone House. On those nights, the men in white delivered generous doses of tranquillisers, and the most notoriously agitated nutters were placed in solitary.

The night was busy with screams of distress and running feet in the corridors. Often, the sirens wailed. By dawn, the night staff were on their knees.

Sonny had told me to go out the next morning, at first light, and hang about in the grounds near the service entrance on Invicta Road.

I had no idea what he was planning, nor how he would get me out through the entrance. The double gates consisted of metal grilles about seven feet high, mostly kept locked shut. At the time appointed for deliveries, a guard occupied the sentry box between the outer and inner gates. When a supplier arrived, he would drive his van through the outer gate and wait until it had shut behind him. Then his papers would be examined in minute detail, and the second grille would open. When the van emerged again, the guard would search it from top to bottom.

Sonny replied that he knew all that, and asked me to trust him.

That evening, before we parted, he took me in his arms and thanked me for all I done for him. I had taught him the meaning of friendship, again. I had taught him patience and compassion. He was highly emotional. He spoke without thinking.

I didn't want to leave without him. I asked him to come too. He sighed. He'd had enough of running away, he wanted to stay there. He was afraid of the outside world. He had done his time, he felt better at Stone House and would end his days there. But I had a mission, and I had to see it through.

I followed his instructions. As soon as the morning alarm rang, I headed out into the park. I wandered about for a good hour. Just as I was losing patience, the sirens wailed, but the sound was different this time. They were not signalling an escape.

I heard the cries. Thick smoke billowed from the administrative building, a kind of red-brick villa with white-painted wooden bay windows, and a clock topped with a little bell-tower on the roof.

I moved nearer to the building. Suddenly, flames burst from the first floor, behind the library windows, and I saw Sonny's silhouette standing in the inferno. I didn't understand what he was doing there, trapped by the fire.

People went wild, shouting and running in all directions: the men in white, the inmates and the administrative staff. In just a few minutes, the courtyard was filled with panic-stricken, helpless onlookers.

The firemen were on the scene in just ten minutes. Only the main gates were wide enough for the engines to pass through. One of the guards raced to open them, then ran back to the courtyard to watch the show.

The gates stayed open, and I walked out, feeling strangely calm and serene. I supposed Sonny had it all planned, that he knew how he would get out of there. It was just a ploy.

Only later did I make the connection between his last words to me, and his sacrifice.

On the outside, Thomas was waiting for me. I got into his car. A Mini Cooper. By coincidence, the last make of car I had seen at the airport before my arrest. I thought that after all this time, they would surely have stopped production.

Thomas pulled away at speed. He had left clothes for me on the back seat. He was nervous, and distant. He disapproved of what we were doing, but he owed his father a debt. He would drop me in the centre of London, and after that, they were quits; I would be on my own.

I asked no questions. Sonny had told me his story. Thomas had signed the papers committing his father to Stone House.

He took me to a busy London street. I looked around, but didn't recognise the neighbourhood. I got out of the car. Thomas gave me a few bank notes, closed the door and drove off without a second glance.

I took a deep breath. I was in London. Nothing had changed, yet everything was different. I recognised the architecture, one or two monuments, a few façades, but the decor and atmosphere were not the same.

Everything had speeded up. Men were running. Women were

running. Children were running. Everyone seemed tense, fevered, anxious, just like Thomas. They terrified me.

The cars, buses and walls were plastered with advertising posters singing the praises of unfamiliar products and devices whose purpose it was difficult to make out.

No one paid any attention to me. No one smiled or looked relaxed, the way we had when London belonged to us.

Drowning in the human tide, I thought of Sonny and his silhouette dancing in the flames.

95: COME HOME

I hid in one of the parks. When night fell, I went down into the Underground. I was hungry and thirsty. I wandered through the passageways.

At the bottom of one staircase, a couple of musicians were giving their all. They were long-haired and gaunt, with a few sparse teeth between them. If not for the difference in their height, they might have passed for twins.

I stopped, and I listened. Their singing was off, and their playing was just as bad, but they made a likeable, energetic duo. Their style was in striking contrast to the world around them. Their broad grins showed off their meagre assortment of teeth, as if they were the happiest men alive.

The first was called Roger, a guy of about my age. He sang and played the banjo. The other was Jonathan. He sang the harmonies and accompanied them on the tambourine. They played a repertoire of country standards.

After a few songs, they packed up their stuff and moved on.

I followed them.

They headed off down another passage, and began playing again. Their set continued for a good part of the evening. After each new song, I handed over one of Thomas's bank notes.

It didn't take long to liquidate my capital. When I had given them my last pound, I turned on my heels and walked away. Roger caught up with me, and asked who I was, why I was following them, why I had given them the money?

I told him the first thing that came into my head. I had been a great drummer. I came from Paris, where I'd played with Clapton. I missed the music. I was harmless.

Jonathan joined us. They looked at one another and nodded, knowingly. They seemed to understand what I was saying.

Roger took me to one side. London wasn't like Paris. In London, the Underground stations weren't dormitories. People like us had to live on the margins, in dark side streets, or down by the Thames. People like us were told to move on, we couldn't hang around in public places, and we had to watch out when we were begging for money, in case we were cautioned by the police, or forcibly moved on.

They could see I was at a loss, and invited me to go with them. They took me under their wing. I became one of them.

They were headquartered under Blackfriars Bridge.

A great many others lived there too, mostly solitary, but some were organised into clans. Roger said never a day went by without a fight breaking out, scores being settled. They were impressed by how tall and broad I was. We struck an agreement – they would show me how to survive, and I would serve as their bodyguard.

Day after day, they showed me the best soup runs in London, the most comfortable places to sleep and how to get drunk for next to nothing.

With them, I relived my time with Candy on the Paris boulevards. I was their escort. I kept an eye on the surrounding scene, and warned them when a police patrol was approaching. More than once, I sent a gang of kids running when they tried to take the guys' money.

At the end of each evening, alcohol coursing through our veins, we snuggled into our sleeping bags and laughed fit to burst. Drink and laughter helped us bear the cold. Roger liked to string me along. He told me they'd dug a tunnel under the Channel, and a woman had been Prime Minister.

Life was tough, often desperate. There was no future, and no way back. But with hindsight, I treasure the weeks I spent with them. They marked a moment of freedom between two prisons.

Apart from the cold that left me frozen to the core, I was a free man, I took pleasure in life once more. The time I spent with Roger and Jonathan restored some of my humanity.

One December night, towards the end of my stay, a gang of tough-looking types burst onto the scene under the bridge. We thought they were racketeers, or plain-clothed cops. The heavies gave us all the eye and inspected the place thoroughly. A few moments later, a kid in jeans, sweatshirt and a knitted hat joined them.

Roger and Jonathan couldn't believe their eyes. They breathed in my ear that the kid was 'Prince William', the son of the Prince of Wales. Another of their jokes, I thought. Their future king was roughing it under the bridges of London. The kid didn't sleep a wink all night, it was about minus four, and he was half-dead with cold.

After New Year, I told them my mother was ill and I wanted to go back to Brussels. They seemed surprised, but asked no questions. A few days later, they introduced me to Looping.

Looping was small, bald and tattooed from head to foot. He came from Aberdeen and knew the best ways to get across the Channel. He was surprised by my request. Generally, he was tasked with getting people from France to England. No one had ever asked to go the other way.

First, he told me I just had to hop on a train. Then he realised I had no papers.

I had a bit of money stashed away, but it was not enough. Roger negotiated with him. I don't know what deal they struck, but Looping said he could help.

I waited a few weeks. One morning, Looping came to fetch me. We went to Victoria Station. From there, we took a coach, and got out in a small village. We went to a hangar where a man was waiting for us. He loaded me into the back of a lorry headed for Dover. The driver *seemed to know what was going on, though he paid me no attention.*

In Dover, I would have to be patient, and wait in the truck. I was not to get out. The journey took several hours, altogether. In Calais, I was handed over to a young guy on a motorbike, who rolled his shoulders. He took me to the station. He had a hard look about him, but he was more open and communicative than the truck driver.

I had kept back a few notes. I explained to him what I wanted to do. In the station, he helped me find the telephone number of the cemetery. He waited patiently as I made call after call, and didn't seem annoyed by the difficulty I had making myself understood.

After nightfall, he took me to a freight wagon bound for Brussels. He had a pass key that opened the metal doors. Before leaving, he gave me a bottle of cheap spirits for company. I thanked him and hid behind a pile of packing cases.

When the train came to a halt, I waited for a couple of hours as instructed.

I emerged from the wagon. I had finished the bottle. I was blind drunk. I walked the streets in the direction of the station. The Tour du Midi towered above the blackened walls and run-down façades. I had watched it being built, just before I left.

Night fell. The sky was heavy with the promise of rain.

After forty-eight years of wandering, I had come home.

96: THE WORD WAS INCOMPLETE

Bernier seemed not to have heard.

Dominique took his hand and quietly repeated what he had said.

'We need to talk, my friend.'

The man stared straight ahead.

'You're going to get a visit from someone you know.'

Dominique was sure the man could hear what he was saying. He let the information sink in.

X Midi batted his eyelids several times and seemed to wake up.

'Dr Taylor is coming here tomorrow. You know him. He says he treated you in the summer of 2009.'

X Midi seemed to search back into his past. Suddenly, his eyes widened, and Dominique saw the first signs of alarm.

His temples were beaded with sweat. After a while, the man seemed to calm down.

He stared at Dominique, then shifted his eyes to the cupboard.

Dominique was quick to respond.

'You want to talk to me?'

Yes.

Dominique opened the cupboard, took out the alphabet board and placed it in front of X Midi.

He began listing the vowels and consonants, forcing himself to be patient.

Bernier seemed to hesitate. Dominique ran through the whole alphabet, with not a letter chosen.

Dominique began the series over, from the beginning.

'Take your time, Jacques. I'll take it slowly, I'll ask you to confirm or refuse each letter.'

This time, X Midi chose the letter F.

Next came the I, the N, and the K.

'FINK. Is that your first word?'

A blink for 'yes'. He seemed exhausted.

'Do you want to stop?'

The man refused. He wanted to continue.

M.

He closed his eyes and paused for a long while.

'Shall we go on?'

A.

Y.

He was sweating more and more profusely. The sweat trickled down his neck, despite Dominique's efforts to sponge his skin.

'MAY? Want to stop?'

The man signalled 'No.'

B.

E.

'MAYBE?'

The man closed his eyes.

Dominique stopped listing the letters.

He had no idea if X Midi had finished, or if the word was incomplete.

97: MY MISTAKE

He never treated me. He never spoke to me. He would cross the court-yard, straight as a ramrod, looking at no one. If he thought he might be interrupted in his work, he would have put me to death without a second thought.

Now, the truth lies in the two words I couldn't complete. This is the end of my road. Journey's end. I have failed.

If it hadn't been for the car racing the wrong way outside the station, I would have reached my goal. Everything would have been different.

I would have gone to see my mother in the cemetery, and she would have forgiven me.

I would have seen my brother again, and told him I loved him. I would have taken him in my arms, the way Sonny showed me. I would have asked him to forgive me for the wall of silence I hid behind so often, and he would have forgiven me. He would have told me about his life, and I would have told him some of mine. We would have shared our childhood memories. He would have talked about the wild beasts that lurked under my bed. I would have reminded him of the porn magazines he used to read under the covers. We would have remembered the mounted police parading by, the soup-seller's van and the baker's horse. I would have talked to him about my coloured cray-ons, and our mother's smile. We would have laughed about our wild afternoon dancing rock'n'roll, our father's cold rages and my jumbled words.

And then I would have turned myself in. I would have confessed my crimes. *Perhaps my sins, too. Upright in the face of God and men, I would have taken responsibility for my actions, and paid my debt.*

I'd have taken up reading again. Made up for lost time. I would have reread the classics and discovered new masterpieces. Listened to my old rock tracks and relived my memories.

Later, I would have gone to see Sonny at Stone House.

He would have explained what happened, the conjuring trick that got him out of there. I would have told him about my weeks in London, my time with Jonathan and Roger. We'd have made an indestructible four-piece.

When everything was settled, I would have gone looking for Mary.

I would never have mentioned the back-up gig again, the recording session, my research, my notes, the ghost words, or the dead who walked with me along the way.

I paid a heavy price for my mistake.

98: WE'RE LOSING HIM

Dominique was concerned after his talk with Bernier. He continued his rounds, but without his usual ebullience. Towards noon, a nurse came to tell him Marie-Anne Perard was looking for him.

He saw from the moment he entered her office that the news was not good.

Marie-Anne Perard was waiting for him with Gérard Jacobs. Both wore closed, anxious expressions. Dominique saw no sign of Dr Taylor.

The director greeted him dully and asked him to sit down.

'Dominique, what I have to tell you is not pleasant. Dr Taylor has just left this room.'

'I knew he was coming today. I'm guessing he hasn't brought good news.'

'Indeed. Dr Taylor is the chief consultant at a psychiatric hospital near London. M. Bernier was one of his patients.'

'Go on, I'm listening.'

'M. Bernier escaped almost two years ago, in August 2009. They have been looking for him ever since. They found him thanks to our announcement in the paper.'

She picked up a cardboard folder lying on the desktop.

'You're the only person who has managed to get through to him, and I know you like him.'

Dominique smiled.

'Dominique likes everyone.'

'I know, Dominique, it's one of your great qualities. Your patients feel it, and it helps them enormously. M. Bernier has a long psychiatric history. Dr Taylor has passed me his medical records.'

She opened the file and glanced down one sheet.

'It's in English, but here's the gist. Jacques Bernier suffers from heboidophrenia, a particular form of schizophrenia. The illness generally manifests itself in adolescence. Diagnosis is by listening and observation, there are no lab tests. Often, the patient's entourage will detect the first signs that something is wrong. Which explains why nothing was found when Bernier was seen by doctors at Petit-Chateau. He would have been in the very earliest stages.'

Dominique sighed.

'I know the condition. I treated one or two young sufferers in France. One boy was seventeen. He had been drinking since the age of ten. When he was drunk, or had taken drugs, he became violent, and suffered hallucinations. No one wanted him. His parents rejected him, and residential homes wouldn't take him in.'

'Violent reactions are quite frequent,' Perard continued, 'but the illness presents differently in different people. Generally, there are behavioural problems. Sufferers think people are plotting against them. They suffer visual or aural hallucinations. There is an absence of expressivity or emotion, problems with concentration, memory problems, confused thinking or speech, difficulty expressing themselves and sometimes ticks or repetitive movements. During psychotic episodes, the patient's perception is disconnected from reality. In Bernier's case this led to instances of criminal psychopathology.'

Gérard Jacobs spoke next. 'Dr Taylor has outlined Bernier's past history for us. He's had a fairly extraordinary life. Until the age of eighteen his difficulties were not especially noticeable, though he was profoundly introverted and often spoke incoherently. The problems worsened later. As you know, he disappeared on the day he was due to enter military service. He took a train to Paris and became involved with a group of beatniks. He became a drug dealer, sold drugs to lycée students and was implicated in a rape case that led to a suicide in circumstances that were suspicious to say the least. He escaped arrest and fled to London. He fell in with a new crowd, drank heavily and took drugs. He changed his identity and became Jacques Berger. He came to light again in Berlin, where he used LSD and claimed to have taken part in a recording session organised by a government agency. Back in London, he seriously injured a small-time dealer, and attacked and stole money from a man in whose house he had previously stayed. He had false identity papers made, called himself René Schnegg and fled to Switzerland. His delusions worsened, and he evolved a global conspiracy theory. Despite this, heaven knows how, he found work as a night porter in a grand hotel in Montreux. A few months later, he fled yet again. The police caught up with him and arrested him when he tried to return to London. There was no trial. Expert psychiatric examination declared him irresponsible for his actions, and he was interned.'

Dominique looked doubtful. There was a piece missing from the story.

'Did Dr Taylor tell you anything about a journalist named Michael Stern?'

Both seemed surprised. Marie-Anne Perard reached for the folder and leafed through it.

'Absolutely. When Bernier travelled back to London he was in possession of a daily newspaper that reported a killing spree that had occurred in Belfast. When he was arrested, he told the police he had arranged a meeting with Michael Stern, the journalist who committed the murders. A diversionary tactic that proved his alienated mental state.'

'And that proves there was definitely no actual contact between him and the journalist?'

'There was none. Only what existed in his own head.'

Dominique shook his head sorrowfully.

'Poor Jacques! He's still talking about it forty years on. I'm surprised by what you've told me, but that doesn't change anything as far as I'm concerned. His past is his own affair. For me, he's a patient, and it's my job to ease his pain.'

Marie-Anne Perard spoke up.

'That's entirely to your credit, Dominique.'

She rose, signalling the end of their interview. The police officer spoke up.

'In any case, you have done a great job. Without you, we would never have identified this man.'

Dominique got to his feet.

He glanced around the room with a questioning air.

'And where is this Dr Taylor now?'

'He wanted to see M. Bernier before he left. Lydia went with him. I wanted to introduce you, but he was in a hurry. He's probably left by now, his train is at 2:00p.m.'

The telephone rang as they moved to the door. Marie-Anne Perard apologised and turned back.

Dominique left the office and accompanied Jacobs to the exit.

The police officer shook his hand.

'Thank you for your help. This hasn't turned out the way we imagined, but that's life.'

He left, and crossed the car park to his vehicle.

Dominique was staring after him when he heard Marie-Anne Perard calling him.

'Dominique!'

She hurried towards him.

'Come with me, it's Bernier!'

Their pace quickened.

'What's up?'

'Something's happened to him.'

There were people hurrying, and voices raised. Footsteps rang out along the corridor.

They pushed their way into the room. The resuscitation trolley was installed, and a doctor was bending over X Midi. An oxygen mask had been placed over his face. The doctor was pushing down, one hand over the other on the man's chest, to the precise rhythm used for cases of cardiac arrest. Two nurses were assisting him.

Marie-Anne Perard jerked her head at one of the two, and shot her a questioning look.

The nurse looked back miserably.

'I think we're losing him.'

99: MY EYES

The outline of a shadow behind him. He stands up. I see Sonny's silhouette in the semi-darkness. Stepping forward. He looks like he always did. He's young, smiling, well dressed. He looks back, and stretches out a hand. Mary comes forward. Her dazzling beauty bursts into the light. She shrugs one shoulder and smiles at Sonny. They have an understanding. Mary strokes her hand over my hair. She signals behind her and my mother comes forward, smiling. All three seem to be playing some kind of prank. I feel their hands on my chest. Ma kisses me on the forehead. I know her sweet smell. I've waited so long. I don't want to hurt you any more. She places her hand on my face, and closes my eyes.

EPILOGUE

Dominique and Léna emerged from JFK airport on Wednesday, June the twenty-second, 2011, at noon.

Contrary to their friends' dire warnings, the flight hadn't seemed unbearably long, and the passport formalities took barely twenty minutes.

They climbed into a taxi and headed for Manhattan. The freeway and the Queensboro Bridge were busy with traffic, and it was 2:00p.m. before they reached their hotel.

The summer tourist crowds hadn't yet arrived in New York. Dominique had searched online and found a comfortable hotel on the Upper West Side, opposite the Lincoln Center.

They found their room, unpacked and decided to stretch their legs with a walk in Central Park.

Since that February weekend in Le Coq, Dominique and Léna had been inseparable. Both said it had been love at first sight. They shared an infectious zest for life, and a great deal else besides. They adored one another's company, and were the best of friends. They planned to move in together in September, when the lease on Léna's apartment was up.

As expected, the news spread like wildfire at the clinic, but the couple's their professionalism, and their undimmed enthusiasm for their work, had stopped the wagging tongues soon enough.

They strolled for two hours in Central Park, marvelling at the quiet shade in the midst of the bustling city. They reached the Reservoir, left the park on the east side, strolled down Fifth Avenue and took a look around Columbus Circle mall before returning to their hotel to freshen up.

Around 6:00p.m. – feeling the effects of the jet lag – they ate a light meal in a restaurant near the hotel and got to bed around eight, where they fell fast asleep.

They woke together at dawn, bright and refreshed. They made love, and took a long shower. They left the hotel around eight, and ate breakfast in a Starbucks nearby.

They began their programme for the day: they would walk down Broadway to the Empire State Building, and kiss on the terrace of the forty-sixth floor, as promised ever since they had watched *Sleepless in Seattle*.

Dominique stopped every few paces to take pictures or marvel at the tiniest details of everyday life. Léna laughed, and poked gentle fun.

It was their first holiday together, and New York fascinated them.

Jacques Bernier's death had been recorded on Tuesday, February the twenty-second at eight minutes past one in the afternoon. The medical examiner's report gave pulmonary embolism as the cause of death. He concluded that there was no connection between the cause of death and the patient's emotional shock following Dr Taylor's visit.

The next day, Dominique organised a collection among the staff at the clinic. He had used all his charm and powers of persuasion to secure the amount needed. But he still had to persuade Marie-Anne Perard and Gérard Jacobs, to help overcome a few administrative hurdles.

It took about a week, but ended in success. Jacques Bernier was buried in Ixelles cemetery, beside his mother.

Dominique, Léna, Marie-Anne Perard, Gérard Jacobs and

two nurses attended the ceremony. When the coffin was lowered, Dominique was invited to say a few words.

Taken unawares, and uncomfortable speaking in public, he said simply:

'Rest in peace, Jacques, my friend.'

They stopped by their hotel towards the end of the morning, and devoured the sandwiches they had bought. Around 2:00p.m., Léna headed for Times Square to go shopping, and Dominique set off in the opposite direction.

He crossed Central Park and walked up Fifth Avenue towards the Metropolitan Museum.

He paid the 'suggested' admission fee, glanced at his watch and checked the museum map. Room 915 was on the first floor, on the mezzanine level.

He walked through a series of rooms filled with priceless artworks, sculptures and glass cases loaded with objects. He crossed a broad terrace flanked by marble columns and climbed a monumental staircase.

Dominique had pored over Jacques Bernier's file for weeks. He had analysed the sequence of events, studied the facts and examined the doctors' conclusions.

He was intrigued by a number of details. Some of the facts didn't concur, or were flatly contradictory. He had decided not to make contact with Dr Taylor, nor to bother Gérard Jacobs with his doubts and questions. For them, the case was closed.

He had spent a long time pondering Bernier's last two words.

What did FINK and MAYBE mean? The names, if they were indeed names, were absent from the case file.

He had contacted the human resources manager at the Palace hotel in Montreux, to find out the dates on which

Jacques Bernier, a.k.a. René Schnegg, had started work, and left. The man told him that Bernier had left Montreux on March the eleventh, 1968, not the eighteenth. He tried asking if the names Fink or Maybe meant anything to him. That was when he discovered who Fink was.

According to the file, Bernier had taken a morning flight to London on the eighteenth of March, 1968, from Vienna, to cover his tracks. There was a six-day blank in the chronology. What had Bernier been doing?

The second word, *Maybe*, remained a mystery.

Room 915 contained works of contemporary art. It was one of the smaller galleries in the museum, rectangular in shape, with a glassed-in area running along one wall. Blinds had been lowered against the bright sunshine.

Dominique spotted the canvas straightaway.

René hung on a side panel, to the right of two works by Andy Warhol. The painting was ten feet high high and six feet wide.

Dominique walked towards it in disbelief.

The portrait looked exactly like a photograph. Even inches from the canvas, he found it hard to believe it was a painting. Every detail was captured with striking realism, from the strands of hair to the creases around the neckline and the reflection of the camera flash visible in the man's eyes.

More astonishing even than the technique was the fact that here before him was Jacques Bernier, younger, but immediately recognisable.

In the portrait, his mouth was half open. He looked stunned, even half-crazed.

A label gave a few details.

Andrew Fink. American. Born 1940
René, 1969–70

Acrylic on canvas
Private collection, New York

'Welcome to Andy's Corner!'

Dominique spun around.

A tall, thin man was smiling at him.

He wore a beard and had long, reddish-grey hair. His pale face contrasted with his billowing, vivid red shirt. Wide khaki shorts revealed his stick-thin legs. He was wearing Birkenstock sandals and held a rucksack in one hand.

Dominique smiled back.

'You're Andrew Fink?'

'And you must be Dominique!'

'Yes. You speak perfect French.'

'I speak it better than I write it, is that what you're saying?'

'Well, your accent is better in real life!'

'American keyboards don't have accents, and every New York artist is a terrible, Francophile snob...'

Dominique laughed out loud.

'I'm very happy to meet you.'

Andrew Fink shook his hand and gestured to his painting.

'So, did you recognise René?'

'Yes, he was a friend.'

'Come and sit down.'

They sat on the padded bench facing a self-portrait by Andy Warhol.

Fink looked Dominique up and down.

'So you came all the way from Brussels to talk to me about René?'

'I've dreamed of coming to New York for a long time. I took advantage of the opportunity.'

'I see. What do you want to know?'

'As I said when I wrote, René was a patient of mine. He was

tetraplegic, and could only communicate by blinking. Shortly before he died, he gave me your name. I discovered you knew him in Montreux, but I didn't know why he had given me your name.'

The painter took a deep breath.

'It's an old story. I knew René over forty years ago. I thought I'd be rich and famous, back then. I was the leading light in the American Hyperrealist movement. I thought our art would be recognised and live for ever. We had our moment of glory. For a year or two, people talked about us, but we were forgotten soon enough. We were like downbeat, second-rate singers. A hit or two, and it was over. Except it only takes a few hours to write a song, but it takes months to paint a canvas like that.'

Dominique looked saddened.

'It's really impressive, I've never seen anything like it.'

'The critics killed us. We had no manifesto. Most of us worked in isolation, we didn't know one another. We presented cold, mechanical observations of the world around us, free of subjective analysis.'

He rubbed his hands as if to chase the thought from his mind.

'Well, that's all over now! Let's talk about René.'

'Did you live together?'

'No, not in Montreux anyhow. He shared my apartment in Vienna for a very short while. I don't remember much about him. He was a secretive guy. He never said much, didn't confide easily. I tried several times to find out about his past, but his story changed every time. Sometimes he hardly seemed to know his own name.'

He paused for a moment.

'Between you and me, I think he had some kind of problem. But I liked him a lot. He was a nice guy. We only saw each other once or twice a week. We would drink beers and smoke dope.

I talked to him about my painting. Sometimes, he would talk to me about rock music, and literature, when he'd had plenty to drink. One day, he left and I never saw him again.'

'So why your name?'

Fink looked awkward.

'Before he left, he gave me something.'

'Something? What?'

'Well it's all a long time ago, but a promise is a promise, and I always keep mine.'

'What do you mean?'

Fink stared Dominique in the eye.

'I have to ask you a question and you're allowed only one answer.'

Dominique's eyes widened.

'OK, go on, I'm listening.'

'What was the first rock song?'

Dominique burst out laughing.

'What?! You're asking me what the first rock song was, and I'm only allowed one answer! I have no idea!'

Fink stared at him.

Dominique could see he was deadly serious.

He was about to give up when the answer came to him in a flash of inspiration.

'I think I know.'

'Go on.'

'Perhaps it's not the full title, but I think it begins with "Maybe".'

Fink smiled.

'I get you. I'm like you, I don't know anything about rock music, but I can only hand over this item on one condition, a kind of password. 'Maybellene', by Chuck Berry. I thought about that again recently, in fact. Chuck was on TV publicising his latest tour.'

Fink bent forward and picked up the ruck sack. He placed it on his knees, opened it and took out a stack of school exercise books held together with a rubber band.

'Here.'

He handed them to Dominique.

'He didn't say whether I could read them, but I'm an inquisitive guy, so I did. Well, I tried. But the writings inside are very confused.'

Dominique removed the band and opened one of the exercise books.

The pages were filled with dense handwriting punctuated with numerous crossings-out. He leafed through the book. The writing changed on every page; sometimes it was square and straight, sometimes right-leaning or left-leaning, with different-sized characters. On some pages, there were only a few words, written in huge letters. In addition to the crossings-out, some pages were packed with drawings, figures and diagrams, or notes added in red in the margins.

Fink sighed.

'See, none of it is particularly clear. Basically, he says he made a record with a group in Berlin. Something happened at the studio. He tries to explain what. I didn't understand much of it, but I didn't read it in any great detail.'

Dominique weighed the books in his hand.

'Well, he had a lot to say.'

'Take my advice, don't pay too much attention to it. He wasn't in his right mind. It's all fantasy. But do what you want with it. The books are yours now. Just promise me one thing.'

'What's that?'

'If one day, you ever make sense of it all, get back in touch with me.'

'I promise.'

They stood up and shook hands.

'Thanks for your help, Mr Fink.'

'You're welcome. I kept my promise to René.'

Fink glanced at the painting.

'One day, I took a picture of him when he wasn't looking. He didn't like being photographed. He was a strange guy.'

They waved and went their separate ways.

Dominique became lost in the maze of galleries, and had to ask a gallery guard for the exit.

Outside, the sun dazzled his eyes.

At the bottom of the steps, a gospel choir were inviting the crowd to clap along. Dominique joined in, and bought their CD when they had finished singing. He put on his sunglasses, tucked the books under his arm and headed off down Fifth Avenue, oblivious to the men following close behind.

ACKNOWLEDGMENTS

I admit to the occasional Web and Wikipedia search, for the background to my books. But reconnaissance on the scene of the action, and interviews with key witnesses, are of a whole other order of importance.

And so I must thank Guy Mazairac, an emergency specialist at the university hospital in Namur, who treated the hero of this story on the forecourt of Midi station, and gave him the name X Midi. A big thank you to Benjamin Legros, neurologist at Erasmus Hospital, who administered X Midi's initial treatment. And to Pierre Schepens, a psychiatric doctor and chief consultant at the clinic in the Forêt de Soignes, for accepting X Midi into his establishment and allowing me to visit him there. And finally, Marianne Parache, neurologist and LIS specialist, who enabled X Midi to tell me his story.

A nod and a wink to Michel, wherever he may be, who left us too soon and may recognise himself in Dominique.

For the rock'n'roll years of X Midi's youth, I give heartfelt congratulations to Marc Ysaye and all the team at Classic 21 rock radio. Devoted listening to their fabulous station provided a wealth of anecdotes from the history of rock, for the pages of *Back Up*.

A big thank you to Lydie and Maxime for their thorough reading and good advice.

And finally, a personal message to my original publisher: Pierre, the message you sent after reading *Back Up* takes pride of place on my desk. I don't need to read it, I know it by heart. *Thank you for this daily elixir of youth.*